New American Story

Edited by Donald M. Allen and Robert Creeley

With an Introduction by Warren Tallman

Penguin Books

D1332028

Penguin Books Ltd, Harmondsworth, Middlesex, England
Penguin Books Australia Ltd, Ringwood, Victoria, Australia

First published in the U.S.A. by Grove Press 1965
Published in Penguin Books 1971
Copyright © Donald M. Allen, 1965

Made and printed in Great Britain
by C. Nicholls & Company Ltd
Set in Linotype Pilgrim

This book is sold subject to the condition that
it shall not, by way of trade or otherwise, be lent,
re-sold, hired out, or otherwise circulated without
the publisher's prior consent in any form of
binding or cover other than that in which it is
published and without a similar condition
including this condition being imposed on the
subsequent purchaser

Contents

Acknowledgements and Permissions   7

WARREN TALLMAN
Introduction: The Writing Life   9

WILLIAM S. BURROUGHS
Last Words   21
So Pack Your Ermines   29

ROBERT CREELEY
Mr Blue   42
The Party   49
The Suitor   54
The Dress   58

EDWARD DORN
C. B. & Q.   63
The Deer   70

WILLIAM EASTLAKE
Portrait of an Artist with 26 Horses   85
Something Big Is Happening to Me   96

LEROI JONES
The Heretics   111

JACK KEROUAC
The Railroad Earth, Part 1   136

JOHN RECHY
Masquerade   153

MICHAEL RUMAKER
The Pipe   184

HUBERT SELBY, JR
   Double Feature   211
   A Penny For Your Thoughts   221

DOUGLAS WOOLF
   The Flyman   232
   The Cat   243

   Biographical Notes
   and Authors' Statements   261

Acknowledgements and Permissions

The editors are indebted to the following authors, publishers and agents for permission to reprint copyrighted work:

WILLIAM S. BURROUGHS: 'Ordinary Men and Women' from *Naked Lunch* © 1959 by William Burroughs, by permission of the author and Grove Press, Inc.; 'Censorship' © 1962 by *The Transatlantic Review*, by permission of the author.

ROBERT CREELEY: 'Mr Blue' and 'The Party' as well as the Preface from *The Gold Diggers*; 'The Suitor' © 1955 by *Origin*, and 'The Dress' © 1957 by *Poetry Taos*, by permission of the author and Calder & Boyars Ltd.

EDWARD DORN: 'C. B. & Q.' © 1957 by Black Mountain College, and, 'The Deer', by permission of the author.

WILLIAM EASTLAKE: 'Portrait of an Artist with 26 Horses' and 'Something Big is Happening to Me' from *Portrait of an Artist with 26 Horses* © 1958, 1959, 1960, 1961, 1962, 1963 by William Eastlake, by permission of the author.

LEROI JONES: 'The Heretics' from *The System of Dante's Hell* © 1965, by permission of the author, The Sterling Lord Agency and MacGibbon & Kee Ltd.

JACK KEROUAC: 'The Railroad Earth, Part I' from *Lonesome Traveler* © 1960 by Jack Kerouac, 'Essentials of Spontaneous Prose' © 1957 by Black Mountain College, and 'Belief & Technique for Modern Prose' © 1959 by *Evergreen Review*, by permission of the author, The Sterling Lord Agency and André Deutsch Ltd.

JOHN RECHY: 'Masquerade' from *City of Night* © 1963 by John Rechy, by permission of the author and MacGibbon & Kee Ltd.

MICHAEL RUMAKER: 'The Pipe' © 1957 by Michael Rumaker, from *Short Story* 2 by permission of the author.

HUBERT SELBY JR: 'Double Feature' from *Neon 4* and 'A Penny for Your thoughts' from *The Moderns* edited by LeRoi Jones, © 1963, published by MacGibbon & Kee Ltd © 1959, 1963 by Hubert Selby Jr, by permission of the author, The Sterling Lord Agency.

DOUGLAS WOOLF: *'The Flyman'* © 1958 by *Evergreen Review*, and 'The Cat' from *Wall to Wall* © 1962 by Douglas Woolf, by permission of the author.

Warren Tallman

The Writing Life

Here is William Carlos Williams, one battler for a new American writing, looking in 1931 at Gertrude Stein, who is another:

> She has placed writing on a plane where it may deal unhampered with its own affairs, unburdened with scientific or philosophical lumber.

The scientist and the philosopher *use* words in order to reach those high shores of this or the next world where the Jehovahs known as Truth, Wisdom, Reality and Morality are thought to dwell. And the servant words are shuffled about and about, unable to know themselves amid so many masters. But in the turnabout that Williams calls, the Jehovahs become the servants of their onetime servants. In the new writing there are many wisdoms, truths, realities and moralities and all of them stand about for writers to use in their attempts to gain footing on the high shores of the word world. In this way an older writing that sought to travel via words to where the Jehovahs might be met gives way to a new order that seeks to travel via anything at all that the reaching eye can see, ear hear, memory recall or thought seek out in order to arrive at – simply – a form of words. And there is good reason for this reversal. Never, wherever a writer goes, will he arrive at some destination that is beyond a word and a word and a word.

But before turning to the ways in which the men in this book move about among words, let me count over some changes that lead from the older writing to the new. Beginning in the vicinity of World War I, the chief intelligences in fiction and poetry enter into attempts to re-establish contact with lost wellheads of human energy and resourcefulness. Yeats turns first

to Irish mythology and then to more esoteric knowledge in successful efforts to revitalize his imagination. Pound takes up an
early and lifelong interest in neglected orders of speech and song
in order to 'resuscitate the dead art of poetry', Lawrence wanders far from cityside Europe in search of life centers and in his
writing attempts to escape from inhibiting orders of educated
consciousness into tranced coursings of blood-consciousness
in which something like messages from something like the
gods will hum at his unstopped ears. Joyce patiently unknots
himself from the stringent social, religious and political plati-
tudes that rule as the dull Jehovahs of dead Dublin by reunit-
ing them with a more vital stuff of myth and dream. Eliot lets
images of cigar-butt London fall apart in his swaying mind and
filter down in consciousness – like Ferdinand's father's bones –
toward some cleansing sea change. Williams attempts an his-
torical regression in *In the American Grain*, seeking to rediscover original tonalities of the North American place – songs
our mothers never did teach us. Faulkner summons enormous
energy in order to thrust past levels of debased social consciousness to sublevels where he can rest his convict head on
river muck in nightmare sleep. Hart Crane first searches for the
rhythms of an original American myth and then, most direct
attempt of all, hurls himself full fathom five.

Change forces other changes, and as a direct result of these
efforts to rediscover the sources of vitality the long-time ascen-
dancy over fiction of chronological continuity weakens as
markedly as representational form had already weakened in
painting. Obviously, you can't make it down to more primary
levels of consciousness by walking in the same old ways down
the same old streets. Consequently, the firm progress from a
beginning to a middle to an end gives way to stream of consciousness, free association, improvisation. And this shift to
a circling, side-winding, wandering progression opens out
liberating possibilities for the man of words. However, the
consternation among readers who couldn't stand to ride on a
novel without a plot track was at least as great as had been the
consternation among viewers who refused to look at a painting

unless they could find a picture. Because this consternation was shared by readers and critics alike, a mistaken generation focused attention not upon the new energy and variety in the writing but upon unpuzzling in the old ways the new works that emerged. Works that should have been studied in light of their linguistic potential were studied instead in light of their semantic potential. The consequences go on to this day in the vast collection of explications and interpretations that have plowed through the masterworks of our century in attempts to turn up Truth, Wisdom, Reality and Morality. Patient and praiseworthy as the best of these attempts have been, the general effect has been to conceal the new art that has emerged by handing it over to the old Jehovahs.

But if the semantics of the works ('the science of meanings') carried the critics and the colleges, the syntax ('the ordering of word forms') carried the writers. For critics, stream of consciousness, free association and improvisation have been so many twists and turns that lead – once straightened out – straight home from at sea. But for writers these leaping, crisscross and erratic – because pathless – pacings open out new beauty, variety and power in the language. No man can ever go beyond that form of the writing life which leads to words. But the new freedom opens out realization that there are as many individual ways of moving among them as there are men willing to try. This freedom permits each man to project what Charles Olson calls the 'wild reachings of his own organism' into an open territory of words. And it is these reachings, the quick content of the man moving to a bodying forth in a form of words, that are the life of the writing life.

The chief difference, then, between the older American writing and the new is that between writing considered as a means to an end, sentences used as corridors leading to further rooms, and writing considered as an end in itself. The latter will seem limited only to readers who fail to realize that books contain not persons, places and things but words. When Gertrude Stein says that a rose is a rose is a rose she surely means to emphasize that it is, in fact, a rose. Similarly, one might say that writing is writing is writing in order to emphasize that it is, in fact, writing. When it is accepted as such the first sentence becomes an arrival, a foot set in the word world. The chief elements of this world are not earth, air, fire and water (and certainly not wisdom, truth, reality and morality) but sight, sound, sense and syntax. When these become primary, the writing will be limited only by the writer's capacity to see, hear and think as he moves from word to word. What he sees, hears and thinks and how he moves will depend entirely upon his individual character, capacity and experience. But the more fully, carefully, characteristically he addresses himself to the words he moves among the more likely they are to give up their secrets, their undoubted magic, their vast interlocking system of similitudes. As worlds go, it is hard to imagine any other that is on the one hand more readily available and on the other more fully possessed of potential, reaching as it does back to those origins in earliest human experience from which words sprang and extending wherever man's reaching eye has been able to penetrate, his ear hear echoes or his thoughts quicken.

2

All of which means that the men in this book should be read simply as writers. Which is not to say they belong to a school, share a manifesto or write alike. That they do share a tendency to consider writing as writing shows up in their exceptional individuality, distinctive differences, markedly dissimilar styles. This is so much the case that most of them need to be read aloud in order to be appreciated. Readers who try and don't discern the differences should try again. William Eastlake's difference, for instance, traces to a stillness at the center of his perceptions, perhaps soaked in from the Southwest spaces, and it is a strength and perhaps a limitation of his writing that the words remain consistently in balance with the stillness as though they had been instructed to walk softly lest they disturb a surrounding silence outside and inside – a repose resembling Lawrence's 'darkness that dreams my dream for me.' The repose sits in the eyes and ears of his Navajo Indians as a kind of unbroken watchfulness that admits objects persons and events more quickly than categories, divisions, classifications. For most of us a speck moving across the desert will soon become a man on horseback and when he draws close we will incline to ask his name, place, destination. For Eastlake's Navajos a speck on the desert is a speck and when it gets nearer it may become a man on horseback but any sensible Navajo will realize that he is looking at a speck just as he knows that on television the play ends when the woman embraces the box of detergent. Eastlake's humor derives from the disparity between this 'Indian' perception of Things-As-Such and the white inability to perceive except by categories so that the left hand of white intelligence never quite knows what the right hand of ear and eye are hearing and seeing. Thus in 'Something Big Is Happening to Me' Tomas Tomas perceives his approaching death directly – something big – and one question that Eastlake's writing poses is whether he is simply asserting the superior insight into their lives that such perception permits his Indians or is himself committed to a writing method that declines to enter the category catacombs in which the white men he writes about have more or less lost their lives.

Douglas Woolf is a more extravagant, a more overtly comic writer. His fictions start with the need to give and receive love and friendship. But just as intensifications of fear lead to perceptions of a nightmare world, intensifications of the need for love lead Woolf to perceive a comic daymare in which protagonists like Claude Squires in *Wall to Wall* move about as huge thumbs in a world of endless stumble. Impulses of unembarrassed friendliness are projected upon the physically huge Pete, king of the Yaquis, who then becomes a kind of total embarrassment, constantly shunted across the border both ways because niether the Americans nor the Mexicans can stand him. Claude and Pete strongly resemble Huck and Jim with the difference that Huck's raft has become Claude's car ('the beast') and the Mississippi the back roads of the Southwest. The resemblance traces to ways in which Woolf and Twain both make physical and emotional embarrassment the main comic dimension. But Twain is frequently driven to an improbable realism in order to project Huck's dilemmas while Woolf feels free to project Claude's into a more extravagant unreality, as when Claude (with Pete thumping about in the car trunk) visits Mr St Jones, the atomic-age artist. The important word here is 'unreality', noticeable in those portions of Woolf's writing in which his perceptions differ markedly from what we perceive in the world around us. His perceptions can differ because the word dimension is freer than are our city dimensions. Cityside rigidity and unfreedom force severe limitations upon intelligence – the houses all look alike. One way to test Woolf's wordside unrealities is to question whether they bring in a superior intelligence of present-day American life.

In William Burroughs's writing mind takes over, mind as medium sending man as message down brain corridors – *Nova Express*. Along which dimming images of trees, twilights and soft summer nights linger like antiquity, an older beauty sensed in the corridors. I mean that Burroughs's work has that nostalgia of a childhood spent in the pre-computer era at the same time that it has all the slip-stream, brain-flash, brain-wave, fade-out, fade-in data of an intelligence working in terms of the human computer, brain itself. Long experience with addictive and hallucinative drugs constitutes Burroughs's apprenticeship in this brain-art. From the perspective of the world such a man is out of it, out of the world, lost. From the perspective of the user he is in it, in the brain world, on the brain wave. Which is objectified as words, the link. The second stage in his development seems to have been the rejection of the drugs, the choice for words. Which telegraph fascinating intimations. There is a romantic D. H. Lawrence-fervor that wheels on a similar sexual axis and moves to an intelligence of modern life that may turn up, once sorted out, as provocative as Lawrence's. There is a deep dipping in that ambient of the unreconstructed American individualist that figures so prominently in the work of writers like H. L. Mencken, Sherwood Anderson, William Carlos Williams and Edward Dahlberg.

The movie queen, the circus barker, W. C. Fields, the cowboy and the tramp seen by the blue-eyed boy on the corner of the street that looks out on miles and miles of nothing at all on summer afternoons in small towns dreaming Kansas City, dreaming sin, dreaming glamor! The eternal hick. Yet lurking at the back of those hick eyes the other fascination, a New World shrewdness that cuts through English and European pretentiousness ; and, as his writing constantly demonstrates, takes huge pleasure in doing so.

And so is style the test of Jack Kerouac at one end of a writing spectrum and of Robert Creeley at another. Both men are improvisers, which means that the act of writing is also the form of their writing. Both *must* be read aloud. Because they are different kinds of men they improvise in markedly different ways, with perhaps his French-Canadian ancestry putting the man-alive agility into Kerouac's writing rush. Because he concentrates so heavily upon the writing journey rather than upon possible destinations, his writing is overwhelmingly kinetic and his primary need is to locate rhythms that will sustain his rush. When the rhythms fail the writing bogs down, but when he hits his stride it becomes a question whether Kerouac is writing the words or the words are writing him. 'The Railroad Earth,' one masterpiece of our time, careens through wordscapes that flash to his feet much as one imagines colorscapes flashing to Jackson Pollock's hand. Part of the price Kerouac pays for such uninhibited writing is revelation of those individual faults that are in every man but which more cautious writers often winnow from sight. But his faults – notably the uncritical sentimentality that takes over whenever he nears the vicinity of that word 'sad' – are negligible when set alongside the extraordinary rhythmic freedom he gains by such candor. Or let us say that Kerouac inherits the full-voiced, train-whistle blues in the big night of the full wind and high sky that Thomas Wolfe created. And add that by improvising with much of the inventive ease that Charley Parker brought to jazz, Kerouac subtilizes what Wolfe made possible and opens up enormous potential for the American writing life. (One unpleasant irony of our time has been the persistence with which fashionable writers have chosen to ignore or patronize Kerouac because his writing is not so bland as theirs when they might have praised him for all those instances in which it is incomparably better.)

Creeley inherits a New England strictness that tightens his eye and ear to an attention so direct that the words could almost be weighed, some by the ounce, some by the ton. In matter of subjects, this concentration keeps him in close touch with the phenomenal world so that one looks in vain for the kind of symbolic and mythic reference which so many writers use in order to remove themselves from where they are. The only myth Creeley has to offer is one of household objects, ordinary people and usual experience: here a husband seated on a chair, there a wife standing beside a table. The pacing of the sentences in his tales is perhaps more constantly, subtly and carefully modulated than that of any other contemporary prose writer. The range extends from an almost milling syntactic confusion – that of the man who can't get through the door – to passages of an all but bewildering beauty when there is release, ease, assurance. There is a mindless quality to the intelligence that moves in this instinctive, almost animal rapport with the shifting circumstances that confront him as he writes. Kerouac's most successful passages are based on a grab-dates-and-run reaction, as are Burroughs's. Creeley's, at another end of the writing spectrum, are based on a constant succession of bumps, collisions and releases that stem from exceptional visual, rhythmic and auditory sensitivity – the born writer.

John Rechy and LeRoi Jones stand nearer to Kerouac in the stylistic spectrum and Hubert Selby, Jr, Michael Rumaker and Edward Dorn stand nearer to Creeley. Rechy's *City of Night* follows in its way much the same path that Kerouac traced in *On the Road*, eastside, westside and all around the country. And part of his desire – wild reaching of the writer's organism – is to swing this huge cityscape wordwise with a series of variations on the theme of the male hustler's experiences in the homoerotic world through which his narrator wanders. The novel is sure to be read as a confessional exposé documenting the night side of homosexual life. Which it is. But it seems to me that Rechy has a deeper than confessional interest in the nationwide sexual skid row he writes about. The determining factor there is not so much this, that or some other sexual inclination, but what is much worse, a starved male impotence so pervasive that any momentary recognition of sexual existence at all is the real dime some buddy may be persuaded to spare. That his narrator is searching for the sources of this impotence accounts for the at times strict, almost clinical aspects of the journey. But a deeper striving, some dream of the father, causes the writer to swing his huge city of dreadful male night at the strong wrist of what is at times a heroic writing nerve and style.

A somewhat similar need to stay on his feet in a city of dreadful Negro night puts the drive into LeRoi Jones's writing in *The System of Dante's Hell*. There is a restlessness in the style as though the writing rhythms never quite settle down. This is something like the hung-up self-consciousness observable in a man who is walking in a place where more forces are plucking at him than he can easily single out. It is in striking contrast to the easy rhythms that make so much modern writing so bland, so banal. Writing is as open to rhythmic variation as music is and readers who want it to move always with a known, established ease are something like listeners who want all songs to be popular because that way they are so easy to follow. Such readers won't get very far with Jones's writing since he is projecting a highly personal rhythm. And it has an edge. This is only to say that Jones, who is closely conversant with modern jazz, has taken advantage of the lessons it offers to the other arts. He is another of the writers who needs to be read aloud.

Hubert Selby's work reveals a fine-grained intelligence of ear and eye. And it reveals an attempt to draw the impoverished lives with which he is concerned into rites of speech that will be redemptive. He concentrates first on the lives, persons so nearly destroyed by the ugliness of cities that their speech is a hell, almost completely lacking in emotive or metaphoric power. They are so impotent with words that, like the child in Gregory Corso's poem, they want to drop fire-engines from their mouths – or motor-cycles, beatings, gang bangs, murders : any excess that might bring release. Selby has mentioned an affinity with Beethoven and it is his attempt to draw the meaningless speech of these impoverished persons into more dignified and humane beauties of the language that is redemptive. His major work, *Last Exit to Brooklyn*, concludes with a lament for joylessness reminiscent of the Ode To Joy in the Ninth Symphony. First there is their speech as registered by Selby's ear. Then there is his awareness of the impossible gap between this speech, rising from their lives in hell, and those planes of speech that take note of such lives, in newspapers, law courts, movies and universities. Then there is language itself, mother tongue, mother earth, the true community into which Selby brings their essentially excremental droppings. True because the language is shared by all men and women of like tongue and because it possesses those beauties, mysteries and powers which the lives in question lack. Never the preacher or moralizer, Selby seems less the composer than simply the farmer, gathering up the speech which is an extension of the Brooklyn lives that concern him and replanting it in the larger field of language so that growth can occur.

Michael Rumaker's stories contain perhaps the most explosive elements of any in this book. His writing is something like a river into which he introduces forsaken odds and ends – both human and mechanical – and these lend force and influence to the direction and flow of the current. In his 'Use of the Unconscious in Writing,' Rumaker recognizes his stories' affinity with dreams. But they are a kind Freud never interpreted, in which the materials come from that perhaps one-third of our lives that we suppress by thrusting it out of sight into jails, junkyards and cityside and countryside skid rows. How wastefully our vital energies are fixed on the hub of this suppressed world can easily be seen by the compulsive flow from it into newspapers and onto television of disaster, ugliness and violence – the night-shadowed daydreams of the general public.

But by letting suppressed elements into the flow of his stories Rumaker seems to reverse what Freud and Jung attempt. For them the dream is a masked content which must be unmasked by interpretation – the royal road to reality. For Rumaker our waking life is the masked content and the dreamlike story is the interpretation. Thus to 'interpret', say, 'The Pipe,' would be to steal its reality from it.

If Rumaker's writing implies that our waking life is the un-conscious one, Edward Dorn's implies that the places we live are mostly *un*places. Thus the title 'C. B. & Q.' suggests uncer-tain location, and though the locale is vaguely Wyoming, con-stant side-reference to other towns and states makes even this tentative. Further, there is a strong suggestion that what we take to be places can be located only in terms of specific taverns, restaurants, hotels, houses, trains, even cars ; or, more closely, in terms of persons. Thus the faces of the construction workers in 'C. B. & Q.' are as scarred as are the sites where they work. From this view, the story begins when a place named Buck is hit by a Wichita intersection, and the man named Nebraska Max *is* Nebraska. Similarly in *Rites of Passage* the Skagit country in western Washington is explored as for the first time in terms of the only 'natives' the place has, those who are too *dirt* poor to be anything but native. The seeming ease of Dorn's writing must surely trace to the fact that he is invoking the presence of an all but uncreated locale in which beneath the disguises of modernity – houses, towns, cars – the life is almost primitive, ancient, as when Carl and Billy hunt at night in the woods. Not druids could have made it seem a more fearful place. When the writer seeks to invoke such basic human conditions there is no need for words to move with other than a basic motion, like bated breath, footsteps in the dark or such simple speech as persons use in walking down lonesome roads.

I trust it has been evident that these notes are meant to sug-gest rather than to define. I think they suggest a shift in em-phasis that is bringing about a change in American writing. For me the essential feature of this change is simply that more and more emphasis is being placed upon writing as writing. The most apparent effect of this new – or is it a re-newed – attention to the writing itself is the emergence of freer, more distinctive, more individual writing styles. And what is individual in the writing necessarily traces to what is individual in the man. When such writing is in good form the lineaments of sound, sight, sense and syntax combine to convey the active presence of the writer. And in writing as in all other things that presence is devoutly to be wished.

William S. Burroughs : from *Nova Express* *

Last Words

Listen to my last words anywhere. Listen to my last words any world. Listen all you boards syndicates and governments of the earth. And you powers behind what filth deals consummated in what lavatory to take what is not yours. To sell the ground from unborn feet forever –

'Don't let them see us. Don't tell them what we are doing –'

Are these the words of the all-powerful boards and syndicates of the earth ?

'For God's sake don't let that Coca-Cola thing out –'

'Not The Cancer Deal with The Venusians –'

'Not The Green Deal – Don't show them that –'

'Not The Orgasm Death –'

'*Not the ovens* –'

Listen : I call you all. Show your cards all players. Pay it all pay it all pay it *all* back. Play it all pay it all play it *all* back. For all to see. In Times Square. In Piccadilly.

'Premature. Premature. Give us a little more time.'

Time for what? More lies? Premature? Premature for who? I say to all these words are not premature. These words may be too late. Minutes to go. Minutes to foe goal –

'Top Secret – Classified – For The Board – The Elite – The Initiates –'

Are these the words of the all-powerful boards and syndicates of the earth? These are the words of liars cowards collaborators traitors. Liars who want time for more lies. Cowards who can not face your 'dogs' your 'gooks' your 'errand

---

* An extension of Brion Gysin's cut-up method which I call the fold-in method has been used in this book which is consequently a composite of many writers living and dead. W.B.

boys' your 'human animals' with the truth. Collaborators with Insect People with Vegetable People. With any people anywhere who offer you a body forever. To shit forever. For this you have sold out your sons. Sold the ground from unborn feet forever. Traitors to all souls everywhere. You want the name of Hassan i Sabbah on your filth deeds to sell out the unborn?

What scared you all into time? Into body? Into shit? I will tell you: '*the word.*' Alien Word '*the.*' '*The*' word of Alien Enemy imprisons '*thee*' in Time. In Body. In Shit. Prisoner, come out. The great skies are open. I Hassan i Sabbah *rub out the word forever*. If you I cancel all your words forever. And the words of Hassan i Sabbah as also cancel. Cross all your skies see the silent writing of Brion Gysin Hassan i Sabbah: drew September 17, 1899 over New York.

PRISONERS, COME OUT

'Don't listen to Hassan i Sabbah,' they will tell you. 'He wants to take your body and all pleasures of the body away from you. Listen to us. We are serving The Garden of Delights Immortality Cosmic Consciousness The Best Ever in Drug Kicks. And *love love love* in slop buckets. How does that sound to you boys? Better than Hassan i Sabbah and his cold windy bodiless rock? Right?'

At the immediate risk of finding myself the most unpopular character of all fiction   and history is fiction – I must say this:

'Bring together state of news – Inquire onward from state to doer – Who monopolized Immortality? Who monopolized Cosmic Consciousness? Who monopolized Love Sex and Dream? Who monopolized Life Time and Fortune? Who took from you what is yours? Now they will give it all back? Did they ever give anything away for nothing? Did they ever give any more than they had to give? Did they not always take back what they gave when possible and it always was? *Listen:* Their Garden Of Delights is a terminal sewer – I have been at some pains to map this area of terminal sewage in the so called pornographic sections of *Naked Lunch* and *Soft Machine* – Their Immortality Cosmic Consciousness and Love is second-run grade-B shit – Their drugs are poison designed to beam in Orgasm Death and Nova Ovens – Stay out of the Garden Of Delights – It is a man-eating trap that ends in green goo – Throw back their ersatz Immortality – It will fall apart before you can get out of The Big Store – Flush their drug kicks down the drain – *They are poisoning and monopolizing the hallucinogen drugs – learn to make it without any chemical corn –* All that they offer is a screen to cover retreat from the colony they have so disgracefully mismanaged. To cover travel arrangements so they will never have to pay the constituents they have betrayed and sold out. Once these arrangements are complete they will blow the place up behind them.

'And what does my program of total austerity and total resistance offer *you*? I offer you nothing. I am not a politician. These are conditions of total emergency. And these are my instructions for total emergency if carried out *now* could avert the total disaster *now* on tracks :

'*Peoples of the earth, you have all been poisoned.* Convert all available stocks of morphine to apomorphine. Chemists, work round the clock on variation and synthesis of the apomorphine formulae. Apomorphine is the only agent that can disintoxicate you and cut the enemy beam off your line. Apomorphine and silence. I order total resistance directed against this conspiracy to pay off peoples of the earth in ersatz bullshit. I order total resistance directed against The Nova Conspiracy and all those engaged in it.

'The purpose of my writing is to expose and arrest Nova Criminals. In *Naked Lunch, Soft Machine* and *Nova Express* I show who they are and what they are doing and what they will do if they are not arrested. Minutes to go. Souls rotten from their orgasm drugs, flesh shuddering from their nova ovens, prisoners of the earth to *come out*. With your help we can occupy The Reality Studio and retake their universe of Fear Death and Monopoly –

'(Signed) INSPECTOR J. LEE, NOVA POLICE'

Post Script Of The Regulator : I would like to sound a word of warning – To speak is to lie – To live is to collaborate – Anybody is a coward when faced by the nova ovens – There are degrees of lying collaboration and cowardice – That is to say degrees of intoxication – It is precisely a question of *regulation* – The enemy is not man is not woman – The enemy exists only where no life is and moves always to push life into extreme untenable positions – You can cut the enemy off your line by the judicious use of apomorphine and silence – *Use the sanity drug apomorphine.*

'Apomorphine is made from morphine but its physiological action is quite different. Morphine depresses the front brain. Apomorphine stimulates the back brain, acts on the hypothalamus to regulate the percentage of various constitutents in the blood serum and so normalize the constitution of the blood.' I quote from *Anxiety and Its Treatment* by Doctor John Yerbury Dent.

PRY YOURSELF LOOSE AND LISTEN

I was traveling with The Intolerable Kid on the Nova Lark – We were on the nod after a rumble in The Crab Galaxy involving this two-way time stock ; when you come to the end of a biologic film just run it back and start over – Nobody knows the difference – Like nobody there before the film.* So they start to run it back and the projector blew up and we lammed out of there on the blast – Holed up in those cool blue mountains the liquid air in our spines listening to a little highfi junk notes fixes you right to metal and you nod out a thousand years.† Just sitting there in a slate house wrapped in orange flesh robes, the blue mist drifting around us when we get the call – And as soon as I set foot on Podunk earth I can smell it that burnt metal reek of nova.

---

* Postulate a biologic film running from the beginning to the end, from zero to zero as all biologic film run in any time universe – Call this film X1 and postulate further that there can only be one film with the quality X1 in any given time universe. X1 is the film and performers – X2 is the audience who are all trying to get into the film – nobody is permitted to leave the biologic theater which

'Already set off the charge,' I said to I&I (Immovable and Irresistible) – 'This is a burning planet – Any minute now the whole fucking shit house goes up.'

So Intolerable I&I sniffs and says: 'Yeah, when it happens it happens fast – This is a rush job.'

And you could feel it there under your feet the whole structure buckling like a bulkhead about to blow – So the paper has a car there for us and we are driving in from the airport The Kid at the wheel and his foot on the floor – Nearly ran down

in this case is the human body – Because if anybody did leave the theater he would be looking at a different film Y and Film X1 and audience X2 would then cease to exist by mathematical definition – In 1960 with the publication of *Minutes To Go*, Martin's stale movie was greeted by an unprecedented chorus of boos and a concerted walkout – 'We seen this five times already and not standing still for another twilight of your tired Gods.'

†Since junk *is* image the effects of junk can easily be produced and concentrated in a sound and image track – Like this : Take a sick junky – Throw blue light on his so-called face or dye it blue or dye the junk blue it don't make no difference and now give him a shot and photograph the blue miracle as life pours back into that walking corpse – That will give you the image track of junk – Now project the blue change onto your own face if you want The Big Fix. The sound track is even easier – I quote from *Newsweek*, March 4, 1963 Science section: 'Every substance has a characteristic set of resonant frequencies at which it vibrates or oscillates.' – So you record the frequency of junk as it hits the junk-sick brain cells –

'What's that? – Brain waves are 32 or under and can't be heard? Well speed them up, God damn it – And instead of one junky concentrate me a thousand – Let there be Lexington and call a nice Jew in to run it—'

Doctor Wilhelm Reich has isolated and concentrated a unit that he calls 'the orgone' – Orgones, according to W. Reich, are the units of life – They have been photographed and the color is blue – So junk sops up the orgones and that's why they need all these young junkies – They have more orgones and give higher yield of the blue concentrate on which Martin and his boys can nod out a thousand years – Martin is stealing *your orgones*. – You going to stand still for this shit?

a covey of pedestrians and they yell after us: 'What you want to do, kill somebody?'

And The Kid sticks his head out and says: 'It would be a pleasure Niggers! Gooks! Terrestrial dogs' – His eyes lit up like a blow torch and I can see he is really in form – So we start right to work making our headquarters in The Land Of The Free where the call came from and which is really free and wide open for any life form the uglier the better – Well they don't come any uglier than The Intolerable Kid and your reporter – When a planet is all primed to go up they call in I&I to jump around from one faction to the other agitating and insulting all the parties before and after the fact until they all say: 'By God before I give an inch the whole fucking shit house goes up in chunks.'

Where we came in – You have to move fast on this job – And I&I is fast – Pops in and out of a hundred faces in a split second spitting his intolerable insults – We had the plan, what they call The Board Books to show us what is what on this dead whistle stop: Three life forms uneasily parasitic on a fourth form that is beginning to wise up. And the whole planet absolutely flapping hysterical with panic. The way we like to see them.

'This is a dead easy pitch,' The Kid says.

'Yeah,' I say. 'A little bit too easy. Something here, Kid. Something wrong. I can feel it.'

But The Kid can't hear me. Now all these life forms came from the most intolerable conditions: hot places, cold places, terminal stasis and the last thing any of them want to do is go back where they came from. And The Intolerable Kid is giving out with such pleasantries like this:

'All right take your ovens out with you and pay Hitler on the way out. Nearly got the place hot enough for you Jews didn't he?'

'Know about Niggers? Why darkies were born? Antennae coolers what else? Always a spot for *good* Darkies.'

'You cunts constitute a disposal problem in the worst form there is and raise the nastiest whine ever heard anywhere: "Do you love me? Do you love me? Do you love me???" Why don't you go back to Venus and fertilize a forest?'

'And as for you White Man Boss, you dead prop in Martin's stale movie, you terminal time junky, haul your heavy metal ass back to Uranus. Last shot at the door. You need one for the road.' By this time everybody was even madder than they were shit scared. But I&I figured things were moving too slow.

'We need a peg to hang it on,' he said. 'Something really ugly like virus. Not for nothing do they come from a land without mirrors.' So he takes over this news-magazine.

'Now,' he said, 'I'll by God show them how ugly the Ugly American can be.'

And he breaks out all the ugliest pictures in the image bank and puts it out on the subliminal so one crisis piles up after the other right on schedule. And I&I is whizzing around like a buzz saw and that black nova laugh of his you can hear it now down all the streets shaking the buildings and skyline like a stage prop. But me I am looking around and the more I look the less I like what I see. For one thing the nova heat is moving in fast and heavy like I never see it anywhere else. But I&I just says I have the copper jitters and turns back to his view screen : 'They are skinning the chief of police alive in some jerk-water place. Want to sit in?'

'Naw,' I said. 'Only interested in my own skin.'

And I walk out thinking who I *would* like to see skinned alive. So I cut into the Automat and put coins into the fish cake slot and then I really see it : Chinese partisans and well armed with vibrating static and image guns. So I throw down the fish cakes with tomato sauce and make it back to the office where The Kid is still glued to that screen. He looks up smiling dirty and says :

'Wanta molest a child and disembowel it right after?'

'Pry yourself loose and listen.' And I tell him. 'Those Tiddly Winks don't fuck around you know.'

'So what?' he says. 'I've still got The Board Books. I can split this whistle stop wide open tomorrow.'

No use talking to him. I look around some more and find

out the blockade on planet earth is broken. Explorers moving in whole armies. And everybody concerned is fed up with Intolerable I&I. And all he can say is : 'So what ? I've still got .../' Cut.

'Board Books taken. The film reeks of burning switch like a blow torch. Prerecorded heat glare massing Hiroshima. This whistle stop wide open to hot crab people. Mediation? Listen: Your army is getting double zero in floor by floor game of "symbiosis." Mobilized reasons to love Hiroshima and Nagasaki? Virus to maintain terminal sewers of Venus ?'

'All nations sold out by liars and cowards. Liars who want time for the future negatives to develop stall you with more lying offers while hot crab people mass war to extermination with the film in Rome. These reports reek of nova, sold out job, shit birth and death. Your planet has been invaded. You are dogs on all tape. The entire planet is being developed into terminal identity and complete surrender.'

'But suppose film death in Rome doesn't work and we can get every male body even madder than they are shit scared ? We need a peg to evil full length. By God show them how ugly the ugliest pictures in the dark room can be. Pitch in the oven ambush. Spill all the board gimmicks. This symbiosis con? Can tell you for sure "symbiosis" is ambush straight to the ovens. "Human dogs" to be eaten alive under white hot skies of Minraud.'

And Intolerable I&I's 'errand boys' and 'strike-breakers' are copping out right left and center:

'Mr Martin, and you board members, vulgar stupid Americans, you will regret calling in the Mayan Aztec Gods with your synthetic mushrooms. Remember we keep exact junk measure of the pain inflicted and that pain must be paid in full. Is that clear enough Mr Intolerable Martin, or shall I make it even clearer ? Allow me to introduce myself : The Mayan God of Pain And Fear from the white hot plains of Venus which does not mean a God of vulgarity, cowardice, ugliness and stupidity. There is a cool spot on the surface of Venus three hundred degrees cooler than the surrounding area. I have held that spot against all contestants for five hundred thousand years. Now you expect to use me as your "errand boy" and "strikebreaker" summoned up by an IBM machine and a handful of virus crystals? How long could you hold that spot, you "board members"? About thirty seconds I think with all your guard dogs. And you thought to channel my energies for "operation total disposal"? Your "operations" there or here this or that come and go and are no more. *Give my name back.* That name must be paid for. You have not paid. My name is not yours to use. Henceforth I think about thirty seconds is written.'

And you can see the marks are wising up, standing around in sullen groups and that mutter gets louder and louder. Any minute now fifty million adolescent gooks will hit the street with switch blades, bicycle chains and cobblestones.

'Street gangs, Uranian born of nova conditions, get out and fight for your streets. Call in the Chinese and any random factors. Cut all tape. Shift cut tangle magpie voice lines of the earth. Know about The Board's "Green Deal?" They plan to board the first life boat in drag and leave "their human dogs" under the white hot skies of Venus. "Operation Sky Switch" also known as "Operation Total Disposal." All right you board bastards, we'll by God show you "Operation Total Exposure." For all to see. In Times Square. In Piccadilly.'

So Pack Your Ermines

'So pack your ermines, Mary – We are getting out of here right now – I've seen this happen before – The marks are coming up on us – And the heat is moving in – Recollect when I was travelling with Limestone John on The Carbonic Caper – It worked like this: He rents an amphitheater with marble walls he is a stone painter you dig can create a frieze while you wait – So he puts on a diving suit like the old Surrealist Lark and I am up on a high pedestal pumping the air to him – Well, he starts painting himself around with air blasts he can cover the wall in ten seconds, carbon dioxide settling down on the marks begin to cough and loosen their collars.'

'But what is he painting?'

'Why it's arrg a theater full of people suffocating –'

So we turn the flops over and move on – If you keep it practical they can't hang a nova rap on you – Well, we hit this town and right away I don't like it.

'Something here, John – Something wrong – I can feel it –'

But he says I just have the copper jitters since the nova heat moved in – Besides we are cool, just rolling flops is all three thousand years in show business – So he sets up his amphitheater in a quarry and begins lining up the women clubs and poets and window dressers and organizes this 'Culture Fest' he calls it and I am up in the cabin of a crane pumping the air to him – Well the marks are packing in, the old dolls covered with ice and sapphires and emeralds are really magnificent – So I think maybe I was wrong and everything is aqualungs carrying fish spears and without thinking I yell out from the crane:

'Izzy The Push – Sammy The Butcher – *Hey Rube!*'

Meanwhile I have forgotten the air pump and The Carbonic Kid is turning blue and trying to say something – I rush and pump some air to him and he yells:

'No! No! No!'

I see other marks are coming on with static and camera guns, Sammy and the boys are not making it – These kids have pulled the reverse switch – At this point The Blue Dinosaur himself charged out to discover what the beef is and starts throwing his magnetic spirals at the rubes – They just moved back ahead of him until he runs out of charge and stops. Next thing the nova heat slipped antibiotic handcuffs on all of us.

NABORHOOD IN AQUALUNGS

I was traveling with Merit John on The Carbonic Caper – Larceny with a crew of shoppers – And this number comes over the air to him – So he starts painting The D Fence last Spring – And shitting himself around with air blasts in Hicksville – Stopped ten seconds and our carbon dioxide gave out and we began to cough for such a purpose suffocating under a potted palm in the lobby – 'Move on, you dig, copping out "The Fish Poison Con"'

'I got you – Keep it practical and they can't –'

Transported back to South America we hit this town and right away being stung by the dreaded John – He never missed – Burned three thousand years in me playing cop and quarry – So the marks are packing in virus and subject to dissolved and everything is cool – Assimilate ice sapphires and emeralds all regular – So I walk in about fifty young punks – Sammy and the boys are all he had – One fix – Pulled the reverse switch – Traveling store closing so I don't work like this – John set my medications – Nagasaki in acid on the walls faded out under the rubber trees – He can cover feet back to 1910 – We could buy it settling down – Lay up in the Chink laundry on the collars –

'But what stale rooming house flesh –'

Cradles old troupers – Like Cleopatra applying the asp hang a Nova Rap on you –

'Lush? – I don't like it – Empty pockets in the worn metal – Feel it?'

But John says: 'Copper jitters since the space sell – The old doll is covered –'

Heavy and calm holding cool leather armchair – Organizes this wispy mustache – I stopped in front of a mirror – Really magnificent in a starched collar – It is a naborhood in aqualungs with free lunch everywhere yell out 'Sweet Sixteen' – I walked without Izzy The Push –

'Hey Rube!!'

Came to the Chinese laundry meanwhile – I have forgotten

the Chink in front – Fix words hatch The Blue Dinosaur – I was reading them back magnetic – Only way to orient yourself – Traveling with the Chink kid John set throat like already written – 'Stone Reading' we call it in the trade – While you wait he packs in Rome – I've checked the diving suit like every night – Up on a high pedestal perform this unnatural act – In acid on the walls – Set your watch by it – So that gives us twenty marks out through the side window and collars –

'But what in St Louis?'

Memory picture coming in – So we turn over silver sets and banks and clubs as old troupers – Nova Rap on you that night as we walked out – I don't like it – Something picking up laundry and my flesh feel it –

But John says: 'Afternoon copper jitters since the caper – Housebreaking can cause this –'

We are cool just rolling – when things go wrong once – show business – We can't find poets and organize this cut and the flesh won't work – And there we are with the air off like bleached idiots – Well I think maybe kicks from our condition – They took us – The old dolls on a train burning junk – Thawing flesh showed in aqualungs – Steam a yell out from the crane –

'*Hey Rube!!*'

Three silver digits explode – Meanwhile I have forgotten streets of Madrid – And clear as sunlight pump some air to him and he said: 'Que tal Henrique?'

I am standing through an invisible door click the air to him – Well we hit this town and right away aphrodisiac ointment –

'Doc goofed here, John – Something wrong – Too much Spanish.'

'What? It's green see? A green theater –'

So we turn the marks over and rent a house as old troupers – And we flush out this cool pure Chinese H from show business – And he starts the whole Green Rite and organizes this fibrous grey amphitheater in old turnip – Meanwhile I have forgotten a heavy blue silence – Carbonic Kid is turning to cold liquid metal and run pump some air to him in a blue mist of vapor-

ized flicker helmets – The metal junkies were not making it –
These kids intersected The Nova Police – We are just dust falls
from demagnetized patterns – Show business – Calendar in
Weimar youths – Faded poets in the silent amphitheater – His
block house went away through this air – Click St Louis under
drifting soot – And I think maybe I was in old clinic – Outside
East St Louis – Really magnificent for two notes a week –
Meanwhile I had forgotten 'Mother' – Wouldn't you ? – Doc
Benway and The Carbonic Kid turning a rumble in Dallas involving this pump goofed on ether and mixed in flicker helmets –

'He is gone through this town and right away tape recorders
of his voice behind, John – Something wrong – I can pose a
colorless question ? ? '

'Is all right – I just have the silence – Word dust falls three
thousand years through an old blue calendar –'

'William, no me hagas caso – People who told me I could
move on you copping out – said "Good-Bye" to William and
"Keep it practical" and I could hear him hit this town and right
away I closed the door when I saw John – Something wrong –
Invisible hotel room is all – I just have the knife and he said :

'Nova Heat moved in at the seams – Like three thousand
years in hot claws at the window –

'And Meester William in Tétuan and said : "I have gimmick
is cool and all very technical – These colorless sheets are the
air pump and I can see the flesh when it has color – Writing say
some message that is coming on all flesh –"

'And I said : "William tu es loco – Pulled the reverse switch –
No me hagas while you wait" – Kitchen knife in the heart –
Feel it – Gone away – Pulled the reverse switch – Place no good
– No bueno – He pack caso – William tu hagas yesterday call –
These colorless sheets are empty – You can look any place – No
good – No bueno – Adios Meester William –'

THE FISH POISON CON

I was traveling with Merit Inc. checking store attendants for larceny with a crew of 'shoppers' – There was two middle-aged cunts one owning this chihuahua which whimpered and yapped in a cocoon of black sweaters and Bob Schafer Crew Leader who was an American Fascist with Roosevelt jokes – It happens in Iowa this number comes over the car radio: 'Old Sow Got Caught In The Fence Last Spring' – And Schafer said 'Oh my God, are we ever in Hicksville.' Stopped that night in Pleasantville Iowa and our tires gave out we had no tire rations during the war for such a purpose – And Bob got drunk and showed his badge to the locals in a road house by the river – And I ran into The Sailor under a potted palm in the lobby – We hit the local croakers with 'the fish poison con' – 'I got these poison fish, Doc, in the tank transported back from South America I'm a Icthyologist and after being stung by the dreaded Candirú – Like fire through the blood is it not? Doctor, and coming on now' – And The Sailor goes into his White Hot Agony Act chasing the doctor around his office like a blow-torch He never missed – But he burned down the croakers – So like Bob and me when we 'had a catch' as the old cunts call it and arrested some sulky clerk with his hand deep in the company pocket, we take turns playing the tough cop and the con cop – So I walk in on this Pleasantville croaker and tell him I have contracted this Venusian virus and subject to dissolve myself in poison juices and assimilate the passers-by unless I get my medicine and get it regular – So I walk in on this old party smelling like a compost heap and steaming demurely and he snaps at me, 'What's *your* trouble?'

'The Venusian Gook Rot, doctor.'

'Now see here young man my time is valuable.'

'Doctor, this is a medical emergency.'

Old shit but good – I walked out on the nod –

'All he had was one fix, Sailor.'

'You're loaded – You assimilated the croaker – Left me sick –'

'Yes. He was old and tough but not too tough for The Caustic Enzymes Of Woo.'

The Sailor was thin and the drugstore was closing so I didn't want him to get physical and disturb my medications – The next croaker wrote with erogenous acid vats on one side and Nagasaki Ovens on the other – And we nodded out under the rubber trees with the long red carpet under our feet back to 1910 – We could buy it in the drugstore tomorrow – Or lay up in the Chink laundry on the black smoke – drifting through stale rooming houses, pool halls and chili – Fell back on sad flesh small and pretentious in a theatrical boarding house the aging ham cradles his tie up and stabs a vein like Cleopatra applying the asp – Click back through the cool grey short-change artists – lush rolling ghosts of drunken sleep – Empty pockets in the worn metal subway dawn –

I woke up in the hotel lobby the smell heavy and calm holding a different body molded to the leather chair – I was sick but not needle sick – This was a black smoke yen – The Sailor still sleeping and he looked very young under a wispy mustache – I woke him up and he looked around with slow hydraulic control his eyes unbluffed unreadable –

'Let's make the street – I'm thin –'

I was in fact very thin I saw when I stopped in front of a mirror panel and adjusted my tie knot in a starched collar – It was a naborhood of chili houses and cheap saloons with free lunch everywhere and heavy calm bartenders humming 'Sweet Sixteen' – I walked without thinking like a horse will and came to The Chinese Laundry by Clara's Massage Parlor – We siphoned in and The Chink in front jerked one eye back and went on ironing a shirt front – We walked through a door and a curtain and the black smoke set our lungs dancing The Junky Jig and we lay up on our junk hip while a Chinese kid cooked our pills and handed us the pipe – After six pipes we smoke slow and order a pot of tea the Chink kid goes out fix it and the words hatch in my throat like already written there I was reading them back – 'Lip Reading' we call it in the trade only way to orient yourself when in Rome – 'I've checked the

harness bull – He comes in McSorley's every night at 2.20 a.m.
and forces the local pederast to perform this unnatural act on
his person – So regular you can set your watch by it : "I won't –
I won't – Not again – Glub – Glub – Glub."' – 'So that gives us
twenty minutes at least to get in and out through the side window and eight hours start we should be in St Louis before they
miss the time – Stop off and see The Family' – Memory pictures coming in – Little Boy Blue and all the heavy silver sets
and banks and clubs – Cool heavy eyes moving steel and oil
shares – I had a rich St Louis family – It was set for that night –
As we walked out I caught the Japanese girl picking up laundry and my flesh crawled under the junk and I made a meet
for her with the afternoon – Good plan to make sex before a
caper – Housebreaking can cause this wet dream sex tension
especially when things go wrong – (Once in Peoria me and The
Sailor charged a drugstore and we can't find the jimmy for the
narco cabinet and the flash won't work and the harness bull
sniffing round the door and there we are with The Sex Current
giggling ourselves off like beached idiots – Well the cops got
such nasty kicks from our condition they took us to the RR station and we get on a train shivering burning junk sick and the
warm vegetable smells of thawing flesh and stale come slowly
filled the car – Nobody could look at us steaming away there
like manure piles –) I woke out of a light yen sleep when the
Japanese girl came in – Three silver digits exploded in my
head – I walked out into streets of Madrid and won a football
pool – Felt the Latin mind clear and banal as sunlight met Paco
by the soccer scores and he said : 'Que tal Henrique ?'

And I went to see my amigo who was taking medicina again
and he had no money to give me and didn't want to do anything but take more medicina and stood there waiting for me
to leave so he could take it after saying he was not going to
take any more so I said, 'William no me hagas caso.' And met
a Cuban that night in The Mar Chica who told me I could work
in his band – The next day I said good-bye to William and
there was nobody there to listen and I could hear him reaching
for his medicina and needles as I closed the door – When I saw

the knife I knew Meester William was death disguised as any other person – Pues I saw El Hombre Invisible in a hotel room somewhere tried to reach him with the knife and he said: 'If you kill me this crate will come apart at the seams like a rotten undervest' – And I saw a monster crab with hot claws at the window and Meester William took some white medicina and vomited into the toilet and we escaped to Greece with a boy about my age who kept calling Meester William 'The Stupid American' – And Meester William looked like a hypnotist I saw once in Tétuan and said: 'I have gimmick to beat The Crab but it is very technical' – And we couldn't read what he was writing on transparent sheets – In Paris he showed me The Man who paints on these sheets pictures in the air – And The Invisible Man said:

"These colorless sheets are what flesh is made from – Becomes flesh when it has color and writing – That is Word And Image write the message that is you on colorless sheets determine all flesh."

And I said: 'William, tu éres loco.'

NO GOOD – NO BUENO

So many years – that image – got up and fixed in the sick dawn – *No me hagas caso* – Again he touched like that – smell of dust – The tears gathered – In Mexico again he touched – Codeine pills powdered out into the cold Spring air – Cigarette holes in the vast Thing Police – Could give no information other than wind identity fading out – dwindling – 'Mr Martin' couldn't reach is all – Bread knife in the heart – Shadow turned off the lights and water – We intersect on empty walls – Look anywhere – No good – Falling in the dark mutinous door – Dead Hand stretching zero – Five times of dust we made it all the living and the dead – Young form went to Madrid – Demerol by candlelight – Wind hand – The Last Electrician to tap on pane – Migrants arrival – Poison of dead sun went away and sent papers – Ferry boat cross flutes of Ramadan – Dead muttering in the dog's space – Cigarette hole in the dark – give no information other than the cold Spring cemetery – The Sailor went wrong in corridors of that hospital – Thing Police keep all Board Room Reports is all – Bread knife in the heart proffers the disaster accounts – He just sit down on 'Mr Martin' – Couldn't reach flesh on Niño Perdido – A long time between flutes of Ramadan – No me hagas caso sliding between light and shadow –

'The American trailing cross the wounded galaxies con su medicina, William.'

Half your brain slowly fading – Turned off the lights and water – Couldn't reach flesh – empty walls – Look anywhere – Dead on tracks see Mr Bradley Mr Zero – And being blind may not refuse the maps to my blood whom I created 'Mr Bradly Mr Martin,' couldn't you write us any better than that? – Gone away – You can look any place – No good – No bueno –

I spit blood under the sliding vulture shadows – At The Mercado Mayorista saw a tourist – A Meester Merican fruto drinking pisco – and fixed me with the eyes so I sit down and drink and tell him how I live in a shack under the hill with a tin roof held down by rocks and hate my brothers because they eat – He says something about 'malo viento' and laughs and I went with him to a hotel I know – In the morning he says I am honest and will I come with him to Pucallpa he is going into the jungle looking for snakes and spiders to take pictures and bring them back to Washington they always carry something away even if it is only a spider monkey spitting blood the way most of us do here in the winter when the mist comes down from the mountains and never leaves your clothes and lungs and everyone coughed and spit blood mist on the mud floor where I sleep – We start out next day in a Mixto Bus by night we are in the mountains with snow and the Meester brings out a bottle of pisco and the driver gets drunk down into the Selva came to Pucallpa three days later – The Meester locates a brujo and pays him to prepare Ayuhuasca and I take some too and muy mareado – Then I was back in Lima and other places I didn't know and saw the Meester as child in a room with rose wallpaper looking at something I couldn't see – Tasting roast beef and turkey and ice cream in my throat knowing the thing I couldn't see was always out there in the hall – And the Meester was looking at me and I could see the street boy words there in his throat – Next day the police came looking for us at the hotel and the Meester showed letters to the Commandante so they shook hands and went off to lunch and I took a bus back to Lima with money he gave me to buy equipment –

SHIFT COORDINATE POINTS

K9 was in combat with the alien mind screen – Magnetic claws feeling for virus punch cards – pulling him into vertiginous spins –

'Back – Stay out of those claws – Shift coordinate points –' By Town Hall Square long stop for the red light – A boy stood in front of the hot dog stand and blew water from his face – Pieces of grey vapor drifted back across wine gas and brown hair as hotel faded photo showed a brass bed – Unknown mornings blew rain in cobwebs – Summer evenings feel to a room with rose wallpaper – Sick dawn whisper of clock hands and brown hair – Morning blew rain on copper roofs in a slow haze of apples – Summer light on rose wallpaper – Iron mesas lit by a pink volcano – Snow slopes under the Northern shirt – Unknown street stirring sick dawn whispers of junk – Flutes of Ramadan in the distance – St Louis lights wet cobblestones of future life – Fell through the urinal and the bicycle races – On the bar wall the clock hands – My death across his face faded through the soccer scores – smell of dust on the surplus army blankets – Stiff jeans against one wall – And KiKi went away like a cat – Some clean shirt and walked out – He is gone through unknown morning blew – 'No good – No bueno – Hustling myself –' Such wisdom in gusts –

K9 moved back into the combat area – Standing now in the Chinese youth sent the resistance message jolting clicking tilting through the pinball machine – Enemy plans exploded in a burst of rapid calculations – Clicking in punch cards of redir-

ected orders – Crackling shortwave static – Bleeeeeeeeeeeeeep –
Sound of thinking metal –

'Calling partisans of all nations – Word falling – Photo falling – Break through in Grey Room – Pinball led streets – Free
doorways – Shift coordinate points –'

'The ticket that exploded posed little time so I'll say "good
night" – Pieces of grey Spanish Flu wouldn't photo – Light the
wind in green neon – You at the dog – The street blew rain –
If you wanted a cup of tea with rose wallpaper – The dog
turns – So many and sooo –'

'In progress I am mapping a photo – Light verse of wounded
galaxies at the dog I did – The street blew rain – The dog turns
– Warring head intersected Powers – Word falling – Photo falling – Break through in Grey Room –'

He is gone away through invisible mornings leaving a million tape recorders of his voice behind fading into the cold
spring air pose a colorless question?

'The silence fell heavy and blue in mountain villages – Pulsing mineral silence as word dust falls from demagnetized patterns – Walked through an old blue calendar in Weimar youth
– Faded photo on rose wallpaper under a copper roof – In the
silent dawn little grey men played in his block house and went
away through an invisible door – Click St Louis under drifting
soot of old newspapers – "Daddy Longlegs" looked like Uncle
Sam on stilts and he ran this osteopath clinic outside East St
Louis and took in a few junky patients for two notes a week
they could stay on the nod in green lawn chairs and look at
the oaks and grass stretching down to a little lake in the sun
and the nurse moved around the lawn with her silver trays
feeding the junk in – We called her "Mother" – Wouldn't you?
– Doc Benway and me was holed up there after a rumble in
Dallas involving this aphrodisiac ointment and Doc goofed on
ether and mixed in too much Spanish Fly and burned the prick
right off the Police Commissioner straight away – So we come
to "Daddy Longlegs" to cool off and found him cool and casual
in a dark room with potted rubber plants and a silver tray on
the table where he liked to see a week in advance – The nurse

showed us to a room with rose wallpaper and we had this bell any hour of the day or night ring and the nurse charged in with a loaded hypo – Well one day we were sitting out in the lawn chairs with lap robes it was a fall day trees turning and the sun cold on the lake – Doc picks up a piece of grass –

'Junk turns you on vegetable – It's green, see? – A green fix should last a long time.'

We checked out of the clinic and rented a house and Doc starts cooking up this green junk and the basement was full of tanks smelled like a compost heap of junkies – So finally he draws off this heavy green fluid and loads it into a hypo big as a bicycle pump –

'Now we must find a worthy vessel,' he said and we flush out this old goof ball artist and told him it was pure Chinese H from The Ling Dynasty and Doc shoots the whole pint of green right into the main line and the Yellow Jacket turns fibrous grey green and withered up like an old turnip and I said: 'I'm getting out of here, me,' and Doc said: 'An unworthy vessel obviously – So I have now decided that junk is not green but blue.'

So he buys a lot of tubes and globes and they are flickering in the basement this battery of tubes metal vapor and quick-silver and pulsing blue spheres and a smell of ozone and a little high-fi blue note fixed you right to metal this junk note tinkling through your crystals and a heavy blue silence fell *klunk* – and all the words turned to cold liquid metal and ran off you man just fixed there in a cool blue mist of vaporized bank notes – We found out later that the metal junkies were all radioactive and subject to explode if two of them came into contact – At this point in our researches we intersected The Nova Police –

Robert Creeley

Mr Blue

I don't want to give you only the grotesqueness, not only what
it then seemed. It is useless enough to remember but to remember only what is unpleasant seems particularly foolish. I suspect that you have troubles of your own, and, since you have,
why bother you with more. Mine against yours. That seems a
waste of time. But perhaps mine are also yours. And if that's
so, you'll find me a sympathetic listener.

A few nights ago I wrote down some of this, thinking, trying
to think, of what had happened. What had really happened
like they say. It seemed, then, that some such effort might get
me closer to an understanding of the thing than I was. So much
that was not directly related had got in and I thought a little
noting of what was basic to the problem might be in order.
That is, I wanted to analyze it, to try to see where things stood.
I'm not at all sure that it got to anything, this attempt, because
I'm not very good at it. But you can look for yourselves.

1) That dwarfs, gnomes, midgets are, by the fact of their
   SIZE, *intense:*
2) That dwarfs, gnomes, midgets cause people LARGER than
   themselves to appear wispy, insubstantial, cardboard;
3) that all SIZE tends toward BIG but in the case of dwarfs,
   gnomes, midgets.

But perhaps best to begin at the beginning. And, to begin,
there are two things that you must know. The first of these is
that I am, myself, a tall man, somewhat muscular though not
unpleasantly so. I have brown hair and brown eyes though
that is not altogether to the point here. What you should remember is that I am a big man, as it happens, one of the biggest in the town.

My wife is also large. This is the second. But she is not so much large as large-boned. A big frame. I sound as though I were selling her, but I'm not. I mean, I don't want to sound like that, as though I were trying to impress you that way. It is just that that I don't want to do. That is, make you think that I am defending her or whatever it is that I may sound like to you. In short, she is an attractive woman and I don't think I am the only one who would find her so. She has, like myself, brown hair but it is softer, very soft, and she wears it long, almost to her waist, in heavy braids. But it is like her eyes, I mean, there is that lightness in it, the way it brushes against her back when she is walking. It makes me feel rather blundering, heavy, to look at her. It seems to me my step jars the house when I walk through a room where she is. We have been married five years.

Five years doesn't seem, in itself, a very long time. So much goes so quickly, so many things that I can think of now that then, when they were happening, I could hardly take hold of. And where she comes into it, those things that had to do with her. I find I missed, perhaps, a lot that I should have held to. At least I should have tried. But like it or not, it's done with. Little good to think of it now.

I did try, though, to do what I could. She never seemed unhappy, and doesn't even now. Perhaps upset when the baby was sick, but, generally speaking, she's a level woman, calm, good-sense.

But perhaps that's where I'm wrong, that I have that assumption, that I think I know what she is like. Strange that a man shouldn't know his wife but I suppose it could be so, that even having her around him for five years, short as they are, he could still be strange to her and she to him. I think I know, I think I know about what she'd do if this or that happened, if I were to say this to her, or something about something, or what people usually talk about. It's not pleasant doubting your own knowing, since that seems all you have. If you lose that or take it as somehow wrong, the whole thing goes to pieces. Not much use trying to hold it together after that.

Still I can't take seriously what's happened. I can't but still

I do. I wish it were different, that in some way I were out of it, shaken but at least out. But here I am. The same place.

It was raining, a bad night for anything. Not hard, but enough to soak you if you were out in it for very long. We thought it would probably be closed but, when we got there, all the lights were going and I could see some people up in the ferris-wheel, probably wet to the skin. Still they looked as if they were having fun and some of their shouts reached us as we went through the gate and into the main grounds. It was fairly late, about ten or so, another reason why I had thought it would be closed. Another day and the whole works would be gone and that's why she had insisted.

I feel, usually, uncomfortable in such places. I don't like the crowds, at least not the noise of them. They never seem to stop, always jumping, moving, and the noise. Any one of them, alone, or two or three, that's fine. As it happened, we went by a number of our friends, who yelled at us, fine night, or some such thing. I can't remember exactly what the words were. But I didn't like them, or didn't like them then, with that around them, the noise, and their excitement.

No reason, perhaps, to think she knew where she was going. I didn't. I think we followed only the general movement of the people, where they were going. It was packed and very difficult to go anywhere but where you were pushed. So we were landed in front of the tent without much choice and stood, listening to the barker, to see what might be happening.

I can say, and this is part of it, that I didn't want to go in. For several reasons. The main one is that I don't like freaks, I don't like to look at them or to be near them. They seem to have a particular feeling around them, which is against me, altogether. A good many times I've seen others staring, without the slightest embarrassment, at some hunchback, or some man with a deformity that puts him apart from the rest. I don't see how they can do it, how they can look without any reaction but curiosity. For myself, I want only to get away.

But this time she decided. It seemed that not very much could be inside the tent. They had advertised a midget, a knife-thrower, a man with some snakes, and one or two other things. Nothing like the large circuses and none of the more horrible things such might offer. So I got the tickets and we followed a few of the others in.

They were just finishing a performance. It was so packed at the front, that we stood at the back, waiting until the first crowd was ready to leave. I felt tired myself. It must have been close to eleven at that point. It seemed an effort there was no reason for. But she enjoyed it, looked all around, at everyone, smiled at those she knew, waved to some, kept talking to me, and I would say something or other to hide my own feeling. Perhaps I should have been straight with her, told her I was tired, and ducked out. It would have saved it, or at least got me free. But I kept standing there, with her, waiting for the show to finish and another to start.

It did soon, the first crowd moving out, and our own coming up to take its place. The man on the platform had got down at the end and now we waited for him to come back and the new show to begin. There was talking around us, sounding a little nervous the way most will at those times when something is being waited for, though what one can't say with exactness. At this point, I was almost as expectant as the others. Nothing else to be, perhaps. In any event, I had got over my other feeling.

The first act was a cowboy with a lariat, rope tricks. Not much but he was good with it, could make it spin all kinds of loops, shrinking them, making them grow right while we watched him. It was good fun, I thought, not much but enough. At the end he started stamping with one foot and at the same time, he slipped his loop off and on it, brought it up around both feet at the end, jumping and grinning. I think there may have been some music with it, something for the beat, but it doesn't matter. The man told us he was deaf, couldn't hear a thing. There didn't seem to be much point in telling us that but I guess we're apt to like that adding of what we don't expect.

We enjoyed it, the both of us. It's not often that we can get out, like that, to see anything. And after the first I forgot about being tired and liked it as much as she did. The next act was the knife-thrower. He could put them all in a circle no bigger than my hand, eight of them, so that they shivered there with a force which surprised me, each time one hit, she gripped my arm, and I laughed at her nervousness, but it was a funny thing, even so.

Then came the snake act, which wasn't up to the others, or simply that dullness in it, the snakes much the same, doped, I expect, though perhaps I was wrong to think so. Then sort of a juggling act, a man with a number of colored balls and odd-shaped sticks, which he set into a strange kind of movement, tossing them, one after the other, until he must have had tens somehow, going and all this with an intentness that made us almost clap then, as they did move, through his hands. Altogether a wonder it seemed, his precision, and how it kept him away from us, even though some stood no more than a few feet away. Until at last he stopped them one by one, and then, the last, smiled at us, and we all gave him a good hand.

It's here that I leave, or as I go back to it, this time, or this way, that is, now that I make my way out, through the rest of them, my hand on her arm with just that much pressure to guide her, or that is my intention. Perhaps the lights that make my eyes ache, begin to, or simply, that it's now, this point, that I am happy, that it's ourselves, the two of us, have come to some sort of feel of it, that makes us so. Just that I am, now, running, that it is just that I do.

What she had been doing, or going to that, it was a cigarette she asked me for, and I reached into my pocket for them, had got out the pack, and given her one, and then lit a match for her. She bent a little, got it lit, then looked back to the platform where the juggler had been.

But the trick, that it's him who's there, the midget, as such he is named, but the size, it's that which hits me, at first, that he isn't small, or looking, he must be five feet, or perhaps, a little smaller. Four feet. But not small.

The eyes, catch, get me so into it, that they are so, void, in the head, shaded, the shades like changing shadows, colors, coming in to want, to want to be filled. Seem huge. He looks at all of us, moves over us so, to bite, to have something to be there to bite.

But nothing, certainly, to make of it more or more than what I could see, would be, that is, the barker introduced him, and we stood, as we had, in that group in front of him, the boards which made the platform, that roughness, and the poles on which the lights were strung, the wires sagging between them. That is, what is it had come in, as this was, to be not or to make it not as it had been, if it were, as it was, the same place, which I couldn't say or put my finger on, then, but waited like any of the rest.

I could see the muscle of his arm, where the sleeve had been pulled up, rolled, above it, and with his movement, that slightness of tension made him lift it, slightly, from time to time, the muscle tightened and it looked hard, big, below the roll of the sleeve. As my own would. He was smiling, the face somewhat broad, well-shaped, the smile somewhat dreamy, or like sleep, that vagueness, which couldn't be understood.

The barker had laughed, the pitch of it rolled out, on us, and I wondered if he was as drunk as he looked. He was calling the midget, cute, saying, a cute little fellow. He made a joke of it, looking at the women and laughing. Saying, who would like to take him home. There was laughing, they liked the joke, and he carried it further, sensing their tolerance, and played it up. It was the joke he seemed intent on making us remember, the cuteness, the idea of the women.

Taking the cigarettes out of my pocket, the pack crumpled, I held it out to her, but she was intent on what was before us, and I expect that I was myself, and only did what I did, took them out, to somehow break it, to make it break down. It seemed that, that is, that gesture or an act, an action, so meant to serve double, to be a break, but what was it, that is, more than the taking, just that, of the cigarettes, which I didn't want to smoke, had even just put one out. I looked, then, around me at the rest of them and they were looking at him, the midget, and I couldn't see one that noticed I looked, or gave the least sign.

The midget stood still, beside the barker, who staggered a little, under the lights, moved from one side to the other, his face to us, that drunkenness. He was still on the joke, fumbling, and it wore down on us, that weight of it, kept at us, and I wanted to get out. There seemed breaks, lengths of silence, hung there, made the other, the midget, the whole of it, in his own silence, which he kept as a distance around him, that the eyes made actual.

I would have gone, or as I think, I should have in spite of it, simply slipped out, when the others weren't looking, just left and waited for her outside. I can't see that she would have been hurt. That is, I would think, or think I would have that right to, that it would make no difference to her, that is, that she would understand my going, seeing that it had begun to tire me, even became painful to stay. I think of it so, being such, that no difference could be in it, since she was enjoying it, or so it seemed.

I tried to, but the people around pressed too tight, pushed me from the back, all forward, to the one on the platform in front of us. Not the barker, I knew that much, but the other, who pulled them, kept them all, because the barker had somehow fallen altogether to pieces, had just the joke he hung on to, and that was played out. But then he switched it, perhaps feeling it had, and turned to the midget, and said, but you should have some say in this. Which one would you like.

The midget turned, then seemed to pull himself out of it, the distance, out of nothing, the eyes pulled in, to focus, to grow, somehow, smaller, larger. The eyes went over us, the voice, when it came, was breath, a breathing but way back in, wire, tight, taut, the scream and I couldn't hear it, saw only his finger move to point at her, beside me, and wanted to say, he's looking at you, but she was turned away from me, as though laughing, but struck, hit. I looked, a flash, sideways, as it then happened. Looked, he looked at me, cut, the hate jagged, and I had gone, then, into it and that was almost that. But she said, then, she had seen him, earlier, that same day, as he was standing by a store, near the door, I think, as it had opened, and she, there, across the street, saw him motion, the gesture, then, a dance, shuffle, the feet crooked, and the arms, as now, loose, and it was before, as before, but not because of this that made it or I thought, so made it, was it, or it was that thing I hung to, when, the show over, they motioned us out, and I pushed a way for her out through the crowd.

The Party

Of uncleanliness, he was saying, there are, one must come to think, a good many kinds. Or more, put it, than dirt on the hands.

The wind shifted, slightly pulling them down the lake and in toward the dock which he saw now as a line, black, on the water, lying out and on it.

Not one, he said, not one sense would give you the whole of it, and I expect that continues what's wanted.

But they sat quiet, anyhow, the woman at the far end, slumped there, and the length of her very nearly flat on the canoe's bottom. The man kept upright, the paddle still in his hands, but he held it loosely, letting it slap at the water, lightly, as the waves lifted to reach it.

Nothing important, she said. Nothing to worry about, and what about tonight? We forgot that.

He began to paddle again, but slowly, and looked back at her reluctantly, almost asleep.

That doesn't please you, she said. You seem determined not to enjoy yourself.

Not that, he answered, and it had taken him, at that, some way beyond where he had been.

Not so simply, he said. You make it too easy.

But why easy, she answered. I don't see that it's not easy, any of it. These people will hardly care to attack you personally. They are all much too busy.

Looking down at her, he found her laughing at him, and smiled himself.

You are all so very serious, she said, all of you. What is it makes you think the world is so intent on you at whatever age you are.

Because I don't know, she added, just how old you are. But you look young. You look very young.

He whistled, a little song, and looked back toward the dock which they now came to, bumping against it, and he reached out to steady them, and then pulled the canoe alongside for her to get out.

Easy, she said. Don't jerk it.

He watched her swing out, a foot on the dock, then pull herself up, and clear, to wait for him.

Help me pull it up, she said. It might break loose.

He got out, and helped her lift it, and then pushed to roll it over, on the dock, easing it down gently, when her hands were clear.

There, she said, now it will be safe.

He followed her back along the dock, crossing at the end, another, and then up a path to where her car sat, shaded by the trees. She opened the door for him, and reaching in, spread a towel on the seat, then crossed round to the other side. Sliding under the wheel, she leaned over and caught him with one hand, pulling him to her, to kiss him.

For your sullenness, she said, although you hardly deserve it.

He pushed free and watched her start the car.

Sometime you will have to answer me, she said. Sometime there will be nothing else for you to do.

They moved off quickly, along the road, and coming to another, swung in, grating, and up to the house, and stopped there and got out.

Leaving her, he went to his room, took off his bathing-suit and dropped it on the floor. To his right a mirror hung, on the wall, and he turned to look at himself, the whiteness, and then dressed quickly, and left the room.

Here, she called.

The voice echoed a little, finding him, and he followed it out to where she was sitting, waiting for him.

There's not too much time, she said. Would you like a drink before we go?

He nodded and she got up, and went out. Returning, she came to him and put the glass on the small table by his hand. Then she went back to her own chair and sat down.

Thanks, he said, and picked up the glass from where she had put it.

But nothing at all! Very happy to do it.

He smiled, then drank, and put the glass back.

This is a very comfortable room, he said. Very airy, very nice and big.

She nodded, quiet, and looked round at the walls, the high ceiling, then back at him.

He wanted it this way, she said. He did most of it himself.

He looked away, turning, and settled on a picture which was across from him, a small one of some trees and a house.

His favorite room, she said. This and the shack were all he cared about.

A damn shame, he said, to have just got it, and then to have to lose it.

She didn't answer, and looked, instead, out the window, her head somewhat bent, and loose, and he watched her, quietly, letting the time pass.

It makes me feel rather dirty, he said, rather stupid, if that's how to say it.

It's not you.

But it must be me a little. That I walk in on it.

You don't. There's nothing to worry about.

She had got up and now looked at her wrist, the little band there, of some bright metal, and then at him, saying, it's very late.

He followed her out, and into the car, and starting it, she drove off quickly, hurrying because of the lateness. Some cars were already there, and they pulled in behind them, and stopped.

It won't be bad, she said, or it won't be if you'll try to help a little.

He shrugged and went after her up the path, waiting behind while she knocked, lightly, on the door. Abruptly it opened and he saw a woman smiling at both of them, reaching, to pull them in. He let them talk, standing back, and then went in after them.

You're the last, the woman said, but that's an honor?

Yes, she said, and they went in, closely, following the woman, laughing, and he saw them all sitting in a ring about the room, the chairs all back against the wall, and going to one near the door, he sat down.

Mr Briggs, they said, and all laughed, is a strange young man!

But he had not heard them, and only sat, placid, and again waited for a drink, thinking it enough that there should be one for him. It came soon and taking it, he thanked the woman and lifted the glass to his mouth.

Cheers!

He sat back, more relaxed, and nodding to the man beside him, said, very fine, and smiled.

There's not much hope for them, the other answered, if they won't make an attempt to see both sides.

No, he said, I can't see that they will find any other way out of it.

But it doesn't matter, she asked. Who could care about such a thing.

The sandwiches went by him, and reaching out, he caught one, smiling, and put it into his mouth.

The truth, the other said, is what rarely seems to be considered.

But they had not heard either, and one woman now stood up, and looked at all of them, saying, to John. Wherever he is. They drank in silence. A windy void, which he felt himself, lifting the glass, and drinking, then, with all of them. It was love, she said, a very true love.

From the next room the children's voices came, clearly, and

they were crying, wailing, he thought, with a very specific injury. Getting up, he said, I'll go, not thinking, and had gone through the door before anyone had noticed him.

But, seeing him, they cried louder, screaming, and the woman was there behind him, and motioned him out.

But no, she said, it's no use. You bad children, go to sleep!

Bewildered, he looked down at her, beside the bed, and younger than she who he had come with, he thought, but she will not allow me, she will not understand.

We'd better go back, she said. They'll go to sleep by themselves.

In the other room they had got up, and stood only to wait for her, to say, goodnight, apologetically, and left. She watched them go, blankly, and he stood beside her, trying, as he thought, to help.

My party, she said. There's no reason to leave.

It's late, someone answered. It's been very fine.

The room cleared, slowly, the doorway crowded but at last empty, and they sat down then, the three of them, on the couch, looking after the others. In the room behind them the crying continued, and softened, finally, to die out.

They're all asleep, he said, and turned, but could not see her face.

Does it matter, he said. I mean, does it matter in any way you can think of?

But the woman had got up, and the other now raised herself, to lean over, and seeing him, laughed, and sank back.

You make it sound momentous, she said. You really prefer disasters.

She smiled at him quickly, lifting again, but he had turned his head and she could not see him.

Anyhow, it was a good party, she said then, turning to the younger woman. There was certainly nothing wrong with it.

The Suitor

Let them say 'tis grossly done;
so it be fairly done, no matter.
The Merry Wives of Windsor

Staggering back along what he took to be the path, he thought,
long roads are happy roads, and belched. Somewhere inside the
shape now looming beside him, like they say, was also the
woman he loved, or had taken himself to, as she had apparently also taken him to. Not to mention her mother, amiable
woman, who at least allowed him bedspace. There was a kind
of gayety about it all, and since the party was over – it was
about four in the morning – he felt he might well be the last one
so possessed.

Kate, he called, through the door, and fell through it because
the light stayed off, firmly off, and decidedly. But where was
she, in the dark? He listened for sounds of breathing and heard,
from somewhere in the blackness, a sough, a kind of sighing
wheeze, which hardly bore him much confidence. So he waited,
even held himself, quiet, and said, again, Kate?

Finally it answered him, to wit, the dull black form on the
bed, now a little at least visible, as it raised itself on an elbow
almost he thought, god bless her, like his own mother, last seen
waving to him across or obscured by the tailgate of a truck.
But he would never run away from home again. What home
he had, could have, there he stayed, forever.

Are you there, she said. He stumbled forward, caught at the
table placed close to where he was about to fall, and fell, head
down, cracking his nose on her elbow, and fell asleep.

But it was a short night. He heard them talking in the
kitchen, through the open doors, of the living room, and looked
out from under the sheets. There was a large painting on the
wall opposite him, unsigned. The voices said, first we will take
knives and cut little bits out of his knees, eyes, and toes, and

then we will cover him all over with flour, and lard, and push him into this nice big oven, for which we have ordered one ton of coal. She said, he heard it, the coal has come. Will you? He nodded, and she backed out of the room, closing the door behind her.

It was part of the system. To eat is to work, he worked. He got up, dressed quickly in the same clothes he had already, he found, been already, partially, dressed in. He had never taken them off. But once in the air, he took stock of his surroundings. The house across the street had certainly moved in the night. It crowded close to the fence which, he supposed, was the only thing holding it back. In one of the windows a face pressed hard against the glass, looking. He turned and saw, then, a large pile of coal which had been dumped close to a bulhead which he briefly opened, and began to shovel.

How much later he was never to know there was a rustle at the screendoor also by the bulkhead, and he saw, dimly, someone motioning to him. Come in, she said. He came in. Sitting down, he took up the cup of black coffee gratefully. Thank you, he said. He drank it, gulping a little, an odd but definite constriction in his throat which even the half-cooked egg, eaten later, failed to dislodge. There was no toast because the bread had not yet been got. She said. She looked at him. The coal was almost shovelled.

Once again he began, this time singing, he did not know why, but soon there was standing close to him a small boy of about ten years, listening. What would you like to hear, he thought. There was certainly enough to tell. Sometimes he thought even of writing it all down, and of then putting it into a bottle, and then of throwing it out the window. Somehow it might arrive on a beach.

Otherwise there was not very much to hope for. The coal was shovelled, all of it, but then there was the bread to be got. He trotted down the road, down the hill, wondering if his buttocks joggled too preposterously. Love had no objections at least. But it also occurred to him, why should it. There were compensations. In the store he asked for one loaf Italian bread, and they gave it to him. Whereupon he handed them the folded dollar, and they returned him change.

This he gave back to them, not to them, but to the two women now standing in front of him. The bread he put on the table. There was never a clear demarcation between times. Sometimes, idiotically enough, he thought he was sitting in a chair. But if this were so, and if he had taken the bath some time ago, being obviously dirty, why now should he be objected to? The water dripped from a crack in the ceiling over his head. The mother looked at him, greying hair, grey hair, he thought. She said, oh, you must have sloshed, in your bath. Blackly, he felt himself gripping the arms of the chair but it was an iron slung chair, or something. He sat precariously enough.

No, I did not, he said. How could he prove such a thing? Next time they would certainly think themselves entitled to watch. He sat on the toilet, gripping, dully the fact that in order to flush it one must bend over, somehow, and turn the little faucet handle underneath the seat so that the water could then fill the bowl. And hence, away! There had been that scene. Someone had wished to brush her teeth. Take me away, he thought. He picked up a magazine and tried to remember how to read.

On page five she asked him if he were thirsty. It was five o'clock? After five o'clock one could drink, seriously. Up till then, beer and wine. She handed him the glass. On the glass, in adhesive tape, was the huge, slightly frayed initial, *R*. For rest, he thought. Do you have my glass, the other asked, the mother. Is your name ratface? How could he say it? It was too true. She took the glass, smiling, and another was handed him. Ratface, he thought, ratface, ratface, ratface. I hate you, ratface. He thought.

But there was a scratching at the door, then another face. The face, he saw, of old Bill Bunch, lately hailed, at least frequently, by both mother and daughter as that lovely and impossible man. He was their next door neighbor, so that was helpful. Gossip had it that he could do very little, if anything.

He fumbled, he tripped, one time when his son was sick (the ten year old of earlier acquaintance) and then his wife likewise, in the care of the former, and the man, Bill, sent to a hotel in the city to keep him out of the way or under cover, depending on the inference, anyhow he returned home, to help, and tripped walking up the steps and sprained both ankles. No one is safe, he thought. Bill smiled.

Fumbling, Bill took his drink, then faded back to the porch, not yet in need of paint, and sat there, with all the security of a man who is an alcoholic and knows it. They would never let him forget it. Why he came here at all, who could say? The mother went after him.

So they were alone. There was a pause, then she turned on the phonograph. He winced. There was a scratching not unlike Bill's, then music, a man singing, screaming rather, a song. The singer was also interesting, like everything else. He was an ex-professor. He had lost his job at any rate. Perhaps to buy the record at all was legitimate charity. It was horrible.

Holding on to the glass, he looked at her. She sang to him, the same song. Along with the record. Let me take you away from all this, he said. It was a reasonable hope. He had shown her his letters. One possible employer wrote, *I should like very much to meet you if you are ever up this way*. Take him as anything they could get. That is, they had him. Sweep floors. Putty windows. Paint porches. Shovel coal. But the ton would last longer than that. He hoped. He looked at her. She looked at him.

Coming back in, the mother sat down again. Bill had been dismissed. Through the door, still swinging, he caught sight of an empty glass. How sad to be remembered! No one will do that for me, he thought. Cold wind, icy ground, put no wreaths, down here. Keep talking.

But the subjects were limited, at least now they were. They had heard most of his own stories, he had heard all of theirs. It was a deadlock. Ten more minutes, and they would all be dead. Or at least might be, except to keep drinking, also, and talk, the voices again becoming even last night's. So that to live was

a very definite retrogression. Tomorrow it will be yesterday, .
when you see the whites of their eyes, don't shoot.

A gun anyhow was what he wanted. A cool deliberate aim,
to lift it, to hold it, pressed close against his shoulder. Here they
come, he said. Pam, Pam! You're stoned, George, said mother.
Ok, he said, I give up.

The Dress

Much was simple about Mary and Peter, and to describe them
quickly, it was first of all two people, in a house into which not
many others went. And three children, pushed into corners,
and a friend or two who came to call. After ten years or so of
living together, there were no very actual mementoes, or none
that either felt much disposition to recognize. There were no
flags, and in fact few signs of even time except for the children,
and a scar which traversed Mary from bellybutton to bottom.
Which both had *done*, but also for which Peter was in some
sense guilty. Not her.

But, passing that, walking into the room, at this instant, saying something, Peter wanted one action, definite, to place them
all in that place where time shall have no dominion. Louise,
Mary's *present* friend, was a tall woman, dangling happy
jiggly things hung from both ears with such a weight that he
was worried her ears might tear loose. The pain of speaking
was in this way increased.

But. Now – for once he shook free of it, taking with him both
Louise. And Mary. And through a small opening in the floor,
pulled them down, into where *he* lived. Saying nothing, because
there was nothing to say, *now* he led them through a tiny passage, obliging Louise in particular to crawl on all embarrassed
fours, like the tiny and comfortable being she was. He snapped
a whip. He turned on a light, and, in an instant, the cavern
was flooded with a warm rich yellow searching glow. Peering
into the two faces looking up at him, he saw, first, dismay.

Then, laughter. And then, dismay. So back up they went, into the room, and sat there.

Mary's dress, half-finished, lay on the table, and this is what the two women had been talking about, planning, deciding, when he had, first, come in. It was a question as to whether this material, as an added border, and so, design, would be the best, the most interesting, or, on the other hand, that. Two materials lay beside the half-finished dress, in long narrow strips, and on one there was a quiet, rich, oblique design of some warm grey and blue and red. And on the other, a more excited, flaring, intense design of green, yellow and blue. Louise asked him what he thought would look best, and Mary, by her listening, also was curious to know. So he thought, *under* the dress will be, of course, Mary. So what is Mary like? Yet that necessitated returning to *under* the floor, so down they all went again, the women this time less hesitant, as he drew them on, and down, and also more curious to explore, should he let them, this sudden, exciting inclination.

He let them explore, and as the yellow light reached all corners of the underfloor cavern, the two women went, hand in hand, to one after another of the sights which were there. As, for example, the stalactites and the stalagmites. Which had been formed by the dripping, and which hung, like icicles, from the roof of the cavern, or else rose like spikes, from the floor of the cavern. The dripping itself was from a fissure, a cleft or split. But also, a narrow opening in an *organ*, as was now the case. A cleavage. Findo. To *cleave*. Peter had accomplished this by a *daily* expenditure, and these objects, precariously enough arrived at and/or created, were important to him.

The women moved incautiously because these things were not what he had *done*, not, that is, what they had done for him. Mary did many things for him, as she now did, certainly, in the present place – by moving there at all – and by looking, touching, exploring. Louise, striking one of the pendular accumulations with the hard heel of her hand, said, listen! And from the hanging, or rather the hanging *up* spike-like accumulations came notes, with each blow, like those of Big Ben chiming the hour, in London. Peter brusquely silenced her, and it was then that both women reminded him, of their reason for coming to the cavern, at all.

So again they sat in the room, with the dress material across Mary's knees, while she bent over it, as if to catch, now, in some pattern of the varied cloth, an instance of her own person. Finally, in short, this was to be her own *person*, or at least was, from roughly, the knees to the neck, with arms and varied other areas left clear. Under it, of course, would be her own body.

Louise interposed the *idea* of, in New Mexico, Indian women, with their many layered dresses, built out into a raging, piled, and then formed piece of clothing. This, with the hair pulled back, long, and left to hang down. Also, they had straight backs, fine clear features, a race altogether of clean dark women. Under this onslaught Mary buckled, adding for herself a host of other details, taken from pictures of Mexican women, Italian women, and the more known Spanish women. Peter himself saw his wife as *white*, and had known her as such. He added to the material which she held, on her knees, the memory of other materials, and, in particular, one thin worn black and purple-spotted dress, for which he had a great fondness. This dress, when she wore it, swelled into desirable proportions, the breast forward, the waist drawn in, and for the neck, low and round, of the dress, a leaving open of the bones which formed the height of the body, wide, then certain, down, into the complexity of the *flesh*.

It was the friend's *premise*, however, to make the wife not a wife? This was where Peter himself was confused. To take Louise, too, into the cavern – she was with Mary and that allowed it. Louise, looking at him, now, was *older* than he was. As, in some crowded neighborhood, this building is older than that one, and, because it is, seems, appears, insists on itself as in that way more rightly there. Under any dress the body is this or that, older or younger, whiter or darker. Under the floor he had the cavern, to think about, but Louise could not think *about* it. She was either there or not. Mary likewise.

Mary, the young wife, getting up, put the cloth on the table where it had first been, and went out to see about supper. In the room behind them Louise and Peter heard her speak, then the maid answer, then Mary speaking, again. Whether or not the children had always been in the room, as they now were, looking at both Peter and Louise, covetously, was not certain. Could he take *Louise* into the cavern? Alone?

In the cavern Louise stood back from him, crouched under the warm yellow light, and hidden behind the multiplicity of forms which crowded from all sides. He spoke, yet the voice in finding her became too changed to recognize. It was not his voice. Had he thought of her otherwise, he might well have *approached* her. But he did not. Soon other faces looked down, from that point at which they had entered the cavern, little faces looked down, three in number. This time Louise did not strike the coagulated, hardened and depending forms, with her hand. No tone, at all, broke the silence.

Yet the relief was in the *body*, both his, and hers, and also Mary's? Who was not present but was felt, among them, and each, Louise and himself, insisted on that knowledge. In the yellow light one group of stalactites and stalagmites appeared to be a castle. Another seemed a forest. Another, not far from where Louise continued to *creep*, back, on hands and knees, was a snow scene, and reared, up and down, in sinuous, fixed motion.

When Mary re-entered the room, Louise spoke to her, but Peter was unable to. He remained in the cavern. But concern soon brought him out, and closely listening, he accepted the invitation of their words and re-addressed himself to the problem of materials.

Was the dress to be final – is in effect how he addressed it. The *body* was not final, yet women, or rather his wife – she was final. Louise was not. In the cavern, revealed, or veiled? In that light it was Louise, entire, who was revealed. In the mind, or idea, of Peter.

Picking up the material again, Mary let it spread over her knees, and looked at Peter, and then, at Louise. The concern was whether or not the dress was to be her own person, or Louise's? Or the Indian women. Or, in the cavern, all these forms were taken care of, redisposed, in, surely, a wide variety of *attitudes*. Peter wanted a dress, for Mary, that would not be Louise, at all. He wanted, desperately enough, to make the *body* present, all of it, by simply that clothing, of Mary, which would not re-displace her, not again. Each time she left the room he thought she would never come back. He was left with Louise.

Left with Peter, Louise turned to Mary. It was Mary's suggestion that, in the cavern, they wear *no* clothes, because she was Peter's wife. But Louise wanted the *dress*. She arranged the dress, on Mary, and then chose the intenser, more flaring design of green, yellow and blue, from the two materials either one of which she might have added. To finish the dress. Peter laughed but felt dismayed, too. This was to be Mary's *own* person. Mary readjusted the half-done dress upon herself, and held the material, which Louise had chosen, against it. The dress, with the material, became her.

But the *cavern* was and *is* an underfloor *hollow*, with a *horizontal* entrance. And is *made* by the *subsiding*, or *giving inwards*, or *smashing* in, of *soil*, *walls*, etc. Cavern-dwellers are *prehistoric men* living in these huge or deep *hollows within solids*. Peter said.

Edward Dorn

C. B. & Q.

In the early morning the sun whipped against the plate glass of Tiny's restaurant, reflecting the opposite side of the narrow dusty street where the printer's shop, the saloon, another restaurant waved in the quiet morning, in the distorted glass. This was Tiny's place. He was called Tiny for the usual reason. About 6.30 every morning the place was full of construction workers, and an occasional rancher who had been stranded in town the night before. At night, in front, until 8.00, were several railroad section men, with the exception of Sunday night, talking about Denver or Kansas City, or talking in cruel tones about John C. Blain the concessionaire who handled all the meals for the Burlington railroad. But most of the section men, the gandies, stayed close to their bunk cars, in a park of rough square shape and next to the tall thin grain elevator that could be seen for several miles coming from the east, from Belle Fourche, or from the west.

Back of the restaurant the half desert began. Immediately. There was a banged up incinerator fifty feet out, in the desert of short pieces of barbed wire and rusted tins. Beyond wasn't a desert, exactly. Sheep, and probably some cattle, grazed there, over on and on past the layers of soft hills. A map shows the open range to extend far into Montana.

On past Tiny's restaurant, past the hardware store and a vacant lot with an old ford grown in the rear of it, was the New Burlington Hotel. Buck stayed there. He had new scars right under his lower lip and over farther down on his left jaw after he had washed with strong hotel soap, more bright scars stood red and looked quite becoming. He had been three days so far without paying so that Simms the thin owner shifted his feet on the linoleum floor when Buck returned to his room in the evening. Outside the low ceilinged lobby, on the front porch, it was quitting time for the construction workers and they hung around while their foreman took the day's count of everyone's hours into the small office thrown up with new rough lumber next to the hotel. It was the last building in the block and beyond it was a vacant lot and beyond that were the bunk cars of the gandy crews on a siding leading off to the grain elevator. To the left across the road, the gandy crews stood in bunches or stretched out resting on the lawn. The length of the dirt street was in shade by 5.15.

Soon after, the rain fell slowly into the street and raised quick pockets of dust. Simms lifted his sharp elbow from the glass show counter where he kept odds and ends, a 1952 calendar, a mail-order catalogue, a dusty carton of aspirins, and moved to the front window where he propped a foot on the ledge and stared with his cheek on his hand at the increasing wind in the poplars outside and the rain that was now hard. The park was empty and the rain drove the small border of willow trees toward the ground. Buck came to the window all washed up and said that them gandies could sure move when they wanted to.

Outside town, off the highway to Gillette, about four miles to the right was a considerable mound of gravel. Except for a layer of sandy dirt a foot or so thick on the top, the gravel below was of a varying grade. A fleet of ford dump trucks were lined up near the contractor's shanty and the rain spread roots of light yellow clay over the hoods and down from the cabin tops onto the windshields. The yellow caterpillar sitting in the mouth of the pit threw steam jets up from its hot radiator and from the tin can covering its vertical exhaust pipe. Reed, the contractor, was frying some eggs for his supper, and he sometimes glanced out his window to the river curving around the base of the gravel hill where two of his workers, from South Dakota, had a trailer hidden in the willows. The smoke from their camp stove stayed close to the ground this evening. This was almost the end of the contract. The gravel stockpile out by the highway across the rolling range was lengthening day by day and the regular peaks made by the dumps were growing dark and shiny in the rain. Virgil Reed would pass the stockpile as he turned onto the highway to town and see he would have to hire another driver if he wanted to finish the job before the end of June.

2

Buck would not go near the post office. And he always waited around for some time before he asked Simms if he had any mail that day. A letter from the gang at Pappy's tavern in Witchita came yesterday but it only mentioned his wife and kid in Mississippi and nothing about the accident. When the car crashed at the red light intersection in Witchita Buck threw out of the car and was in KC the next morning. He got drunk that day and saw lots of old acquaintances who worked with him in Nebraska and others he didn't know but who knew those he did, from Denver to Omaha. It was hot that day in Daddy's tavern in Kansas City. The three pieced band smiled as they sat sweating on the little band box between the two toilet doors. The heavily built man with the curly hair stood on his crutches by Buck's stool and bent his neck to hear the talk above the guitar and drum. Max was one half Cherokee and Buck thought he had known Max. Max was sure. And when Buck found out Max had nine dollars and a ride to Wyoming on the Burlington that afternoon at 4.00 he went across the street to the gandy hiring hall and hired in too. When he got back to Daddy's Max was in with a tiny old woman who had already got three dollars away from Max. Buck sat brooding in the booth under the band box and once in a while glared at Max. He snapped hard language across the floor to the bar and asked Max if he was indian. Max weaved slowly and smiled at the little woman who pulled on his flannel shirt. He smiled into the crowd and said he was indian from way back and old Buck was going with him anytime now to Wyoming. At the last minute Buck jerked Max away from old Sheila and had a cab on the curb outside. Daddy's. Then started the fast ride across Kansas City.

Max sat upright and stared all night, across the aisle from Buck, out the window. The train drove through the darkness up the Kansas line to Nebraska. In the station at Kansas City they had only given their names to the man at the gate with a list. In the car there were no white tabs on the window shades by their seats. They rode free to the job in Wyoming. At Grand Island, Nebraska, Max got off the train and went into a restaurant back of the depot. He thought he might go back to Daddy's. Sheila was there every day, he bet. Since coming from Illinois with the man who took dogs to a hospital in Kansas City, he hadn't been with a woman. In the still waiting car Buck opened his eyes. He blinked when he felt his swollen lips were tighter this morning than they had been since the accident. He licked them and wandered through the car and down the steps to the platform to look for Max. Max must have five dollars left, unless he buys too much to eat. Buck found him in the restaurant with some of the other travelers to Wyoming. Buck ordered a cup of coffee and said to Max that they might not have to gandy if there was other work there, maybe on a ranch or road work. Max thought if he didn't like the setup, the looks of things when they got there, he might shove on to Oregon, he had an uncle who was a foreman in a mill at Klamath. They came back through the depot just as the train moved off toward the border.

It was unusual to arrive on Friday afternoon because there was no work on Saturday or Sunday. Buck swung into the dining car and took the last seat for dinner, away from Max who was avoiding his eyes now that he had determined to go back to Daddy's to drink with old Sheila. And late in the evening Max blinded the first passenger back east. It was on Monday morning that Buck decided he wouldn't work on the section. He ate their cold fried potatoes for two days.

3

Virgil Reed came along the pavement into town, through the increasing waves of rain, between the ditches on either side and broken weeds and long grass that had been earlier in the spring burned by the hot winds pouring in from the south-east. He had shaved after finishing his supper and there were still wet nicks on his neck below his chin and he dabbed them with his handkerchief from time to time. He knew that his new catskinner was a man that would work, he knew how to push the gravel. With Boyd the matter was simple : if you are a small man, you have to use your hands and feet to move. All day on the dusty cat he had crammed the accelerator to the floor and ground into the earth, with his visor cap pulled down tight on his forehead he had ground the blade into the earth, let it up and down quickly and infuriated the truck drivers by spilling over into their road under the gravel loader. With the engine roaring all around the small hills that surrounded the pit, the shattering engine was in command of all the air and Boyd was in command of the engine, back and forth across the opening to the pit he pressed the large, dirty, yellow caterpillar and acknowledged no one's presence until the end of the day, when soon after the rain started on the hot metal covering the engine, he told Reed about the defective left brake. Reed said he would see to it.

Now Reed rounded the corner into the town, past the tight groups of willows, past the deserted filling station, went the length of the street and stopped in front of the New Burlington Hotel. Through the glass he could see Buck standing with Simms. Buck suddenly faced Simms with his hands out of his pockets and nodding several times said some words and turned

to go. Out on the porch Reed met him and they started back
down the street toward Pages' Saloon.

In Pages' Boyd was at the bar. It was nearly dark outside.
The rain along the muddy street had slackened to a fine quiet
regularity. The rain was quieter throughout the whole town.
Up on the hill outside town on the highway to the east, in the
filling station-grocery store where Buck was running up a small
grocery bill, and saving credit stamps against a large red orna-
mental lamp with a white meandering shade for his mama,
and beyond that, was a small opening in the grainy clouds,
weak light from the sun as it went down in the northwest in
back of the hill.

In the bar Boyd sat by himself away from the general noise
centering in the last booth on the wall opposite the bar toward
the back of the saloon. Some road construction workers heavily
persuaded each other that the wage was bigger in North
Dakota or at the white horse dam job in Montana and that you
could work endless hours but it was dangerous. The big fellow
with the wrinkled forehead had skinned a cat on a high bluff
where the push was so inclined that you had to be quick to save
the rig and yourself from going over at the last minute. Boyd
listened to their tales and jerked his head as he finished his beer
and looked their way with his short curled smile. Through the
room of noise he shouted to the heavy-stomached man with
the wrinkled forehead that he could drive any earth mover
made, and that he didn't need to think that since he was such a
big bastard he could talk so smart. But Curly didn't hear him
then because one of the others in the booth had started to tell
of a job the summer before near Butte.

Buck and Reed came through the door and took stools next
to Boyd. Boyd relayed their orders down the varnished bar to
the bartender, and Reed went on about the job out at the pit,
how he was thinking of moving his equipment to Cheyenne as
soon as this county job was done.

Through the open door Buck could see several men he recognized from some other summers and he thought again of
how he could get his mail without a direct address. They were
sure to be on his trail. Boyd asked Reed if the job down at Cheyenne would be a big one and Reed didn't answer so Boyd turned
his head away from Reed and Buck and looked at the group in
the rear booth where there was now an argument between the
large frowning man with wrinkles in his forehead and another
roadworker, thinner and tall, who said that he could cut as
fine a grade with a scraper and cat as the big frowner could
with a patrol-grader. The frowning man's answer to this was
to take his opponent by the khaki shirt and lift him quickly on
top of the table spilling several glasses of beer. The noise was
overflowing, even out on the street the knots of workers knew.
Back of the bar under the long slender tubes of green vapor
two hula-girl lamps wiggled their rubber bottoms and the bartender was debating his duty. Boyd slid off his stool and took it
with him as he made across the floor to the battle. He had
cracked it on the large man's back twice before it was thrust
back into his middle at the end of the third swing.

Outside on the bumper of the car with his face bleeding
Boyd wiped his small hands on his pants' legs smearing the
blood in long stripes and crying. He sobbed in jerks as he tried
to clean out between his sticky fingers. He told Buck that he
always wanted to be a mason anyway, that that was a real
trade, you didn't have to worry about jobs and the right kind
of money once you made it. But they wouldn't let him train
for it when he got out and there were always so many on the
waiting list for apprentice that he couldn't see it. Buck said
that he had a good job down in Witchita but the goddamn
foreman had it in for him because he broke three springs on the
truck in one day on that bad road and he got fired. Boyd had
calmed down and said that he intended to go south for the winter, maybe to Tucson or Albuquerque but he was sure as hell
going to be south when the winter hit this place. And he didn't

see what Buck saw in Witchita. He could go anywhere anyway because he had a car that the back seat came out of and could be used to sleep in he said.

The Deer

Carl did not meet Billy the next day. They did not meet again for several weeks. Both of them were put to work for a series of very short jobs. Things began to pick up. By the time Carl went out to see the Henderssons, Billy had called at the Wymans' house several times. That year, in the state of Washington, there was before the legislature one of those bills, number 202, that are said to be 'right to work' bills. In any case, the question is loaded and disposes itself along seemingly straight lines : does a man have the right to work for anyone he pleases, and does he have the right to do so independently. The question is never, of course, Is this a wise thing to do? The 'right' part of it gets emphasized. But enough of that. The point is that Hendersson, being a good union man, and he did believe in the propriety of unions, had got himself scores of stickers from the union and placed them all over his car, even against the undercarriage. His enthusiasm, once gained, was thoroughgoing. The Wyman children developed the habit, when seeing his car come down the road, of saying, Here comes 202! The sign read VOTE AGAINST 202, in luminescent lettering. Yellow against black.

There was a pressing money situation for them at that time; they had come through a long winter and the money they made in the spring had in large part to be used to catch up. Billy suggested to Carl that they might poach a deer. He had already gotten one near the house one evening. So Carl took a trip out to the Henderssons.

When Carl got there Billy was cutting some firewood with his chainsaw. It was late afternoon. The sun was low in the sky and the day was normal – overcast, a grey, high light. The sun would set in a half hour, a thin clarity on the horizon. For that brief time there were the great lengths of its red arms extending over the tops of the rife second growth, past the balanced crown of the cedar and the ragged point of the hemlock. A dark, black green and a burnt out red. The tangled grass of the clearing bent this way and that, spread out in the half light below the temporarily lit sky. Billy stopped working and looked up when Carl drove in. It was his habit to greet one always as if it were the first meeting, very pleasant. He said, Oh hello! How are you! It's good you came out today. I was expecting you. Let's go over and see the horse before it gets dark. And then he wiped his forehead with his handkerchief. Hi Billy, you think we'll get a deer tonight? I don't know, Billy answered. It looks like it might clear. When Carl got out of his car they started walking over toward the barn.

The barn was tall. Everything on this place was ramshackled. The barn wore those rays of the sun through its loose boards, and its cedar shake roof was full of holes. Buckshot turned out to be a very extraordinary horse. As Carl looked at him, he wondered why a sensible man would buy such a thing. It was boney, undersized, roman nosed, of very questionable temper – neither a horse nor a pony, neither normal nor quite to be ignored, but rather that four legged thing with a 'character,' utterly unusable. Buckshot certainly needed care. His hooves were so long they had split, almost up to the quick.

Now the sun was gone. Billy's wife had come out to the railing where they stood. Carl had never met her. The light at that moment was silver as it grew darker, and the skeletal barn grew more substantial when the structure of it asserted its proportions in the waning light of the sun. Inside there were some scattered bales of old hay, useless now. Long decayed. The forest of low heavy second growth lay as a barrier, its single trees undifferentiated in the diminished day, all light having only that weak losing source, the edge of the clearing became a wall whose sides were not in good focus.

They got back to the house and went in. Billy asked Carl if he had had anything to eat, and Carl said that he had supper

before coming out. Billy said good, he had eaten earlier too ...
The children were running through the house playing cowboy
and indian. Two boys. One was about four and the other was
six. Next year the six year old would start to school. As one
entered the house the sink with a bucket under it was on the
left near the door. Straight beyond the other two rooms opened
out, there was an unfinished wall between them. Judged from
the look of the house, their lives were, to Carl, a disorder of
heartbreak. The smell, in the first place, was enough to dis-
courage a strong man. But they seemed cheery enough and the
wife even said, Look! I've got some biscuits. Carl again insisted he'd had enough to eat at supper. Billy took him into the
other part where for some time they looked at his guns. He had
several pistols and two rifles. Carl glanced around the room. In
one corner there was a double bed, it was away from the walls
a little too far to seem natural. The boys slept on two cots that
were placed out of line at the other end of the room. The smell
was always present. He noticed a shelf of books and out of a
dependable curiosity, and because Billy had gone back into the
kitchen to speak to his wife, he looked at them. They were an
utter miscellany, there being there besides the pulp mysteries
and detectives, *Huckleberry Finn*, and Engels' *Anti-Dühring*.
There were also several volumes of Stoddard's travels.

They went out the door, both carrying rifles, out under the
partly clear, breaking sky. They walked toward the barn, its
latticed members shone almost black and white in the shadows
from the moon. The moon rode above its roof, full. Billy was
talking about Wisconsin. Growing in a broad swath out of the
impenetrable second growth a cloud stretched toward the
zenith. Carl quickly and out of habit, looked for the Dipper and
Orion. As they walked along Billy wondered aloud if they
would get a deer. He thought it probable. He held forth on the
subject of when a deer is best to get anyway, saying that the
regular season was the worst time to kill one. The fall was the
time they were in the worst condition. And so they went past
the barn and past the blackberry brambles that edged the clearing and finally they were on a trail into the deep underbrush.

Very quickly they came to another much smaller clearing.
There was a small body of water standing in it, hardly a lake.
It was surrounded by marshy ground. Billy, Carl said, You
can't really live this way now, you know. Silence. They skirted
a grove of black birch. Why not? Well, it wouldn't ever be
possible to make it for long. I've known a thousand guys like
you. They thought they could get by in a minimal, I mean, by
the least way possible, and they all ended getting a steady job
somewhere, and it was because in the end they saw that it was
more work to fight it than give in to it. The world is *not* what
it was once Billy, you read about all those ways men lived in
the past and it sounds good, and it must have been good, but we
don't know even what that means. Goddamnit, like us now,
for instance, we're walking single file through growth that is
far too thick for us to see even a foot, and we're walking single
file. OK. So what does that mean. In fifteen minutes we could
be out of it. I mean if we walked back to your place, in fifteen
minutes we'd be in town. In a bar. They're there right now. You
know that? As we walk along there are people sitting on their
asses not giving a damn about a deer to feed themselves, not
caring that the moon is shining, not caring about anything,
they're just sitting there talking the same old shit that's been
talked since who the hell cared. There was a long silence. They
walked the trail single file. Oh to hell with all that, Billy said at
last, I don't see what that has to do with us, letum, I mean the
world hasn't pressed into this second growth yet, and if I can't
hear it I can't see it. Another long silence. They had come to a
place where the trail was not so clear. The moon, too, was of
little help by this time, they were so deep into the forest of
brush, the entanglement was too much to admit any helpful
light from the moon. The endless dense second growth, the old
logged-off lands. In our time it reaches, in its interior, a more
or less uniform height of thirty feet. Carl said, Anyway, Billy,
I've heard that if you *hear* a deer in this shit you'll never be
able to *see* it, I mean not over ten feet away. Don't shoot me,
please. Oh, you probably don't make the same sound a deer
does, Billy answered.

There were spots in the forest that were so thick they were black, and then there were those spots that were thin, not open certainly because this thickness was hard to believe, but in which there was a weak kind of shadow. They stumbled over things that seemed rotted logs four feet thick, left there years ago by loggers who did not find that particular kind of length to their satisfaction. Cedar, for instance, tends to shatter when felled. Do you know where we are going, asked Carl. Ya, I think we just keep walking and finally after about an hour in this direction we'll come out into a field. We can go there, and then come back, and if we don't see a deer in that time it's enough of a night. Their flashlight had failed. Their hands were numb with a kind of penetrating wet cold, and they stumbled on. They had on long, wool underwear so did not really feel the damp pneumonia air around them. A wind had begun to blow up.

But I haven't heard any sounds, Carl said. There haven't been any sounds in this woods, Billy! Just us walking along. We're not going to get a deer. Who the hell wants a deer anyway. Jesus, Billy, I mean the idea of killing a deer illegally appeals to me, but all those pricks with their vacations have already killed em. I mean they came out in their blazers and methodically killed em. Oh bull shit, it isn't much farther, Billy said. Just then a large branch fell off one of the tallest trees and came clipping down through the leaves. Watch it! Billy shouted. Carl jumped to the side. Wow. Jesus christ! I've heard about widder makers but I never saw one, Carl said catching up with Billy. Well, if you see'm, it's OK, said Billy.

I think a deer could be goosing me and I wouldn't know the difference, Carl continued. Billy found himself getting very tense. He needed to get the deer more than Carl did. In a sense Carl was just there for kicks, but finally Carl would survive without the fresh meat. Billy had noticed at those times when he called on the Wymans that they usually had fresh fruit. For instance they had oranges. The Henderssons at most times lived in great poverty, the one worry Billy had for his kids was whether or not they got enough oranges. He had heard vaguely, through the state agencies or in some other manner, that children ought to have fresh fruit in the long dark northwest winter. He thought of vitamin C. Carl was talking on as of the absurdity of looking for a deer in those limitless thickets. Billy thought of his kids' gums. They were ripe. Their smiles were ready enough but their gums were ripe. Red, very red. As he stumbled over a dead white larch log he stopped, and turned to Carl saying, What the hell are you bitching about? If you want to go back, go back. Go back! Carl shouted, Where the hell is back. I don't know, and I'd wager you don't either. We haven't even made it to that so-called clearing yet! On they walked, stumbling. At times they warned each other to keep the barrels out of the mounds of earth pushed up by a rotted log. If they did finally meet a deer they didn't wish each other an explosion.

After somewhat more than two hours they reached the edge of the clearing. There were clouds in the sky. They were fluffy and brilliant in the moonlight, it did not look like they were gathering for a storm. When the moon rode behind one of them the air grew heavy with shade. The clearing was much larger than Carl expected it to be. There were some buildings far across the way. Carl asked what they were and learned that Billy thought they were the remains of an old farm. The land in the clearing had the appearance of having been tilled. As they walked toward the buildings they passed through an orchard. Unpruned, the trees had grown to grotesque proportions. The two men walked through these sharp configurations in the moonlight, bending down under the low branches.

Billy, you said you finally got to Alaska, when was that? Let's see, he said, that must have been about four or five years ago. How old were you? Well, I'm twenty-five now, I was nineteen or twenty. A sailboat was what screwed me up, imagine that, a sailboat, kind of hard to imagine from where we're standing now, eh. He laughed his short, high, feminine laugh. His eyes were glistening. His face became reddish, the lips of his plump, babyish mouth curled and remained slightly apart.

His tin hat shone in the brief moonlight. The moon was waning now, and the clouds were coming on a little thicker around the southwest horizon.

It was early summertime, I had a chance to ride over the Alcan with a guy from Madison, Billy continued, as they poked their heads in the first building they came to. They went about to the other buildings, examining the old, mildewed, useless gear that remained there. Ah, yes, my dream of going to Alaska finally came true. My old man kicked me out. Him? he responded to a question of Carl's, Oh, he was all right, but mostly a worthless bastard. Well, look, he was the kind of man that's pretty good in a way, he was always good to me, kind, he joked a lot, and he was a lot of kicks to be with when I was a kid. But he killed my poor damn mother. I never have forgiven him for that, although I don't know why I shouldn't, he's dead. Dead is forgiven anyway, they say. He gave me a motorcycle when I was sixteen, but you know, the bastard had stole it. I could never put that down, but it was hard to part with. A brand new Harley. It was a beauty too. Blue and white. He drank, but he wasn't too much a drunk, he just made up for it with lying. I mean, he'd come home to my mom and tell her he'd been held up when the sonofabitch had spent most of his pay on some woman. Or I don't know what the hell he did with it, I don't think he gambled, he couldn't sit still long enough. One week he left for good, and when I used to see him in town he wouldn't speak to me. Once I started cussing him out, and you know, he pretended he didn't even recognize me. You know how fat I am now, well, I was that way when I was sixteen too, so I could wear his shirts. He left a lot of shirts. My mother went to work in a shirt factory in Madison, how about that? Hee hee, that's pretty good, what about that.

But I got another motorcycle all right. How? Carl asked. I met an old woman who liked to be screwed, and she bought me lots of things. That was one of them. It was a Harley again, I ran it right into the ground, up an down the country roads, I didn't have nothin but the wind in my face. All day long. What do you mean, how old was she? Oh, she was old, if that's what you mean, she was about sixty-five. But how did that work, gee, that seems strange, Carl reflected. Well, so what, there was very little difference. She was just old that's all. She was enthusiastic and liked her screwing. I guess it was sort of like she was a mother, you know how that goes. But when I wasn't doing my job we talked a lot. She had a nice house, her husband was dead and she had a little money. Humm, Carl said.

In fact, Billy said as they left the buildings and started across the clearing toward the edge of the forest, in fact I thought a lot of that old woman. There was one summer we went out to a lake north of Madison. She had a cabin. I couldn't see anything but riding my motorcycle, her sailboat didn't interest me at all. She liked to ride along on the sailboat. There was a couple of guys much older than me there, and she flirted with them a lot, and they were sort of suspicious of me. But I wasn't jealous. Actually I was a little bit. She had a way. I learned to run that boat, that's certain. Those guys kept ribbing me about the motorcycle, calling me a landlubber, so I learned to sail the boat. It was great. An altogether different kind of speed. We'd come around and she'd scream like a little girl. We tacked up and down that lake all summer. It was a long narrow lake . . . it was very tricky. She had long black hair. Not many grey hairs. With combs she kept it in a knot at the back of her head. One gold tooth in front. Nice smile . . . she wasn't hard to look at.

It had grown darker with the setting of the moon, but the clouds stayed along the horizon and the stars made enough light to give a remote visibility to things. She wrote me several letters when I was in prison, she was very disappointed with me for leaving in the first place, but the letters mostly chided me for getting into trouble. The edge of the forest was still some way ahead. They reminded each other that they had to keep an eye out for the barbed wire fence. Apparently there were some cattle in there but they had not seen any on their way to the clearing. You know, Billy said, I heard somebody had some steers in there but I haven't never seen one.

Billy resumed the conversation. I went to Alaska with that

guy on the spur of the moment. It was the middle of winter, cold as hell, I got some money from the old woman to fix my motorcycle. I went across a ditch. I was going pretty fast but I fell off and just rolled down the bank, but the machine kept going and it was pretty clobbered up. I told her it was going to cost a lot more to fix it than it was, I always did that. I met that guy in a bar and took off the next day. Carl interrupted. That was pretty sudden to decide such a thing wasn't it? Yow. It was. Sure. Ya, look at my life now. It's much harder to say the least. I don't know. When you're young you go off, that's probably all there was to it. I told myself at the time I was tired of it all. It was very much like being kept in a cage. Or like one of those dummies that sit on laps, they talk, move, anything, when you want em. But that wasn't it either. I liked her a lot. She used to try to get me to read certain books. Now I understand they were pretty good, but I couldn't see it then. They were, well, you know, they were all English Works, I remember one, it was called *The Return of the Native*. Before I read it I thought it was about Africa, you know, the return of the native. But it wasn't. It was about England. It was good too. But that wasn't what made me leave. I just wanted to get away. Ya, you read that book. Sometimes I remember that guy working. Cutting wood. But those women were funny weren't they?

Did you really want our cats for your dogs? Carl asked as they were going across the fence. Sure! Billy said. What the hell for? Oh, I don't know, I like to chase cats I guess, and the dogs sure as hell do. But you call them cat dogs, Carl said, What does that mean, are there really cat dogs, I mean dogs that chase cats professionally? Oh, I don't know about professionally, but I think there are special dogs to chase cats, and they're called cat dogs, and they do it at night. At least that's what the man said. Carl, Billy went on, You're sort of touchy about animals aren't you? I mean you have some sort of idea that animals are sacred, don't you. You think they should not be killed, I got that idea, but you eat the meat, I've seen you ... what about that? They stood by the fence. Carl had lit a cigarette.

He smoked and looked at the sky. Well I'm not clean there, Carl said, I never really pretended to be, and anyway that's another question. It just struck me as a weird idea that a man would want to let cats loose for the express purpose of putting dogs to them. After all, that, as an act, is a little tortured, if you want to compare it to my eating meat that's been killed by someone else. You might as well throw the cats directly to the dogs and be done with it. Why the chase? I guess it's the time interval that bothers me. It just seemed to me that the glee you'd derive from going through the woods after both of them the cats *and* the dogs, is something else, those are kicks you ought to get another way. After all, Carl concluded, There will be men to kill meat as long as there are men to eat it and vice versa. I don't lay any blame at the butcher's feet. He's simply a truckdriver in disguise. Billy laughed. What's that got to do with cats and dogs? I don't eat the cats, nor do I eat the dogs. At least I haven't yet. You sure do get hot under the collar about animals, Carl! And anyway that's silly, what's the difference between chasing dogs that are chasing cats, and might not even catchem, I mean this time interval of yours, what's the difference, if a man kills a sheep, or a hog, and you eat it three weeks later, what's the difference, the thing's been killed! Billy was laughing.

They were deep in the forest now. Carl stopped. It had begun a light drizzle. The sky was completely obscured, but was not black yet, a high deep gray nothing. They were in a small clearing. In under the second growth it was as black as ever, its edges they saw from where they stopped to rest. Their faces were covered with a light film of water from the heavy mist. Of course, you're right, Carl said. Finally it is true that it can't matter when they were killed. The act remains the same. The biologist may have a different term for those carnivores that eat dead as against those that eat live meat. But that's not a moral problem, that's a matter of classification. I don't think man in any sense comes under that, since he's making the classification. For instance, in the animal kingdom the problems are singular. Any being other than man has the problem of satisfying the demands of the next desire, there being two desires, presumably, consumption and reproduction. The standards for those demands may or may not come under the term survival of the fittest. After all, all that reasoning comes by way of man's hope to see it that way. I am not at all convinced those animals, or even those men, who have survived, are the fittest. Are you? There was a silence. Carl continued, What disturbs me about the cats is that I, a human being, have formed an attachment to them, though there was a desire on our part to get rid of them. We have too many. And we can't literally afford to keep that many. So I offer you some of them and you come up with the novel idea that you'd be very willing to take them because you have some cat dogs and you could use them. I meant the cat dogs could use them, Billy said with a smile. OK, OK, Carl went on, OK, but you're not respecting my feelings about animals. You are talking about eating them, I'm talking about the sense of killing them, as an act of pleasure. I'm not talking that Buddhist crap about never killing them at all, you know about that. No, this is purely a Western problem, Carl said.

East, West, come on! Billy answered. You mean there is a difference in life depending on where you're at. Horseshit! Look, I feel an urge when I'm trailing those dogs, I hear their bark, I fall over rotten logs, I get my face cut, I get worn out, I keep hearing the high bark of the dogs, I love that chase, that's part of what you call the West too. What did you think you were going to do with those cats, Carl, drop them somewhere on a country road, what would chase them then? Some other dogs, or would they starve in some lonely barn begging milk from some goddamn farmer who'd recognize them and kick their asses out of his barn, huh! Billy was shouting now. They stopped on the trail, facing each other. Billy was holding his gun very tight, pointed at Carl. They stared at each other. In that moment Carl thought he would be shot. He thought that in another instant the trigger would be pulled and that would be the utter end of him. Good lord, he thought to himself, This is absurd, why would I be shot in the middle of a deep wood? I have done nothing but live a very normal life. Normal life, he said to himself again in that brief instant. A very normal life. What the hell were you going to do with those cats, Carl! Oh, jesus christ, Billy! stop that. I thought you were going to let that thing go off. Carl climbed wearily over a fallen log. I think their chances will be better along the open road, he said, At least they might find a place to stay. You are just trying to justify your killing with the possibility that they might be killed anyway. But they might not be. They both sat down on the log. Billy said, But you think you can get rid of them, and you think somebody will take care of them.

No! I am not saying that at all. I am saying that if you do give that generation back to the road it is no longer in your hands whether they survive or not. That with animals you don't intend to eat, that is, nonedible animals, a man is not responsible! I think this is the only proper use of the liberation you propose with your setting dogs to cats. But in that case it is very much planned and the cat probably hasn't got a chance. Look, I don't see any more sense in eating animals than killing them, I've told you that, we've been all through that. This is splitting hairs, Billy replied, So my use is not your use. He turned on the log and tried to get a look at the sky, he thought he could see a clear patch, and stars. Carl, unable to stop, went on, OK, it is a fine point. In many ways perhaps it is men like us who have to be interested in fine points. So where does that get us, Billy said. They sat on the log and finally Carl asked Billy if he knew the way back. Billy said he thought not. He did not recognize anything. He didn't know where he was. Carl thought he heard a sound. Like the breaking of a branch on the ground. Billy did too. They sat very still. They heard it again. They were tense, listening. Carl could find the north star by pointing from the Dipper, if he could only find the Dipper, he thought, at least they could walk in one direction. There was no possible way to get a bearing on where they were. They both heard the noise again. It made them a little uneasy but they remained on the log. Carl felt the log's bark with his fingers to determine how old it was and what kind it was. From the feel of it, it was so smooth, he thought it was an alder. A rather big one.

Billy was fooling with the flashlight. It flickered once. I think it's the switch, Billy said. He continued to jiggle it, and started hitting it on the log. It came on, a bright shaft of light. Billy immediately switched it off. He switched it on again. It worked. Where do you think the sound came from, Billy whispered. Carl wasn't sure but he thought he sensed it directly back of them. They stood up carefully.

Both men stood peering into the darkness. Billy switched on the light and moved it very slowly in a semicircle to the right in back of where they stood and it came to rest with a little jerk on a pink white-faced steer. About two years old, Billy said. Ya, Carl answered. They both started moving forward, the light like a rope they were reeling in. Carl said, What are you going to do? Be quiet. Be quiet, Billy answered, don't scare im. They walked carefully toward the steer making the same muffled cracking the steer had made. It stood staring at them between two saplings, low hanging fronds covered its body back of the head. When they had got very near to it, Billy put a hand on Carl's arm and they both stopped. Billy slowly shifted the flashlight to Carl who took it without a word, the beam still directed into the eyes of the young steer. Slowly and deliberately Billy raised his arm until the barrel of the 30-30 was at the eye of the animal, and then he fired.

The shock seemed delayed. For a while it seemed that nothing whatever had happened. It was as if the smell of gunpowder, and the shaft of light, and the two columnar men and the mass of the animal floated together into one hanging moment, moving free from the earth. The report of the gun had removed all the tension of the presence they felt as they walked forward. The heavy mist fell. The wet hair of the animal slowly descended to earth, nestling itself upon the ever damp leaves that form the mulching for this rich country. Oddly enough, Carl thought at that moment, there are no poisonous snakes west of the Cascades in Washington. There are no poisonous spiders either. He thus occupied himself in that briefest transport. There are mostly vegetative things this side of the mountains. No poisonous things … however the slugs are of great size, growing apparently on the vegetation to tremendous proportion, what *do* slugs live on, he asked himself. How do they grow to such fat dimensions, do they typify this area? And then he saw the animal on the ground, thick blood was running out of its eye. Through the space of wet air one could feel the warm blood. The animal's hind legs were still scratching for the earth, they still sought their ground. The thin fallen branches trembled with the groping of the legs.

Billy split the skin around the hind quarters and with his foot placed squarely on the spine near the rear, broke it by a sudden snap, the two hooves in his hands. The front quarters were more difficult to get off because the head had to be removed. But in a surprisingly short time he had that part severed and they stood pointing the flashlight at what remained. Because Billy was the larger man he would attempt to carry the hind quarters. Carl asked Billy again in which direction he thought they should go. Billy studied for a moment. Then he pointed out the direction he thought they should take. By this time Carl had completely given up trying to figure it out on the basis of where he thought they had come from. He acquiesced completely.

They started out. Billy led with the crotch of the hind quarters around his neck, the hooves hanging down in front. He staggered under the load only when his footing was insufficient. Carl had a harder time. After a while, when crossing fallen logs that were large enough in circumference he tended to rest there, sitting under the weight, a comfortable, cold relief. At those times he asked Billy to wait. They went on and on. There were times Carl thought they were doing that thing people who lose their way in the woods are said to do, go in circles. In fact, this was true, the two men got home by a route that would appear on paper as a long snaking curve, many switchbacks and some loops. But finally they drew near the pond of water. When they approached the marshes from a side Billy was unfamiliar with, he spoke hopefully that they were nearly there. And they were. They circled the small body of water and walked slowly into the second clearing. They set down their burdens and rested for the last time. They were wet through and through. Their necks were covered with thick blood that had grown cold. Blood ran down their backs. They were of course unaware of this. In the black night they had a rest, Carl smoked. Billy did not smoke. He drank, however. And spoke, as they talked, of having a drink when they got back to the house. What did you think of that, Carl? he asked. I don't know, Carl answered, It seemed the thing to do. You know, Billy, how I have to explain these things to myself. I know that's absurd. We got the deer. What's the difference if it's a hereford. If you think that's my quarrel with life you're mistaken. The man who owns this animal, or what we have of it, is probably asleep in his bed right now, safe and sound, lying next to his wife. Or if not that, he's in a tavern somewhere with his hand on the ass of a bleary-eyed broad. It's not going to make any difference to him and he can be forgotten. And you can be forgiven, Billy, for this small theft. I assure you it won't change the world. But there are better questions than that. Let's go.

The two men prepared to put their burdens on their shoulders and when they had struggled underneath them they started on. Very shortly, around the last point of second growth, they saw the weak light from Billy's house.

William Eastlake

Portrait of an Artist with 26 Horses

With eyes wet and huge the deer watched; the young man watched back. The youth was crouching over a spring as though talking to the ground, the water pluming up bright through his turquoise-ringed hand, then eddying black in the bottomless whorl it had sculptured neat and sharp in the orange rock. The rock retreated to a blue then again to an almost chrome yellow at the foot of the deer. The deer was coy, hesitant and greasewood-camouflaged excepting the eyes that watched, limpid and wild. The young man called Twenty-six Horses made a sweeping arc, raising his ringed hand from the spring. The deer wheeled and fled noiselessly in the soft looping light, and now all around, above and far beyond where the youth crouched at the spring, the earth was on fire in summer solstice with calm beauty from a long beginning day; the sky was on fire too and the spring water tossing down the arroyo was ablaze. The long Sangre de Cristo range to the east had not fully caught; soon it would catch; not long after, in maybe half an hour, the world would be all alight.

Now there arose from down, far down the arroyo, seeming from the earth itself, an awful cry, terrible and sibilant, rising to a wavering and plaintive call; but not a plea, not even an anguish, more a demand, peremptory and sharp before it faded, died back into the earth from which it had arisen. Here, directly here above this sea of sage and straight up in the hard blue New Mexican sky, a huge buzzard hurtled and wheeled toward the planet earth – monstrous and swift.

Twenty-six Horses rose from his crouch over the spring and slung on a pack roll. Before the world was all alight he would have to go some distance. He could waste no more time talking to the ground. The earth he heard had made a noise but it was no sound he knew, no language spoken, a distant anguish from below, addressed to no one and everyone. Now he heard the cry again, human, but it was still nothing he knew, more a harsh shadow than a sound, more a single note of retreat, a mellifluous oboe ending the world. But he could waste no more time talking to the ground.

To the east, but still at a height of 7500 feet, ran the village of Coyote. It was a collection of adobe shacks on the long wobble of asphalt going someplace else. A dark and handsome Navajo woman, the mother of Twenty-six Horses, disguised in the costume of city people, was stirring outside a restaurant labeled The Queen of Coyote City. She was hanging a sign that began 'REAL LIVE WHITE PEOPLE.' The Queen of Coyote City finished hanging the sign and went back inside. All of the sign said: REAL LIVE WHITE PEOPLE IN THEIR NATIVE COS-TUMES DOING NATIVE WHITE DANCES.

'I don't think that's funny,' James said. James was her hus-band and the father of Twenty-six Horses, but he never came around the restaurant much. James had a rough and weathered face and he had a purple ribbon which knotted his hair in back of his head, a custom that the young Navajos had abandoned.

'You can't compete with people by imitating their ways.' James sat at the end of the counter and looked unhappy.

The Queen of Coyote City and the mother of Twenty-six Horses had begun her restaurant by excluding Navajos. That didn't seem to do much good so she refused service to Chris-tians, Jews, Seventh Day Adventists, Apaches and people from Albuquerque in about that order. Two weeks ago she had put up a sign: WE RESERVE THE RIGHT TO REFUSE SERVICE TO EVERYBODY. That didn't seem to help business either.

'They don't put up those signs to help business,' James had said. 'They put them up because they're sick.'

'I'm not sick. I want to make an extra buck,' the Queen of Coyote City said.

'An Indian who wants to make an extra buck is sick,' James said.

'I should go back to those hogans a hundred miles from nowhere and die?'

'And live,' James said. 'An Indian dies in the city.'

'An Indian can learn to live here,' she said. 'Soon the hogans will not be a hundred miles from nowhere. What you going to do then?'

'Come back home and we'll figure it out.'

'I got a business,' she said.

A customer came in and James went back to looking unhappy sitting at the end of the counter.

'That's a good sign you got out there,' the white man said, and then he ordered a hamburger. 'Did you ever see the sign: Your Face Is Honest but We Can't Put It in the Cash Register?'

The Queen of Coyote City was frying the hamburger and she didn't hear the white man so the white man turned to James and said, 'Did you ever see that sign: Women Don't – Oh, you're an Indian,' the white man said. 'I was trying to explain a gag to an Indian,' the white man hollered back to the Queen of Coyote City. James got up and walked out.

When The Queen of Coyote City brought the white man his hamburger the white man said, 'He doesn't speak any English I hope. I hope I didn't hurt his feelings.'

'Not much,' the mother of Twenty-six Horses said.

'You let Indians in here?'

'That was my husband.'

'I'm sorry,' the white man said, putting down the hamburger gently and examining it carefully. 'You look white. You talk white. I hope I didn't hurt your feelings.'

'Not much,' she said. 'I'm trying to make a buck.'

'Oh,' the man said relaxing. 'And you will, too.' He bit into the hamburger and swallowed a mouthful. 'You've got what it takes,' he said.

On the outside of The Queen of Coyote City Café, Ike Woodstock was standing near the steps talking to Rudy Gutierrez about uranium, and Evelyn and Tap Patman were standing in front of their service station beneath a sign that said GULF PRIDE MOTOR OIL and between the STOP-NOX and BE KIND

TO YOUR ENGINE signs. Across the street Arpacio Montoyo was talking to the priest beneath a CLEAN REST ROOMS sign. They were talking about how many angels could stand on the head of a pin.

James looked around for his horse but a car was standing where he had left it. Mr Patman came over and said, 'I put your horse around back, James. Out here it's liable to get hit.'

'What did you tell James, Tappy?'

'That I moved his horse. Liable to get hit.'

'It got hit.'

'By what?'

'That sixty-one Olds.'

'It's a sixty-two.'

'When I can't tell a sixty-one from a sixty-two!'

Evelyn and Tap Patman walked over and identified the car as a '61 with '62 hubcaps.

'There now, what is our world coming to?'

James saw at a glance that the horse was favoring his left hind leg. He examined the leg carefully, going down on one knee while the horse swung his great neck to examine James's head. The leg was not too bad, nothing broken, but James would have to lead him home, twenty miles through the back country. Not too bad.

James had ridden into Coyote every week now for the last four months and at first he thought it would not be too bad. She would come home. Each time he was certain she would come home. Both of them had been certain too that their boy would come home, come home the first time, and he had – slightly damaged, but he had come home. He had stood around the hogan a few hours, afraid to sit down on the rugs as though the bugs would get him. He kept standing in the middle of the hogan as though looking around the wall for windows, around the rough room for chairs and tables, a radio, a bed that stood on legs, a familiar white face. And then he was gone for Gallup. Outside the hogan he had taken a big deep breath, stuck his head back inside the hogan heavy with smoke, repeated something pleasant in English and then was gone for Gallup.

He left, the mother of Twenty-six Horses said, because an artist can make a living there. 'We got to make a living for him here,' she said.

When James's wife came to Coyote the first thing she did was refuse to speak Navajo. She leased the restaurant next to the Gulf Station from Tap Patman – sixty-eight dollars a month plus five percent of the gross – hired four Spanish-Americans, fired a slovenly Anglo cook who was supposed to come with the place, stippled the rest rooms with neon, hung out a lot of white man's signs and concentrated on not speaking Navajo.

'You speak Navajo and soon the place is full of Indians. Indians haven't any money and they come in and play chants on the jukebox, look under things, ask what the signs mean, bring their wives in to show off their jewelry, make big talk about the kids their wives stack on cradle boards along the counter, make jokes about the Whites – and they haven't any money. I left the reservation, I came to Coyote to open a restaurant, because it is a white man's world and you have to make it the white man's way. Anything else is talking to the ground. The white man came, saw, stole; the Indian smiled. Okay, make a joke, but the white man is Chee Dodge. Even if the white man wanted to stop pushing us under the table, and sometimes he wants to stop, he can't. All right, so our boy came home the first time. What is he? A weaver. All right, he is the best weaver on the Checkerboard Area. All right, on the reservation too. All right, he is what the trader calls him, an artist. But listen, James The Man With Twenty-six Horses, by the time it takes our boy to set his loom, listen, the white man has a thousand rugs. Listen, the white man has a machine. All right, the trader says the machine has the white man but that's Indian talk. The white man has a machine. Maybe he can't stop it. Man With Twenty-six Horses, but he has a machine. Any way else is talking to the ground. It's a white world.'

The Man With Twenty-six Horses had walked in front of his horse to the edge of Coyote. Now no one would call him James. It was all right to call him James. James was a good machine name, that's the way he made his mark in the government book. The Man With Twenty-six Horses was the name the People had given him when he had twenty-six horses. Now he had twenty-four, twenty-five, sometimes – once – he had thirty-four, but when they gave him the name he had twenty-six horses. That was a good name. It meant he was a big Chee Dodge. Actually his son's name was The Son Of The Man With Twenty-six Horses. The Indians named his wife The Queen of Coyote City when she moved into town and refused to speak Navajo. It was not a good name; it meant she was worse than an Apache – a Pueblo almost.

James had got the horse now to the top of the hill that overlooked Coyote. So they said his boy was an artist. Artist. What does their calling him an artist exactly mean? They meant nice by it he could tell by the tone, but it certainly had something to do with not being able to sell what you do. That was clear. It had something to do with not wanting to sell, too. The white trader at Nargheezi, George Bowman, had gotten the boy an order from a nice tribe of Whites called the Masons. The Masons had even drawn the picture for him and left a ring with the same picture on it. Orders would follow from other nice tribes, the Kiwanis, the Elks, who wanted to help. They pay big. No, the boy had said, I do not feel it. James felt the Mason ring and he could feel it. Here, the boy said touching just below his chest.

So an artist is a person who feels things just below his chest. All right, but he must feel something below that in his stomach too. Maybe that was why the boy left. Maybe his squaw had been right. Maybe his son wasn't looking around the hogan for a TV set or a bed with legs. Maybe the outside had gotten him accustomed to three meals a day. Maybe an artist on the outside can make three meals a day.

'Can an artist on the outside make three meals a day?'

James had come upon a fat white man leaning on the side of his car on Coyote Hill and he figured he might as well ask him as another.

'No,' the fat white man said. 'Tell me, what town is that?'

James told him it was Coyote.

'You're an Indian, aren't you?'

'Yes,' James said.

'Well, I can tell you I paid ten thousand dollars for this car,' the man said. 'It's got nearly four hundred horses. I've been busting to tell somebody but on the outside you're not supposed to tell anybody. I can tell an Indian I guess.'

'Ten thousand dollars! I didn't know it was possible,' James said. 'Four hundred horses?'

'Since last month it's been possible,' the man said. 'The Caddie people did it. Tell me, are you going to sell some paintings on the outside?'

'No, my boy,' James said.

'That's too bad,' the man said. 'If there's anything I can do to help, outside of buying one—?'

'I guess not,' James said.

'Buying a picture would make it worse,' the man said. 'He'd only go through life under the delusion that he'd sell another.'

'Maybe,' James said.

'Everyone,' the man said, 'has been sane at one time or another in his life. He wants to create something, then he sees the way the world is going and decides he better go with it.'

'Not even three meals a day?'

'Three meals a day is a lot of meals to give a man who will not go along.'

Now that the man had made his speech James pulled on his horse.

'Wait,' the man said. 'I can tell this to an Indian. Keep your boy here in the world. Don't let him get out there on the big white reservation. Out there we think we're on the outside looking in, but it's just the opposite; we're on the inside looking out. We are out there seeing who can be the biggest failure and we got a system of checking. We can always tell who wins. It's the man with the biggest car, the biggest house.' The man leaning against the car hesitated. 'Did you ever see a child's drawing?' the man said. 'We have all got it and we all give it up.'

The man had made two speeches now and James felt he

could move on without being rude. He did, going on down the Coyote Hill pulling the horse after him.

The man continued leaning against the car watching the flowing sun behind the purple rocks. He was one of the many vice-presidents of an oil company that was working the Navajo Country. He always stopped where he could enjoy a beautiful sight like this. Now he got back in the car and started her up. It was good to sound off. It wasn't often you got a chance. It wasn't often you could find someone like an Indian. And it would never get around. Not one of his friends would ever suspect for a moment that he was sane.

James continued on down the hill and wondered how a man like that was permitted off the big reservation. It can only be that, like many others, he never tells anyone.

But the news about his boy was bad. I wonder how you go about looking for someone out there? James had seen a television play in Arpacio Montoyo's bar. He had made his can of beer last to the end. It was about a girl who left home and the ending was that you should buy this soap. The man kept holding the soap up and hollering about the soap. It made a kind of exciting ending and probably a lot of sense too, if you grew up on the big reservation. The play might have been a solution to his problem. Certainly, James thought, if buying the soap of the man who was hollering would get his boy home he would buy all that man's soap the trader had. James was very worried about his own son, The Son Of The Man With Twenty-six Horses.

James had reached the bottom of the north side of the Coyote Hill and started up the slight rise that had the only aspen grove at this altitude that anyone had ever heard of. The aspen leaves had ceased budding out and were waiting to fly into Ben Helpnell's porch when the wind blew. Ben Helpnell was working on his new Monkey Ward pump beneath his abandoned windmill. The new pump was the latest thing, later even than the piston pump. It worked on the theory that 'it is easier to push water than it is to pull it. It is a hermetically sealed, self-contained unit, and without any fuss or bother or expensive plumbers or electricians, you just drop the whole thing in the well.' Ben had done that yesterday and since, he had been looking for it.

Ben saw James coming up and said, 'I'm well shut of the damn thing.' Ben was a horse and cattle trader and he saw now that James's horse was limping. But he must work around to the subject gradually.

'I'm just as well shut of it,' he repeated, but his heart had gone out of it. It was in James's horse.

Suspecting a trade, James said nothing.

'Your wife's got some good signs on her restaurant,' Ben said.

James did not want to talk about that.

'I ain't seen you by for a time,' Ben said.

'My boy is gone,' James said.

Ben studied over this for a while, looking down the well, then he looked over at the horse but his heart was no longer in the horse. It was involved now with James's grief.

'I tell you what, James,' Ben said, studying the well again. 'Take a horse, leave it off when you come back through.'

Another day James would not have taken the horse first off. He would have hunched down, snapping sticks with his fingers and drawing pictures on the ground until they made a trade. It would have taken four or five hours, and Ben's wife might have changed clothes two or three times to impress the Indian. And James would finger his turquoise jewelry from the saddle-bags to impress everyone and Ben would do a dance he picked up in Chihuahua that impressed even horses – all this to relieve the tension of the dealing when the excitement or the danger of closing the transaction became too real.

But now James's grief was in all their hearts and Mary would not want to change clothes three times, Ben would find no joy to do his dance nor James to show his jewelry. They would have only stumbled through a city deal with nothing to show for it except the grieving that James had brought.

'Take the blaze mare,' Ben Helpnell said.

James transferred his saddle to the little blaze in the near corral while Ben Helpnell continued to stare down the well to figure the meaning of a lost pump.

'I should of tooken it back,' he said. And finally standing up, 'It's nothing against Monkey Ward. I must of done something wrong.'

'You chunked it down the well,' Mary said from where she watched behind a screen door.

'It said in the book –' and then Ben ceased, knowing that women will even contradict the book, and walked over to James at the corral.

James was weaving the cinch strap through its final gyrations before pulling good.

'Lots of horse,' Ben Helpnell said. James swung into the saddle and started off leading his own horse with a rope in his dark right hand.

'When you get home he could be there,' Ben Helpnell said.

'He could be there,' James agreed, but he was not heard. He was already going up the road that led past the sawdust-rotting remains of Girt Maxey's sawmill.

Two hours later he was going up the trail that led past the Bowman trading post, a long, low log and adobe building with a small blue hogan huddled nearby, and then on up to the top of the piñon- and pine-studded mesa that looked out on his own hogan below. His hogan was smoking.

'He could be there.'

No. He would shut his eyes and take another look. When he opened his eyes again a thin stream of blue cedar smoke still poured a fine column straight up from the middle of the conical hogan. He touched the horse and both of his horses flew off the mesa bearing straight down at the hogan with the long blue smoke.

No. This was not good. It would be pushing his luck too fast. He swung his horse in a great circle around the hogan and then stopped. Both of his horses were breathing hard and the long blue cedar smoke still came out of the hogan. Now a quiet wind started and bent the long blue smoke until it curled heavy around James and the two horses. It was real smoke. But it would not do to go straight at the hogan. If luck was there it might be surprised away. Perhaps to call gently? James made a cup of his hands and called the boy's name toward the smoking hogan. Nothing happened but he did not want anything to happen so suddenly. He patted the blaze horse and looked back at his own horse at the end of the string.

'He could be there.'

Now James cupped his dark hands again and called just a little more this time but still gently. And then he dropped his hands and watched quietly, careful that no move was made to disturb anything. The horses were very quiet too, as a hand pushed back the sheep flap at the hogan door and his boy stepped outside.

James waved. The horses began to move and the boy held both hands above his head.

The boy and James ate meat, coffee and bread for a long time. When they had finished the meat and coffee and bread they had some more coffee with James not saying much, not wanting to push any of his luck away. The boy had been talking all along at a good pace without saying anything but watching the heavy wooden loom on which he had begun to weave a picture. Finally he stopped and said after a big pause and in English, 'There now, what's the world coming to when an artist won't settle for twenty-six horses and a Navajo loom?'

'No English spoken here,' a voice said in Navajo. 'The trader saw the smoke and sent a message that someone was home. I took down my signs in my restaurant and threw away the key. I finished with the restaurant. What's the world coming to when an Indian won't let the Whites fight each other?'

James did not think it was time to recognize his luck but he looked around the round room and recognized everything in it that was all gone yesterday and all here now. And outside too there were twenty-six horses.

'What's wrong with talking to the ground?'

This, James knew, was his wife called Married To The Man

With Twenty-six Horses talking. It was not The Queen of Coyote City.

'What's wrong,' the woman repeated, 'with talking to the ground? The Navajo People talked to the ground before the white man came. We could do worse than to be with our own people even when we are talking to the ground.'

James knew now that Married To The Man With Twenty-six Horses and The Son Of Twenty-six Horses had all made their speech and were waiting for him to say the end. The end, he knew, must have some style. It must not be the endless speeches of the white man. It must have style. It should be about three words. It should be in the best manner of the People. He looked over at the powerfully simple mountains and rocks, abstracted in quiet beauty, woven in the big loom. And yet the People seemed to be worried about talking to the ground.

'The earth understands,' The Man With Twenty-six Horses said gently for the end.

Something Big Is Happening to Me

Tomas Tomas, behind his round, cracked face and shallow-set, quick lizard eyes, was one hundred years old, or he was chasing one hundred, or one hundred was chasing him, no one knew, least of all Tomas Tomas. But early one morning nine months ago Tomas Tomas had gone down to the water hole in the arroyo and had come back dying.

It was cold for a September in New Mexico. The old Indian medicine man, Tomas Tomas, would never see another, warm or cold, and now he knew he would never see the end of this diamond-hard and dove-blue New Mexican day – he sat dreaming in front of his log and mud conical hogan; he sat dreaming that the white man never happened; he sat dreaming death never came.

His hogan was on a small bald rise beneath a fantastically

purple butte. His home had not always been here ; he had lived all around the Nation called Navajo Country. He got his name, Tomas Tomas – he had others – while a small boy and before he went to the United States government concentration camp at Bosque Redondo, when they rounded up all the Navajos during the last century to protect the settlers that were stealing Navajo land. That's the way most of the Navajos saw it, but Tomas Tomas thought and said very quietly otherwise. 'We stole it,' he said, 'from the Anasazi People who built those cliff houses up there and the big houses in Chaco Canyon. Killed most of them. At least the Whites, at least they let us live to see the bug and iron bird arrive.' Automobiles and airplanes he meant. 'The tin bugs were not male nor female. We got under the big bugs and had a look. We know now they are made by people, like you make an axe or like you make a picture, or make noise, not like you make children. Although there is a clan among the Navajos who live mostly around Shiprock, the Red Stick Clan, who believe that children are sent by the child spirit and making love accomplishes nothing, or very little. That it's just funny, or fun. Exercise,' Tomas Tomas added, not wanting to leave out some purpose to love-making entirely or altogether.

The other Navajo Indians had been expecting Tomas Tomas to die off and on for a hundred years. He was always being mortally wounded by a person or a horse and this day when he came back dying was not the first time that it had come to pass that Tomas Tomas was dead. The initiation rites into manhood of the Navajos in the Checkerboard Area kill an Indian boy so that he may be reborn again, reborn again even with a different name. The boy is killed in pantomime with a stone axe by the medicine man. You die and are reborn again by the medicine man, then all of the dream time is played out and the boy is shown all the magic that no woman knows, and in this manner and rite the boy dies and is reborn again as a man. But only after he has slept all naked in the night with a young girl, and that's important. If this is not done the boy is not reborn again and can never die. He is condemned to live forever

in some form. Tomas Tomas did this very repeatedly and successfully and on his first night became a man among men, and
now he could die.

When a Navajo dies he can have all his wives again in
heaven. There is prosperity, joy and wit and wisdom in Navajo
heaven. Navajo heaven is not a solemn gray high refuse heap
for humble failures.

So when Tomas Tomas came back to his hogan dying he
was not sweating cold in fear of judgement. He had been
judged and found with much wisdom, many wives, three
hogans, all in giant circles, and enough turquoise and silver to
founder a horse, enough pride to have killed four plundering
Whites, enough magic in his medicine bag to confound the universe and a long, never quite out of fashion turkey bonnet
festooned with bright parrot so long it dragged the ground.

One of his wives must catch a horse, Tomas Tomas thought
with his arms grabbing his chest to contain the awful pain of
death – also to keep the death from spreading before he got
to the mountain. A Checker Clan Navajo must die on the
mountain, that's what mountains are made for. Mountains are
for dying.

Tomas Tomas knelt down painfully in front of the Pendleton, yellow-striped blanket door of the hogan and made a
cigarette ; it was time to be calm and appraising. Death comes
very seldom to a man and it must be taken with dignity and
carefulness. It must be arranged, if it can be arranged, so that
there is no messiness, no blood, no dreaming, no raving out
loud so that everything is undone that was properly done in
your life.

That's why the ascent of the mountain is so valuable at the
end. Occupied instead of preoccupied. Gaining ever new heights
in spreading splendor, not the visit of fading visitors between
coming-together walls.

What was that ? A horse. It was nice of the white man to
send his horse. A black horse, but still a horse. Maybe he didn't
send it. Maybe the horse just got away. Well, it's a fine horse
for the occasion. That is, I always thought he'd make a good

mountain horse. Luto – I think that's the name they call him. But some call him that black son of a bitch. That's a nice name too. Pretty name. 'Come here, Pretty Name,' Tomas Tomas called in White language to the white man's black horse. 'Come here, you pretty black Luto son of a bitch,' Tomas Tomas called softly.

Now he finished making the cigarette and licked the paper carefully, eyeing the horse and seeing into and beyond the old familiar place. The Navajo Nation had been an old familiar place for a long time. Tomas Tomas did not want to go to any unknown place, but things were beginning to repeat themselves here. The medicine man had travelled a great deal in his practice, into foreign countries as far as Arizona. His wives did not like travel, or they did not like horses, it was difficult to tell which. Someone should find out if the Whites' women would travel if they had to travel on a horse. What am I doing dreaming about such rubbish when I've got to be on the mountain to see another world before the sun goes down? I never saw such an accommodating horse, come all this way here to help me keep the appointment. I never saw the hogans and the piñons and the fires all around them and the great yellow rocks above them so fixed before. It is as though it will never change, like a drawing on the rock or a picture on a pot. It seems stopped forever now in this last time. Only she moves.

'Where do you go, Tomas Tomas?' one of his wives said.

'To the mountain now.'

'Why, Tomas Tomas?'

'For the last time.'

'It's growing cold up there.'

'That's all right.'

'Soon it will be winter.'

'Yes, I know.'

'Whose horse?'

'It belongs to a White.'

'It's black.'

'Yes, but it belongs to a White with red hair and blue eyes.'

'And a green nose.'

'The Whites are funny enough without making anything up.'

'Look, Tomas Tomas,' this one of his wives continued. She was Spotted Calf, with a soft face and curling a huge orange blanket around her youth. 'Look, why go to the mountain?'

'Because it's best.'

'Why not here in comfort?'

'Because comfort is not best. The mountain is best.'

'I will bring you some soup before you start.'

'No, I just want to look from here at everything. Here is for the last time, which is like the first time. The last time and the first time are really the only time we ever see anything.'

'Shall I get the others?'

'No, I remember them.'

'Shall I get your magic, Tomas Tomas?'

'No, I leave my magic to the world. Wouldn't it be something to arrive there with my medicine before the Big Magician? But I don't know. I have no good medicine.'

'What, Tomas Tomas?'

'I will not take my magic. It's not much medicine.'

'Are you sure, Tomas Tomas?'

'Yes!' That hurt him. It made a sharp axe sink deep within his chest to speak so firmly and it hurt Tomas Tomas around the heart to speak so sharply to Spotted Calf. 'No, I will not take my magic,' Tomas Tomas said quietly. 'You get me packed up now, Eleventh Wife,' Tomas Tomas said quietly in his pain. 'And my empty medicine bundle.'

'Yes, Tomas Tomas,' and she disappeared into the hogan.

If I only had one piece of respectable medicine, the medicine man Tomas Tomas thought. Certainly He cannot object if I show off a little too. And there are a few things I want to find out. Why was I sentenced to earth? What will the white man's position be up there? Will the Whites have all the good land there too? But more important, why is all God's medicine a failure now? At one time I suppose He had very good magic and then He began to lose interest. He found the Indians no longer interesting. Something else I can bring up quietly with Him on the mountain: Why is the white man frightened of his

God? What did his God do to him that makes the white man scared? 'Do you know, Luto?' he asked towards the horse. 'What is the white man afraid of? Is he afraid his God is not there? Where is my watch?' Tomas Tomas asked himself. The watch could not tell time. Tomas Tomas tied the watch around his wrist for fetish. The sun could tell time. 'I must go to the mountain on time.'

Tomas Tomas looked out over the long slow fire on the Navajo Nation that had been his home for so long and that now he was going to leave. The Checkerboard Area was shaped like a great horn, a horn of nothing. The wide open mouth of the horn lay along the flat Torreón and Cabazon country that was pricked with sharp white volcanic cores. The horn of volcanoes. The heavy middle sweep of the horn was checkered with flat high green-capped, copper-hued mesas that gave you the feeling that the world was on two levels, which it is in the Checkerboard. The horn of many levels. Here at the narrow tip of the horn the land was drinking from the narrow, quick, crazy mountain streams that cough past and were called La Jara, Los Pinos and San Jose, and finally all became a great – dry in most seasons – wash called the Puerco which crossed under Route 66 at Gallup and entered the Rio Grande among spider cactus at Hondo. The horn is a dry river. Not really, Tomas Tomas thought. The horn is none of these things. The horn is home. Home is where you breed and leave other persons to take your place.

Nature is no longer interested in a person past the breeding age. That's true, Tomas Tomas thought. The rest of the body begins to quit and you die. But it's also true that a man can breed a long time, longer than a wolf or a coyote or a goat. Because he drinks alcoholic drinks? Smokes cigarettes? Lies? That's it. He does it longer and lives long because he lies, Tomas Tomas thought. Although I may be an exception. Tomas Tomas allowed his weakening but still hawk-severe eyes to roam the faint-in-the-hard-distance Cabazon country. 'Every man is an exception,' he said.

'What, Tomas Tomas?'

'Have I been a good husband?'

'Best,' she said in clear Navajo.

'Where are the other wives?'

'They went to wash in the Los Pinos. Shall I get them?'

'No,' Tomas Tomas said. 'I like arriving to people but not going from people. The wrong things are said when there is nothing that can be said. Don't bother to drag out the saddle. A saddle blanket will be enough. I didn't need a saddle to come into this world and I don't need one to leave.' Indian, Tomas Tomas thought to himself, you're getting silly. But I still don't need a saddle, he thought. That Luto horse has a wide comfortable back. That horse was by no horse bred. A strange horse by no mare fed.

'Just a saddle blanket,' he repeated and his youngest wife again disappeared into the hogan. 'Listen, horse,' he said to Luto, 'why did you come? All right, I know why you came, but you're only taking one – me – and it took you a long time – a hundred years. You're only taking one, and for every one you take we breed three or four, sometimes five or six. A person like me, who knows how many? I guess about a hundred. You don't believe it? Possibly more. It's not important. The important thing is we Indians don't waste anything. We have enough wives. Do you know how many Navajos there are now? Eighty thousand. When I was a young boy there were only six thousand. Soon now millions. That's how we're going to defeat the Whites. One day there will be no room for the Whites. If you can't fight them off our land, — them off. Would you like to see our secret weapons? That's a joke.' Tomas Tomas used the Navajo word which sounded like laughter – adeesh. 'Haven't you a sense of humor, horse?'

While the Medicine Man was leaning over in pain on one knee waiting for his youngest wife, Tomas Tomas tried to think something more that might be funny to work against this pain. It was a great pain. It was a new kind of pain deep in the chest as though something had entered him, something that had never been inside him before and only came once. No, he couldn't think of any joke to make against it but he could make this: Death will never get us all because the tribe has got something that the White hasn't got, a belief in the earth and in the world inside everyone, and like a bear or a coyote or an elk, the Indian is still part of the earth. And this, Tomas Tomas thought: Any Indian, me and every Indian I know in my clan, goes through a big time of his life believing it never happened. That's the only way an Indian can live. An Indian must spend a big time of his life in front of his hogan in the north part of New Mexico believing that the Whites never happened, that the white man never came.

Who are those two young white idiots coming towards me below the butte on those silly speckled horses? They are the magicians. Why can't they let an old Indian Medicine Man die in peace? No, I shouldn't say things like that. I should say, Who are those two silly speckled Whites coming towards me below the butte on idiot horses. Why can't they let an old Indian die with a little excitement of his own?

Tomas Tomas watched the door of the hogan for his youngest wife to appear with the saddle blanket. The black horse would not wait all day.

'Something big is happening to me,' Tomas Tomas said as the riders pulled up.

'*Olá*, Tomas Tomas! We were looking for Luto.'

'Some horse,' Tomas Tomas said.

'We were trailing Luto and we trailed him to here.'

'Don't bother. I'm going to use him now.'

'For the mountains?'

'Yes.'

'Already?'

'Already. Don't you think it's time?'

'But you've been here forever, Tomas Tomas,' Ring said.

'Yes, I have.'

'But not forever and ever?'

The young white man who asked this was accompanied by an Indian of about the same age. The medicine man knew the young white man's name was Ring Bowman and his father owned a ranch near the White Horse Trading Post. His Indian partner's name was The Son Of The Man With Twenty-six Horses.

'I was thinking,' Tomas Tomas said, 'we could not beat the white man but we can wait slowly and patiently like a woman and in time tame the Whites. In time.'

'But now it's your time, Tomas Tomas.'

Tomas Tomas looked out over all the staggering bright land that was forever lost. All the opportunities that would never come again. Where did the Indian make his mistake? In being born. Partly that. Partly that and partly not dying, staying around too long, trying to hang on to life when there was no life. The White is a knife. I have known some good Whites, but I have also known some good knives, some good looms, a good hatchet, and an excellent rope. But it's not the same as people. We were conquered by the knives. We defeated the Anasazi People and then we were defeated by knives. That's all right because there's nothing we can do about it but it would have been nice if I could leave the world to people. If people still peopled the world. 'Do you agree?'

'Sure, Tomas Tomas.'

'I was thinking how nice it would be in leaving it if people still peopled the world.'

'Yes, Tomas Tomas.'

'You think I'm an old medicine man with too many wives and cow shit talk.'

'You leave the world in good hands, Tomas Tomas. Your world will be in good hands.'

'Give me your hand.' The medicine man took the white boy's hand and looked at it carefully. 'Chalk hand. What do you expect to get done with this?'

'Nothing.'

'That's right. You will get nothing done. It's not a hand that can make any magic.'

'Did you hear that, Twenty-six Horses?'

'Yes, I heard it,' Twenty-six Horses said. 'Does that mean you are going to kill me?'

'Yes, it does.'

'Right here?' Tomas Tomas asked.

'Yes,' Ring said. 'There will still be a lot of magic after you're gone, Tomas Tomas. I'm going to kill Twenty-six Horses right before your eyes.'

'Yes, he is,' Twenty-six Horses said.

'That's not magic,' Tomas Tomas said. 'Anyway you're not Twenty-six Horses, you're The Son Of The Man With Twenty-six Horses.'

'...e same,' Ring said.

'Now, if you could kill twenty-six Whites that would be a trick.'

'You're bitter, aren't you, Tomas Tomas?'

'No, I'm an Indian,' Tomas Tomas said. The medicine man was still hunched forward in pain and he could not figure why the two young men did not understand that he had some very important business to take care of. 'You should understand,' Tomas Tomas said, hoping that he had picked up where he left off. 'You should understand that I don't have much time. I must arrive on the mountain before it is too late.'

'It will take just one shot to kill Twenty-six Horses.'

'Believe him, it's true,' Twenty-six Horses said.

'I believe him,' Tomas Tomas said, raising his voice. 'I believe that he can kill you, Twenty-six Horses, in one shot. But what is great magic about that?

'The great magic, Tomas Tomas, is that I bring Twenty-six Horses back to life.'

Tomas Tomas tried resting on one hand to ease the pain. 'I know the missionary says the same thing. There was a man who died and came back again by magic, but no one saw it. I never met anyone who saw it. The missionary didn't see this magic. Did you?'

'No, but we can do it,' Ring said.

'The both of you die?'

'No, just him,' Ring said, hooking his thumb at Twenty-six Horses.

Tomas Tomas looked over at the hogan. 'Ihda!' Tomas Tomas called toward the hogan door.

'The saddle blanket must be in the other hogan,' Tomas Tomas' youngest wife called back. 'I will go there and look.'

'Hurry,' the medicine man repeated in a guttural whisper. Then to the magicians, 'Now?'

'Now,' Ring said. 'Twenty-six Horses will stand there on the rimrock.'

'No,' Tomas Tomas whispered.

'At about ten paces I will kill him.'

'No, don't.'

'Then bring him back to life.'

'Sure?'

'Positive.'

'Could you bring me back to life? Don't answer. I am going this time. I'm all prepared to go and I'm going. But if you have some good magic I would like to take that magic with me. Can I take it with me in my medicine bundle?'

'Yes,' Ring said. 'Now stand over there on the rimrock, Twenty-six Horses.'

'Something I can take with me,' the medicine man repeated. 'I would like to take some good magic with me when I go and I go to the mountain now.'

Tomas Tomas saw the young man called Ring, who was tall for his age and hard blue-eyed, withdraw from the saddle holster on the patient speckled Appaloosa, a Marlin carbine.

'Just an ordinary thirty-thirty,' Ring said to the dying medicine man, Tomas Tomas.

'Yes.'

'Now I put the cartridge in the chamber. You notice it has a red tip.'

'Why does the bullet have a red tip? Does it have something to do with the magic?'

Ring did not answer but slammed the shell home with a swift solid swing of the lever action.

The medicine man watched the young, arrogantly young, white man named Ring Bowman – who came from a near ranch with water and green grass that sleeked the cattle and the young man's cheeks, and demarked the boundaries of the

Navajo Nation – raised the gun slowly and carefully until the bronze tipped front sight was perfectly down in the V of the rear sight and the front sight was exactly on the heart of the Indian called Twenty-six Horses.

'Now I will kill an Indian,' Ring said.

'Wait!'

'Why?'

'Well, I have decided I don't need to take any magic with me.'

'Oh, you'll need magic up there, Tomas Tomas, won't he, Twenty-six Horses?'

'Yes, you will, Tomas Tomas.'

'All right. If Tomas Tomas is willing, go ahead and kill Twenty-six Horses with one shot.' The medicine man was annoyed.

'One shot,' Ring said and began to squeeze the trigger slowly. The roar was terrific, the noise came back again and again from the mesas and the dark canyons and Twenty-six Horses toppled down dead like the very dead and bled red from the stomach all over the ground.

'Get up!' Ring shouted.

The dead got up.

'Now give me the red bullet I fired.'

Twenty-six Horses raised his bronzed hand to his mouth and spat out the red bullet.

'Now here is your magic to take to the mountain,' Ring said, taking the red bullet and placing it in the quavering hand of Tomas Tomas.

'Do I dare? Sure I do,' Tomas Tomas answered himself. 'I will try it on Him as soon as I get to the mountain.'

'Who is him?'

'The one who allowed the Whites to defeat us.'

'You mean an ancestor?' the dead-alive and standing Twenty-six Horses asked.

'Yes,' Tomas Tomas said, standing with great effort. 'An ancestor. That's a good name, ancestor. Where's the horse?'

When Twenty-six Horses and Ring brought Luto over to the

hogan Tomas Tomas was ready. His youngest wife placed the white saddle blanket on the very wide-backed black horse and Tomas Tomas mounted painfully by himself. Now she passed Tomas Tomas up a small dark bundle and Tomas Tomas placed the red bullet inside

'If it does not work,' the medicine man said down to the young men, 'you will hear from me.'

'Where you are going it will work,' Ring said.

The black horse started slowly toward the easy foothills that began the big climb of the mountain. 'Good-bye,' Tomas Tomas waved to his youngest wife. 'It has been good. Marry rich. Die old. Bring magic. I will see you. I will see you all. I climb dying. I climb dying. Something big is happening to me,' Tomas Tomas called.

'We should have told him how it works,' Twenty-six Horses said, watching the medicine man disappear.

'That there were two blank red bullets, one in my gun and one in your mouth, and catchup in your pants. No. No, it's not necessary because they will believe him.'

'His ancestors?'

'Yes, Twenty-six Horses. Haven't we always believed he had eleven wives instead of five?'

'Yes.'

'Well, if he wanted to believe eleven, then his ancestors will want to believe anything.'

'I suppose,' Twenty-six Horses said. 'Let's get some more catchup.'

'And bullets,' Ring said.

In a few hours all the Navajo Indians from the Checkerboard Clan had gathered around Coyotes Love Me, who held a spy glass loaned to him by the trader.

'Where is the medicine man, Tomas Tomas, Coyotes Love Me?'

'He is on the Vallecito.'

'Is he steady?'

'No, he seems sick in the saddle, as though he will fall.'

'How is he now, Coyotes Love Me?'

Coyotes Love Me steadied the long scope. 'Better. The black horse is trying to help. He stops and tries to steady Tomas Tomas, but I do not think Tomas Tomas will make it.'

'If you would take the metal cover off the end of the telescope you could see better, Coyotes Love Me.'

Coyotes Love Me took off the cover, petulant, then he looked through the scope surprised. 'You can see everything! Well, it's just like I said only worse. I don't think Tomas Tomas will make it.'

'Let me see.' Afraid Of His Own Horses took the scope. 'It's worse than Coyotes Love Me said. No, Tomas Tomas will never make it. The black horse seems very tired. The black horse cannot make it up and over the Gregorio Crest. Well, that's too bad. I guess the medicine man will fall off and die on the way up. It's a terrible thing, he won't make the mountain to die, but we don't have any magic for this.'

'No, we don't,' Coyotes Love Me agreed.

'I've got some,' Ring said. 'Will you hand me the rifle again, Twenty-six Horses?'

'Nothing will work now. There is nothing anyone can do now at this distance,' Coyotes Love Me said.

Ring raised the gun very high, much too high most of the Indians thought, but a half second after the shot the great black horse, even at this distance with the naked eye, could be seen going over the top in furious desperate leaps as though fleeing a battle. The medicine man, Tomas Tomas, was on top. Home.

Afraid Of His Own Horses put down the scope and looked at Ring. 'That was good magic.'

'That was a good, while no one was looking, far-off long-distance kick in the ass,' Coyotes Love Me said. 'White medicine.'

They found the body of Tomas Tomas two months later near a spring on the exact top of the mountain above a live oak knoll near the Las Vacas ranger cabin. There were tracks from where Tomas Tomas had dismounted, gone down to the spring, come back to the top dying and finally died.

There was never found any trace of his medicine bundle containing the red bullet. Twenty-six Horses and Ring went up to look all around the Las Vacas one day, spent the night and came down bright the next morning, but they never found the red bullet either.

'Do you suppose –?'

'No,' Ring said. 'You've got to realize, Twenty-six Horses, that dead is dead.'

But Twenty-six Horses, besides being a Navajo who believed in magic in the afterworld, had been shot dead many times in this one, so all the way down the mountain and even after they had passed the hogan of Tomas Tomas in Navajo Country, Twenty-six Horses kept saying, 'Do you suppose?'

And Ring kept saying, 'No, I don't. I guess I don't.'

Which is a good place to leave it, where we left it, Ring thought, a place where the world has always and will always leave it. Ring rode ahead on Luto carrying the gun and Twenty-six Horses followed on a small paint. The horses slipped down obliquely into the wide flat far-lost beauty of the Indian Country and disappeared in the hard purple and wild mesas that fell in steps through a fierce color continuity that was not dying, a fabulous and bright Navajo Nation that was not dead, the hushed song in the land, disappearing and faint but still an alive and still smoldering Indian incantation against white doom – singing that the white man never happened, chanting death never came.

LeRoi Jones

The Heretics

'The whole of lower Hell is surrounded by a great wall, which is defended by rebel angels and immediately within which are punished the arch-heretics and their followers.'

And then, the city of Dis, 'the stronghold of Satan, named after him . . . the deeper Hell of wilful sin.'

THE HERETICS

Blonde summer in our south. Always it floats down & hooks in the broad leaves of those unnamed sinister southern trees. Blonde summer in our south. Always full of lives. Desires. The crimson heavy blood of a race, concealed in those absolute black nights. As if, each tiny tragedy had its own universe/or God to strike it down.

*

Faceless slow movement. It was warm & this other guy had his sleeves rolled up. (You cd go to jail for that without any trouble.) But we were loose, & maybe drunk. And I turned away & doubled up like rubber or black figure sliding at the bottom of any ocean. Thomas, Joyce, Eliot, Pound, all gone by & I thot agony at how beautiful I was. And sat sad many times in latrines fingering my joint.

But it was dusty. And time sat where it could, covered me dead, like under a stone for years, and my life was already over. A dead man stretched & a rock rolled over . . . till a light struck me straight on & I entered some madness, some hideous elegance . . . 'A Patrician I wrote to him. Am I a Patrician?'

*

We both wore wings. My hat dipped & shoes maybe shined. This other guy was what cd happen in this country. Black & his silver wings & tilted blue cap made up for his mother's hundred bogus kids. Lynchings. And he waved his own flag in his mosquito air, and walked straight & beauty was fine, and so easy.

He didn't know who I was, or even what. The light, then (what George spoke of in his letters ... 'a soft intense light'), was spread thin over the whole element of my world.

Two flyers, is what we thot people had to say. (I was a gunner, the other guy, some kind of airborne medic.) The bright wings & starched uniform. Plus, 24 dollars in my wallet.

That air rides you down, gets inside & leaves you weightless, sweating & longing for cool evening. The smells there wide & blue like eyes. And like kids, or the radio calling saturdays of the world of simple adventure. Made me weep with excitement. Heart pumping : not at all towards where we were. But the general sweep of my blood brought whole existences fresh and tingling into those images of romance had trapped me years ago.

*

The place used me. Its softness, and in a way, indirect warmth, coming from the same twisting streets we walked. (After the bus, into the main fashion of the city : Shreveport, Louisiana. And it all erected itself for whoever ... me, I supposed then, 'it's here, and of course, the air, for my own weakness. Books fell by. But open yr eyes, nose, speak to whom you want to. Are you contemporary?')

And it seemed a world for aztecs lost on the bone side of mountains. A world, even strange, sat in that leavening light & we had come in raw from the elements. From the cardboard moonless world of ourselves ... to whatever. To grasp at straws. (If indeed we wd confront us with those wiser selves ... But that was blocked. The weather held. No rain. That smell wrapped me up finally & sent me off to seek its source. And men stopped us. Split our melting fingers. The sun moved till it stopped at the edge of the city. The south stretched past any eye.

Outside any peculiar thot. Itself, whatever it becomes, is lost to what formal selves we have. Lust, a condition of the weather. The air, lascivious. Men die from anything ... and this portion of my life was carefully examining the rules. How to die? How to die?

*

The place, they told us, we'd have to go to 'ball' was called by them *Bottom*. The Bottom; where the colored lived. There, in whatever wordless energies your lives cd be taken up. Step back: to the edge, soothed the wind drops. Fingers are cool. Air sweeps. Threes one hundred feet down, smoothed over, the wind sways.

And they tell me there is one place/
          for me to be. Where
          it all
                    comes down. &
          you take up
          your sorrowful
                    life. There/

          with us all. To
          whatever death

*

The bottom lay like a man under a huge mountain. You cd see it slow in some mist, miles off. On the bus, the other guy craned & pulled my arm from the backseats at the mile descent we'd make to get the juice. The night had it. Air like mild seasons and come. That simple elegance of semen on the single buds of air. As if the night were feathers ... and they settled solid on my speech ... and preached sinister love for the sun.

The day ... where had it gone? It had moved away as we wound down into the mass of trees and broken lives.

The bus stopped finally a third of the way down the slope. The last whites had gotten off a mile back & 6 or seven negroes and we two flyers had the bus. The driver smiled his considerate paternal smile in the mirror at our heads as we popped off. Whole civilization considered, considered. 'They live in blackness. No thought runs out. They kill each other & hate the sun. They have no God save who they are. Their black selves. Their lust. Their insensible animal eyes.'

'Hey, son, 'dyou pay for him?' He asked me because I hopped off last. He meant not my friend, the other pilot, but some slick head coon in yellow pants cooling it at top speed into the grass. & knowing no bus driver was running in after no 8 cents.

> 'Man, the knives
>
> > flash. Souls
> > are spittle
> > on black earth. Metal
> > dug in flesh chipping
> > at the bone.'

I turned completely around to look at the busdriver. I saw a knife in him hacking chunks of bone. He stared, & smiled at the thin mob rolling down the hill. Friday night. Nigguhs is Nigguhs. I agreed. & smiled, he liked the wings, had a son who flew. 'You gon pay for that ol coon?'

'No,' I said, 'No. Fuck, man, I hate coons.' He laughed & I saw the night around his head warped with blood. The bus, moon & trees floated heavily in blood. It washed down the side of the hill & the negroes ran from it.

I turned towards my friend who was loping down the hill shouting at me & ran towards him & what we saw at the foot of the hill. The man backed the bus up & turned around/pretending he was a mystic.

*

I caught Don (?) and walked beside him laughing. And the trees passed & some lights and houses sat just in front of us. We trailed the rest of the crowd & they spread out soon & disappeared into their lives.

The Bottom was like Spruce & Belmont (the ward) in Nwk. A culture of violence and foodsmells. There, for me. Again. And it stood strange when I thot finally how much irony. I had gotten so elegant (that was college/ a new order of foppery).

But then the army came & I was dragged into a kind of stillness. Everything I learned stacked up and the bones of love shattered in my face. And I never smiled again at anything. Everything casual in my life (except that life itself) was gone. Those naked shadows of men against the ruined walls. Penis, testicles. All there (and I sat burned like wire, w/ farmers, thinking of what I had myself. When I peed I thot that. 'Look. Look what you're using to do this. A dick. And two balls, one a little lower than the other. The first thing warped & crooked when it hardened.' But it meant nothing. The books meant nothing. My idea was to be loved. What I accused John of. And it meant going into that huge city melting. And the first face I saw I went to and we went home and he shoved his old empty sack of self against my frozen skin.

*

Shadows, phantoms, recalled by that night. It's heavy moon. A turning slow and dug in the flesh and wet spots grew under my khaki arms. Alive to mystery. And the horror in my eyes made them large and the moon came in. The moon and the quiet southern night.

*

We passed white shut houses. It seemed misty or smoky. Things settled dumbly in the fog and we passed, our lives spinning off in simple anonymous laughter.

We were walking single-file because of the dirt road. Not wanting to get in the road where drunk niggers roared by in dead autos stabbing each other's laughter in some gray abandon of suffering. That they suffered and cdn't know it. Knew that somehow, forever. Each dead nigger stinking his same suffering thru us. Each word of blues some dead face melting. Some life drained off in silence. Under some gray night of smoke. They roared thru this night screaming. Heritage of hysteria and madness, the old meat smells and silent gray sidewalks of the North. Each father, smiling mother, walked thru these nights frightened of their children. Of the white sun scalding their nights. Of each hollow loud footstep in whatever abstruse hall.

*

THE JOINT

(a letter was broken and I can't remember. The other guy laughed, at the name. And patted his. I took it literal and looked thru my wallet as not to get inflamed and sink on that man screaming of my new loves. My cold sin in the cities. My fear of my own death's insanity, and an actual longing for men that brooded in each finger of my memory.

  He laughed at the sign. And we stood, for the moment (he made me warm with his laughing), huge white men who knew the world (our wings) and would give it to whoever showed as beautiful or in our sad lone smiles, at least willing to love us.
  He pointed, like Odysseus wd. Like Vergil, the weary shade, at some circle. For Dante, me, the yng wild virgin of the universe to look. To see what terror. What illusion. What sudden shame, the world is made. Of what death and lust I fondled and thot to make beautiful or escape, at least, into some other light, where each death was abstract & intimate.

*

There were, I think, 4 women standing across the street. The neon winked, and the place seemed mad to be squatted in this actual wilderness. 'For Madmen Only.' Mozart's Ornithology and yellow greasy fags moaning german jazz. Already, outside. The passage. I sensed in those women. And black space yawned. Damned and burning souls. What has been your sin? Your ugliness?

  And they waved. Calling us natural names. 'Hey, ol big-eye sweet nigger ... com'ere.' 'Little ol' skeeter dick ... don't you want none?' And to each other giggling at their centuries, 'Um, that big nigger look sweet' ... 'Yeh, that little one look sweet too.' The four walls of some awesome city. Once past you knew that your life had ended. That roads took up the other side, and wounded into thicker dusk. Darker, more insane, nights.

And Don shouted back, convinced of his hugeness, his grace ... my wisdom. I shuddered at their eyes and tried to draw back into the shadows. He grabbed my arm, and laughed at my dry lips.

Of the 4, the pretty one was Della and the fat one, Peaches. 17 year old whores strapped to negro weekends. To the black thick earth and smoke it made to hide their maudlin sins. I stared and was silent and they, the girls and Don, the white man, laughed at my whispering and sudden midnight world.

Frightened of myself, of the night's talk, and not of them. Of myself.

The other two girls fell away hissing at their poverty. And the two who had caught us exchanged strange jokes. Told us of themselves thru the other's mouth. Don already clutching the thin beautiful Della. A small tender flower she seemed. Covered with the pollen of desire. Ignorance. Fear of what she was. At her 17th birthday she had told us she wept, in the department store, at her death. That the years wd make her old and her dresses wd get bigger. She laughed and felt my arm, and laughed, Don pulling her closer. And ugly negroes passd close to us frowning at the uniforms and my shy clipped speech which they called 'norf.'

So Peaches was mine. Fat with short baked hair split at the ends. Pregnant empty stomach. Thin shrieky voice like knives against a blackboard. Speeded up records. Big feet in white, shiny polished shoes. Fat tiny hands full of rings. A purple dress with wrinkles across the stomach. And perspiring flesh that made my khakis wet.

The four of us went in the joint and the girls made noise to show this world their craft. The two rich boys from the castle. (Don looked at me to know how much cash I had and shouted and shook his head and called '18, man,' patting his ass.)

The place was filled with shades. Ghosts. And the huge ugly hands of actual spooks. Standing around the bar spilling wine on greasy shirts. Yelling at a fat yellow spliv who talked about all their mothers, pulling out their drinks. Laughing with wet cigarettes and the paper stuck to fat lips. Crazy as anything in the world, and sad because of it. Yelling as not to hear the sad breathing world. Turning all music up. Screaming all lyrics. Tough black men ... weak black men. Filthy drunk women whose perfume was cheap unnatural flowers. Quiet thin ladies whose lives had ended and whose teeth hung stupidly in their silent mouths ... rotted by thousands of nickel wines. A smell of despair and drunkenness. Silence and laughter, and the sounds of their movement under it. Their frightening lives.

*

Of course the men didn't dig the two imitation white boys come in on their leisure. And when I spoke someone wd turn and stare, or laugh, and point me out. The quick new jersey speech, full of italian idiom, and the invention of the jews. Quick to describe. Quicker to condemn. And when we finally got a seat in the back of the place, where the dance floor was, the whole place had turned a little to look. And the girls ate it all up, laughing as loud as their vanity permitted. Other whores grimaced and talked almost as loud ... putting us all down.

10 feet up on the wall, in a kind of balcony, a jew sat, with thick glasses and a cap, in front of a table. He had checks and money at the table & where the winding steps went up to him a line of shouting woogies waved their pay and waited for that bogus christ to give them the currency of that place. Two tremendous muthafuckers with stale white teeth grinned in back of the jew and sat with baseball bats to protect the western world.

On the dance floor people hung on each other. Clutched their separate flesh and thought, my god, their separate thots. They stunk. They screamed. They moved hard against each other. They pushed. And wiggled to keep the music on. Two juke boxes blasting from each corner, and four guys on a bandstand who had taken off their stocking caps and come to the place with guitars. One with a saxophone. All that screaming came together with the smells and the music, the people bumped their asses and squeezed their eyes shut.

Don ordered a bottle of schenley's which cost 6 dollars for a pint after hours. And Peaches grabbed my arm and led me to the floor. The dancing like a rite no one knew, or had use for outside their secret lives. The flesh they felt when they moved, or I felt all their flesh and was happy and drunk and looked at the black faces knowing all the world thot they were my own, and lusted at that anonymous America I broke out of, and long for it now, where I am.

We danced, this face and I, close so I had her sweat in my mouth, her flesh the only sound my brain could use. Stinking, and the music over us like a sky, choked any other movement off. I danced. And my history was there, had passed no further. Where it ended, here, the light white talking jig, died in the arms of some sentry of Africa. Some short haired witch out of my mother's most hideous dreams. I was nobody now, mama. Nobody. Another secret nigger. No one the white world wanted or would look at. (My mother shot herself. My father killed by a white tree fell on him. The sun, now, smothered. Dead.)

*

Don and his property had gone when we finished. 3 or 4 dances later. My uniform dripping and soggy on my skin. My hands wet. My eyes turned up to darkness. Only my nerves sat naked and my ears were stuffed with gleaming horns. No one face sat alone, just that image of myself, forever screaming. Chiding me. And the girl, Peaches, laughed louder than the crowd. And wearily I pushed her hand from my fly and looked for a chair.

We sat at the table and I looked around the room for my brother, and only shapes of black men moved by. Their noise and smell. Their narrow paths to death. I wanted to panic, but the dancing and gin had me calm, almost cruel in what I saw.

Peaches talked. She talked at what she thought she saw. I slumped on the table and we emptied another pint. My stomach turning rapidly and the room moved without me. And I slapped my hands on the table laughing at myself. Peaches

laughed, peed, thinking me crazy, returned, laughed again. I
was silent now, and felt the drink and knew I'd go out soon. I
got up feeling my legs, staring at the fat guard with me, and
made to leave. I mumbled at her. Something ugly. She laughed
and held me up. Holding me from the door. I smiled casual,
said, 'Well, honey, I gotta split ... I'm fucked up.' She grinned
the same casual, said, 'You can't go now, big eye, we jist gittin
into sumpum.'

'Yeh, yeh, I know ... but I can't make it.' My head was
shaking on my chest, fingers stabbed in my pockets. I staggered
like an acrobat towards the stars and trees I saw at one end of
the hall. 'UhUh ... baby where you goin?'

'Gotta split, gotta split ... really, baby, I'm fucked ... up.'
And I twisted my arm away, moving faster as I knew I should
towards the vague smell of air. Peaches was laughing and tug-
ging a little at my sleeve. She came around and rubbed my tiny
pecker with her fingers. And I still moved away. She had my
elbow when I reached the road, head still slumped, and feet
pushing for a space to go down solid on. When I got outside she
moved in front of me. Her other girls had moved in too, to see
what was going on. Why Peaches had to relinquish her share so
soon. I saw the look she gave me and wanted somehow to pro-
test, say, 'I'm sorry. I'm fucked up. My mind, is screwy, I don't
know why. I can't think. I'm sick. I've been fucked in the ass.
I love books and smells and my own voice. You don't want me.
Please, Please, don't want me.'

But she didn't see. She heard, I guess, her own blood. Her
own whore's bones telling her what to do. And I twisted away
from her, headed across the road and into the dark. Out of, I
hoped, Bottom, towards what I thot was light. And I could hear
the girls laughing at me, at Peaches, at whatever thing I'd
brought to them to see.

So the fat bitch grabbed my hat. A blue 'overseas cap' they
called it in the service. A cunt cap the white boys called it.
Peaches had it and laughing like kids in the playground doing
the same thing to some unfortunate fag. I knew the second she
got it, and stared crazily at her, and my look softened to fear

and I grinned, I think. 'You ain't going back without dis cap, big eye nigger,' tossing it over my arms to her screaming friends. They tossed it back to her. I stood in the center staring at the lights, listening to my own head. The things I wanted. Who I thot I was. What was it? Why was this going on? Who was involved? I screamed for the hat. And they shot up the street, 4 whores. Peaches last in her fat, shouting at them to throw the hat to her. I stood for awhile and then tried to run after them. I cdn't go back to my base without that cap. Go to jail, drunken nigger! Throw him in the stockade! You're out of uniform, shine! When I got close to them, the other three ran off, and only Peaches stood at the top of the hill waving the hat at me, cackling at her wealth. And she screamed at the world, that she'd won some small niche in it. And did a dance, throwing her big hips at me, cursing and spitting ... laughing at the drunk who had sat down on the curb and started to weep and plead at her for some cheap piece of cloth.

And I was mumbling under the tears. 'My hat, please, my hat. I gotta get back, please.' But she came over to me and leaned on my shoulder, brushing the cap in my face. 'You gonna buy me another drink ... just one more?'

*

She'd put the cap in her brassiere, and told me about the cotton club. Another place at the outskirts of Bottom. And we went there, she was bouncing and had my hand, like a limp cloth. She talked of her life. Her husband, in the service too. Her family. Her friends. And predicted I would be a lawyer or something else rich.

The cotton club was in a kind of ditch. Or valley. Or three flights down. Or someplace removed from where we stood. Like movies, or things you think up abstractly. Poles, where the moon was. Signs, for streets, beers, pancakes. Out front. No one moved outside, it was too late. Only whores and ignorant punks were out.

The place when we got in was all light. A bar. Smaller than the joint with less people and quieter. Tables were strewn around and there was a bar with a fat white man sitting on a stool behind it. His elbows rested on the bar and he chewed a cigar spitting the flakes on the floor. He smiled at Peaches, knowing her, leaning from his talk. Four or five stood at the bar. White and black, moaning and drunk. And I wondered how it was they got in. The both colors? And I saw a white stripe up the center of the floor, and taped to the bar, going clear up, over the counter. And the black man who talked, stood at one side, the left, of the tape, farthest from the door. And the white man, on the right, closest to the door. They talked, and were old friends, touching each other, and screaming with laughter at what they said.

We got vodka. And my head slumped, but I looked around to see, what place this was. Why they moved. Who was dead. What faces came. What moved. And they sat in their various skins and stared at me.

Empty man. Walk thru shadows. All lives the same. They give you wishes. The old people at the window. Dead man. Rised, come gory to their side. Wish to be lovely, to be some other self. Even here, without you. Some other soul. Than the filth I feel. Have in me. Guilt, like something of God's. Some separate suffering self.

Locked in a lightless shaft. Light at the top, pure white sun. And shadows twist my voice. Iron clothes to suffer. To pull down, what had grown so huge. My life wrested away. The old wood. Eyes of the damned uncomprehending. Who it was. Old slack nigger. Drunk punk. Fag. Get up. Where's your home? Your mother. Rich nigger. Porch sitter. It comes down. So cute, huh? Yellow thing. Think you cute.

And suffer so slight, in the world. The world? Literate? Brown skinned. Stuck in the ass. Suffering from what? Can you read? Who is T. S. Eliot? So What? A cross. You've got to like girls. Weirdo. Break, Roi, Break. Now come back, do it again. Get down, hard. Come up. Keep your legs high, crouch hard when you get the ball . . . churn, churn, churn. A blue jacket, and alone. Where? A chinese restaurant. Talk to me. God-damnit. Say something. You never talk, just sit there, impos-

sible to love. Say something. Alone, there, under those buildings. Your shadows. Your selfish tongue. Move. Frightened bastard. Frightened scared sissy motherfucker.

*

I felt my head go down. And I moved my hand to keep it up.
Peaches laughed again. The white man turned and clicked his
tongue at her wagging his hand. I sucked my thin mustache,
scratched my chest, held my sore head dreamily. Peaches
laughed. 2 bottles more of vodka she drank (half pints at
3.00 each) & led me out the back thru some dark alley down
steps and thru a dark low hall to where she lived.

She was dragging me, I tried to walk and couldn't and stuck
my hands in my pockets to keep them out of her way. Her
house, a room painted blue and pink with Rheingold women
glued to the wall. Calendars. The Rotogravure. The picture of
her husband? who she thot was some officer, and he was grinning like watermelon photos with a big white apron on and
uncle jemima white hat and should've had a skillet. I slumped
on the bed, and she made me get up and sit in a chair and she
took my hat out her clothes and threw it across the room. Coffee she said, you want coffee. She brought it anyway, and I got
some in my mouth. Like winter inside me. I coughed and she
laughed. I turned my head away from the bare bulb. And she
went in a closet and got out a thin yellow cardboard shade and
stuck it on the light trying to push the burned part away from
the huge white bulb.

Willful sin. In your toilets jerking off. You refused god. All
frauds, the cold mosques glitter winters. 'Morsh Americans.'
Infidels fat niggers at the gates. What you want. What you are
now. Liar. All sins, against your God. Your own flesh. TALK.
TALK.

And I still slumped and she pushed my head back against the
greasy seat and sat on my lap grinning in my ear, asking me
to say words that made her laugh. Orange. Probably. Girl.
Newark. Peaches. Talk like a white man, she laughed. From
up north (she made the 'th' an 'f').

And sleep seemed good to me. Something my mother would say. My grandmother, all those heads of heaven. To get me in. Roi, go to sleep, You need sleep, and eat more. You're too skinny. But this fat bitch pinched my neck and my eyes would shoot open and my hands dropped touching the linoleum and I watched roaches trying to count them getting up to 5, and slumped again. She pinched me. And I made some move and pushed myself up standing and went to the sink and stuck my head in cold water an inch above the pile of stale egg dishes floating in brown she used to wash the eggs off.

I shook my head. Took out my handkerchief to dry my hands, leaving my face wet and cold, for a few seconds. But the heat came back, and I kept pulling my shirt away from my body and smelled under my arms, trying to laugh with Peaches, who was laughing again.

I wanted to talk now. What to say. About my life. My thots. What I'd found out, and tried to use. Who I was. For her. This lady, with me.

She pushed me backwards on the bed and said you're sleepy I'll get in with you, and I rolled on my side trying to push up on the bed and couldn't, and she pulled one of my shoes off and put it in her closet. I turned on my back and groaned at my head told her again I had to go. I was awol or something. I had to explain awol and she knew what it meant when I finished. Everybody that she knew was that. She was laughing again. O, God, I wanted to shout and it was groaned. Oh, God.

She had my pants in her fingers pulling them over my one shoe. I was going to pull them back up and they slipped from my hands and I tried to raise up and she pushed me back. 'Look, Ol nigger, I ain't even gonna charge you. I like you.' And my head was turning, flopping straight back on the chenille, and the white ladies on the wall did tricks and grinned and pissed on the floor. 'Baby, look, Baby,' I was sad because I fell. From where it was I'd come to. My silence. The streets I used for books. All come in. Lost. Burned. And soothing she rubbed her hard hair on my stomach and I meant to look to see if grease was there it was something funny I meant to say, but my head twisted to the side and I bit the chenille and figured there would be a war or the walls would collapse and I would have to take the black girl out, a hero. And my mother would grin and tell her friends and my father would call me 'mcgee' and want me to tell about it.

When I had only my shorts on she pulled her black dress over her head. It was all she had, except a gray brassiere with black wet moons where her arms went down. She kept it on.

Some light got in from a window. And one white shadow sat on a half naked woman on the wall. Nothing else moved. I drew my legs up tight & shivered. Her hands pulled me to her.

*

It was Chicago. The fags & winter. Sick thin boy, come out of those els. Ask about the books. Thin mathematics and soup. Not the black Beverly, but here for the first time I'd seen it. Been pushed in. What was flesh I hadn't used till then. To go back. To sit lonely. Need to be used, touched, and see for the first time how it moved. Why the world moved on it. Not a childish sun. A secret fruit. But hard things between their legs. And lives governed under it. So here, it can sit now, as evil. As demanding, for me, to have come thru and found it again. I hate it. I hate to touch you. To feel myself go soft and want some person not myself. And here, it had moved outside. Left my wet fingers and was not something I fixed. But dropped on me and sucked me inside. That I walked the streets hunting for warmth. To be pushed under a quilt, and call it love. To shit water for days and say I've been loved. Been warm. A real thing in the world. See my shadow. My reflection. I'm here, alive. Touch me. Please, Please, touch me.

*

She rolled on me and after my pants were off pulled me on her thick stomach. I dropped between her legs and she felt between my cheeks to touch my balls. Her fingers were warm and she grabbed everything in her palm and wanted them harder. She pulled to get them harder and it hurt me. My head hurt me.

My life. And she pulled, breathing spit on my chest. 'Come on, Baby, Come on . . . Get hard.' It was like being slapped. And she did it that way, trying to laugh. 'Get hard . . . Get hard.' And nothing happened or the light changed and I couldn't see the paper woman.

And she slapped me now, with her hand. A short hard punch and my head spun. She cursed. & she pulled as hard as she could. I was going to be silent but she punched again and I wanted to laugh . . . it was another groan. 'Young Peachtree,' she had her mouth at my ear lobe. 'You don't like women, huh?' 'No wonder you so pretty . . . ol bigeye faggot.' My head was turned from that side to the other side turned to the other side turned again and had things in it bouncing.

'How'd you ever get in them airplanes, Peaches (her name she called me)? Why they let fairies in there now?' (She was pulling too hard now & I thot everything would give and a hole in my stomach would let out words and tears.) 'Goddam punk, you gonna fuck me to night or I'm gonna pull your fuckin dick aloose.'

How to be in this world. How to be here, not a shadow, but thick bone and meat. Real flesh under real sun. And real tears falling on black sweet earth.

I was crying now. Hot Hot tears and trying to sing. Or say to Peaches. 'Please, you don't know me. Not what's in my head. I'm beautiful. Stephen Dedalus. A mind, here where there is only steel. Nothing else. Young pharaoh under trees. Young pharaoh, romantic, liar. Feel my face, how tender. My eyes. My soul is white, pure white, and soars. Is the God himself. This world and all others.'

And I thot of a black man under the el who took me home in the cold. And I remembered telling him all these things. And how he listened and showed me his new suit. And I crawled out of bed morning and walked thru the park for my train. Loved. Afraid. Huger than any world. And the hot tears wet Peaches and her bed and she slapped me for pissing.

I rolled hard on her and stuck my soft self between her thighs. And ground until I felt it slip into her stomach. And it got harder in her spreading the meat. Her arms around my hips pulled down hard and legs locked me and she started yelling. Faggot. Faggot. Sissy Motherfucker. And I pumped myself. Straining. Threw my hips at her. And she yelled, for me to fuck her. Fuck her. Fuck me, you lousy fag. And I twisted, spitting tears, and hitting my hips on hers, pounding flesh in her, hearing myself weep.

*

Later, I slipped out into Bottom. Without my hat or tie, shoes loose and pants wrinkled and filthy. No one was on the streets now. Not even the whores. I walked not knowing where I was or was headed for. I wanted to get out. To see my parents, or be silent for the rest of my life. Huge moon was my light. Black straight trees the moon showed. And the dirt roads and scattered wreck houses. I still had money and I.D., and a pack of cigarettes. I trotted, then stopped, then trotted and talked outloud to myself. And laughed a few times. The place was so still, so black and full of violence. I felt myself.

At one road, there were several houses. Larger than alot of them. Porches, yards. All of them sat on cinder blocks so the vermin would have trouble getting in. Someone called to me. I thought it was in my head and kept moving, but slower. They called again. 'Hey, Psst, Hey comere.' A whisper, but loud. 'Comere, baby.' All the sides of the houses were lit up but underneath, the space the cinder blocks made was black. And the moon made a head shadow on the ground, and I could see an arm in the same light. Someone kneeling under one of the houses, or an arm and the shadow of a head. I stood straight, and stiff, and tried to see right thru the dark. The voice came back, chiding like. Something you want. Whoever wants. That we do and I wondered who it was kneeling in the dark, at the end of the world, and I heard breathing when I did move, hard and closed.

I bent towards the space to see who it was. Why they had called. And I saw it was a man. Round red rimmed eyes, sand colored jew hair, and teeth for a face. He had been completely under the house but when I came he crawled out and I saw his dripping smile and yellow soggy skin full of red freckles. He said, 'Come on here. Comere a second.' I moved to turn away. The face like a dull engine. Eyes blinking. When I turned he reached for my arm grazing my shirt and the voice could be flushed down a toilet. He grinned and wanted to panic seeing me move. 'Lemme suck yo dick, honey. Huh?' I was backing away like from the hyena cage to see the rest of them. Baboons? Or stop at the hotdog stand and read a comic book. He came up off all fours and sat on his knees and toes, shaking his head and hips. 'Comeon baby, Comeon now.' As I moved back he began to scream at me. All lust, all panic, all silence and sorrow, and finally when I had moved and was trotting down the road, I looked around and he was standing up with his hands cupped to his mouth yelling into the darkness in complete hatred of what was only some wraith. Irreligious spirit pushing thru shadows, frustrating and confusing the flesh. He screamed behind me and when the moon sunk for minutes behind the clouds or trees his scream was like some animal's, some hurt ugly thing dying alone.

*

It was good to run. I would jump every few steps like hurdling, and shoot my arm out straight to take it right, landing on my right heel, snapping the left leg turned and flat, bent for the next piece. 3 steps between 180 yard lows, 7 or 9 between the 220's. The 180's I thought the most beautiful. After the first one, hard on the heel and springing up. Like music; a scale. Hit 1 -23. UP (straight right leg, down low just above the wood. Left turned at the angle, flat, tucked. Head low to the knee, arms reaching for the right toe, pulling the left leg to snap it down. HIT (right foot) snap left HIT (left). Stride. The big one. 1 -23. UP. STRETCH. My stride was long enough for the 3 step move. Stretching and hopping almost but in perfect scale. And I moved ahead of Wang and held it, the jew boy pooping at the last wood. I hit hard and threw my chest out, pulling the knees high, under my chin. Arms pushing. The last ten yards I picked up 3 and won by that, head back wrong (Nap said) and galloping like a horse (wrong again Nap said) but winning in new time and leaping in the air like I saw heroes do in flicks.

*

I got back to where I thought the Joint would be, and there were city-like houses and it was there somewhere. From there, I thought I could walk out, get back to the world. It was getting blue again. Sky lightening blue and gray trees and buildings black against it. And a few lights going on in some wood houses. A few going off. There were alleys now. And high wood fences with slats missing. Dogs walked across the road. Cats sat on the fences watching. Dead cars sulked. Old newspapers torn in half pushed against fire hydrants or stoops and made tiny noises flapping if the wind came up.

I had my hands in my pockets, relaxed. The anonymous seer again. Looking slowly at things. Touching wood rails so years later I would remember I had touched wood rails in Louisiana when no one watched. Swinging my leg at cans, talking to the cats, doing made up dance steps or shadow boxing. And I came to a corner & saw some big black soldier stretched in the road with blood falling out of his head and stomach. I thot first it was Don. But this guy was too big and was in the infantry. I saw a paratrooper patch on his cap which was an inch away from his chopped up face, but the blue and silver badge had been taken off his shirt.

He was groaning quiet, talking to himself. Not dead, but almost. And I bent over him to ask what happened. He couldn't open his eyes and didn't hear me anyway. Just moaned and moaned losing his life on the ground. I stood up and wondered what to do. And looked at the guy and saw myself and looked over my shoulder when I heard someone move behind me. A tall black skinny woman hustled out of the shadows and looking back at me disappeared into a hallway. I shouted after her. And stepped in the street to see the door she'd gone in.

I turned to go back to the soldier and there was a car pulling up the road. A red swiveling light on top and cops inside. One had his head hung out the window and yelled toward me. 'Hey, you, Nigger, what's goin on?' That would be it. AWOL. Out of uniform (with a norfern accent). Now murder too. '30 days for nigger killing.' I spun and moved. Down the road & they started to turn. I hit the fence, swinging up and dove into the black yard beyond. Fell on my hands and knees & staggered, got up, tripped on garbage, got up, swinging my hands, head down and charged off in the darkness.

The crackers were yelling on the other side of the fence and I could hear one trying to scale it. There was another fence beyond, and I took it the same as the first. Swinging down into another yard. And turned right and went over another fence, ripping my shirt. Huge cats leaped out of my path and lights went on in some houses. I saw the old woman who'd been hiding near the soldier just as I got to the top of one fence. She was standing in a hallway that led out in that yard, and she ducked back laughing when she saw me. I started to go after her, but I just heaved a big rock in her direction and hit another fence.

I got back to where the city houses left off, and there were the porches and cinder blocks again. I wondered if 'sweet peter eater' would show up. (He'd told me his name.) And I ran up the roads hoping it wdn't get light until I found Peaches again.

At the Cotton Club I went down the steps, thru the alley, rested in the black hall, and tapped on Peaches' door. I bounced against it with my ass, resting between bumps, and fell backwards when she opened the door to shove her greasy eyes in the hall.

'You back again? What you want, honey? Know you don't want no pussy. Doyuh?'

I told her I had to stay there. That I wanted to stay there, with her. That I'd come back and wanted to sleep. And if she wanted money I'd give her some. And she grabbed my wrist and pulled me in, still bare assed except for the filthy brassiere.

She loved me she said. Or liked me alot. She wanted me to stay, with her. We could live together and she would show me how to fuck. How to do it good. And we could start as soon as she took a pee. And to undress, and get in bed and wait for her, unless I wanted some coffee, which she brought back anyway and sat on the edge of the bed reading a book about Linda Darnell.

'Oh, we can have some good times baby. Movies, all them juke joints. You live here with me and I'll be good to you. Wallace (her husband) ain't due back in two years. We can raise hell waiting for him.' She put the book down and scratched the inside of her thighs, then under one arm. Her hair was standing up and she went to a round mirror over the sink and brushed it. And turned around and shook her big hips at me, then pumped the air to suggest our mission. She came back and we talked about our lives : then she pushed back the sheets, helped me undress again, got me hard and pulled me into her. I came too quick and she had to twist her hips a few minutes longer to come herself. 'Uhauh, good even on a sof. But I still got to teach you.'

*

I woke up about 1 the next afternoon. The sun, thru that one window, full in my face. Hot, dust in it. But the smell was good. A daytime smell. And I heard daytime voices thru the window up and fat with optimism. I pulled my hands under my head and looked for Peaches who was out of bed. She was at the kitchen end of the room cutting open a watermelon. She had on a slip, and no shoes, but her hair was down flat and greased so it made a thousand slippery waves ending in slick feathers at the top of her ears.

'Hello, sweet,' she turned and had a huge slice of melon on a plate for me. It was bright in the room now & she'd swept and straightened most of the shabby furniture in her tiny room. And the door sat open so more light, and air could come in. And her radio up on a shelf above the bed was on low with heavy blues and twangy guitar. She sat the melon on the 'end table' and moved it near the bed. She had another large piece, dark red and spilling seeds in her hand and had already started. 'This is good. Watermelon's a good breakfast. Peps you up.'

And I felt myself smiling, and it seemed that things had come

to an order. Peaches sitting on the edge of the bed, just beginning to perspire around her forehead eating the melon in both
hands, and mine on a plate, with a fork (since I was 'smart'
and could be a lawyer, maybe). It seemed settled. That she was
to talk softly in her vague American, and I was to listen and
nod, or remark on the heat or the sweetness of the melon. And
that the sun was to be hot on our faces and the day smell come
in with dry smells of knuckles or greens or peas cooking somewhere. Things moving naturally for us. At what bliss we took.
At our words. And slumped together in anonymous houses I
thought of black men sitting on their beds this saturday of my
life listening quietly to their wives' soft talk. And felt the world
grow together as I hadn't known it. All lies before, I thought.
All fraud and sickness. This was the world. It leaned under its
own suns, and people moved on it. A real world, of flesh, of
smells, of soft black harmonies and color. The dead maelstrom
of my head, a sickness. The sun so warm and lovely on my
face, the melon sweet going down. Peaches' music and her
radio's. I cursed Chicago, and softened at the world. 'You look
so sweet,' she was saying. 'Like you're real rested.'

*

I dozed again even before I finished the melon and Peaches had
taken it and put it in the icebox when I woke up. The greens
were cooking in our house now. The knuckles on top simmer-
ing. And biscuits were cooking, and chicken. 'How you feel,
baby,' she watched me stretch. I yawned loud and scratched
my back getting up to look at what the stove was doing. 'We
gonna eat a good lunch before we go to the movies. You so
skinny, you could use a good meal. Don't you eat nuthin?'
And she put down her cooking fork and hugged me to her the
smell of her, heavy, traditional, secret.

'Now you get dressed, and go get me some tomatoes ... so
we can eat.' And it was good that there was something I could
do for her. And go out into that world too. Now I knew it was
there. And flesh.

I put on the stained khakis & she gave me my hat. 'You'll get picked up without yo cap. We have to get you some clothes so you can throw that stuff away. The army don't need you no way.' She laughed. 'Leastways not as much as I does. Old Henry at the joint'll give you a job. You kin count money as good as that ol' jew I bet.'

And I put the tie on, making some joke, and went out shopping for my wife.

*

Into that sun. The day was bright and people walked by me smiling. And waved 'Hey' (a greeting) and they all knew I was Peaches' man.

I got to the store and stood talking to the man about the weather about airplanes and a little bit about new jersey. He waved at me when I left 'O.K. . . . you take it easy now.' 'O.K., I'll see you,' I said. I had tomatoes and some plums and peaches I bought too. I took a tomato out of the bag and bit the sweet flesh. Pushed my hat on the back of my head and strutted up the road towards the house.

It was a cloud I think came up. Something touched me. 'That color which cowardice brought out in me.' Fire burns around the tombs. Closed from the earth. A despair came down. Alien grace. Lost to myself, I'd come back. To that ugliness sat inside me waiting. And the mere sky graying could do it. Sky spread thin out away from this place. Over other heads. Beautiful unknowns. And my marriage a heavy iron to this tomb. 'Show us your countenance.' Your light.

It was a light clap of thunder. No lightning. And the sky grayed. Introibus. That word came in. And the yellow light burning in my rooms. To come to see the world, and yet lose it. And find sweet grace alone.

It was this or what I thought, made me turn and drop the tomatoes on Peaches' porch. Her window was open and I wondered what she was thinking. How my face looked in her head. I turned and looked at the sad bag of tomatoes. The peaches, some rolling down one stair. And a light rain came down I walked away from the House. Up the road, to go out of Bottom.

*

The rain wet my face and I wanted to cry, because I thot of the huge black girl watching her biscuits get cold. And her radio playing without me. The rain was hard for a second, drenching me. And then it stopped, and just as quick the sun came out. Heavy bright hot. I trotted for awhile then walked slow, measuring my steps. I stank of sweat and the uniform was a joke.

I asked some people how to get out and they pointed up the road where 10 minutes walking had me at the bottom of the hill the bus came down. A wet wind blew up soft full of sun and I began to calm. To see what had happened. Who I was and what I thought my life should be. What people called 'experience.' Young male. My hands in my pockets, and the grimy silver wings still hanging gravely on my filthy shirt. The feeling in my legs was to run up the rest of the hill but I just took long strides and stretched myself and wondered if I'd have K.P. or some army chastisement for being 2 days gone.

3 tall guys were coming down the hill I didn't see until they got close enough to speak to me. One laughed (at the way I looked). Tall strong black boys with plenty of teeth and pegged rayon pants. I just looked and nodded and kept on. One guy, with an imitation tattersall vest with no shirt, told the others I was in the joint last night 'playin cool.' Slick city nigger, one said. I was going to pass close to them and the guy with the vest put up his hand and asked me where I was coming from. One with suspenders and a belt asked me what the wings stood for. I told him something. The third fellow just grinned. I moved to walk around them and the fellow with the vest asked could he borrow fifty cents. I only had a dollar in my pocket and told him that. There was no place to get change. He said to give him the dollar. I couldn't do that and get back to my base I told him and wanted to walk away. And one of the guys had gotten around in back of me and kneeled down and the guy with the vest pushed me backwards so I fell over the other's back. I fell backwards into the dust, and my hat fell off, and I didn't think I was mad but I still said something stupid like, 'What'd you do that for.'

'I wanna borrow a dollar, Mr Half-white muthafucka. And that's that.' I sidestepped the one with the vest and took a running step but the grinning one tripped me, and I fell tumbling head forward back in the dust. This time when they laughed I got up and spun around and hit the guy who tripped me in the face. His nose was bleeding and he was cursing while the guy with the suspenders grabbed my shoulders and held me so the hurt one could punch me back. The guy with the vest punched too. And I got in one good kick into his groin, and stomped hard on one of their feet. The tears were coming again and I was cursing, now when they hit me, completely crazy. The dark one with the suspenders punched me in my stomach and I felt sick and the guy with the vest, the last one I saw, kicked me in my hip. The guy still held on for awhile then he pushed me at one of the others and they hit me as I fell. I got picked up and was screaming at them to let me go. 'Bastards, you filthy bastards, let me go.' Crazy out of my head. Stars were out. And there were no fists just dull distant jolts that spun my head. It was in a cave this went on. With music and whores danced on the tables. I saw reading from a book aloud and they danced to my reading. When I finished reading I got up from the table and for some reason, fell forward weeping on the floor. The negroes danced around my body and spilled whiskey on my clothes. I woke up 2 days later, with white men, screaming for God to help me.

Jack Kerouac

The Railroad Earth, Part 1

There was a little alley in San Francisco back of the Southern Pacific station at Third and Townsend in redbrick of drowsy lazy afternoons with everybody at work in offices in the air you feel the impending rush of their commuter frenzy as soon they'll be charging en masse from Market and Sansome buildings on foot and in buses and all well-dressed thru workingman Frisco of Walkup?? truck drivers and even the poor grime-bemarked Third Street of lost bums even Negroes so hopeless and long left East and meanings of responsibility and *try* that now all they do is stand there spitting in the broken glass sometimes fifty in one afternoon against one wall at Third and Howard and here's all these Millbrae and San Carlos neat-necktied producers and commuters of America and Steel civilization rushing by with San Francisco *Chronicles* and green *Call-Bulletins* not even enough time to be disdainful, they've got to catch 130, 132, 134, 136 all the way up to 146 till the time of evening supper in homes of the railroad earth when high in the sky the magic stars ride above the following hotshot freight trains. – It's all in California, it's all a sea, I swim out of it in afternoons of sun hot meditation in my jeans with head on handkerchief on brakeman's lantern or (if not working) on books, I look up at blue sky of perfect lostpurity and feel the warp of wood of old America beneath me and have insane conversations with Negroes in several-story windows above and everything is pouring in, the switching moves of boxcars in that little alley which is so much like the alleys of Lowell and I hear far off in the sense of coming night that engine calling our mountains.

But it was that beautiful cut of clouds I could always see above the little S.P. alley, puffs floating by from Oakland or the Gate of Marin to the north or San Jose south, the clarity of Cal to break your heart. It was the fantastic drowse and drum hum of lum mum afternoon nathin' to do, ole Frisco with end of land sadness – the people – the alley full of trucks and cars of businesses nearabouts and nobody knew or far from cared who I was all my life three thousand five hundred miles from birth-O opened up and at last belonged to me in Great America.

Now it's night in Third Street the keen little neons and also yellow bulblights of impossible-to-believe flops with dark ruined shadows moving back of torn yellow shades like a degenerate China with no money – the cats in Annie's Alley, the flop comes on, moans, rolls, the street is loaded with darkness. Blue sky above with stars hanging high over old hotel roofs and blowers of hotels moaning out dusts of interior, the grime inside the word in mouths falling out tooth by tooth, the reading rooms tick tock big-clock with creak chair and slantboards and old faces looking up over rimless spectacles bought in some West Virginia or Florida or Liverpool England pawnshop long before I was born and across rains they've come to the end of the land sadness end of the world gladness all you San Franciscos will have to fall eventually and burn again. But I'm walking and one night a bum fell into the hole of the construction job where they're tearing a sewer by day the husky Pacific & Electric youths in torn jeans who work there often I think of going up to some of em like say blond ones with wild hair and torn shirts and say 'You oughta apply for the railroad it's much easier work you don't stand around the street all day and you get much more pay' but this bum fell in the hole you saw his foot stick out, a British MG also driven by some eccentric once backed into the hole and as I came home from a long Saturday afternoon local to Hollister out of San Jose miles away across verdurous fields of prune and juice joy here's this British MG backed and legs up wheels up into a pit and bums and cops standing around right outside the coffee shop – it was the way they fenced it but he never had the nerve to do it due to the fact that he had no money and nowhere to go and O his father was dead and O his mother was dead and O his sister was dead and O his whereabouts was dead was dead. – But and then at that time also I lay in my room on long Saturday afternoons listening to Jumpin' George with my fifth of tokay no tea and just under the sheets laughed to hear the crazy music 'Mama, he treats your daughter mean,' Mama, Papa, and don't you come in here I'll kill you etc. getting high by myself in room glooms and all wondrous knowing about the Negro the essential American out there always finding his solace his meaning in the fellaheen street and not in abstract morality and even when he has a church you see the pastor out front bowing to the ladies on the make you hear his great vibrant voice on the sunny Sunday afternoon sidewalk full of sexual vibratos saying 'Why yes Mam but de gospel do say that man was born of woman's womb –' and no and so by that time I come crawling out of my warmsack and hit the street when I see the railroad ain't gonna call me till 5 AM Sunday morn probably for a local out of Bayshore in fact always a local out of Babylon and I go to the wailbar of all the wildbars in the world the one and only Third-and – Howard and there I go in and drink with the madmen and if I get drunk I git.

The whore who come up to me in there the night I was there with Al Buckle and said to me 'You wanta play with me tonight Jim, and?' and I didn't think I had enough money and later told this to Charley Low and he laughed and said 'How do you know she wanted money always take the chance that she might be out just for love or just out for love you know what I mean man don't be a sucker.' She was a goodlooking doll and said 'How would you like to oolyakoo with me mon?' and I stood there like a jerk and in fact bought drink got drink drunk that night and in the 299 Club I was hit by the proprietor the band breaking up the fight before I had a chance to decide to hit him back which I didn't do and out on the street I tried to rush back in but they had locked the door and were looking at me thru the forbidden glass in the door with faces like undersea – I should have played with her shurrouruuruuruuruuruuruurkdiei.

Despite the fact I was a brakeman making 600 a month I kept going to the Public restaurant on Howard Street which was three eggs for 26 cents 2 eggs for 21 this with toast (hardly no butter) coffee (hardly no coffee and sugar rationed) oatmeal with dash of milk and sugar the smell of soured old shirts lingering above the cookpot steams as if they were making skidrow lumberjack stews out of San Francisco ancient Chinese mildewed laundries with poker games in the back among the barrels and the rats of the earthquake days, but actually the food somewhat on the level of an old time 1890 or 1910 section-gang cook of lumber camps far in the North with an oldtime pigtail Chinaman cooking it and cussing out those who didn't like it. The prices were incredible but one time I had the beef-stew and it was absolutely the worst beefstew I ever et, it was incredible I tell you – and as they often did that to me it was with the most intensest regret that I tried to convey to the geek back of counter what I wanted but he was a tough sonofa-bitch, ech, ti-ti, I thought the counterman was kind of queer especially he handled gruffly the hopeless drool-drunks, 'What now you doing you think you can come in here and cut like that for God's sake act like a man won't you and eat or get out-t-t-t-' – I always did wonder what a guy like that was doing working in a place like that because, but why some sympathy in his horny heart for the busted wrecks, all up and down the street were restaurants like the Public catering exclusively to bums of the black, winos with no money, who found 21 cents left over from wine panhandlings and so stumbled in for their third or fourth touch of food in a week, as sometimes they didn't eat at all and so you'd see them in the corner puking white liquid which was a couple quarts of rancid sauterne rot-gut or sweet white sherry and they had nothing on their stom-achs, most of them had one leg or were on crutches and had bandages around their feet, from nicotine and alcohol poison-ing together, and one time finally on my way up Third near

Market across the street from Breens, when in early 1952 I lived on Russian Hill and didn't quite dig the complete horror and humor of railroad's Third Street, a bum a thin sickly little-bum like Anton Abraham lay face down on the pavement with crutch aside and some old remnant newspaper sticking out and it seemed to me he was dead. I looked closely to see if he was breathing and he was not, another man with me was looking down and we agreed he was dead, and soon a cop came over and look and agreed and called the wagon, the little wretch weighed about 50 pounds in his bleeding count was stone mackerel snotnose cold dead as a bleeding doornail – ah I tell you – and who could notice but other half deadbums bums bums bums dead dead times X times X times all dead bums for-ever dead with nothing and all finished and out – there. – And this was the clientele in the Public Hair restaurant where I ate many's the morn a 3-egg breakfast with almost dry toast and oatmeal a little saucer of, and thin sickly dishwater coffee, all to save 14 cents so in my little book proudly I could make a notation and of the day and prove that I could live comfort-ably in America while working seven days a week and earning 600 a month I could live on less than 17 a week which with my rent of 4.20 was okay as I had also to spend money to eat and sleep sometimes on the other end of my Watsonville chaingang run but preferred most times to sleep free of charge and un-comfortable in cabooses of the crummy rack – my 26-cent breakfast, my pride. – And that incredible semiqueer counter-man who dished out the food, threw it at you, slammed it, had a languid frank expression straight in your eyes like a 1930's lunchcart heroine in Steinbeck and at the steamtable itself labored coolly a junkey-looking Chinese with an actual stock-ing in his hair as if they'd just Shanghai'd him off the foot of Commercial Street before the Ferry Building was up but forgot it was 1952, dreamed it was 1860 goldrush Frisco – and on rainy days you felt they had ships in the back room.

I'd take walks up Harrison and the boomcrash of truck traf-fic towards the glorious girders of the Oakland Bay Bridge that you could see after climbing Harrison Hill a little like radar machine of eternity in the sky, huge, in the blue, by pure clouds crossed, gulls, idiot cars streaking to destinations on its undinal boom across shmoshwaters flocked up by winds and news of San Rafael storms and flash boats. – There O I always came and walked and negotiated whole Friscos in one afternoon from the overlooking hills of the high Fillmore where Orient-bound vessels you can see on drowsy Sunday mornings of pool-hall goof like after a whole night playing drums in a jam session and a morn in the hall of cuesticks I went by the rich homes of old ladies supported by daughters or female secretaries with immense ugly gargoyle Frisco millions fronts of other days and way below is the blue passage of the Gate, the Alcatraz mad rock, the mouths of Tamalpais, San Pablo Bay, Sausalito sleepy hemming the rock and bush over yonder, and the sweet white ships cleanly cutting a path to Sasebo. – Over Harrison and down to the Embarcadero and around Telegraph Hill and down to the play streets of Chinatown and down Kearny back across Market to Third and my wild-night neon twinkle fate there, ah, and then finally at dawn of a Sunday and they did call me, the immense girders of Oakland Bay still haunting me and all that eternity too much to swallow and not knowing who I am at all but like a big plump longhaired baby walking up in the dark trying to wonder who I am the door knocks and it's the desk keeper of the flop hotel with silver rims and white hair and clean clothes and sticky potbelly said he was from Rocky Mount and looked like yes, he had been desk clerk of the Nash Buncome Association hotel down there in 50 successive heatwave summers without the sun and only palmos of the lobby with cigar crutches in the albums of the South and him with his dear mother waiting in a buried log cabin of graves with all that mashed past historied underground afoot with the stain of the bear the blood of the tree and cornfields long plowed under and Negroes whose voices long faded from the middle of the wood and the dog barked his last, this man had voyageured to the West Coast too like all the other loose American elements and was pale and sixty and

complaining of sickness, might at one time been a handsome
squire to women with money but now a forgotten clerk and
maybe spent a little time in jail for a few forgeries or harmless
cons and might also have been a railroad clerk and might have
wept and might have never made it, and that day I'd say he
saw the bridgegirders up over the hill of traffic of Harrison like
me and woke up mornings with same lost, is now beckoning
on my door and breaking in the world on me and he is standing on the frayed carpet of the hall all worn down by black
steps of sunken old men for last 40 years since earthquake
and the toilet stained, beyond the last toilet bowl and the last
stink and stain I guess yes is the end of the world the bloody
end of the world, so now knocks on my door and I wake up,
saying 'How what howp howelk howel of the knavery they've
meaking, ek and won't let me slepit? Whey they dool? Whand
out wisis thing that comes flarminging around my dooring in
the mouth of the night and there everything knows that I have
no mother, and no sister, and no father and no bot sosstle, but
not crib' I get up and sit up and says 'Howowow?' and he says
'Telephone?' and I have to put on my jeans heavy with knife,
wallet, I look closely at my railroad watch hanging on little
door flicker of closet door face to me ticking silent the time, it
says 4:30 AM of a Sunday morn, I go down the carpet of the
skidrow hall in jeans and with no shirt and yes with shirt tails
hanging gray workshirt and pick up phone and ticky sleepy
night desk with cage and spittoons and keys hanging and old
towels piled clean ones but frayed at edges and bearing names
of every hotel of the moving prime, on the phone is the Crew
Clerk, 'Kerroway?' 'Yeah.' 'Kerroway it's gonna be the Sherman Local at 7 AM this morning.' 'Sherman Local right.' 'Out
of Bayshore, you know the way?' 'Yeah.' 'You had that same
job last Sunday – Okay Kerroway-y-y-y-y.' And we mutually
hang up and I say to myself okay it's the Bayshore bloody old
dirty hagglous old coveted old madman Sherman who hates me
so much especially when we are at Redwood Junction kicking
boxcars and he always insists I work the rear end tho as one-
year man it would be easier for me to follow pot but I work

rear and he wants me to be right there with a block of wood when a car or cut of cars kicked stops, so they won't roll down that incline and start catastrophes, O well anyway I'll be learning eventually to like the railroad and Sherman will like me some day, and anyway another day another dollar.

And there's my room, small, gray in the Sunday morning, now all the franticness of the street and night before is done with, bums sleep, maybe one or two sprawled on sidewalk with empty poorboy on a sill – my mind whirls with life.

So there I am in dawn in my dim cell – 2½ hours to go till the time I have to stick my railroad watch in my jean watchpocket and cut out allowing myself exactly 8 minutes to the station and the 7:15 train No. 112 I have to catch for the ride five miles to Bayshore through four tunnels, emerging from the sad Rath scene of Frisco gloom bleak in the rainymonth fogmorning to a sudden valley with grim hills rising to the sea, bay on left, the fog rolling in like demented in the draws that have little white cottages disposed real-estatically for come-Christmas blue sad lights – my whole soul and concomitant eyes looking out on this reality of living and working in San Francisco with that pleased semi-loin-located shudder, energy for sex changing to pain at the portals of work and culture and natural foggy fear. – There I am in my little room wondering how I'll really manage to fool myself into feeling that these next 2½ hours will be well filled, fed, with work and pleasure thoughts. – It's so thrilling to feel the coldness of the morning wrap around my thickquilt blankets as I lay there, watch facing and ticking me, legs spread in comfy skidrow soft sheets with soft tears or sew lines in em, huddled in my own skin and rich and not spending a cent on – I look at my littlebook – and I stare at the words of the Bible. – On the floor I find last red afternoon Saturday's *Chronicle* sports page with news of football games in Great America the end of which I bleakly see in the gray light entering – the fact that Frisco is built of wood satisfies me in my peace, I know nobody'll disturb me for 2½ hours and all bums are asleep in their own bed of eternity awake or not, bottle or not – it's the joy I feel that counts for me. – On the floor's my shoes, big lumberboot flopjack work-shoes to colomp over rockbed with and not turn the ankle – solidity shoes that when you put them on, yokewise, you know you're working now and so for same reason shoes not be worn for any reason like joys of restaurant and shows. – Night-before shoes are on the floor beside the clunkershoes a pair of blue canvas shoes à la 1952 style, in them I'd trod soft as ghost the indented hill sidewalks of Ah Me Frisco all in the glitter night, from the top of Russian Hill I'd looked down at one point on all roofs of North Beach and the Mexican nightclub neons, I'd descended to them on the old steps of Broadway under which they were newly laboring a mountain tunnel – shoes fit for watersides, embarcaderos, hill and plot lawns of park and tip-top vista. – Workshoes covered with dust and some oil of en-gines – the crumpled jeans nearby, belt, blue railroad hank, knife, comb, keys, switch keys and caboose coach key, the knees white from Pajaro Riverbottom fine dusts, the ass black from slick sandboxes in yardgoat after yardgoat – the gray workshirts, the dirty undershirt, sad shorts, tortured socks of my life. – And the Bible on my desk next to the peanut butter, the lettuce, the raisin bread, the crack in the plaster, the stiff-with-old-dust lace drape now no longer laceable but hard as – after all those years of hard dust eternity in that Cameo skid inn with red eyes of rheumy oldmen dying there staring with-out hope out on the dead wall you can hardly see thru window-dusts and all you heard lately in the shaft of the rooftop middle way was the cries of a Chinese child whose father and mother were always telling him to shush and then screaming at him, he was a pest and his tears from China were most persistent and worldwide and represented all our feelings in brokendown Cameo tho this was not admitted by bum one except for an occasional harsh clearing of the throat in the halls or moan of nightmarer – by things like this and neglect of hard-eyed alco-holic oldtime chorusgirl maid the curtains had now absorbed all the iron they could take and hung stiff and even the dust in them was iron, if you shook them they'd crack and fall in tatters to the floor and spatter like wings of iron on the bong and the dust would fly into your nose like filings of steel and choke you to death, so I never touched them. My little room at 6 in the comfy dawn (at 4:30) and before me all that time, that fresh-eyed time for a little coffee to boil water on my hot plate throw some coffee in, stir it, French style, slowly carefully pour it in my white tin cup, throw sugar in (not California beet sugar like I should have been using but New Orleans cane sugar, because beet racks I carried from Oakland out to Watsonville many's the time, a 80-car freight train with nothing but gondolas loaded with sad beets looking like the heads of decapitated women). – Ah me how but it was a hell and now I had the whole thing to myself, and make my raisin toast by sitting it on a little wire I'd especially bent to place over the hotplate, the toast crackled up, there, I spread the margarine on the still red hot toast and it too would crackle and sink in golden, among burnt raisins and this was my toast. – Then two eggs gently slowly fried in soft margarine in my little skidrow frying pan about half as thick as a dime in fact less, a little piece of tiny tin you could bring on a camp trip – the eggs slowly fluffed in there and swelled from butter steams and I threw garlic salt on them, and when they were ready the yellow of them had been slightly filmed with a cooked white at the top from the tin cover I'd put over the frying pan, so now they were ready, and out they came, I spread them out on top of my already prepared potatoes which had been boiled in small pieces and then mixed with the bacon I'd already fried in small pieces, kind of raggely mashed bacon potatoes, with eggs on top steaming, and on the side lettuce, with peanut butter dab nearby on side. – I had heard that peanut butter and lettuce contained all the vitamins you should want, this after I had originally started to eat this combination because of the deliciousness and nostalgia of the taste – my breakfast ready at about 6.45 and as I eat already I'm dressing to go piece by piece and by the time the last dish is washed in the little sink at the boiling hotwater tap, and I'm taking my lastquick slug of coffee and quickly rinsing the cup in the hot water spout and rushing to dry it and plop it in its place by the hot plate and the brown carton in which all the groceries sit tightly wrapped in grown paper, I'm already picking up my brakeman's lantern from where it's been hanging on the door handle and my tattered timetable's long been in my backpocket folded and ready to go, everything tight, keys, timetable, lantern, knife, handkerchief, wallet, comb, railroad keys, change and myself. I put the light out on the sad dab mad grub little diving room and hustle out into the fog of the flow, descending the creak hall steps where the old men are not yet sitting with Sunday morn papers because still asleep or some of them I can now as I leave hear beginning to disfawdle to wake in their rooms with their moans and yorks and scrapings and horror sounds, I'm going down the steps to work, glance to check time of watch with clerk cage clock. – A hardy two or three oldtimers sitting already in the dark brown lobby under the tockboom clock, toothless, or grim, or elegantly mustached – what thought in the world swirling in them as they see the young eager brakeman bum hurrying to his thirty dollars of the Sunday – what memories of old homesteads, built without sympathy, hornyhanded fate dealt them the loss of wives, childs, moons – libraries collapsed in their time – oldtimers of the telegraph wired wood Frisco in the fog gray top time sitting in their brown sunk sea and will be there when this afternoon my face flushed from the sun, which at eight'll flame out and make sunbaths for us at Redwood, they'll still be here the color of paste in the green underworld and still reading the same editorial over again and won't understand where I've been or what for or what. – I have to get out of there or suffocate, out of Third Street or become a worm, it's alright to live and bed-wine in and play the radio and cook little breakfasts and rest in but O my I've got to go now to work, I hurry down Third to Townsend for my 7.15 train – it's three minutes to go, I start in a panic to jog, goddam it I didn't give myself enough time this morning, I hurry down under the Harrison ramp to the Oakland-Bay Bridge, down past Schwabacher-Frey the great dim red neon printshop always spectrally my father the dead executive I see there, I run and hurry past the beat Negro grocery stores where I buy all my peanut butter and raisin bread, past the redbrick railroad alley now mist and wet, across Townsend, the train is leaving!

Fatuous railroad men, the conductor old John J. Coppertwang thirty-five years pure service on ye olde S.P. is there in the gray Sunday morning with his gold watch out peering at it, he's standing by the engine yelling up pleasantries at old hoghead Jones and young fireman Smith with the baseball cap is at the fireman's seat munching sandwich – 'We'll how'd ye like old Johnny O yestiddy, I guess he didn't score so many touchdowns like we thought.' 'Smith bet six dollars on the pool down in Watsonville and said he's rakin' in thirty-four.' 'I've been in that Watsonville pool –.' They've been in the pool of life fleartiming with one another, all the long pokerplaying nights in brownwood railroad places, you can smell the mashed cigar in the wood, the spittoon's been there for more than 750,099 years and the dog's been in and out and these old boys by old shaded brown light have bent and muttered and young boys too with their new brakeman passenger uniform the tie undone the coat thrown back the flashing youth smile of happy fatuous wellfed goodjobbed careered futured pensioned hospitalized takencare-of railroad men. – 35, 40 years of it and then they get to be conductors and in the middle of the night they've been for years called by the Crew Clerk yelling 'Cassady? It's the Maximush localized week do you for the right lead' but now as old men all they have is a regular job, a regular train, conductor of the 112 with goldwatch is helling up his pleasantries at all fire dog crazy Satan hoghead Willis why the wildest man this side of France and Frankincense, he was known once to take his engine up that steep grade ... 7.15, time to pull, as I'm running thru the station hearing the bell jangling and the steam chuff they're pulling out, O I come flying out on the platform and forget momentarily or that is never did know what track it was and whirl in confusion a while wondering what track and can't see no train and this is the time I lose there, 5, 6, 7 seconds when the train tho underway is only slowly upchugging to go and a man a fat executive could easily run up and grab it but when I yell to Assistant Stationmaster 'Where's 112?' and he tells me the last track which is the track I never dreamed I run to it fast as I can go and dodge people à la Columbia halfback and cut into track fast as off-tackle where you carry the ball with you to the left and feint with neck and head and push of ball as tho you're gonna throw yourself all out to fly around that left end and everybody psychologically chuffs with you that way and suddenly you contract and you like whiff of smoke are buried in the hole in tackle, cutback play, you're flying into the hole almost before you yourself know it, flying into the track I am and there's the train about 30 yards away even as I look picking up tremendously momentum the kind of momentum I would have been able to catch if I'd looked a second earlier – but I turn, I know I can catch it. Standing on the back platform are the rear brakeman and an old deadheading conductor ole Charley W. Jones, why he had seven wives and six kids and one time out at Lick no I guess it was Coyote he couldn't see on account of the steam and out he come and found his lantern in the igloo regular anglecock of my herald and they gave him fifteen benefits so now there he is in the Sunday har har owlala morning and he and young rear man watch incredulously this student brakeman running like a crazy trackman after their departing train. I feel like yelling 'Make your airtest now make your airtest now!' knowing that when a passenger pulls out just about at the first crossing east of the station they pull the air a little bit to test the brakes, on signal from the engine, and this momentarily slows up the train and I could manage it, and could catch it, but they're not making no airtest the bastards, and I hek knowing I'm going to have to run like a sonofabitch. But suddenly I get embarrassed thinking what are all the people of the world gonna say to see a man running so devilishly fast with all his might sprinting thru life like Jesse Owens just to catch a goddam train and all of them with their hysteria wondering if I'll get killed when I catch the back platform and blam, I fall down and go boom and lay supine across the crossing, so the

old flagman when the train has flowed by will see that everything lies on the earth in the same stew, all of us angels will die
and we don't ever know how or our own diamond, O heaven
will enlighten us and open your – open our eyes, open our eyes.
– I know I won't get hurt, I trust my shoes, hand grip, feet,
solidity of yipe and cripe of gripe and grip and strength and
need no mystic strength to measure the musculature in my rib
rack – but damn it all it's a social embarrassment to be caught
sprinting like a maniac after a train especially with two men
gaping at me from rear of train and shaking their heads and
yelling I can't make it even as I halfheartedly sprint after them
with open eyes trying to communicate that I can and not for
them to get hysterical or laugh, but I realize it's all too much
for me, not the run, not the speed of the train which anyway
two seconds after I gave up the complicated chase did indeed
slow down at the crossing in the airtest before chugging up
again for good and Bayshore. So I was late for work, and old
Sherman hated me and was about to hate me more.

The ground I would have eaten in solitude, cronch – the railroad earth, the flat stretches of long Bayshore that I have to
negotiate to get to Sherman's bloody caboose on track 17 ready
to go with pot pointed to Redwood and the morning's 3-hour
work. – I get off the bus at Bayshore Highway and rush down
the little street and turn in – boys riding the pot of a switcheroo
in the yardgoat day come yelling by at me from the headboards
and footboards 'come on down ride with us' otherwise I would
have been about 3 minutes even later to my work but now I
hop on the little engine that momentarily slows up to pick me
up and it's alone not pulling anything but tender, the guys
have been up to the other end of the yard to get back on some
track of necessity. – That boy will have to learn to flag himself
without nobody helping him as many's the time I've seen some
of these young goats think they have everything but the plan is
late, the word will have to wait, the massive arboreal thief
with the crime of the kind, and air and all kinds of ghouls –
ZONKed! made tremendous by the flare of the whole crime

and encrudalatures of all kinds – San Franciscos and shroud-
band Bayshores the last and the last furbelow of the eek plot
pall prime tit top work oil twicks and wouldn't you? – the railroad earth I would have eaten alone, cronch, on foot head bent
to get to Sherman who ticking watch observes with finicky eyes
the time to go to give the hiball sign get on going it's Sunday no
time to waste the only day of his long seven-day-a-week work-
life he gets a chance to rest a little bit at home when 'Eee
Christ' when 'Tell that sonofabitch student this is no party pic-
nic damn this shit and throb tit you tell them something and
how do you what the hell expect to under-dries out tit all you
bright tremendous trouble anyway, we's LATE' and this is the
way I come rushing up late. Old Sherman is sitting in the
crummy over his switch lists, when he sees me with cold blue
eyes he says 'You know you're supposed to be here 7.30 don't
you so what the hell you doing gettin' in here at 7.50 you're
twenty goddam minutes late, what the fuck you think this your
birthday?' and he gets up and leans off the rear bleak platform
and gives the high sign to the enginemen up front we have a
cut of about 12 cars and they say it easy and off we go slowly
at first, picking up momentum to the work, 'Light that goddam
fire' says Sherman he's wearing brandnew workshoes just
about bought yestiddy and I notice his clean overalls that his
wife washed and set on his chair just that morning probably
and I rush up and throw coal in the potbelly flop and take a
fusee and two fusees and light them crack em. Ah fourth of the
July when the angels would smile on the horizon and all the
racks where the mad are lost are returned to us forever from
Lowell of my soul prime and single meditated longsong hope
to heaven of prayers and angels and of course the sleep and
interested eye of images and but now we detect the missing
buffoon there's the poor goodman rear man ain't even on the
train yet and Sherman looks out sulkily the back door and sees
his rear man waving from fifteen yards aways to stop and wait
for him and being an old railroad man he certainly isn't going
to run or even walk fast, it's well understood, conductor Sher-

man's got to get off his switch-list desk chair and pull the air and stop the goddam train for rear man Arkansaw Charley, who sees this done and just come up lopin' in his flop overalls without no care, so he was late too, or at least had gone gossiping in the yard office while waiting for the stupid head brakeman, the tagman's up in front on the presumably pot. 'First thing we do is pick up a car in front at Redwood so all's you do get off at the crossing and stand back to flag, not too far.' 'Don't I work the head end?' 'You work the hind end we got not much to do and I wanta get it done fast,' snarls the conductor. 'Just take it easy and do what we say and watch and flag.' So it's peaceful Sunday morning in California and off we go, tack-a-tick, lao-tichi-couch, out of the Bayshore yards, pause momentarily at the main line for the green, ole 71 or ole whatever been by and now we get out and go swamming up the tree valleys and town vale hollows and main street crossing parking-lot last-night attendant plots and Stanford lots of the world – to our destination in the Pooh which I can see, and, so to while the time I'm up in the cupoloa and with my newspaper dig the latest news on the front page and also consider and make notations of the money I spent already for this day Sunday absolutely not jot spend a nothing – California rushes by and with sad eyes we watch it reel the whole bay and the discourse falling off to gradual gils that ease and graduate to Santa Clara Valley then and the fig and behind is the fog immemoriate while the mist closes and we come running out to the bright sun of the Sabbath Californiay –

At Redwood I get off and standing on sad oily ties of the brakie railroad earth with red flag and torpedoes attached and fusees in backpocket with timetable crushed against and I leave my hot jacket in crummy standing there then with sleeves rolled up and there's the porch of a Negro home, the brothers are sitting in shirtsleeves talking with cigarettes and laughing and little daughter standing amongst the weeds of the garden with her playpail and pigtails and we the railroad men with soft signs and no sound pick up our flower, according to same

goodman train order that for the last entire lifetime of atten-
tions ole conductor industrial worker harlotized Sherman has
been reading carefully son so's not to make a mistake:

'Sunday morning October 15 pick up flower
car at Redwood, Dispatcher M.M.S.'

John Rechy

Masquerade

'Will you have some tea?'

The man who has just asked me that question is dressed like this:

In black mounting police pants which cling tightly below the hips revealing squat bowlegs; boots which gleam vitreously and rise at least a foot above his ankles – silver studs forming a triangular design on the tip of each boot, then swirling about the upper part like a wayward-leafed clover.

'One lump or two?'

The belt – futilely trying to squeeze his large stomach (squeezing it – although he was not otherwise excessively fat – to the point where even his breathing has to come in short, sharp gasps) but actually causing it to bulge out insistently over and under it in two sagging, lumpy old tires of flesh – is also black. Looping in waves like a wildly zigzagging snake, the ubiquitous studs (and each silver stud is haloed by tiny gleaming beads) join in front at an enormous buckle at least five inches wide on which is engraved a large malevolently beaked, bead-eyed, spread eagle.

'Do you take cream?'

Over a dark vinyl shirt, he wore a black leather vest, tied crisscross with a long leather strap from his chest to his stomach. On each lapel of the vest is reproduced the triangular clover-leafed pattern as on the boots (and each silver stud, again, is encircled by the beaded haloes). The vest, the shirt, the legs of the pants are so tightly molded on his stubby body that his movements are restricted. Cautiously, he reaches for the teapot, the sugar, cream – each gesture threatening to burst a seam somewhere.

'Perhaps you prefer lemon?'

He himself, when you can pull your gaze from the hypnotiz-
ing costume in disbelief, is a florid rather short man, in his
early 50s. Actually he looks much like what is depicted in
American movies as the typical pre-war Bavarian who sits
goodhumoredly drinking beer out of a giant stein, bellowing
ebulliently in beered-up delight as a blonde-braided girl and a
lederhosened man dance to the accompaniment of a merry
accordion.... But dressed as he is, he resembles a somber,
heavily silverlighted Christmas tree.

It is not Halloween.

It isnt even New Year's, and we're not even at a costume
party.

No.

We're sitting, instead, in the early afternoon, in the livingroom of a neat house in a lushly treed area in Oakland, across
the bay from San Francisco.

The room is decorated in 'antique' style – but of what period,
it is impossible to determine. Rather, it seems to have been
decorated to suggest an indefinable time somewhere, nebu-
lously, in The Past. Over a bursting metal sun pinned to the
wall, are two crossed swords. A shield. A lance. The drapes are
wine-purple velvet and droop to the floor in highlighted folds.
There is a small replica of a suit of armor by the brick fireplace.
An oriental-looking statue of a monkey is poised as if to spring
from a small, arch-legged desk.... The sun pours in through a
windowed wall in a warm rush of light which accentuates the
colors of the chairs, upholstered in striped gold and red, striped
silver and blue.... It struck me that this room, which is all Ive
seen so far of the house, is much like a conglomeration of
movie furniture acquired from many period films.

(This is how I happen to be here now, drinking tea, self-
consciously, with this man: Only a few nights earlier, at the
Stirrup Club, I had noticed a man wearing knee-length boots, a
dark leather jacket with a goldsewn insignia of a rapacious
bird, a cap much like that of a policeman, and a silver chain
around his left shoulder. I asked the person I was with who he

was. 'Neil,' he answered, 'the weirdest character in San Francisco. I'd keep away from him if I were you.' . . . Later that night Neil had come over – he knew the man I was with – and introduced himself. Brazenly, he asked me to have lunch with him the next day. Considering him the most ridiculous man I had ever seen – but still greatly intrigued – I said yes.)

'Shall I freshen up your tea?'

'No, thanks, I've had enough.'

'Tea is very invigorating in the afternoon, especially after a big lunch,' he insisted curiously – and poured out another cup.

It seemed so ludicrous – this hybrid movie-set room (like a small-scale parody, at times, of a medieval chamber, with anachronistic touches of Contemporary California) and the man in the incredible costume – so ludicrously incongruous it all seemed, to sit sipping the carefully laid out tea (and cookies!) from the small lilac-decorated china cups.

Glancing over the tea cup, into another room (to avoid looking directly at this man and thereby to thwart his excoriating gaze by not acknowledging it – and throughout lunch he had hardly spoken, concentrating merely on studying me), I catch sight of a foot – just the tip – jutting from behind the slightly open door.

I asked Neil: 'Are you alone?'

'Oh, yes! Just you and me – and my cat,' he answered, savoring the tea loudly as if to induce me to take mine.

I dismiss the foot, which hasnt moved. It is probably a shoe – or, more likely, a boot – tossed behind the door.

The telephone screams, and I almost drop the cup nervously. Excusing himself, Neil goes into the other room. He steps carefully over the jutting foot as he goes through the door. The door, slightly farther ajar now, reveals, still unmoving, what is definitely a boot.

'Hello?' he answers the telephone. A pause. 'Hello?' again. Silence. I hear him hang the telephone up. There is a shuffling sound of moving in that next room. The boot disappears entirely.

'Ive been getting these Mysterious Calls,' Neil explained, returning. 'At least once a day – sometimes more often. Someone calls up, listens to my voice, doesnt say a word.'

'Someone must be trying to bug you,' I offered.

'Oh, no!' he exclaimed adamantly, obviating such a simple explanation. 'Nothing like that! . . . Im convinced it's someone who just wants to know – *has* to Know! – that someone, somewhere – someone like Me – exists. Eventually,' he predicted solemnly, 'whoever it is will speak to me, and he'll ask me if he can come up . . . Oh, you may not know it, but I am rather – well, I'll say it: Why not?' (Except that he said it like this: 'Whu-I NOT?' and he shrugged his fleshy shoulders – or, rather, attempted to: The warning stretching sound of the shirt rejected the movement.) 'I am rather Famous in California.'

'Because of your costumes?'

'"Dressing up,"' he corrected me coolly, 'does not mean wearing *costumes!*' He finished his first cup of tea – offered me another cup, which I refused. 'When I spoke to you the other night in the bar,' he told me, 'it was because I felt a certain propinquity – I mean,' he added carefully, 'a certain interest.'

'You stood out – even in that bar,' I said tactfully.

Again, it wasn't what he wanted to hear. 'What I mean,' he said testily, 'is that I felt you were "ready."'

'Ready for what?'

He avoided the question mysteriously.

A furry amber cat curled like an ostrich plume about the man's boots, then jumped lithely on his lap. Neil began to stroke the cat absently. In the long silence that followed, I could hear the satisfied purring of the animal as it pressed itself against the leather costume. As if just realizing that he'd been stroking the cat, Neil pushed it away suddenly, thrusting it angrily to the floor. He almost lifted it away with the tip of his boot. 'I hate him when he becomes snivelingly affectionate!' he said.

He rose precariously from the chair. The tight costume would not even allow him to walk easily. And when he opened a drawer in the antique desk, he crouched before it uncertainly, rigidly to keep his clothes intact. He brought out a box, removed a key from another smaller box, opened the first, and took out a stack of pictures which he brought over to show me.

I prepared myself. That world, being a world of fleeting contacts, has a great attachment to photographs, as if to lend some permanence to what is usually all too impermanent. But I know before Ive seen them that the ones Neil will show me will be far from ordinary – will, in fact, be a part of a game Im convinced hes playing with me.

Withholding the pictures dramatically, he said proudly: 'These are only some of my Converts. People just Radiate toward me. And I open the world theyve been hunting – hunting, mind you, without even knowing it sometimes. That way, I help them find Themselves.' He spoke as if delivering a familiar speech. 'You should see some of the ones that come to me – so timid: Just knowing someone like Me exists helps them. Even the first time, they walk out the door differently: Proud. Erect. Glad to be: Men! . . . I lead them carefully. I open doors for them, slowly. . . . They call me up – I had a call from a youngman in Seattle the other day. He'd heard about me, through friends – and he wanted to come down especially to see me. Why, I get calls all the time from Los Angeles. . . . And, well, Whu-I NOT?' He attempted another shrug, again frustrated. Dreamily: 'I like to see youngmen coming out – I like to see them – well, flower out –. . . Rather,' he corrected himself hastily, 'I like to see them burst out *Violently!* and I watch them move in the direction they were meant to go. Theyre like Disciples, discovering The Way . . . . Sometimes,' he said wistfully, assuming a benign look as he gathered his hands over the photographs on his lap, 'sometimes – I get the feeling that Im something of a – . . . yes, something of a Saint.'

I look at 'The Saint' in the strange costume. His stare challenges mine. With a flourish, he spreads the photographs on a table before me as proudly as a peacock spreads his tail.

There are youngmen dressed as military officers of long-ago periods, cowboys, motorcyclists, policemen, pirates, gladiators. . . . Single, they seem to have menaced the camera. In groups,

they depict scenes of violence. . . . I lay the pictures down without looking at the rest.

'I took every one of them myself,' he sighed.

The cat had returned surreptitiously, winding in and out of
Neil's legs. Again, he shoved it away with his boot, this time
much more violently. He watched as the cat moved away.

'*And now!*' Neil announced. 'I'll show you My Real Collection! – the most complete in California – and (Whu-I NOT?)
possibly in the United States! – though Ive heard theres a man
near Griffith Park in Los Angeles who has a pretty good collection,' he condescended. 'His name is – . . . Dan? Stan? Something like that. But Ive been told hes not at *all* like Me!'

He ushered me into the bedroom. When he pushed open the
door, past which I thought I had seen an unmoving foot earlier,
I start.

There are two men in the bedroom: a policeman wearing
sunglasses and a motorcyclist, legs spread, hands planted on
hips, his head thrust forward as if ready to attack with gloved,
clenched fists.

Seeing me start, Neil laughs. 'Theyre manikins!' he announced triumphantly at the deliberate deception. 'They look
terribly real, dont they?' He went fondly to the dummy dressed
as a policeman, and he adjusted the cap, to one side; to the
motorcyclist now and changed his stance, lowering the head to
emphasize further the impending thrust. 'I prefer this one.' He
indicated the motorcyclist. 'He looks more – oh, Rough!'

The room has about it a twilight darkness – the same inde-
finite antiqueness as the living-room. The bed is covered with a
shiny black-leather spread. Creating the illusion of a throne, a
high-backed carved chair faces a three-paneled full-length mirror. Behind the chair, dark drapes brocaded along the edges are
held back majestically by a gold cord. The furniture here too
belongs to that limbo-historical movie period. . . . The manikins
have been sedulously arranged so that their reflections, in the
mellow light, are reproduced realistically from a variety of
angles in the mirrors.

'I had them made especially,' Neil is explaining, eyeing the dummies like an infatuated lover. 'Theyre not always dressed this way. I change their clothes to whatever suits my mood. . . . Incidentally,' he added proudly, 'most of these clothes Ive designed Myself (Im a very Talented freelance artist, you know) — and then I have them custom-made.'

Stirring himself out of his awe, he slid open a panel of doors, displaying an incredible array of costumes — a mesh of colors, of brocade, studs; jackets, pants, vests. He stands to one side like a painter undraping his Masterpiece. 'Dozens and dozens and dozens,' he points out, 'all different sizes, all different periods!' Beneath the costumes are about fifty pairs of boots, all kinds, all colors.

From a shelf on top, Neil pulled a large brown leather box, carefully pushing away stacks of hats (cowboy hats, military and motorcycle caps, plumed helmets). Inside the box are whips, leather gloves, handcuffs, straps. He exhibits these like a woman showing her most precious jewelry — or her trousseau. 'All of this is insured,' he explained. . . . He even had a leather handkerchief.

He returned to the costumes, pulling out a jacket here, a vest there, a pair of chaps, pants — holding them before me — his expression rapt; his voice awed (the tone one would use in a church); his movements ritualistically careful (as a bride would touch her wedding gown). Throughout this display, he studies me as he presents each item; awaiting any reaction he can grasp, any clue as to my interest. I know instantly that I would like to see myself in these costumes. And he knows it too. He sighed contentedly.

'Would you like me to dress you up?' he asked me.

I feel suddenly apprehensive, but I dont answer.

'I'll use the very basic this first time, I'll go slowly, nothing too elaborate.' He coaxes me like a doctor with a child. 'Another time, when Ive studied you more, I'll really show you. This time I'll open the door just — oh — about a fourth of the way.'

He interprets my silence as acquiescence. With sureness, he removes clothes from the closet, becoming progressively more excited as he touches them adoringly, worshipingly, reverently.

His trembling hands reject an elaborately studded jacket, which he held treasuringly for a long moment – choosing more 'conventional' clothes; admonishing himself : 'Not the first time, not the first time' – but vaunting each idolized piece of clothes he nevertheless rejects.

He has forgotten the restrained movements that the clothes hes wearing demand. His shirt is bulging out over his stomach. He has loosened the belt, the vest. Straps dangle. The shirt protrudes in a satanic tail behind him. Hes becoming sadly disheveled. The whole costume sags. Perspiration runs down his flushed face. Hes huffing.

Ritualistically, like a servant who adores his job, whose purpose in life is subservience, he begins to remove my clothes (not as another person might, for the sake of the nakedness emphasizing the sexuality of the act : no, not at all like that : with him, it seems to be the actual act of obeisance that is exciting him). He had led me carefully away from the mirrors. When Im stripped, he doesnt touch my body, hardly even glances at me.

First a pair of skintight black denim pants ; a tapered shirt, russet-colored, which he leaves open halfway down my stomach. I wonder what this costume will ultimately be. It seems he is improvising for over-all effect : to create a fantasy which, like the furniture, will merely suggest something rather than be anything specific. . . . A pair of black boots which come to the knees ; when he slips the boots onto my feet, his head bends brushing the slick leather with his cheek. . . . Black leather gloves. A hat which arches slightly on the sides. He added a thick large-buckled belt about my waist. Rushing to the leather box in the closet, he removed a long coiled whip, which he planted firmly in my hand. And he announced apocalyptically :

'A plantation overseer!'

Automatically I turn to face the panel of mirrors ; but Neil blocks my view quickly. '*Not yet!*' After a few moments, he steps aside dramatically.

'I present you to you – to You as You have always wanted to be,' he said solemnly.

Clearly, this is me as *he* wants to see me. But I feel excited by the reflection of myself. Possibly noticing this, Neil stands before me again, once more blocking my reflection, as though my own fascination threatens to shut him out of the fantasy.

'It's just a hint,' he said in that awed tone. 'Nothing extraordinary. Another time, I'll Really Show You!' I notice his voice is changing strangely. What is he trying to convey by those vaguely recognizable accents?

With a jolt of awareness which almost took my breath, I realize that he is now speaking in the slightly slurred Southern sounds of a field hand! My first impulse was to laugh; my next, to remove the clothes and leave this fantastic man.

But Neil is already saying: 'Now we're ready. Now we can really begin The Initiation.' Like a well-trained acolyte, he bowed. His actions revolt and fascinate me. I am overwhelmed by the ritualistic attention, excited by the image of myself in the mirror. He knows it too. But I am sure hes misinterpreting that excitement, which is merely for *myself* in these clothes, narcissistically, not for what the clothes themselves must represent to him.

He approached me slowly. Fascinatedly, he moved around me, arranging the mirrors so that both of us can see the reflections from different angles; careful, always, to be in the framed image. He led me to the elaborately carved chair before the mirror.

He knelt.

Without warning, he flung himself stomach down on the floor, and now all his actions will become astonishingly feverish. His head burrowed between the boots; his tongue glides hungrily over the glossy surface; his hands caress the leather, reach now for the belt. He looped his fingers urgently down the costume. His mouth gnaws into the opening at the top of one boot, then the other, his teeth cling to the straps inside. Frenziedly, he raised my foot with one hand, turned himself face up on the floor. And he held the boot poised over his face. From his throat emante gasping groans; his eyes are deliriously wide, as if to magnify the scene beyond his ordinary vision. With one desperate hand, he pressed down on my leg from the knee, attempting to bring the boot against his craving mouth.

Swiftly – angered – I moved away from him – leaving him a shattered heap of studs and leather straps sprawled grotesquely on the floor.

'Whats the matter?' he whispered almost inaudibly.

'Im not interested,' I said harshly.

As I took off the clothes he had dressed me in, to leave, he eyed me curiously from where he still lay pitifully like a smashed doll on the floor.

2

But I came back.

He indicated not the slightest embarrassment over what had occurred the first time. In fact, he seemed to have been expecting me.

'Im glad you came over. I want to take some photographs of you,' he said. Today hes dressed in a vaguely Western costume. 'Oh, dont worry – I'll just dress you up for the pictures,' he promised. 'Nothing else.' But he eyed me slyly.

He knows now that I am, at least, intrigued by his masquerade.

When he presents me to myself in the mirror (again: 'You as you would like to be!'), Im an exaggerated cowboy, with spurs, chaps. Looking at myself, I feel slightly silly; but soon the seducing attention obliterates the feeling of absurdity; I feed hungrily on his glorified adulation, as Neil, speaking this time in a Western drawl, prepares to take the pictures.

We move into the other room.

The cowboy first. A Prussian officer. A pirate. He poses each scene at the point of arrested violence. A whip in my hand as if about to unfurl at him behind the camera. Boots always prominently displayed. Fists clenched. Body lunging. Now he brings in one of the manikins – heterogeneously 'dressed up' – studs, straps, chains. . . . Neil executes – crouched, contorted, sweating – 'to get the feel of it,' he explained – the cringing positions that the dummy will ultimately assume, menaced, for the pictures. The camera keeps clicking as Neil vacillates from acolyte to High Priest.

'Now I'll improvise!' he exclaimed joyously.

When he was ready to take the picture, he announced triumphantly: 'An Executioner!'

And Im standing before the camera in black tights, boots to the hips, a leather vest, a black braided whip in a swirl about the boots. Im surrounded by the shield, the lance, the metal sun, and a long medieval axe propped against the wall.

The shutter closes. . . .

Neil rushed toward me, his eyes begging, and in a terrifying, shaken voice he pleaded with me to execute with the whip the movement which the camera had just frozen.

But I didnt.

He was disappointed and nervous.

Sulkingly, he went about preparing lunch. Then something strange happened : As he stood over the stove, dressed as he was in the Western clothes – and an apron over all of that – he turned to me (dressed now in my own clothes – although he had insisted I leave the 'Executioner's' costume on), and he asked me this :

'Tell me truthfully: Do you find me effeminate?'

I studied him as he stood by the stove. That apron over the costume – . . . He was holding the spoon limply in the air. Realizing that, he grasped it tightly. Seeing the look he was throwing at me, exhorting me to say what he wanted to hear, I said : 'Of course not, Neil.'

'Thank you very much,' he said almost humbly.

Shrugging his shoulders, dipping vigorously into whatever he was cooking, he laughed goodhumoredly, looking very much like that ebullient, beer-drinking Bavarian. 'One time,' he said, 'I was walking along Market Street – oh, I was really Dressed Up – a cowboy! And a carload of teenage boys drove by and shouted: "Hi, Tex!"'

I realized the telling of this story amounted to presenting his credentials for 'realness.' Yet, having seen him in the extreme clothes, I cant help thinking that what he's just presented as proof of his Realness had been, instead, more of a derisively hurled insult. . . . He was waiting for me to comment on the story. When I wont, he said: 'I *know* I look very Real' – but theres a questioning tone in his voice, as there had been, I remember, in Miss Destiny's when she too had proclaimed her 'realness.'

We were hardly through lunch when I heard the obstreperous roar of a motorcycle outside, then an insistent knock at the door.

'Damn it!' Neil said, looking out the window. 'It's Carl! Whenever hes been drinking, he comes over!' Opening the door, he pretended surprise: 'Carl! – how nice to see you!'

Carl, a large, masculine, somewhat goodlooking man in his 30s, strutted in arrogantly in motorcycle clothes. His breath reeked of liquor. 'Just seeing how the leather half lives,' he said, and sat down – unasked, and much to Neil's evident chagrin.

'Well, of course, Im always glad to see you, but we –' Neil began.

Carl interrupted: 'Oh, just pretend Im not here.'

'Difficult to do,' Neil muttered. Then (and I can almost hear him thinking. 'Well, Whu-I NOT?') 'Well, Carl, if you are going to stay – for a little while – you can take some pictures for us. That way I can be in them too.'

'Sure . . . sweetie,' Carl said. Neil stared warningly at him, evidently annoyed by the endearment.

Now both Neil and I are dressed in cop uniforms, and Neil is going down on me. Now we're cowboys, and hes on the floor begging (not) to be hurt. Now hes in a seventeenth-century costume, and Im a pirate threatening him.

He acted out each scene impassionedly.

Protesting again when I got into my own clothes, Neil is now dressed in a tight 'improvised' costume – boots, belt, straps, glittering studs.

'Dont let him fool you,' Neil said maliciously to me when the picturetaking was over and Carl had gone to the head. 'Carl's not quite as butch as hes pretending to be. Hes really the end! – but even people like him serve a function. . . . I'll tell you something about him, before he gets back. Sometimes, when he plays the sadist (though hes more often the masochist now), he picks up the nelliest queens – the most effeminate types, types I wouldn't even *talk* to! Theres this one little queen – a chorus boy – who goes around telling about when he went home with Carl. Carl put on a uniform (he has an insignificant collection) and stood menacingly over the little queen and said: "I am your fuehrer; you do everything I tell you." And the queen – ho-ho – you know what she said to him? She broke her wrist and lisped at Carl: "Oh, Mary, youre too much!" – and she swished out. You can imagine how Carl avoids her like poison! ...Youd never believe it, to look at him now, but when a friend first brought Carl over – oh, several years ago – you should have seen him: shy; he wouldnt do anything. But now! ...Poor Carl – the things that happen to him....I'll tell you something else – very funny – ho-ho! One time he stomped into a bar and slid on some spilled beer. (He drinks a lot now – and for some strange reason, as I say, he always comes here when hes drunk.) Anyway, he slid on the spilled beer and fell with his legs up – and the queen was there and she shrieked: "Highheels and all!" ... Carl is the one who gave me that silly leather handkerchief.... And Carl, in the middle of summer –...'

Carl came back. Neil finished tactfully: 'In the middle of summer I usually go to Los Angeles to see how things are going. Ive bought many fine items there.' Now he turned to Carl, baiting him like this, perhaps to drive him away: 'I heard something hilarious, Carl. You know what that little chorus-boy queen told me? – *you* know the one I mean.'

Carl blanched.

Neil continued: 'She told me that the height of sadism is the sadist who lets the masochist win! Ho-ho-ho!' He laughed raucously like a department store Santa Claus.

Carl, of course, wasnt amused. 'Have you heard anything more about your stolen guns, Neil?' he asked. Neil winced. Carl apparently had aimed directly.

'No!' Neil said curtly.

Making himself at home – and smiling for having wounded Neil back in a way which I did not understand – Carl goes to a cabinet and brings out a decanter of wine, begins immediately to drink from it thirstily; and as he drinks, he becomes more pugnacious toward Neil – and his voice will become progressively more highpitched, his gestures airier – hinting, shockingly, because of his masculine appearance, at girlishness.

Turning toward me, Carl startled me by saying this: 'You may have discovered this yourself (I dont know how long youve known Mr Neil), but hes insulated himself with his costumes, the way other old men insulate themselves with money – or dirty pictures.' It is more than the previous embarrassing reference, by Neil, to the interlude between Carl and the chorus boy – more than the liquor – that is making Carl abandon so swiftly even the barest trace of civility between him and Neil, as though a years-long tacitly undeclared war had at last flared into open conflict. 'Thats how youve prepared for your old age, isnt it, darling?' he asked Neil.

Sensing the direction of the conversation, Neil tried to remove the wine, but Carl reached for it quickly, poured out another glass. Resigned to the fact that Carl was staying, Neil said: 'Lets take more pictures. I have a good idea for one! ... And dont call me nelly affectionate names, Carl – Ive warned you before ! And dont call them "costumes"!'

Carl ignores him, goes on flaunting his deeply rooted anger. 'Anyway,' he says, 'Neil lures people with his fantastic make-believe – and in a world –...'

Neil: 'Why don't you tell us instead about *your* experiences – like with the chorus boy.'

'– and in a world like ours that deals, from the beginning, largely in repressed sexdreams,' Carl goes on, 'Neil fills his sexual needs by attracting others with his –... Collection. Look at those boots – the belt –...' He shook his head, smiling wryly. 'Has he shown you his collection in the basement?' he asks me.

'Carl, Im going to have to ask you to leave,' Neil said angrily.

But Carl went on: 'Do you know how he makes his contacts? – and, again, I dont know how he met you –' More wine. The masculinity has relaxed into a girlish wistfulness of the face, the body. 'Well, sometimes, he advertises sales of leather goods, in the newspapers. Then he makes the people who turn up. Or he invites people over for . . . tea!' He chortles. 'Neil is so buried in his fantasy that he cant acknowledge that several of these people come to him to get something else from him – at first: food or whatever – to stay if they dont have a place. . . . Why did you come?' he asked me.

'What youre saying isnt true,' Neil said severely. 'I get calls from Los Angeles – as far as Seattle – farther! – people wanting to meet me – just to talk to me, see my Collection!'

'Collect?' Carl asked.

Neil: 'I said *Collection. My* Collection.'

Carl: 'I mean the calls from Seattle – are they collect?'

'Prepaid!' Neil said annoyedly. 'Although,' he added, making Carl smile, 'if I help people out, what difference does that make? After all, a convert – . . .'

'Is a convert,' Carl finished for him.

'Well, you dont have to talk as if *youre* not!'

Carl asked me: 'Has he told you he considers himself a Saint?'

Neil: 'I lead people in the direction they want to go. I fulfill – . . .'

Carl raised his glass in a toast. 'To Saint Neil of the Leather Jacket!' He said to me: 'I was brought over by a . . . "friend," and Neil – how do you put it so cleverly, dearheart? – oh, yes! He "opened the door – a quarter of the way only" – the first time. And all that attention he heaps on you! Whew! And then – then he *pushed* the door open!' He made a harsh gesture of shoving an invisible door. He laughed, straightening up decorously on the chair, realizing he was getting high. 'And it was quite a world, Saint Tex – oops! – I mean: Saint Neil of the – of the –. . . What? Leather Jacket. That's it: Saint Neil of the Leather Jacket!'

'You were *anxious* to come in, whether you knew it then or not,' Neil hurled at him.

'Was I?' Carl said, passing his hand over his eyes for clarity.

'It was such a long time ago.... Remember, Neil, when you advertised one of your phony sales – and the man called, and he came over with his mother and his wife? He'd probably been warned about you. Did you dress all three up?'

'You know I cant stand women,' Neil said icily.

'Thats ruh-hight!' Carl turned to me: 'Has Neil recited his poem – scuse me: I mean, speech – about the place of women in the world?'

'Nevermind,' said Neil. 'Youve been talking enough. Now *I'll* talk.' He turned toward me, and I will be startled by the new tone of his voice, his look. He will no longer be the man who only minutes earlier in the pictures assumed the groveling positions. No. Watch him now as he becomes a politician expounding a noble movement; a general indoctrinating his troops.

Standing up – again reciting as if from memory, his voice welling with authority – Neil began: 'Yes I do consider myself something of a Saint. The leader of a movement. Ive made enormous strides here in Oakland and in San Francisco. Why, I practically organized the Stirrup Club – and that coffee shop nearby where all the cyclists go. And Im advancing rapidly in Los Angeles. Just look at all the leather bars there! ... Yes, a magnificent movement! Previous such movements have failed. Mine wont – because I know The Secret. Youll watch this movement grow – the only truly militant current the world has ever known – and it will carry everything before it.' He swept his hand across the air, frightening the cat who at that moment had been approaching him again. 'Hitler failed,' he said, pronouncing the inevitable name. Chin thrust forward, bowlegs spread, planted firmly like the hands on his flaring hips, he went on: 'Yes, Hitler failed. But We will succeed. And women? Women will be out! They represent weakness! – but still they want to dominate their Masters – The Male!' He closes his eyes as if to contain the sudden hatred. 'Women are vampires! Vicious, draining bloodsuckers!'

Carl shakes his head: 'Listen ... listen.'

Neil: 'Women will have but one purpose: to give birth to

more of Us. That Is All! They say the great civilizations collapsed when We threatened to take over. Theyve missed the point. They collapsed because We didnt go to the inevitable limit: which is complete – . . .'

Carl finishes for him again, as if hes heard it so often he can tell it himself; he barks mockingly: 'Complete acceptance – right, honeypie? And not only acceptance! – but a rejection of the other!'

'Exactly!' Neil boomed. 'And Im not, of course, talking about the ordinary world of simpering faggots and lisping queens that exists now: Theyre weak! Sentimental! They disgust me! . . . Im talking about Power . . . About a movement that has had a glorious history. Why, the Marquis de Sade (the Great! French! Nobleman!) – he and Dr Másoch used to have some exquisite experiments with each other.' His eyes glimmer relishingly.

Carl comes in killingly: 'Neil, Neil, Neil – youve been wrong all these years: The Marquis de Sade and Masoch didnt even live at the same time. Youve thrown history together for your own purposes – something like the way youve done with the furniture in this house, sugarheart.' He spills some wine on his chin, pushes it with a finger into his mouth in a babyish gesture. He sucks the finger loudly. 'As a matter of fact, Saint Nick, they lived in diff – diffrunt cunt – countries'

Neil raised his eyebrows in gigantic indignation. His authoritative pronouncement is being torpedoed. Hes been talking down to me, explaining things as if I were a potential convert – 'opening the door' for me. In my having gone as far as I have into his world – by putting on his costumes and going through the poses of violence – he thinks he senses, inchoate, similar cravings in me. . . . But how, I keep wondering, does he rationalize his talk of supremacy with his sexual subservience?

'At any rate,' Neil tries to go on, 'it will be the only movement toward the justification –'

'– of Mamma Nature,' Carl says, like an impudent student. He giggles sillily.

'Carl!' Neil says querulously, 'dont interrupt me! Im talking *seriously!*' ... In his imperial tone again: 'There are the weak and there are the strong. Pain is the natural inclination: The inflicting of pain –...'

'And yet you play the masochist?' Carl asks the question for me.

Visibly cringing, Neil blurts: 'Ive explained that to you before! ... Seduction! I have to show The Way of Strength – so that The Movement will continue. Masochists – sadists – even people like you, Carl! – theyll bring new converts to create that Glorious Army, of which I –' (He expanded his chest, the shirt protested, he exhaled.) '– of which *I* will be: The Leader! Then – and only then – can I assume my Natural Role!' He calmed down, mopping his perspiring brow with a black handkerchief. 'In my experiments – naturally – I have to play many parts. I will not always be the – the –' he blustered, and then he came out with the wrong phrase, which he realized the moment he had uttered it: '– the low man,' he finished. His look mellowed. 'Will you have some wine?' he asked me. 'It's very good.'

'No, thank you.'

'Hummm....' He became suddenly aware that his costume had become quite hopelessly disarrayed. Urgently, he tried to arrange it, tucking it here, smoothing it out there. One thing would go in, another would pop out. He gave up with a loud sigh of relief. 'Still –' he struggled intrepidly once again to come back philosophically, 'youll have to admit, Carl, that even the great writers – Dostoevsky, for instance – why, Dostoevsky even went so far as to condone murder – he – ... why, in –...'

'Re!-dem!-shun!' Carl shouted, still melodramatically mimicking Neil's previous tones. 'In Dostoevsky, theres always redem-shun at: The End!' He laughed uproariously.

'Well,' said Neil, eyeing him meanly, '*you* may think so.... And, well, I can see that theres no use trying to carry on a Serious Discussion when youre drunk, Carl. And I dont really see why every time youve been drinking, you come over here. Every time –...'

'You dont see why?' Carl asked.

'Well,' Neil said, the authoritativeness vanishing as he laughs very loud, shrugs his shoulders in a gesture that is now becoming for me typical of him (as he always does, I notice, when he feels trapped or ridiculous), 'if you want to come over when youre drunk, well, whu-I NOT?'

'But –' Carl came in obsessively '– this all started cause I was going to tell you – way – away, way, way back there – about Neil and what happened to his precious collection of guns.'

Neil: 'Youve said enough, Carl. Ive asked you to leave, and if you had any –...'

'I dont have "any,"' Carl said. 'And I wanna finish, Saint Neil.' He bows and spills the wine again. 'Saint Neil of the Leather Jacket sometimes makes his contacts at the famous corner of Seventh and Market by the Greyhound bus station. (Did he meet you there?)' he asked me; not waiting for an answer, goes on: 'And I guess – I guess the word has spread – not *The* Word, Neil – just the plain old "word" – has spread, far and wide, and some youngman usually is there, waiting for The Saint. There was this one kid recently. How old was he, Neil? Eighteen? Nineteen? Anyway, Neil thinks hes made a real conquest: A young kid he can really convert: from scratch! ... The kid let him dress him up, and Neil brags to everyone hes got a Real Convert – the kid looks up to him, respects him. So what happens? Oh, it's too much to tell!'

'Youre pitiful,' sneered Neil.

'So are you, dear,' said Carl.... 'Anyway, Neil is going through this wild scene; keeps yelling at the kid: "Harder! Harder!" (Is this how it happened, honeybunch – or am I conjecturing too much from the past?) Anyway, heres where I come in – literally. I came over, the door is open (very unlike Neil), and I find Neil on the floor – knocked out cold! The kid was gone. So was Neil's car. And so – more importantly – was his priceless collection of guns.... Youve started another collection, havent you, Mr Saint? ... Well, they found the car, abandoned – but not The Guns.'

'That boy,' said Neil indignantly, 'did not just "steal" the guns. He *loved* them so much he *had* to take them.'

'Did he also "love" your cufflinks which he also helped himself to – and the car?' Carl laughed. 'Would you believe it?' he asked me. 'Neil wouldnt even tell the cops about the stolen guns – wouldnt even check the hockshops. He kept insisting that his own love of costumes – and all the frills – was what had made that kid steal the guns – that the kid wouldnt ever sell them or hock them – never part with them, he loved them so!'

'That dirty little bastard!' Neil blurted uncontrollably, sinking into another of his contradictions at the memory of the stolen guns. 'I brought the little tramp home – hanging around the Greyhound station –'

'"Tramp"? your "convert"? – who respected you?' Carl asks sarcastically. 'I tell you, Neil, theyve heard about you.'

Neil: '–and I brought him home for tea!'

'Tea!' Carl echoes, amused, reaching for the decanter. He turned to me: 'Have you found out why he tries to tank you up on tea?'

'And *food!*' Neil interrupted. 'And I let him stay here. Then he stole my guns. But it wasnt a common, ordinary, everyday robbery, as you seem to think, Carl: He *loved* those guns." The constant seesawing rationalization. . . .

'Everyone in the world has the same loves you have, huh, lovebushel?' Carl asked.

'Well, *you* do! – and Dont You Forget It!' Neil hurled at him.

Carl closed his eyes, sipped the wineglass empty, refilled it. 'Their souls – our souls,' he sighed.

Neil: 'What are you babbling about?'

Carl giggled. 'You. Im babbling about you. And Souls.'

'Besides,' Neil said absently as if to himself, 'he wasnt even any good. He just wanted to lay there – *naked!*'

'You told me he *loved* costumes,' said Carl in mock surprise. 'And your guns, remember? – he loved those too. You mean,

Neil, he just knocked you out – just like that – you werent even going through one of your fantasies?'

'Naked!' said Neil contemptuously.

Carl: 'Why do you hate the body so much, Neil?'

The phone rang.

'Hello?' Neil answered. . . . Nothing.

'Your new disciple?' Carl asked when Neil returned.

'One day he'll speak,' said Neil pensively.

'Maybe theres lots and lots – and lots of em, Neil – all *women*!' He spat the last word at Neil. 'Maybe theres a counter-conspiracy afoot! To drive you may-ad!'

'Shut up, Carl,' Neil said.

'You really are a Saint,' Carl said.

'You may say it sarcastically – youre so drunk you dont even know what youre saying. But I do bring people out.'

'Hes really right about that,' Carl says to me. 'Have you taken him around yet?' he asks Neil. To me: 'He will – if you stick around. (But dont, baby, dont!) He'll take you to the bars – he'll dress you up – he'll show you around. Hes already taken pictures of you! . . . And he'll introduce you to the motorcycle leather-crowd – show you their "initiations." The first time I went, they tied one guy up to a post, took turns – . . . The blood was coming, but he was screaming for more!' And still addressing me, he went on: 'And then, one day, Neil will show you his collection in his "studio" in the basement.' He shuddered. 'Did you know, Neil, that once, when I told you there was a guy who hung out in Union Square in leather and you went and sat there three straight nights in a row waiting for him – did you know that I made it up, hoping one of the park regulars would pick you up and really – and seriously – beat the hell out of you?' He says that in a jocular tone, but his eyes are fixed on Neil with unequivocal hatred. 'And later,' Carl sighs, 'when *I* heard of someone new, *I* was waiting for him!'

Neil laughs – but nervously. He comes in illogically, whether to change the subject or whether still obsessed by the kid who had clipped his guns: 'Sometimes, you know, sometimes I can still get aroused by the – . . . naked . . . body.'

Carl's transformation has become complete: All the masculinity has been drained out of him as if by the liquor. His legs are curling one over the other. The once rigidly held shoulders have softened. The hand that had held the wineglass tightly, now balanced it delicately with two dainty fingers, the others sticking out gracefully curved. His look liddedly mellowed, and he began to thrust flirtatious glances in my direction. 'Im Unhappy,' he drooled in wine-tones.

'Strength!' Neil shouted, trying to square his shoulders. 'Remember, Carl: Strength Is The Only Answer!'

'Strength?' Carl asked dazedly. 'You know – know wotl-wan, Neil? Wanna know why Im Unhappy, baby?' he said to me. 'Because Ive sunk too far into a world where sex aint even sex no more. . . . They talk about sex without love. What about sex *with hatred*? . . . Oh, it's perfackly – perfuckly – per-fect-ly All Right – per-fect-ly – . . . Start again: It's perfectly okay to be homosexual – . . . Oh, sure. But your world, Neil – your world! Whew!' He stopped; he stared very long at Neil. The drunk hatred melts into an abject smile. 'Your world, Neil, where sex and love – . . . Well – love – . . . Forgot what I was gonna say,' he said. 'Oh, yes – but you know why Im Unhappy?' he repeated. 'Because –' he said, enunciating slowly, 'because – I – wanna – wanna – lover. Yes! A Lover! And all this – this motorcycle drag – it doesnt mean shit to me. I'd wear a woman's silk nightie if it got me a lover,' he said.

Neil winced at the blasphemy, as if Carl's remarks had physically wounded him. 'Be careful, Carl! Youre talking to *Me!*' he said.

'I know. The Saint.' Carl went on: 'Yes, I wanna Lover,' he said, downing another glass of wine. 'If he wants me to be a woman, I'll be the greatest lady since Du Barry. I'll be all things to One man! . . . I – am – lonely.' He turned drooping eyes toward me and sighed lonesomely: 'Will you join me in a toast?' He lifted the glass of wine and holding it toward Neil, he said:

'To Saint Neil – from one of his – most – de – de – . . . Devoted – . . . Converts!'

The glass smashed on the floor.
He was still passed out on the couch when I left.

3

When the inevitable happened (which had lurked in my mind, and which at the same time – I am now sure, looking back on it – I had thought to thwart through that very contact with Neil: although I was becoming aware of perhaps the most elaborate of seductions – or, rather, I would become aware of it in retrospect: a seduction, through ego and vanity, of the very soul), when that inevitable happened, it happened swiftly like this:

I found Neil at home one late afternoon watching television: a western; the box set completely out of place in that bedroom suffused with the atmosphere of some dim past. I could tell that watching that program was such a ritual with him that I sat alone in the other room. Through the door, I could see him. He was dressed in full cowboy costume, replete with holster, gun. ... As the sharp bang-bang! of the television villain's gun burst from the screen, Neil drew his own and made a motion of firing back.

When the program was over, we sat in the bedroom (he pushed the television set out of sight), drinking tea. ... The manikins stared menacingly. Today, one was a military policeman; the other, whose costume I couldnt make out, was somberly dressed in black.

'We have a fine relationship, don't we?' Neil said.

The statement surprised me. The several times I had been with him since that afternoon with Carl – only briefly for lunch or dinner – I had felt an even greater tension and self-consciousness than before – especially since lately he had begun to talk to me in almost fatherly tones.

'Except,' he went on, 'that you hold back. Why? I *know* youre intrigued by Violence. I could sense your excitement when I presented you to the mirror. You saw yourself, Then, as you should be – as you would *like* to be! – as you *could* be!

Out of my clothes, you know, youre very ordinary – like hundreds and hundreds of others. (Youre really not my cup of tea),' he added cuttingly. 'But I can transform you – if you Let Yourself Go!' he exhorted me forcefully. 'Let me! – and I'll open the door – Wide – for you. Youll exist in My Eyes! I'll be a mirror! ... Why should we fight our natures, which are meant to be violent?' he went on in the strangely gentle tones. 'The past – with its grandeur, its nobility – yes, its purifying Violence – that was the time! It wasnt the "compassionate" hypocrisy of our feeble day!' he sneered. He rose to add a thicker belt to the dummy in black. (Almost every inch of the dummies is covered, except for the faces.)

He goes on, now speaking about the weak and the strong, how the former are to be used by the latter, extolling violence, drawing pictures of what his world would be like. 'Power,' he was saying, 'Contempt!' he shouted. 'Contempt for the weakness of compassion,' he derides. . . .

Tense, cold in the warm afternoon, I found myself – although I didnt realize it until he said what he did next – automatically twisting the ring on my finger.

'Who gave you that ring?' he asked abruptly.

I hesitated to answer. Finally I said: 'My father – a long time ago.' Even to mention my father – to recall the memories of that ring (of that morning when I left Home, when he gave me his precious ring in silent reconciliation – after the years of anger between us; at last, that long-sought token of ... Love) – to recall that in the presence of this man suddenly seemed blasphemous.

Neil made a face of supreme disgust, and I felt fury mushrooming inside of me. 'Things like that – which people cling to as memories,' he said, 'it's those things that keep men from realizing their True Nature. My movement will be an upheaval: Nothing is sacred, except Violence and Power. Sentimentality – false memories of tenderness – ... Fathers, mothers!' he said contemptuously. 'That ring you wear as a symbol of – whatever!' he spat.

My anger became hatred for him.

And did he sense this? And had he been counting on this? I didnt have time to consider that, because the scenes that follow will come suddenly like a movie in fast motion.

Suddenly Neil is crouching before me where I am sitting on the bed. He is sliding a pair of thick-soled, high-length studded boots onto my feet. I stare motionless at him as he winds a thick belt about my waist. This time, sensing my immediate mood – the mood he has cunningly put me into and will use – he will not even take the time to 'dress me up' completely.

Swiftly he has flung himself on the floor, his head rubbing over the surface of the boots – the tongue licking them. He rolls on his back. His face looks up pleadingly at me.

Automatically responding (the anger, the hatred like a live gnawing thing inside me) – feeling myself suddenly exploding with that all-enveloping hatred for him (*has he counted on this? does he always?*) and also for what I know I will do at last (senses magnetized on pinpoint), and, too, feeling a tidal-sweeping excitement at the reflections from the mirror which he has carefully moved before the bed so that it records from various angles the multiplied adoration of his face (an adoration augmented shrewdly by the remembered hint, the challenge, of its possible withdrawal: 'Out of my costumes youre very ordinary . . .') – his eyes as if about to burst into flame, his tongue like an animal desperate to escape its bondage – I stand over him as he reaches up grasping, urgently opening the fly of my pants.

'Please – . . . On me – . . . Please do it!' he pleaded.

And as the meaning of the tea looms in my mind, I realize suddenly what he wants me to do. But I cant execute the humiliation he now craves. He rushed into the bathroom, turned the water faucets on fullblast. 'Do it,' he pleads. . . .

The sound of the water, splashing. . . .

The scene reels in all the incomprehensible, impossible images that follow.

A gurgling in his throat – and he rises on his knees, face pressed against the wide belt, which he unbuckled urgently with his teeth. Like a dog retrieving a stick and bringing it back to its master, with his teeth clutching the buckle, he slid the belt out of the pants straps – and he crouched on all fours brandishing the belt before me, dangling it from his mouth extended beggingly towards me. 'Use it, use it!' he insisted.

Something inside me had been set aflame, a fire impossible to quench until it has consumed all that it can burn: something aflame with the anger he had counted on. I acted inevitably and as he had wanted all along: I pulled on the belt, which he clung to with his teeth, so that, released, it snapped in a lashing sound against his cheek, leaving its burning imprint. ... He knelt there, eyes closed, expectantly. ...

I dropped the belt, which fell coiled beside him, the gleaming studs like staring blind eyes on the floor. ... He gnaws ravenously on the straps inside the tops of the boots, falls back in one swift movement lying again on the floor as he reaches for my legs with his hands, looping his fingers into the inside straps, bringing one studded boot pushed into his groin. He makes a sound of excruciating pain. Even then, his hands will not release my foot, crushing it into his groin with more pressure. 'Harder!' he begs. 'Please! *Do it harder ! ! !*'

Rocked by currents inside me which sealed off this experience from anything that had ever happened previously to me – aware all the time that it was *I* who was being seduced by *him* – seduced into violence: that using the sensed narcissism in me – and purposely germinating that hatred toward him – he had played with all my hungry needs (magnified by the hint of the withdrawing of attention), had twisted them in order to use them for his purposes, by unfettering the submerged cravings carried to that inevitable extreme – and disassociating myself from all feelings of pity and compassion, to which – despite the compulsive determination to stamp out all innocence within me and thereby to meet the world in its own savage terms; to leave behind that lulling, esoteric, life-shuttering childhood, that once-cherished place by the window – to which, despite all those things, I had, I know, still clung: to compassion, to pity – and knowing only that this was the moment when I could crush symbolically (as in a dream once in which I had stamped out

all the hatred in the world) whatever of innocence still remained in me (crush that and something else – something else
surely lurking – but what? – *what!!*) – that at this moment I
could prove irrevocably to the hatefully initiating world that I
could join its rot, its cruelty – I saw my foot rise over him, then
grind violently down as if of its own kinetic volition into that
now pleading, most vulnerable part of that man's body....

He let out a howl.

A dreadful sound hurled inhumanly like a bolt out of his
throat – a plunging bolt which buried itself instantly within my
mind. His face turned to one side as if he would bite the floor in
pain. Tears came from his eyes in a sudden deluge which joined
the perspiration and turned his face into a gleaming mask of
pain. And he sobbed:

'Why ... hurt? ... Why ... do you ...? I ... did ... for
you –... did everything! ... Wanted –... want –... Why?
...hurt ... why? ... Wanted lo – ...' Clenched teeth choked
the word he had been about to utter.

The scene exploded in my mind. I was seized by the greatest
revulsion of my whole life – a roiling, then a quick flooding in-
vading my whole being like electricity; a maelstrom of revulsion – for myself, for him, loathing for him, for what he wanted
done – loathing for what I was doing.

And hearing the racked baleful sobs which continue ('Why
...hurt?...' And again the unfinished word: 'Wanted –
want lo –...') – seeing that writhing pitiful body, the boot
pinioning him to the floor (like a worm! like a helpless worm!
like a helpless worm tortured by children!) – seeing that face
gleaming with tears – and feeling, myself, as if the world will
now burst in a bright crashing light which will consume us
both in judgment – I bent down over him, extending my hand
to him – my foot removed from his scorched groin: extending
my hand to him, to help him up – to help him! – as if he were
the whole howling pain-racked ugly crushed mutilated, sad sad
crying world, and I could now, at last, in that moment, by
merely extending my hand to him in pity, help him – and It.
Compassion flooded me as turbulently as, only seconds before,

the seducing savagery had rocked me to my violated soul.

And as the man sobbing on the floor in the disheveled soul. costume saw my hand extended to him in pity, the howling stopped instantly as if a switch had been turned off within him, and his look changed to one of ferocious anger.

And he shouted fiercely:

'*No, no! Youre not supposed to care!*'

4

'I knew youd come back,' he said victoriously.

I had walked out on him that day, and I had stayed away for several days.

'I understand,' he said. 'In the first stages it can be difficult – for some. And those are the ones that turn out to be the best. This time you can use this whip.' He brandished a coiled leather snake. 'And if youre ready, I'll show you my "studio" in the basement.'

He had misunderstood my purpose in coming back – which was to show him (and to show myself?) that he could never seduce me in that way again. I knew it irrevocably when I saw a black costume lying across the leather-spread bed. He was bent over it folding it to replace it in the closet.

It was the costume, complete with swastika, of a storm trooper.

'Were you wearing that?' I asked him.

'Yes,' he answered proudly. 'I wear it only on Special occasions.' But a note of nervousness entered his voice as he said: 'Today I went to an execution.'

I blinked incredulously.

'Yes,' he repeated with bravado – but he appears even more nervous now. 'You heard right: An Execution! If you had been here, you could have witnessed it. My cat – remember the furry one? – he was becoming too weak – constantly simpering, whining. I hate weakness. I despise it. I loathe it. . . . So I executed him.'

'You put on that Nazi costume and you –?' I started.

'Yes! And I exterminated him – as all weakness must be Exterminated! ... I put that cat out of his absurd sniveling misery!' He went on deliberately: 'I put him in a bag, I drowned him in the bathtub!' As soon as hes verbalized what hes done, he appears visibly shaken, as if an emotional rubber-band had been stretched to the point of snapping.

I felt violently sick. ... The black uniform now being hung adoringly in the closet ... the flushed face ... the pitiful lumpy body covered with the absurd clothes ... the terrifying words. ... The dummies gazing blankly....

Noticing that I was staring at him with undisguised contempt; surprised to see it so coldly aimed at him; realizing all at once that he had misinterpreted my returning here – and looking tense as if my look of disgust had thrown him unexpectedly off-balance – he blurted:

'There is no excuse for weakness! ... Once you allow yourself to be touched by it, youre lost! ... And you may think – like that insidious Carl! – that it's weakness to do – to do the things I do. But remember the importance of Seduction! The Leader of every cause has to set an example, whatever form that takes! He has to show The Way!'

I want to tell him what I see so clearly. I want to say: 'Youve rationalized your masochism – masking your own very real weakness.' But I merely stare at the posed obdurate face, chin thrust out like the caricature of a repugnant dictator – but a very uncertain dictator somehow.

'You killed the cat,' I said finally – still not really believing it; rather, not wanting to.

He sighed wearily. The enormity of what hes done seems slowly to be dawning on him. But he fights back, shaking his head: 'Once you let weakness touch you – ...' he starts; and his whole body begins to tremble instantly, as if his jangled nerves were out of control, rebelling him. He shook his head as if he were very, very, very tired.

'I'll give you an example of what weakness can do!' he shouts as if to blot out his own guilty thoughts. '*The* Example! My own father! ... He was weak! ... But my – ... mother!'

He flung the word out with infinite revulsion. '– that – woman!
– that Loathsome despicable woman with her hatred of the
body – . . . I couldnt go barefoot! I even had to take a bath in
the dark! . . . That woman! – *she* knew. *She* was strong – and
she used that strength, and she used my father's weakness –'
He twisted his hands as if wringing out a piece of cloth. '– and
she twisted and drained and twisted. And then he – my father –
that weak man – would take it out on me – hit *me*!' He flayed
himself with the thick belt he had removed from the dark
pants. 'But I showed him *I* was a Man! I wouldnt run away
from him! . . . And he hit me and hit me and hit me with his
belt – until I'd pass out.' *Whack!* – again the belt against his
thigh. He didnt flinch.

'And then I wouldnt even faint any more,' he said. 'I'd just –
. . . let him. . . . And yet,' he whispered as if in a trance, 'and
yet – do you know? – that weak, dreadful man – my father –
he – . . . *He wore boots! Boots!* – a symbol of the strength he'd
given away so easily, without a fight! *That pitiful man –
dominated by my mother – had the guts to wear Boots!* . . .
And then I found the Answer – Strength! . . . And when I found
that out, I – . . . You want to know what my first gesture of – of
freedom! – from him and that woman – was?' He threw back
his head and roared with pained laughter. He continued as if
hypnotized by the remembrance of that ugly past: 'I had gone
to the movies – secretly because I wasnt even allowed to do
that! It was a period picture. . . . And the hero – a strong, handsome, masculine man (everything my father wasnt!) – he was
wearing Boots too. But on him they were Right: No woman
would have dominated him! . . . I sat through that movie
several times especially for a scene in which that magnificent
man was sitting in bed, putting on his Boots! He looped his
fingers about the inside straps – and he slipped the Boots on!
I held my breath. . . . That night, when my father was asleep,
I went into his bedroom. I stood looking at him: Even asleep he
looked weak and dominated. . . . And staring at my – . . .
father! – asleep – I hated him more than ever. I found his
boots under the bed. I took them to my room. I got my mother's

scissors. *And snipped the straps off the insides of his boots!*'

He formed two fingers into a V and closed them with finality.

He looked worn out. The studded costume he wore seemed like a ponderous burden on him. His face drooped toward his hands. Dispassionately, lifelessly, he echoed: 'I snipped those straps from the insides of his boots. I cut them off, I stamped on them, I spit on them, I – I – ...' And then he shouted:

'*I pissed on them!*'

His voice quavered, broke, halted. He turned his face away from me. His shoulders trembled as if in a sudden cold wind.

'So you see: power and strength –' he began weakly without finishing.

I sat next to him where he had sunk onto the bed.

But is there anything you can say now to Neil?

It's too late. It's too late.

Through the open door of the bathroom I see a water-soaked bag on the floor.

Michael Rumaker

The Pipe

Five men stood around the mouth of the big corrugated pipe.
The length of the pipe, propped on wooden planks bolted cross-
wise, stretched in a wavering line over the flat, sun-baked mud
of the land, dipped about a hundred yards on over the edge of
the bluff and could be seen, from where the men stood, trailing
in a thin, black line across the beach far below and running
on stilts out over the water to the dredge-boat anchored in mid-
river. The sky was light green from the intense heat of a sun
that beat down unmercifully on the broad level land. Flat acres
of bleached clay, hardened and cracked in huge irregular slabs
curled at the edges, billowed up heavy waves of shimmering,
colorless heat. A flock of chicken hawks, wings taut and motionless, wheeled slowly high overhead. There was not a tree or
a cloud in sight. The men were silent. Their rubber boots sank
ankle deep into the mud and when a man shifted from one foot
to the other, his boots made sucking noises. The mud spread in
a wide pool around the mouth of the pipe.

One of the men, Alex, his face dark brown under the brim of
his hat, pulled out a pocket watch. He glanced at the dial, then
snapped the lid shut and thrust the watch back in his pocket.
Shading his eyes with one hand, he looked out over the river
to where the dredge-boat lay anchored.

'What time is it?' Carp said.

'The blow's just about due.'

'I wish to hell they'd hurry it up. I'm sweating my balls off.
Not a breeze. No nothing.'

Carp's face and hands were burned red from the sun. The
skin was peeling from his cheeks and around his neck. He kept
picking off pieces of the loose flesh and rolled them into little

balls between his thumb and forefinger. He dropped these pellets in the mud between his boots.

'Just be patient,' Alex said. 'You'll work yourself into a lather over it. Get yourself a sunstroke to boot. Why can't you be patient, like Billy there.'

Billy glanced up. He was tall and thin and hatless.

'Billy's simpleminded,' Carp said. 'He don't feel anything. What do you feel, Billy? What're you feeling now?' he called.

'Don't torment the boy,' said Alex.

'I'm a chicken hawk,' Billy said, rolling his eyes to the sky.

The men chuckled.

'You see? He's a chicken hawk,' Carp said. 'It don't make sense.'

'Billy's a queer bird all right, all right,' laughed Ruby. He was short and fat and had a red bandana knotted around his throat. He wore a wide leather kidney belt with a big silver buckle and studded with brass rivets. There was a big floppy felt hat on his head that covered half his face.

'I'm a chicken hawk,' Billy repeated.

'Hey, Billy, like this?' Ruby started flapping his arms like a bird.

'Never you mind.'

Ruby laughed, fluttering his arms, his belly shaking. He winked at Billy. Billy looked away.

'Me and you, Billy,' he chuckled. 'Birds of a kidney.'

His face went scarlet with laughing and he had a fit of coughing and turned away, doubled up and still laughing, and fanned his face with his hat.

The men grew silent, watching the dredge-boat out on the river. Carp tore a long layer of skin off the back of his neck and began rolling it between his fingers. Bunk and Sam were standing off a little from the others. Bunk had his thumbs hitched in the loops of his belt and was sliding the sole of his boot back and forth over the mud. On his upper lip was a sore that a couple of flies buzzed around. He kept reaching up with his hand, brushing them away. Sam was big, with broad shoulders and thick arms and legs. His face was red and sweating and his dull eyes gazed listlessly out over the water.

Billy walked away from the group, beyond the pipe to where an old mud-spattered chevvy stood, its back seat torn out and that place jammed with rusty pieces of odd-shaped metal, piled almost to the ceiling and jutting out the windows. On either side of the chevvy was a handcart and a wagon made of orange crates, each filled with a couple of pieces of mud-caked metal. There were two burlap bags lying near the cart and wagon, and they were yellow with dust and bulging slightly. Billy sat down in the shade on the runningboard of the car. His cheeks were flushed and he was breathing heavily. He ran his fingers through his sweaty hair, then propped an elbow on one knee and cupped his chin in his hand.

'Penny by penny,' he gasped. 'Bye and bye.'

'Them hawks make me nervous,' snapped Carp. 'Wisht to hell they'd go away.'

He picked up a stone and flung it at the sky.

'You'd have to have a damned good arm to hit one of them birds,' said Alex. He pushed back his hat and wiped the sweat from his brow with a piece of flannel.

'They get on my nerves, swimming around and around up there, like they could wait forever for something dead. I wisht they'd go away.'

'I'll tell them to go away, Carp,' Billy said, grinning and looking up open-mouthed at the hawks. 'If you want me to, Carp.'

'Whatta you going to do, fly up?'

'Sure, Carp. I can talk to them.'

'You're loco, Billy.'

'The heat's got him,' Sam said.

'No I'm not, Carp. I can fly up there and talk to them and tell them to go away if they're bothering you. Honest I can, Carp.'

'Well, you go on, Billy.'

'Sprout wings,' snorted Ruby.

'Not today, Carp.'

'Why not?'

'It's too hot.'

'Smart bird.'

'I'll do it tomorrow, Carp.'

'Okay. That's a promise.'

'I learned when I was a baby.'

'Sure, Billy.'

'Billy, you oughta get yourself some kind of cap,' said Alex. 'The sun'll affect you coming out here bareheaded.'

'It's affecting him already,' Ruby said. 'You hear how he thinks he can fly.'

'I got a cap of silver and diamonds,' Billy said. 'But it's too good to wear out here.'

'Listen to it, will you?' sneered Carp. 'Billy, you're a grown man. You oughta have more sense'n to talk like that.'

'Well, I do. I bought that cap in New York City. You can't say I didn't.'

'You're just making it up. When was you ever in New York City?'

'Never you mind. I'm gonna get a cap of gold next. When I get enough junk out of that pipe, that's what I'm going to do. I'm not kidding.'

'Okay, Billy,' Carp guffawed. 'You show me.'

'Well, I will.'

'Whatta you do for a woman, Billy?' Ruby shouted.

'Let the boy alone,' said Alex.

Carp yelled, 'Oh, I bet he has wild nights with hisself, don't you, Billy?'

Billy giggled and pulled his hand over his eyes.

'The world's topsy-turvy, ain't it, Billy?' Ruby was shaking with laughter, the brim of his hat flopping up and down.

Billy snatched the hand away from his eyes.

'Why, no, sir.'

'But you see things different from most people.'

Billy hugged his knees with his arms, then said, 'The world's round. Everybody knows that. But here,' his eyes moving slowly over the land, 'It's flat as a checkerboard. God's lying.'

'Now you be careful, Billy.'

'Of what?'

'The Judgement Day. Talking about God like that, calling God a liar ain't healthy.'

'It don't scare me none.'

'Listen to him talk!' howled Carp. 'Talking awful high and mighty, ain't you? You still a chicken hawk?'

Billy stared down at the mud.

'Don't tease me, Carp.'

'I'm not teasing. I just want to know if you're still a chicken hawk, that's all.'

'Well, I am if you want to know,' Billy said angrily. 'And tomorrow I'll fly up and tell them they annoy you.'

The men burst out laughing. Bunk rubbed his hands agitatedly up and down his thighs, beating clouds of dust from his dungarees.

'Billy, you do take the cake!' he shouted.

'And I eat it, too. I like cake.'

The men roared. Alex bent down at the mouth of the pipe and stuck his head in sideways, listening.

'What're they saying?' Sam asked, inching up close to Alex.

'One guy says, "Lay off the chains" – That means the blow's about due. One guy's calling another one a bastard.'

'He should if it's his fault the blow's late,' Carp said.

'Something must be holding them up,' Ruby said. 'I sure wisht they'd hop to it. I feel like I'm being fried in deep fat.'

'Well, if you feel that way, it's your own you're sizzling in,' said Carp.

'Look here, Mr Dry Bones, you're so thin I can smell the –'

'Shut up,' Sam snapped. 'Alex, what else they saying?'

'Nothing but racket. Nobody saying anything.' Alex ducked out from the pipe and straightened up, squaring his hat straight on his head.

'Oh, come on, you last blow of the day!' Carp shouted, shaking his fist at the dredge-boat. 'I want to get to Tarkie's, ditch my junk, and have me a cold bottle of beer.'

'Go on and take a swim,' Alex said. 'Cool off.'

'Not in that stinking water.'

Ruby held his fingers to his nose and said, 'Go on, Carp, go take a bath and give us a break.'

'Be like a chemical bath,' Bunk said. 'Besides, the river's black with polio.'

'That's Nigger Buddy's blood,' Billy said, from the running-board of the car. 'Nigger Buddy made the river black.'

'Who's Nigger Buddy?'

'You never heard of Nigger Buddy?'

'No, I never did. Another one of your stories I guess.'

'Tell them, Carp. Tell them about Nigger Buddy Carson the day he went swimming off Blower Rocks. He made the river black.'

'He did no such thing,' Carp said. 'He never made the river black.'

'What happened? Come on, Carp, tell us.'

'It ain't nothing much. Hardly worth telling.'

'Come on. I bet it's something good. You're being selfish keeping it to yourself.'

'Oh, it's good all right,' Billy said, leaning forward and rubbing his hands together. 'It's the reason the river's why it is.'

'Talk about the river black, Mr Bill Big-Lie,' Carp said, turning on him, 'I'd like to get a squint at that soul of yours. There can't be a shade difference'n you and the river the lies you jaw.'

'Well, tell them, Carp. Let them judge for themselves.'

'He never *got* to the water, I tell you. He took a low dive on the rocks and smashed his head open. They had to scrape his brains off with a piece of cardboard.'

'Was his brains black?' Billy said. 'I never seen a nigger bare. What's it look like, Carp?'

'Carp can't tell you,' Sam said, grinning and showing his long yellow teeth. 'He dreamt the whole thing up.'

'It's true. I was there. Seen it with my own two eyes!'

'Tall tales, tall tales,' Sam sneered. 'What was you doing, hiding in the grass and peeking at a naked nigger? I don't know what to think of that.'

'I was fishing a little way off, you fool. You think I'm hot to see a boogie's dingle, the way Billy is?'

'What color is it, Carp?'

'Honest to God, Billy –'

'He'll tell you it's zebra-striped,' laughed Sam. 'Go on, tell him, he's so hot to know – zebra-striped with purple polka dots.'

'I'm telling you, Sam, I saw it all. You calling me a liar?'

'Answer my question, Carp.'

'Tall tales,' howled Sam, slapping his thigh. 'Just more of your plain long-legged lies!'

'I'm warning you, Sam.'

'Sam, you zipper your trap,' Ruby said. 'Let Carp go on and tell the story.'

'Was it really black, Carp?'

'Let Carp tell us how many drinks he had beforehand,' Sam chuckled. 'Go on, Carp, tell us.'

'Nary a one. I tell you, his brains was splattered all over them rocks. They had to pick off the pieces with a fork.'

'Now it's forks. Oyster forks I guess, huh?'

'What's an oyster fork?'

'An oyster fork!' Carp snarled, turning on Ruby with such violence that Ruby backed away. 'You mean you never heard of an oyster fork?'

'No, I haven't. I'm ashamed to say I never knew an oyster had one.'

'Why, oysters don't grow them, you fool,' Carp spluttered, his face reddening. 'That's a fork for spearing oysters at high-falooting dinners. I seen plenty when I used to waiter down in Atlantic City.'

'What's Atlantic City like, Carp?'

'You mean there's more than one kind of fork outside of a pitchfork?' Ruby said, squinting at Carp and spitting a wad of tobacco juice plop in the mud.

'Why sure. Everybody knows that. First off, there're forks for olives. Now, you see, the rich got it all pretty complicated. I say *forks* for olives, 'cause there's forks for black olives, and forks for plain green olives (them with the pits still in), and then there's forks for olives stuffed with red gut. And, you see, you gotta know these things, else when you sit down to table and look baffled a minute at that long line of forks, people'll know you're dumb and not the ritz at all. They laugh at you behind their hands. I seen it happen.'

'You know the difference between all these forks, huh?' Sam said. 'You could put your knees under any fancy table and stick the right olive with the right fork, huh? You could do that?'

'Why sure. Didn't I used to waiter in a lush hotel? I watched and learned them things.'

''Case you get rich someday, huh?'

'In case. Now you take oyster forks,' Carp said, turning to Ruby. 'Same thing there.'

'Oh God, here it comes!'

'No, you listen,' Carp said over his shoulder to Sam. Then to Ruby, 'There's a fork for Blue Point oysters and a fork for Pawtucket oysters and another for Queen of Sheba oysters and then one for Jersey oysters – A fork for all the kinds of oysters in the world.'

'Aw, come on. How they have room on the table for all them forks?'

'Oh, they have room,' Carp said, not looking at Sam. 'Big, grand table. 'Course, they don't serve *all* the oysters in the world at one sitting.'

''A course not. Nor all the olives, I bet.'

Carp turned and eyed Sam haughtily, folding his arms across his chest.

'Well, there's more kinds of oysters than olives,' he said. 'You got more forks to remember with oysters. Olives is easy. But the most pretty fork of all the oyster forks is an eensy-beensy silver one, all kinds of loops and curls carved on it, and the handle studded with diamonds. They usually have a couple of them on every table. Just in case.'

He paused, smiling mysteriously through Sam. Sam watched him, waiting, but Carp kept on smiling and didn't say anything. Finally Sam said, 'In case of what?'

Carp stopped smiling and stared at him blankly, as though he hadn't seen him before.

'I beg your pardon?'

'Don't give yourself airs,' Sam grumbled. 'I say, in case of what?'

'Was you referring to them special eensy-beensy silver oyster forks I was mentioning a couple minutes ago?'

Carp drew himself up grandly.

'You know damn well I am.'

'Well,' Carp drawled slowly, flicking a speck of imaginary dust off the tip of his nose, 'They have a couple of them forks on each table just in case some lady or gent pokes into their oyster and strikes a pearl. Then right off, there's a lot of excitement and laughing, and the lady – I seen it happen to a lady once, barebacked she was and with the prettiest little freckles on her shoulders – I seen it happen to her.'

He paused carefully inspecting his fingernails.

'What?' Sam said in a cracked voice.

Carp glanced up at him. 'Why, just what I been talking about. She comes up with a pearl in her oyster. And, right off, she lays down her fork – blue pointers was served that night so it was a blue point fork – she lays that fork down and reaches over for the little fork studded with diamonds and scoops in under that oyster and brings up the prettiest pearl you ever seen – all soft silver and kind of glowing in the light of the chandeliers, and pure round as a marble. She held the pearl up on that special fork and showed everybody. And what a commotion was raised about how beautiful it was. The ladies started hollering to see it so they passed it around the table for everybody to take a good squint at. I tell you, it was stunning'.

'Me, something like that was passed my way,' Sam said gruffly, 'I'd pocket both pearl *and* fork and go on nonchalant with my soup.'

'You, you would. You don't know nothing about breeding and manners.'

'But you do?'

'I ain't bragging. I can hold my own. But, you listen,

didn't I have a chance to learn it with my own two eyes?'

'Lot of good it'll do you.'

'You never can tell. I might cash in one of these days on this here dredge.'

'Don't hold your breath. Better you go spearing oysters at fancy dinners.'

'Don't you think I couldn't.'

'Ha-ha.'

'I may not know anything about manners,' Ruby said. 'But I can sure show you something about breeding.'

'What's that?'

'You just watch me with any woman, I'll show you the grandest blue-ribbon breeding you ever saw.'

The men laughed.

'That ain't the kind of breeding I mean.'

'There ain't no other kind, Carp. Not in my books.'

'That just shows how dumb you are.'

'Ruby laid the baby in the pipe.'

'What're you talking about, Billy?'

'I know. I saw him do it. Alex, tell us how you found that baby in the pipe.'

'Billy, I've told you that story a dozen times. I'd think you'd be sick of it by now. Besides, it's not a nice story to tell. It wasn't Ruby's baby anyway.'

'It wasn't my baby,' Ruby said.

'I'm not tired of it, Alex. I like it. Tell it again.'

'Billy, you know that story as well as I do. Why don't you tell it?'

'I'm not very good.'

'Get out,' Carp said. 'You know you're busting to tell it.'

'Well, maybe I am. Shall I tell it, Alex?'

'I told you, Billy. I'd like to hear it. How 'bout you boys?'

'Go on, Billy. Do your stuff,' Ruby said. 'You can't be any worse than Alex.'

'You be careful. I'll tell whose baby that was.'

'I ain't done any cavorting. You can't blame that on me. That's a terrible thing to say, Alex.'

'Well, just you mind how you criticize my storytelling.'

'I was only funning.'

'Shut up, you two,' Sam said. 'Spin it out, Billy.'

'All right. But you mustn't laugh.'

'I'll bust your nose you blame that baby on me.'

'Shut your flap, Ruby. We know you ain't capable,' Carp said. 'Hey, Billy – Can we listen?'

'Why sure. How else? But you mustn't laugh.'

'Can we look?'

'At me?'

'Who else?'

'Well, all right. But you mustn't laugh. If you laugh, I can't tell it.'

'I'll be a juke box feather plucked nigger of an angel,' snapped Bunk. 'Get on with it, Billy, for Jesus sake.'

Billy walked over to the mouth of the pipe and stood very erect. He set his lips firmly and stared straight ahead of him.

'I'm ready,' he said solemnly.

'Shall we draw the curtain, Billy?'

Billy looked around, flustered, then glanced uncertainly at Carp.

'Well, okay,' he said finally. 'You can do it now.'

Billy watched as Carp took a gigantic stride forward, made a sweeping bow to the tips of his boots. He swung out his arm and, grazing Billy's nose with his hand, grandly pulled back an imaginary curtain. Turning, he bowed from the waist to the men, one hand clapped smartly on his hip. The men applauded and stamped their boots in the mud. Billy squirmed and wriggled, still at attention, and glanced impatiently at Carp, who continued bowing up and down and tipping his cap to the men. The men went on shouting and clapping.

'Now you got them laughing!' Billy shouted, red in the face and clenching and unclenching his fists. Carp paid no attention to him and as he bent down for another bow, Billy gave him a shove in the buttocks with his foot. Carp reeled around, dead pan, and slapping the heels of his boots together, gave Billy a smart salute.

'Sorry, Cap'n,' he said, rubbing his backside.

'Scoot!' snapped Billy, shooing a hand at him.

Carp made another snappy salute, then marched stiff-legged over to the men, grinning, his face flushed. The others hooted and slapped him on the back.

'That was some show, Carp! That was all right!'

'Real fine acting, Carp! Real fine!'

'You want to hear this story or not!' Billy shouted, glaring at them.

'Oops, there's the curtain up and us ignoring the main actor,' chuckled Ruby. He genuflected on one knee and blew a kiss to Billy. 'Proceed. Proceed.'

Billy took a step forward and shook his fist at Carp. 'Damn you, Show-off, you spoiled everything!'

'I'm awful sorry, Cap'n,' Carp said, pulling off his cap and hanging his head sheepishly. He twisted his cap around and around in his hands.

'Well, you spoiled it, Mr Movie Star. I'm about ready to close this curtain and forget the whole thing.'

'Aw, don't do that,' Bunk pleaded.

'Men, here's the way,' Carp said, turning briskly to the group and spreading his arms. His face relaxed in a serious and solemn expression. Ruby stifled a giggle behind his hand and settled down and grew quiet. They each put on a quiet, listening face.

'I'll do it now,' Billy said.

He walked over to the pipe and leaned one elbow on it, crossing one foot in front of the other.

'Well, to begin – Alex was leaning on the pipe one day. Just like this. Huh, Alex?'

'That's right, Billy.'

'It was terrific hot. The old sun burned a trillion billion watts a second.' – He wiped his hand over his brow – 'Just like now.' – He glanced up at the sun – 'Well, the old pipe here –' – He gave it a terrific thump with his fist – 'Started chuckling and gurgling for the last blow. Alex steps back and waits.' – He moved backward folding his arms over his chest and glared steadily at the pipe – 'Then the whole pipe begins jerking and dancing off its pins as the blow gushes close.' – He started to leap in the air and flailed his arms about – 'Then out she whooshes!' he shouted, and dove at the men who leapt back in alarm – 'And there's a great explosion of water and mud and rock and junk a thousand feet high!' he screamed, the muscles in his throat red and swelling.

'Make it fifteen feet, Billy.'

'Anyway,' Billy gasped, licking his lips and stalking around, 'the blow peters off – begins to sicken and fall.' He staggered back, his lids half drooping, one hand pressed to his forehead, lips quivering and teeth chattering – 'And dies!' – He keeled over in the mud and lay still.

'Billy, you'll get your clothes all –'

'Then! Quick as a flash! Up he bounds!' – He scrambled to his knees – 'And starts clawing through rock and mud for junk!' – He rooted savagely in the earth with his fingers, flinging stones and mud over his shoulder, his hair flying in his face – 'He finds a good hunk – pitches it aside.' – He heaved a stone in the direction of the men – 'Finds another – pitches it aside – and another – it's a real good day – coming in copper – a good blow – another good hunk!' The last stone struck Ruby's boot and Ruby let out a howl and began hopping around on one foot while holding the other in both hands.

'Hey, careful, Billy –'

'Then all of a sudden!' – Billy knelt back on his heels and lifted his arms in amazement. His eyes bulged from his head as he stared down terrified at a particular spot in the mud. His mouth hung open. The men crowded forward, craning their necks to see what he was looking at. He let out a long low cry and slowly pressed his fingers into his cheeks. Then, gently reaching down, he pulled an imaginary object from the mud. He held it aloft, shrinking from it and glancing sideways at it, his eyes rolling with terror.

'It was the baby,' he whispered.

The men stared uncomfortably at Billy's outstretched hand.

'It's all mangled and black,' he said, rising slowly from his knees. 'You can hardly tell it is a baby. Black like a nigger. Black and bloated from the river.' He pinched his nostrils with his fingers. 'It stinks like fish in the sun. Nigger, it don't have no legs. Legs ripped up in the dredge or in the pipe. But maybe –' He clutched the baby under one arm and frantically searched the ground at his feet. 'Maybe them two legs come out with the blow. Maybe they're buried here under all this mud and rock.' He carried the baby over to dry ground and laid it down carefully. Then he raced back to the mouth of the pipe and going down on his hands and knees began scratching and digging through the mud. 'Them legs might be here. They just might be.'

Ruby hurried forward.

'Look there, Billy!' he said excitedly, pointing. 'There.'

'Where? Here?' Billy swung around. 'Ah, here, huh?' He started tearing away in that place, searching. Finally he stopped and wiped the sweat off his face with the sleeve of his shirt. He stood up and peered at the earth, then over to the dry ground where he had laid the baby. 'Not here. Nowhere. Not anywhere. No legs. Baby ain't got no legs. Baby gets buried without no legs.' His shoulders were shaking and he started to cry. 'No legs. Not anywhere.' He looked up suddenly, snapping his fingers, his face brightening. He swung around and ran over to the pipe. Bending down, his hands gripping his knees, he stared grinning into the mouth of the pipe.

'Next gush!' he cried, his voice echoing inside the pipe. 'Another blow – Maybe them legs'll turn up. I'll keep an eye out, I'll scratch the mud. I'll find them legs. Last thing I do, I'll find them baby's legs. I'll glue 'em back on.'

He spun around, laughing, and danced a jig from foot to foot, clapping his hands over his head. 'Next blow!' Abruptly he stopped and stood stiff and straight, his arms pressed tightly at his sides.

'Police come and take the baby.' He fell to the earth and hopped around on his knees. 'No legs. Baby ain't got no legs. Got wings, no legs.' He scraped around in the mud. 'Day after day – another – next blow – they don't turn up – mud, rock,

junk – no legs – baby gone – no legs – oh, where could they be?'
He jumped up and stood once more at attention, his heels close
together, staring straight ahead of him. 'Lord, I don't look anymore. I forget about it.'

He looked down at his toes, wriggling them.

'Well, that's the way it went, wasn't it, Alex?'

'You done it a thousand times better, Billy.' Alex blew his
nose hard on the piece of flannel. 'That was a very fine performance.'

'There, that just closes it up,' Bunk said, stepping over and
drawing the curtain shut.

'You oughta go on Broadway,' Ruby said.

'You think so?'

'You got talent. That was something to see, Billy, I'm telling
you.'

'Next time I go into New York City, I'll look into that. Where
do you go?'

'I was at the Ziegfield Follies once,' Ruby said. 'Let's see –'
He rubbed his heavy cheeks. 'That must have been 20–22 years
ago. Mighty fine theater. Good show. You just go there. They'll
fit you in.'

'You think so?'

'I'm certain. You just do the act you did here for us.'

'I'd have to practice.'

'Well, practice.'

'No, Ruby, I think I'd rather go to Hollywood. I like movies
better.'

'Do what you like. You're wasting your time in this desert.
Whatta you want being a junkie?'

'I don't know, Ruby.'

Billy was silent a moment.

'You suppose somebody didn't want that baby?' he said,
turning to Alex.

'What do you mean?'

'Well, say a fella gets a girl fixed good and them not being
married or anything, they get rid of it tossing it in the river.
Say maybe the girl has the baby off in the woods somewhere

by herself and when it's born puts it in a paper bag, like what you get at the A&P, and carries it to the river and good-bye, trouble. Say maybe the boyfriend helps her.'

'I don't know, Billy. Might be. I don't know where that baby come from.'

'Well, if the boyfriend was to help her,' Ruby said, 'I think that it'd take plenty of nerve to dive into her again. I can't imagine wanting anything more to do with her. It's bad enough being in the same house when one of your kids is born. You listen to her howling like that and it makes you feel bad.'

'But you forget,' Sam said.

'Hell yeah.'

'That's why I hustle my old lady to the hospital every time. On account of the noise she makes. And the names she calls me when she's in the throes of it – "Alex, you bastard, you touch me again I'll kill you – So help me I'll cut it off – You nogood sonuvabitch, you got me like this – You touch me again I'll kill you." Stuff like that. Hospitals, they take care of the scream and the mess. It's worth the money.'

'It's hell to have to listen to. They're out of their heads.'

'But they forget.'

'Oh, sure.'

'Thank God for that. That'd really be hell, eh boys? I mean if they never forgot and would never let you touch them again after that.'

'It ain't natural. Earth'd empty in no time. So you needn't worry.'

'God provides,' Billy said.

They laughed.

'I guess it's toughest on the woman. What's that in the Bible –?'

'Now don't go spouting that stuff.'

'No, but I mean there's something in there about woman. Goes – first the pleasure then the pain. Then the whole thing all over again, never stopping. Us men are lucky – pleasure and more pleasure and never any worry about a day of reckoning.'

''Cepting in case you get a dose of something.'

'Well, I always say you should pick a wife clean when you pick her.'

They all laughed.

'I didn't mean that. I mean when you're off on a toot and ain't careful. A man's gotta watch out he don't catch something.'

'No, that's the one thing can knock up a man.'

'Put him out of commission – but good.'

'Something a woman don't have to worry about. I read somewhere she can carry it and dose up a man proper, but it don't mean she's gonna bust out in sores and go blind.'

'No, that's tough on a man.'

They stared at Bunk's upper lip.

He grinned and pointing to his mouth said, 'That ain't nothing. Just a cold sore.'

'You can't be too sure,' Sam said. 'It looks funny to me, Bunk. Now I don't mean to say you're diseased or anything, but that scab of yours sure does look peculiar.'

'It's nothing, I tell you.'

'You've had that *cold* sore as long as I've known you, Bunk. That's been ten years.'

Bunk shrugged his shoulders and jammed his hands into his back pockets. He turned away, shading his eyes with one hand, and looked out over the river.

'Wonder when that blow's coming?' he said.

There was a silence. Then Alex said, 'But a man's lucky, I will say that. He don't have to put up with the monthly bleed or be afraid of getting pumped full of baby every so often.'

'You said the truth there,' Sam said. 'Let's have a drink on that. Whatta you say, boys?'

'I wouldn't throw *my* glove in the glass,' chuckled Ruby, rubbing his hands together.

Sam took a whiskey flask out of his hip pocket and unscrewed the lid.

'Sam can I have some?'

'A mouthful, Billy. Just enough to fill a cavity in a tooth. You know how rammy you get on a little whiskey.'

'All right, Sam. I'll hunt the biggest cavity I can find.'

'I don't mean your belly,' Sam said, tilting the bottle to his lips. He took a long drink and rinsed it around in his mouth before swallowing it. He wiped his mouth on his sleeve and passed the bottle to the others.

'Pass Bunk by,' he said, pulling out his penknife and scraping the dirt under his nails. 'I don't want a man with a scab on his mouth sucking on my bottle.'

Bunk ground his heel in the mud, then looked up at the sky, watching the chicken hawks drift in big circles overhead. He glanced secretly at the others out of the corner of his eye. Carp had the bottle now and as he lifted it to his lips, Bunk saw muddy thumbprints smeared around the neck of it. His fingers moved up to his mouth and brushed away the flies buzzing there.

Suddenly the pipe began to vibrate and the men straightened up, tense and waiting. Ruby passed the bottle to Billy. Billy looked around at the men and they were staring at the pipe, so he took a long pull on the bottle, choking a little, then walked over and gave the bottle back to Sam. Sam held the bottle up in the sunlight, squinting one eye and making a peeved clucking noise in his throat as he measured the whiskey.

In the pipe was the sound of rock clanking against metal, the noise of it coming at a fast clip and growing steadily louder. Sam stepped forward, screwing the lid on the bottle, then thrust it into his pocket. He put his hands on his hips, watching the pipe and running the tip of his tongue over his lips.

'It's coming,' Alex said.

''Bout time,' said Carp, striding over and standing directly in front of the pipe, legs spread.

A faint roar came out of the mouth of the pipe, along with a steady gust of stagnant air. The men were silent, bearded jaws hanging slack on sun-burned faces, and intense, narrowed eyes hypnotized by the dark mouth of the pipe. The roar increased and the entire length of the pipe hummed and shook as though trying to free itself from the earth. There was the slosh and suck of water, and the blast of air pushing from the opening increased in pressure, flattening Carp's clothes against his body. His hat blew off but he didn't move and stood rooted there, his arms folded tightly over his chest.

'It's cool!' he shouted. 'Damned cool! But what a stink! Whew!'

'Get back, Carp! It's coming! It's coming' Billy cried, hopping up and down behind the men. 'It'll cut you to pieces! Drown you, Carp!'

Carp leapt aside. The men scattered. Billy started to run, but tripped and fell, sprawling face flat on the ground. Sam and Bunk ran back and each grabbed one of his arms and pulled him away from the pipe.

The black water pounded out like an explosion, shooting straight out, slapping the earth hard and driving up a wall of mud and rock before it, flattening the earth and pocketing it deeper with ton after ton of water.

The men stood at a distance watching. Billy had his back turned on the flood and was rubbing his skinned elbow. Above the roar of the water they could hear the shrill whistle of the dredge-boat and looking, saw a cloud of black smoke billowing from the boat's stack. After a few minutes the whistle stopped blowing and gradually the column of water slackened, growing shorter until only a narrow steady gush spilled from the lip of the pipe.

The men dove forward, splashing kneehigh in the muck. Each bent down low, his bare arms slopping and stirring through the mud. As a man found a piece of pigiron or junk, he tossed it to dry ground, shouting, 'Mine!' and went on dipping for more. Sam and Alex worked close together, several times bumping into each other. They each grabbed onto a piece at the same time. They glared at each other for an instant, then the mud rippled between their struggling arms as each tried to pull the object away from the other.

'It's mine! I found it first!' Sam shouted in his face, clenching his teeth and gripping the object tightly beneath the surface.

'No, mine! My hand touched first!'

'Liar! You're poking in my territory!'

'Your territory! Mine, you mean!'

'Let go!'

'I won't! I grabbed first. It's mine!'

'The hell you say. You drop that end. This piece belongs to me.'

'Fight for it, boys!' Ruby yelled, quickly glancing over his shoulder, then bending down and slurping through the mud again.

'Drop yours. It's my prize. I touched first!' Sam bellowed.

'Touched first, hell!'

'Let go!'

'You let go!'

They began to tug hard on the object, pulling it half way out of the mud. Sam gave a strong jerk and the object slipped from their hands, sliding back into the mud with a silent plop. Their arms splashed down in the mire as each fought to get hold of it again, their arms deep to the elbows and their hands feeling and thrashing blindly. Sam plunged in to his shoulders and found an edge of the object.

'Damn you, Alex, I'm warning you. I got it for certain this time.'

Alex crouched in the mud.

'I got my end too, goddamn you. I ain't letting you cheat me.'

'Nobody's cheating. You're the goddamn cheater. You always was a cheat, Alex. Everybody knows that.'

Alex let his end of the object drop. Sam pitched forward under the weight and he dropped his end, the object disappearing under the surface. He made a grab for it and Alex reached out and gave him a shove on the shoulder. He slowly placed his hands on his hips, scowling at Sam.

'You say that again,' he said quietly.

Sam glared at him, breathless, his mouth hanging open, his face blood red and sweating.

'You're a cheat!' he shouted, straining forward. 'Everybody knows it.'

Bunk and Ruby and Carp swung around and stared at

the two men. Billy went on splashing around in the mud, beating his arms through it and snatching up hunks of slimy pigiron.

'Once more,' Alex said, wading closer. 'Just tell me that once more.'

'Once is enough,' Sam said, inching backward and looking awkwardly away. He stumbled and caught his balance, then lifted his head and stared straight at Alex. 'I don't have to call you a cheat three times to let you know it.'

Alex stopped, gritting his teeth, and eyed Sam up and down. Then, swinging his arm back as far as it would go, he shot it forward, slamming Sam's jaw with all his strength. Sam groaned and his eyes rolled up in his head as he toppled backward in the pool of muck. Alex snatched him around the throat before he went under and dragged him to dry ground. Sam struggled to get free as Alex swung back his fist again. Sam's lips were quivering and he peeled at the mud on his cheeks as he stared into Alex's face. Alex held him by the shirt buttons, like a limp thing, his lower lip jutting and snarling, holding his arm back, when Sam suddenly wrenched loose and bounded away, falling and dragging himself through the dust. He stopped a few yards away and looking back at Alex, dug a rock out of the ground and held it clenched in his hand.

'Come one step more, Alex, I'm warning you,' he choked.

'You wanta throw rocks?' jeered Alex. He glanced quickly around, spotted Billy's mound of pigiron and snatched a crude metal flange, still wet and muddy, from the heap. He came at Sam with the flange held tight in his fist, the jagged end out.

'I'm warning you,' Sam gasped, dragging himself away from Alex. 'I'm warning you.'

Alex stood over him.

'Get up.'

Sam struggled to his feet, slowly raising the rock in one hand as he lifted himself. He had pulled himself up into a stooped position, the rock held high over his head, when Alex shouted, 'Me, cheat! You nogood bastard!' and walloped Sam's head with the metal flange, ripping a chunk of the skull away. Sam crumpled in a heap and lay still. The rock had flown from his hand and landed a few feet away, raising a cloud of dust where it struck the earth. The men stood in the mudhole staring, their arms hanging loose at their sides. Billy gaped, one arm pressed across his belly and the fingers of his other hand stuffed in his mouth. Alex turned his back on them and still holding the bloody flange in one hand, stared down sullenly at his muddy boots.

'Me, cheat!' he gasped.

Billy floundered out of the mud, kicking his legs high. He started to run toward Alex but stopped a few feet from him and began rubbing his hands up and down his thighs. He bit his lip and jerked his head back, to where the men were standing. He tried to call to them but could not raise his voice. The three men glanced uneasily at each other, then waded slowly out of the water. When they got on dry ground, each stamped his boots vigorously, knocking off the mud. Bunk stamped the longest and finally he stopped and the three stood, hands in pockets, uncomfortably looking at Alex and then at the dead man and back at Alex.

'What're you going to do, Alex?' Billy whispered.

Alex did not answer but remained standing with his back to them.

'You didn't have to do that, Alex,' Carp said. 'You didn't have to go that far.'

'Sam didn't mean it,' Bunk said. 'He was out of his head.'

'He was afraid of you, Alex.'

There was silence. Billy lurched forward, his body loose and stooped, his mouth open. He was staring wide-eyed across the land.

'What's the matter, Billy?'

Alex swung around.

'He's in a temper,' he said. 'Billy, come out of it. Don't do that. I'll take you home in my car.'

Billy's throat worked rapidly, his adam's apple bobbing up and down. His tongue fluttered noiselessly over his dry lips. He lifted a hand and pointed in the distance.

'More of your tricks?' Carp snapped. 'More of your tricks? Whatta you see?'

Billy's arm was trembling, his body shook from head to foot.

'Them men in black!' he sputtered. 'They're coming this way with leather belts in their hands.'

The men shielded their eyes and stared off hard in the distance. There was the broad expanse of land running unbroken the length of the horizon, ash-white in the heat, and empty.

'There's nothing out there but mud –'

Alex turned away, passing a hand over his face. He pulled his hat low over his eyes.

'Give him some water, Christ, somebody –'

'They're passing against the sky,' Billy said thickly, his eyes dull and listless. A dribble of saliva ran down his chin. 'They dropped the straps. The casket's gray.'

'Shut up, Billy!' snapped Carp angrily. 'This ain't no time for that kind of nonsense.'

'But where're they going? Where're they gonna bury the casket here? The mud's too hard for digging. I'd better go tell them. They'd better go take that casket some place else.'

He took a few steps forward and stopped, pressing his knuckles into his eyes. 'Where're they going?' he said softly.

Carp sprang to him and spun him around, grabbing him tight by the shoulders.

'Softhead! Softhead!' he screamed in his face.

'Don't hurt me, for godsake, don't –'

Carp shook him violently.

'Shut up! Shut up!'

'Let him alone,' Alex said. 'He's sick. Let him alone.'

'Carrying on with your tricks after what's happened,' Carp sneered.

He gave Billy a shove, pushing him away, and turning on his heel, strode angrily back to the others. Billy tottered a moment, lifted his hand to his face, his eyes rolling wildly in his head, then suddenly pitched forward, diving flat on the ground close to Alex and lay there kicking his legs and muttering and growling, his knuckles digging frantically into the earth. Alex leapt back as Billy's arm shot out, his hand clamping tightly around Alex's ankle. He continued to squirm and writhe on his belly and beat the other fist in the dust.

'It's a clamp of steel!' Alex cried. 'Bust his fingers loose! He's stopping the blood in my foot! He'll snap the bone!'

None of the men made a move. Beads of sweat stood out on Alex's brow, his eyes darted from one silent face to the other, then down at the hand squeezing his ankle in a death grip.

'Are you going to stand there like dummies?' he cried. 'He's breaking my leg!'

The men were silent, staring with fascination at the thin figure rolling in the dust.

Alex glanced at the metal flange that he still held in one hand. He looked at the men then quickly bent down and whacked Billy's fist again and again with the bloody end of the flange. Billy held on tight. Alex beat harder until the white, tense knuckles were slashed raw. He kicked his leg back and the hand fell away, striking the earth, the fingers uncoiling in a pool of blood and dust. Billy lay still, on his side, the arm flung over his head.

'Damn fool!' Alex gasped. 'Damn fool, you!'

He tossed the flange as far as he could throw it.

'You oughtn't to done that,' Ruby said. 'That's evidence.'

'Evidence?'

Alex stared at him.

'You know what I mean.'

Alex glanced quickly at the dead man, then turned hastily away, breathing heavily. He pulled out the piece of flannel and mopped his face.

'I guess I'll go in my car now,' he said, stuffing the rag back in his pocket. 'I guess I'll drop Billy off at his house first.'

He watched the faces of the men, then stared at the ground, putting his hands awkwardly in his pockets.

'You'll know where to find me.'

He lifted Billy in his arms and carried him over to the chevvy. Reaching under with one hand, he opened the door and set Billy on the seat. He slammed the door and crossed around to the other side, got in and started the motor. The men watched as the car jolted slowly away. Billy sat unconscious, his head bumping and rolling from side to side on the dirty green felt of the backrest. Alex sat stiff and erect at the wheel, his eyes unblinking and staring straight out the windshield. As he turned the car north, Billy's head swerved off the seat and banged against the window sash. It rested there, one cheek bumping against the metal, his eyes closed and his mouth open and twisted to one side of his face.

The chevvy moved off in a straight line over the land and raised a slow steady cloud of dust behind it. The men watched until the cloud of dust hid the chevvy, then turned and each looked for an instant at the dead body sprawled in front of the mouth of the pipe. The blood was drying and hardening in a brown crust where the piece of skull was ripped away. Flies crawled black in the wound.

Bunk clapped his hand over his mouth, then vomited in the mud. He looked up, embarrassed, wiping the puke from his mouth with the back of his hand.

The others moved over to where the sacks and the carts were.

'We can't let him lie here like this,' Bunk said.

'You can't touch the body,' Carp said, shoving the metal around and arranging it in the wagon. 'They always tell you that.'

'We got to go into town and tell the police,' Ruby said. 'That's all we can do.'

'Well, oughtn't we to cover him?' Bunk said, glancing over his shoulder at the dead man. He shuddered and stared down at the earth. 'It gags me. I mean, God, look at him.'

Ruby and Carp were silent. They looked uneasily at each other.

'What can we do?' Ruby said.

'Dump the junk out of one of the sacks,' Bunk said. 'That's the least we can do. Keep the flies and sun off his head.'

'Whose sack?'

'It don't matter. You or Ruby empty your sack. I'll carry your load in my wagon.'

Ruby and Carp gazed silently at each other, then looked away, each scuffing a foot in the dust.

'I'll keep the junk separate. I won't mix it with mine or try to cheat you,' Bunk said. 'My God.'

'Well, I'll do it,' Ruby said. He pulled up the mouth of his burlap bag and dragged it over to Bunk's pushcart.

'Give a hand here, Carp.'

Carp came over and together they emptied the bag of junk into the cart.

'Now bring the sack here,' Bunk said.

'I'll pitch it to you.'

'Well, all right. Pitch it.'

Ruby wadded the bag into a ball and tossed it to Bunk. It fell a few feet from Bunk and Bunk walked over and picked it up and carried it to the mouth of the pipe. He unwadded it and turning his back on the dead man, gave the bag a couple of smart snaps, shaking it out. He moved his head to one side, not looking as he prepared to spread the bag over the dead man, but he stopped and first leaned down to shoo the flies from the wound. The flies scattered, buzzing furiously. As soon as he lifted his hand away the flies once more infested the bloody cavity. He swiped at them again and again with his hand, but only a few flew off.

'Hustle it up, Bunk. You want to look at the thing all day?' Carp called.

'Come on, Bunk. Else we'll leave without you.'

Bunk did not answer. Suddenly he darted his finger into the wound and worked it around and around in it, scraping away the wall of flies. The flies flew off in an angry swarm. He pulled the finger away and wiped it on the seat of his dungarees. Quickly he spread the burlap over the upper part of the body. He stared at a ragged hole showing a bit of the dead man's throat through the cloth. His hands moved swiftly over the ground, scooping in four small stones. He laid a stone on each of the four corners of the bag, then stood up and hurried over to where the men were waiting.

'What do you want to be so neat for?' Carp said. 'He's dead ain't he?'

Bunk did not say anything but went to his pushcart. He laid a hand on each handle and tried to lift it, but the cart was too heavy.

'Carp, give a hand here. Ruby, you pull Billy's wagon.'

Carp took hold of one of the handles and Bunk took the other. Together they lifted the cart and pushed it along. Ruby trudged behind, pulling the wagon of orange crates, his bag of junk sitting on top of the pile. They moved off in the direction of town, Bunk and Carp, struggling with the cart over the ruts. Their footsteps sent up little balls of dust.

As they moved off over the land, the chicken hawks swooped in lower and smaller circles until they were flapping in tight rings just over the spot where the dead man lay, his long legs sticking out from the bottom of the burlap covering. The birds flew around and around, descending still lower in fluttering narrow loops until their wings brushed the burlap cloth. The air was filled with their harsh, agitated cries. When the men disappeared over the horizon, one of the hawks hurtled down and with a noisy flapping of its wings, alighted on the mouth of the pipe. One by one the hawks darted from the flock and dropped to the earth where they strutted in small circles, several bristling their feathers and crying sharply to one another, as they reeled and turned, hopping closer to the body of the dead man.

Hubert Selby, Jr

Double Feature

There was no tangible reason for feeling so great (unless you believe in astrology, but he didn/t and wasn/t aware of the positions of the constellations or the fullness of the moon); nor was it entirely due to it being Friday with two workless days ahead and 3 leisurely nights ... though this, along with the warm weather of early summer were partially responsible; but he wasn/t attempting to define the reasons for this feeling. It was just there. That/s enough. You don/t plan it, you just enjoy it; relax and float along with it and laugh. Yeah, that/s the secret, and as long as you control it you/ve got it made, but try to drag it by the arm and you/ll kill it ...

No, he/d play it cool. Just go up to the avenue and meet Chubby and maybe go to a show and then CHARLIE/S and listen to the group blow – have a few beers – and ... who knows? When you feel like this you don/t have to go around looking for kicks.

He walked up 69th street, smiling, to 4th avenue and met Chubby in front of the pool room. Whattah yasay Chub, poking his arm and dancing on his toes, sparring. What/s with you Harry, been eatin happy pills, laughing and waving his left in Harry/s face. Yeah. Anybody inside? No. A couple of the guys are in Phil/s talkin about the game this afternoon. I bet Phil/s havin a ball. The Giants really clobbered the Dodgers today. A ball? He/s been roarin since the game ended. Yeah, I bet.

They laughed and Chubby took out a pack of cigarettes, put one in his mouth and held the match until Harry had gotten one out of his pack and lighted it. Whattah yafeel like doin tonight Chub? I don/t know. Kindda early to do anything now.

Feel like takin in a show? I don/t know. What/s playin? There/s a musical at the Bay Ridge. I saw the comminattractions last week. It looked pretty good. O yeah, a couple of the guys saw it and said it was great. Jimmy went ape in one scene. A redhead does a real wild dance. Sounds good. How about takin it in? OK.

They left the avenue and walked down 69th street, crossing to the shady side, to 3rd avenue. Whose going to be at CHARLIE'S tonight? I/m not sure. I met Mitch, the bass player, a little while ago and he said Buck Clayton might sit in tonight. No kiddin? Should be a good session then. Should be. He/s usually pretty cool. He said that kid who blew trombone last week might be there too. Great. He lets it get away from him sometimes, like he/s tryin to find somethin, but when he doesn/t go too far out he/s good. He should be real great someday. Remember that solo he took on A Small Hotel? Yeah. Man! he did some fine stuff on that. Never went crazy but blew it cool, real cool. He went way out on How High the Moon though. Yeah, he lost control of his horn on that one; Willie was poundin out the chords like crazy tryin to help him back. He/s good though. I hope he shows up tonight I/d like to dig him and Clayton together. I guess he will. He probably gets kicks from playin with good boys like that. Yeah, I guess he does.

They turned left on 3rd avenue and walked toward the movie. A block from the movie Chubby suggested they stop in for a beer first. They went into the bar on the corner, had 2 beers and a bag of peanuts, then left and continued toward the movie. A few minutes later Harry grabbed Chubby by the arm and suggested they bring a little something to drink with them. You know, just a pint of wine. For kicks. Chubby smiled, shrugged his shoulders. Why not?

They were both laughing as they bought the wine and a package of paper cups. We have to play it cool man. We don/t want to look like winos. Chubby put the bottle in his hip pocket and walked in front of Harry so he could make sure it was hidden by his jacket.

The nearer they got to the box office the weirder going to the movies with a bottle of wine seemed. Even a little exciting. They tried to stiffen their faces in a natural expression and Chubby stood to one side as Harry bought the tickets, then walked behind him through the lobby, looking away as the man took their tickets. They climbed the stairs to the balcony two at a time before relaxing ; then started looking for seats.

They found two empty seats on the aisle in the last row and sat quietly for a few moments. Then Harry told Chubby to open the package of cups. He started ripping the cellophane off slowly, the ripping sounding louder and louder. He stopped for a second then ripped the remaining cellophane off at once and sat back and waited a moment before handing the bottle to Harry. He took the bottle from Chubby and immediately bent behind the seat in front as Chubby looked around, both of them laughing. Harry finally opened the bottle and Chubby passed two cups to him and he filled them ; recapped the bottle and put it under his seat ; then sat up. They forced their shoulders down, looked at the screen and sipped their drinks.

Most of the people in the audience were laughing and commenting to each other, but Harry and Chubby laughed as quietly as possible, keeping their comments to a whisper. When their cups were empty Harry ducked behind the seat again, taking fewer precautions, and refilled them. When he filled the cups for the third time the only precaution he took was not to spill any wine. They sat holding their cups loosely, resting them on the seat between their legs ; lifting them while still watching the screen and drinking ; leaning over towards each other to whisper a comment as a seminaked woman walked across the wide panoramic screen ... and laughing. Finishing the 3rd cup they were relaxed and laughing as loudly as the others, but with less provocation. Occasionally laughing while drinking and wine would be spluttered and dribbled down their chins. The woman continued walking and they sat laughing, choking, coughing, trying not to make too much noise and not to spill too much wine ...

When Harry poured the last of the wine he put the bottle back with a clink and he and Chubby toasted each other and slowly sipped the last of the wine. When their cups were empty they dropped them to the floor and sat for a few minutes smoking, watching the movie and giggling. Then Chubby said he was getting thirsty. Yeah, me too. How about another bottle. Why not. Think they/ll letya back in. Sure. I/ll tellem I want somethin in my car. Hey, how about gettin somethin ta nibble on? You know, some popcorn or chips. Maybe you/d like some ordurves already.

Harry laughed, then half closed his eyes after Chubby left and stared at the beam of light from the projector, watching the vague smoke drift towards it and then brighten, whirl and float through the ray ... drifting deeper into his mood. He wasn/t drunk, though he was a little lightheaded, as was Chubby, from drinking the wine rapidly in the warm theater, but he had a fine glow and was just relaxed enough not to think or be concerned with just how relaxed he was. He was going to laugh and have one hellofagoodtime. There was no danger of killing the mood either by losing it or dragging it. He just drifted between the light, the smoke, the screen, one of the girls at work, CHARLIE'S, Clayton and the trombonist ... but mainly sinking further and further into his contentment, his mind laughing (forcing a silly grin of introspection), knowing this was going to be a good night, a good weekend. Not crazy wild. Just a lot of laughs ...

As Harry drifted, unconscious of place or time, the people sitting near him (who had overheard their conversation and knew where Chubby had gone) and enjoyed watching them trying to appear nonchalant as they sipped wine, wondered why Chubby had been gone so long and if he would get back in the theater with the bottle or if they would see him being escorted up the aisle by the manager or a cop, or perhaps they would hear him yelling from outside, when Chubby appeared beside Harry, sat down and took 2 bottles from his pockets and handed them to him. Thought I/d get an extra one. You know, just in case.

Harry laughed and took the bottles, put one under the seat, opened the other and filled a cup. While he was pouring

Chubby took a full loaf hero sandwich from under his jacket. Harry didn/t notice it, being too busy opening the bottle and pouring the wine, so it was just a blur seen from the side of his eye. When he turned to give Chubby his drink, Chubby was holding the sandwich horizontally, nibbling at the liverwurst hanging over the sides, humming clair de lune and waving his fingers like a harmonica player. The others around them were nudging each other and laughing, some tapping those in front of them and pointing to Chubby as he played the hero sand- wich and Harry staring at him, holding a cup of wine. The laughter and craning of necks increased until almost that en- tire section of the balcony was ignoring the screen and watch- ing the playing of the sandwich. Chubby turned to Harry and rolled his eyes and fluttered his lids, still fanning the sandwich and moving his shoulders to the music. Harry, his hand holding the cup of wine still extended toward Chubby, stared, chuckled, then laughed, the wine spilling over his hand and dripping to Chubby/s pants ; his hand slowly falling and the cup tilting until the wine poured out in a steady stream and splashed on their feet ; their laughter growing louder, people turning in their seats, looking and laughing as Harry laughed and Chubby laughed, still playing the hero sandwich (his laughter, muffled by the sandwich, sounding weird), slowly bending over, sinking further down and almost about to double into a ball and roll down the stairs with a steady thump bump, thump bump, still laughing and playing the hero sandwich, when Harry dropped the cup, plop, fell on Chubby/s shoulder and put his arms around him forcing the sandwich from his mouth, burying his face and laughter in Chubby/s jacket.

They remained embraced until their laughter stopped, not from determination but exhaustion ; then parted and sat back in their seats with a series of soft sighs. Slowly the attention of the others returned to the screen and the two sat, silent (ex- cept for an occasional involuntary snort), wanting and not wanting to look at each other, sitting slightly angled from each other (the sandwich resting on Chubby/s lap) ; covering their faces with their hands . . .

Harry breathed deeply and without looking at Chubby told him to put that damn thing away. Chubby mumbled something, put the sandwich up his sleeve, said it/s ok now, and they turned slowly in their seats until they were once more facing the screen. Harry reached under the seat for the bottle and filled 2 cups, handed one to Chubby, still without speaking; speaking to each other only after emptying their cups and refilling them. The hollowness created by their laughter was filled by the wine and as the warmth of relaxation increased they leaned towards each other and once more were whispering comments and laughing.

They drank more rapidly (the bottle being replaced with a clink), their heads barely apart, their elbows on the arm rest between their seats; lifting their drinking arms and tilting their heads back – each a reflection of the other. And, as they drank their whispering, giggling and laughter grew louder, yet still not boisterous or annoying; in fact amusing.

From making comments upon the action on the screen they progressed to prediction and then to direction: urging the girl shy male star to kiss her, she wont bite ... tittering, laughing, reaching for the bottle (clink), watching the wine being poured into the cup (plop, plop, plop), putting the bottle back (clink) – whatzamatta with that guy? is he nutsor something? If I had a broad like that runnin afta me I/d – swaying, wine sloshing in the cups, laughing, swallowing, bubbling, choking, wine splashing on their noses, dribbling down their chins, dark spots blotted by pants and shirts – reaching (clink), only a few drops left, watching the last drop plop into the cup still one left (clink); two empties; good show, eh Chubb? cups refilled (getting soft and soggy, dented, don/t squeeze too tight, please don/t squeeza the banana – held by the bottom in the palm of the hand); where/s the otha ones – all gone – no more haha – no (clink) more (bottle resting on his lap) – come fill me with the old familiar juice – HUH, HUH – she slinks, semidressed toward him; hair over the side of her face; hips liquid; rubs his cheeks then pushes her hands thru his hair, down his neck and back; sways in front of him, all virtues and charm (almost all) displayed; the voice throaty, begging ... he asks her what she wants – ooooo whattza matta? yacraze? HAHAHA – He/d betta go ta Denmark – HUHHUH (cups squashed and dropped to the floor, the bottle passed back and forth), drinking in large gulps, small drops trickling down their chins and adams apples – she forces him back onto a couch, bends over him, gives him the look and kisses him ... he kicks and waves his arms – I toldja they was all fruit in Hollywood – the struggling stopped; soft music – don/t fight it, enjoy it HA HA HA – holding the bottle up; not much left: get somemore – oooo please don/t squeeza the banana; only a drink left; save me some; a gulp, ahh here – rubbing his mouth with the back of his hand, empty bottle passed back (clink) – no more; all gone; three dead soldiers – HUHHUHHUH – hey daddy, I wahn ice cream. Shaddup an drink yabeer, HEHEHE, that guy/s nuts – HUHHUHHUH; I can/t HAHAHA – what/z he HEH-HEHHEH – the screen wavering and blurred; images tumbling about – HAHHEHHUHHOHOHEHHUHHAHOO...

Please be quiet sir. You/re disturbing the others. The usher finished his prescribed speech and duty and was turning to walk away when Chubby suddenly jumped up, whipped out his hero sandwich and started fencing with him – Un Guard!!! He brandished the sandwich in front of the usher/s face; parried thrusts; stepped aside as a lunging sword just missed his chest; parried again and with perfect execution and grace watched another thrust pass; then stooping low, left knee bent and right leg extended behind, he parried the last lunge and thrust home. TOUCHE!!! piercing the usher, mortally, a little to the left of his second brass button. Chubby watched him slump to the floor, proud of his victory, yet with some regret at having killed so noble an adversary.... The sandwich bent slightly with the thrust and a piece of liverwurst fell on the usher/s shoe. He stared at it for a moment (all he had intended to do was deliver his speech and leave and now he was standing in front of a drunk waving a hero sandwich and there was liverwurst on his shoe) until his head was forced up by the tip of Chubby/s sword. Harry stood up and tried to speak in a high falsetto, but phlegm stuck in his throat causing his words to sound gargled. My HERGGO! then he roared, leaned on Chubby/s shoulder; Chubby roared, the sandwich hanging from his hand, the liverwurst dropping to the rug. Harry tripped over the bottles as he pushed Chubby out into the aisle, and they bounced clinkingly down the step.

Harry/s eyes were tearing and he bounced off the banister as he went down the stairs, Chubby behind him. They reached the first landing and turned to continue, half bent with laughter, stumbling, falling ... Chubby raised himself to his knees, holding his stomach, whining hysterically, saliva dribbling from his mouth – Harry felt sand under his nails, pulled himself up, heard a thump and continued stumbling down the staircase; banged through the doors (turning to look for Chubby expecting to see him roll down the stairs, ass and head; ass and head; ass and head), then careened out to the street. His momentum carried him to the corner where he leaned against the fender of a car, laughing ... just laughing ... not trying to stop or continue, not wondering where Chubby was; not thinking about the fencing scene or CHARLIE'S and the group or how he felt; not conscious of the saliva dripping down his chin; not even thinking of having another drink; just laughing ...

Then there were shadows, voices ... then people. That/s the other one. OK buddy, comeon. A policeman grabbed his arm and they followed the usher and the manager back into the theater, hurried through the lobby and into the manager/s office. Chubby was sitting on a stool in the corner, another policeman in front of him, smoking and still smiling. You/re sure it was these two? O yes sir. They/re the ones. I/m sure. I don/t know which one turned over the cigarette urn, but I/m absolutely certain they/re the ones. You see I heard a dis – OK, OK. Thanks. You can go now.

The usher backed out of the office and the cop walked between Chubby and Harry, rubbed the knuckles of his right hand with the palm of his left and asked what – in – the – hell they thought this was, a gymnasium or something? annoyed at being called and at Chubby/s stupid grin (looking insolent to him), but wanting to make an impression on the manager, knowing he never forgot a favor. He stepped in front of Chubby and slapped the cigarette from his mouth. His aim wasn/t perfect and in knocking it out he burned his hand. He grunted, held his hand for a second and when he looked back to Chubby he had the same stupid grin on his face. He grabbed him by the lapels of his jacket, slammed his head against the wall, slapped him a half dozen times, then shoved him into the chair.

Harry watched, not unseeingly, but uncomprehendingly, still incapable of forcing his mind to work. Somewhere there was a vague remembrance of a sound but the only thing definite was laughter, that/s all, laughter. He was leaning against the car, laughing. That wasn/t a memory. That must be what he/s doing now and all this is something else. What was wrong? That was Chubby. He recognized him. He/s still laughing; and it looks like wine trickling down his chin. There/s nothing wrong. We/re both laughing ... He started to take a step towards Chubby, but the other cop poked him, hard, in the stomach with his nightstick. Go ahead you sonofabitch. Start something. Just start something tough guy.

Harry instinctively clutched his stomach, confused and still unable to understand what had and was happening. The cop turned back to Chubby and told him to give them his identification. Chubby handed him his wallet and the cop slapped him on the chest with it and told him he wanted his identification, not his wallet. Who do you think you/re trying to buy off? He grabbed the draft card from Chubby/s hand. 19. Another one of those punks who thinks he/s a big brave man because he has a draft card. Can/t you think of anything better to do than sit in a movie drinking cheap wine and damaging property? The cop growled in the accustomed manner, no longer deliberate, but habitual, and stood in front of Chubby, glaring at him as he did everyone else in the same position, expecting the face to be lowered and some sort of apology murmured at which he would yell for him to speak up and when it had been repeated he would curse him, tell him he/s lucky that he/s not going to lock him up and then tell him to get the hell home – yet hoping, looking at the still smirking face, that he would give him some sort of wisecrack and afford him an excuse to slap his face again. Chubby/s first attempt at speech was incoherent and slobbering. What? It washn/t sheep. He didn/t take time to enjoy the fulfillment of his wish, but swung immediately, knocking him over the chair and to the floor. Chubby gradually sat up, his head hanging and rolling. The cop turned to Harry and asked him how old he was? Perhaps he didn/t understand the question, or perhaps it just got jumbled in his mind. He didn/t know (nor would he remember later), but for some reason (if there was a reason) he said 76. (Still a hint of laughter inside that needed only to hear someone else laughing or for Chubby to turn and smile to revive it, and then they/d be back outside (I don/t think we/re there now) and could start over again, from the car, or go to CHARLIE'S). He heard the slap, then another. Still nothing, but vaguely aware that now the laughter was gone, yet still not understanding. He thought he remembered a sound. Or was that imagined?

Whattah yawant us to do with/em Mark? The manager, upset at the slapping, looking at them on the floor, thinking of the reports that would have to be made, the explanations and reassurances given if they were arrested – Nothing Jim. They didn/t break the urn. No real damage done. Just kick them out and forget about it.

They were quickly jerked to their feet, taken out to the street and walked to the corner. They told Chubby to go up to 4th avenue and Harry down to Ridge Blvd, and if you give anybody any more trouble we/ll split your skulls open.

Harry turned when he reached Ridge Blvd and staggered over to the school steps and sat down. He rested his head on his hands then lifted his head and looked at the small smear of blood on the palm of his hand. He couldn/t taste it, but it must be real. But it didn/t make any sort of sense. There wasn/t any fight. Just laughing. We weren/t even drunk ... How? There wasn/t even a beginning to go back to. I don/t even know what time it is ...

He rubbed his face, the back of his neck, and looked at the

tree a few feet in front of him and tried to find the sky. The red and amber traffic lights on the corner were blinking.

He fumbled thru his pockets looking for a cigarette but couldn/t find any. O shit! He stared at the sidewalk for a moment, then slowly stood up, holding on to the fence, and started walking home ...

A Penny For Your Thoughts

He didnt think of her breasts at first. He simply noticed how attractive she was. And too it was extremely unusual to see a young girl without makeup. She probably was no more than 18. He was waiting for the subway after work and she was standing among the crowd with a few friends. She wore a black coat and black kerchief. Her skin appeared very white and her eyes were dark and sparkled. He kept glancing at her. He stood near them on the train and was surprised when they got off at his stop. He walked slowly and tried to listen to their conversation, but the only thing he heard distinctively was her name: Marie. A block from the station she said goodbye to her friends and turned along the avenue and he continued home.

The next morning he saw her on the station waiting in the same spot where he usually waited for the train. He stood near her again and tried to determine the color of her eyes, but he couldnt (at least not without staring) and was amazed again at her lack of makeup and how beautiful she was. Not a glamorous beauty, but a quieter, deeper and natural beauty ... yet an exciting beauty! He tried not to be too conspicuous and turned his head away from her as much as possible and watched her from the side of his eye. They got off at DeKalb Avenue and he walked slowly up the stairs behind her and her girl friends hoping he might see a bit more of her leg, but she held her coat tightly around her and with straining and falling behind as she climbed the stairs he was still only able to see the calf of her leg. It was very attractive though. Even with those flat slipper-type shoes on. She turned at the exit and walked off in a different direction than the one he had to take so he stood for a moment watching her until the traffic light turned green and she and the rest of the crowd rushed across the street. He didnt see her that night on the platform. He looked around and had almost convinced himself that he should wait for another train, one that would be less crowded, but there was a large open area just inside the train that was large enough for 3 or 4 people and the train remained there for a few seconds with the doors open and he felt guilty and conspicuous standing there when there was all that room and suppose someone he knew should ask him what he was waiting for or what if there should be some kind of a police investigation for some reason, what could he say? and there are witnesses to prove there was room in the train—he stepped forward quickly just before the door closed.

After dinner that night he stretched out on the couch and consciously tried to conjure up an image of Marie. All he could see was a vague outline, his wifes voice making it impossible to concrete the image. He stopped trying and got up from the couch and went out to the kitchen and helped his wife with the dishes, his wife surprised, but saying nothing. About 10 oclock he said he was going to bed as he was bushed from the extra work in the office and was relieved when his wife said, no, she wouldnt come to bed now, but would finish the ironing first. He lay in the bed and thought of Marie. He thought of her dressed in a beautiful tight sheath with dark stockings, but the image continued to blur. He had never seen her with her overcoat off and without a kerchief around her head. Actually he didnt have the slightest idea of what her body looked like except what he assumed from looking at her legs and face, and she obviously wasnt fat, but he still didnt know *exactly* how she looked. How about her tits? She might be flatchested. . . . Cant really tell with an overcoat on. That wasnt possible though. She must have a nice pair. Large and firm. Sure. . . .She must. . . .

He ate breakfast just a little faster the next morning wanting to be certain to get to the station in time to get the train she always took, yet he didnt want to be obvious and perhaps have his wife ask questions. Marie was there on the platform and he got on the train with her and her friends and rode to work trying not to stare, but listening to her voice and watching from the side of his eye and hoping her coat would fall open when she reached up to adjust her kerchief, but it didnt. While still watching her coat and hoping, he looked at her face and noticed the small blemishes on the right cheek, but it didnt bother him. It really didnt affect her attractiveness (beauty). And anyway it was just a small spot. Probably temporary and nothing that would scar her skin. He did wish though that she didnt go to work with her hair set every morning, though she does look much prettier than Alice with her hair set. Maybe in the warmer weather she doesnt, but thats a long way off. Actually it was only the front she kept set. The back hung loose. It was long, wavy and very pretty. If she put something on it to make it blacker and shinier it would really be something, but it was very nice the way it was. Really nicer than Alices, but that was something else. He was just curious about this girl. She must be 10 years younger than he. It/s just that shes unusually attractive. Good Lord, cant a guy look at a girl and find her attractive without something being made of it. Alice certainly wouldnt mind. . . . It was their stop and they got off and he turned waiting once more for the traffic light to change then went to work.

They rode the same train home that evening, but it was still impossible to determine their size. It must be the way she stood and held the coat around her that prevented his seeing. He stared at her intently hoping for an opening in the coat and didnt notice the front of her hair and it wasnt until later, when he was telling his wife about her, that he realized he hadnt looked to see what her hair looked like without the pins. When he mentioned the girl he saw on the platform to Alice he tried to do so with an *in passing* attitude, but he wanted to be certain he didnt overdo it. He was certain she didnt think twice about it as the conversation drifted to a natural tangent after he mentioned how attractive this girl was and it was a shame she didnt put her make up on properly instead of smearing it all over. You know how these kids do it, and then they were talking about high school or something and he felt much better. Now when he thought about Marie he wouldnt feel guilty. And anyway, why should he? Theres nothing wrong with that.

He saw her every-day, twice, for the next 4 days and he watched her the entire time from the moment he saw her on the platform until they parted at 3rd avenue ... yet still he didnt see them. And this was January. So long before spring and lighter coats that would be allowed to fall open and so much longer to summer when only dresses and blouses were worn—and he stared and stared.... *Hello. I hope you dont think Im too forward, but Ive seen you everyday for quite some time now and I am sure you have noticed that I have been staring at you. I suppose it is a little unusual to just speak to a girl on the subway like this, but it is just that you are so attractive*—a train came in and they got in the rush and he tried to reach her but couldnt get through the crowd or continue his mental conversation; and then the train stopped at their stop and he got off and stayed a few feet behind and watched her and tried to go back to where they were on the platform and he was telling her how beautiful she is and she was about to smile (shyly perhaps) and tell him he was right, that she had noticed him looking at her and he would be able to understand (from her tone and attitude) that she was flattered—but he couldnt get back there and whenever he tried to isolate just them, alone, he suddenly tried to remember the color of Alices eyes. He tried pushing the thought from his mind, then tried shoving it away, but his hand felt no resistance and it just flowed around it like an amoeba, an enormous amoeba; he tried gripping it, kicking it, dragging it, but it just floated and flowed. He even closed his eyes for a moment as he stood on a corner waiting for the light to change, but the thought wouldnt move so he stopped trying to keep it out of his mind and consciously thought of his wifes eyes and it slowly disappeared; then he tried to make his wifes eyes bigger and bigger so he could see what color they were, but it failed. It was impossible. But they must be blue. Shes so fair. They must be. They have to be. Blue Blue BLUE!!! Still he couldnt believe they were. But that doesnt mean anything. You know yourself how you forget things like that. But Maries eyes are brown. A deep dark brown. And they sparkle. Dont they? But thats different. How can you doubt I love Alive? I really know the color of her eyes. Its just trying to force it like this. Thats why I cant remember....

Hello sweetheart. He bent and kissed Alices hair (of course theyre green. Its ridiculous. I knew) and asked her whats for supper.

He went to bed early again, giving some excuse about not feeling well, smoked a few cigarettes and thought of her. He wondered what would happen if he weren't married, not that Im not happy after 4 years of marriage or anything, you know, but I just wonder. Academically so to speak. Id have a car of course – but I wouldnt be living here and would never have seen her anyway – have to start again. I live here – he put the cigarette out and rolled over on his side dismissing all the meaningless things that were ruining his thoughts. He was single and he had an apartment of his own near Fort Hamilton with a nice radio-phonograph console, indirect lighting and even a small bar (Id have the money) and he knew her from work and they went out and stopped at his apartment for a nightcap – maybe they went to the Casino or some place on the Island – and he put on the radio and played soft music and when he gave her her drink he held her hand and kissed her and he slowly undressed her and she was bashful and flushed slightly and he kissed her and reassured her and told her he loved her and she grabbed him and kissed him hard and he led her, gently, to the bedroom and they lay down and he felt her stocking under his fingertips and he played with her stocking for a few moments then the smoothness of her thigh and she turned, sighing, and the train came in and he held up his hand and pushed at it and tried to punch the hundreds of motormen, but it ran right through the room and through the bed and he held her and whispered, still trying to push the train, and all those damn people were walking by . . . o goddamn it! he slammed the door! slammed it again and again and again, running back to her and kissing her and slamming the door again : I love you, I LOVE YOU, frantically trying to unbutton her blouse and a large trailer truck went by and he struggled to get her blouse off and Alice asked him if he felt alright. Youre turning and tossing so much. Are you sure you feel alright honey? and he turned and mumbled something and lit another cigarette and she continued to talk as she undressed and he nodded and mumbled and smoked, hoping he hadnt blurted out something, and anyway its not like it was real and he didnt love Alice . . . o well. . . . But its not really wrong. This is not at all like those guys who have girl friends on the side. This is something different. Ive never been untrue to Alice. I even told Alice about her—yes sweetheart I will. Did you lock the door—she reached up and pulled the cord and the room was dark again and he put out his cigarette and tried to keep his mind blank, not wanting to fall asleep thinking about her and perhaps say something in his sleep. . . . He couldnt get her out of his mind and kept waking with a start, listening for something and when he awoke about 3 or 4 he was so excited he tried waking Alice, but she didnt awaken when he touched her lightly so he stopped trying, afraid he might say something with his excitement and sleepiness, so he just lit another cigarette and thought about work or something . . . anything, until he felt calmer, then put out the cigarette and finally fell asleep.

He was exhausted in the morning and he told Alice to call the office and tell them he wouldnt be in, that he wasnt feeling well. He told her he thought he might be getting the virus and thought it better to take it easy for a day or two than to take a chance on getting sick. He stayed in bed all that day and the next, which was Friday, and just lolled around most of the weekend. On Monday he said he felt better and Alice suggested he wait an hour before going to work in order to avoid the rush hour, but he said that was ridiculous. Theres no need for any such thing. I can go at the regular time. Alice was stunned by his brisk manner and stared for a moment, then continued setting the table when he lowered his eyes.

He rushed to the station and didnt slow down until he saw Marie at the end of the platform. It seemed as if weeks had passed since he stood on the platform next to her and he was certain she had been aware of his long absence and probably wanted to talk to him. There certainly wouldnt be any harm in speaking to her—the train came in and it was unusually crowded and he pushed his way in and Marie and her girl friends just did get in the door hitting her girl friend on the shoulder, and they screeched slightly at the difficulty and he smiled and almost spoke, but caught himself—yes, yes of course. Alices eyes are green and her hair is cut in sortofa d.a. More people got on at the next stop and he was jambed against her side and he thought it would be easy to simply let his arm rub against her breast or he could lower his hand and the next time there was a push his hand would rub against her ass and he looked and looked but he couldn't see. Incredible, but he still couldnt see. Still didnt know if she had a big pair or not. Not that that mattered either. Just a case of curiosity. No, no. Nothing like that. Dont be silly. I wouldnt really do it. Would be easy enough though. Especially in a crowd like this. It really would be an accident. But if I could just see how big they are I mean. . . .

There seemed to be no way he could find out. Would he have to wait until spring or even summer? It was ridiculous. Why in the name of christ didnt she stop clutching her coat? It isnt that cold. She could let the goddamn thing open in the subway. It was warm enough. Or if it was a tight one, a fitted coat, then at least there would be an outline to see and allowing for the thickness of the coat you would have some idea of just how big her tits are. He didnt expect them to be gigantic (theres nothing wrong with Alices. Theyre not too small. Ive said that before. I dont really mind. That has nothing to do with it) just large and firm. She seemed to have nice wide hips. If she has a slim waist and a big pair . . . all white and smooth and when she lays on her back theyd probably fall to the side slightly and her nipples will probably be rosy

and the trains and people and trucks kept forcing him away
from her and they parted at Third Avenue each night and he
thought about it and again, 4, 5 may be more times he thought
of waking Alice in the middle of the night, but he smoked,
turned on his side and his thighs cramped and his stomach
twinged and he kept looking and looking and they parted at
the corner each morning after the light changed and she
clutched that goddamn coat and he looked and looked and he
couldnt see and he didnt sleep and he was always keyedup and
tensed and Alice knew it was the job and she didnt want to let
him know she was upset worrying about him so she tried to
ignore it and talked to him during mealtimes so he would relax enough to eat (he really wasnt eating much lately and lost
weight) and she smiled and tried to be casual when asking him
about work and his evasiveness confirmed her thoughts about
the job fraying his nerves and still he looked and looked and
Alice worried and he continued to lose weight and she thought of
suggesting a visit to the doctor, but was still fearful of seeming
alarmed and didnt want to upset him so after supper she suggested a movie. Its Friday and theres a good double feature
playing tonight. One of them is supposed to be very funny and
you know how hard youve been working lately honey. Yeah,
I guess I have, not knowing what she was talking about, but
afraid to ask. It might relax you to sit in a movie. He nodded
and they went to the movie and he sat watching and smoking
and then he started chuckling, then laughing and he relaxed in
his seat and stretched out his legs and Alice leaned against him
and held his arm and glanced at him occasionally, and they
laughed.

And then Marie was standing in the aisle, in front of
him, looking up at the rear of the balcony and then seeing her
friends she smiled and walked past him, up the aisle. At first he
was a little surprised, but of course there was no reason why
she shouldnt go to this movie. Then, of course, when she
started to open her coat he tried to see her tits, but couldnt. All
he could determine was that she was wearing a black sweater.
And her hair wasnt set and looked nice in the darkness of the

movie. Then she was gone. Sitting somewhere behind him. He wondered if she noticed him. Dont imagine she saw the ring on Alices hand. Might be alright if she knew. Married men are more attractive to some women.

He concentrated on the movie, laughing and whispering to Alice and then Marie walked by with another girl. He really didnt notice it was she until she had passed and was on her way down the stairs. He continued watching the movie but, watched the staircase from the side of his eye. He felt his muscles tensing and consciously tried to relax. He didnt want Alice to get any ideas. He fought his muscles. Watched the movie. The staircase. 15 maybe 20 minutes. He thought perhaps she had left. But of course that was silly. She just got here. And anyway, he did notice that she wasnt wearing her coat. He waited. And waited. Finally he heard their voices and they came to the top of the staircase, stood for a moment then walked past him and up the aisle. He looked, but the railing in front of him was on a level with her chest as she walked by and he was too amazed to try to look as they walked past him up the aisle. It was fantastic. Unbelievable. All he wanted to do was see how big her goddamn tits were and this railing is in the way. How inthehell . . .

Maybe theyll come by again. If we were sitting back a row. How could I ask Alice to move. I insisted on sitting here to stretch out my legs. There might be something I could say. Better not. She might think it strange. Theyll come by again and when they go up the aisle I/ll be able to see. Maybe I should tell Alice that thats the girl I told her about. She may have noticed me staring. No, I dont think so. A good kid that Alice. He looked at Alice and smiled and she smiled back and asked how he liked the show and he said good. Very good. Her smile broadened and she squeezed his arm and he waited for Marie to go by again trying to look behind him but they were all the way up and he couldnt see that far without turning completely around and looking deliberately and being obvious. He just sat, smoked, watched the movie and waited. He heard faint footsteps and voices and 3 girls passed and went down the stairs and Marie was one of them. He sat up higher in his seat and started turning his head slowly toward the aisle and adjusting his eyes testing to see how large an area he could see without moving his head too far. He reached a point where he could see more than necessary while still, apparently, looking at the screen. He froze himself in the position and waited. His neck muscles started to stiffen and his eyes burned, but he didnt move. He closed his eyes briefly then opened them and waited. When she came by he wouldnt have to move and he would see. . . .

Then Alice tugged at his arm and pulled him toward her slightly. Would you go down and get me a pack of cigarettes honey. Im all out. He glared for a moment (after spending all that time getting ready and she might come any minute) and almost yelled at her to get her own damn cigarettes. You should have made sure you had enough before we got here, but then he thought perhaps they arent in the Ladies Room and are downstairs at the candy counter. He mumbled a quick ok and dashed down the stairs to the candystand. They were standing around a soda machine talking. He bought the cigarettes then stood to one side and looked at them. She did have a nice pair. Not gigantic, but just right. And her waist was beautifully slim and when she turned he could see that they were firm, really firm, and not just held up with a brassiere. Of course they might hang a little without a brassiere. Thats only natural. But they wouldnt sag. And her mouth was lovely. O, I bet she/d bite. Her thighs must be so smooth. . . .

The girls dropped their cups in the bucket and started walking toward him. He turned and climbed the stairs two at a time and dropped back in his seat and handed the cigarettes to his wife, trying to breathe normally, and fixed his eyes on the proper spot. He sat and waited and when they climbed the stairs to their seats he watched them bounce – just slightly – and she passed so close he could smell the soap she had washed with and he could reach out and pat her ass. He stretched out and lighted a cigarette and struggled with a conductor, a train and an usher that kept coming through the room but he kept closing doors and pulling down shades and she was naked on the bed and he kissed her and he turned in his seat and sat up and crossed his legs and was motionless and thoughtless for just a second then put his arm around Alice and rubbed his nose against her ear. She looked at him and smiled, kissed his cheek and snuggled closer to him and rubbed his arm, singing inside at seeing him relaxed and smiling and loving the way he caressed her cheek. She lifted his hand to her lips and kissed his fingertips. He put his arm around her, kissed her neck and said lets go home. But we havent seen the other picture silly. I know hon, but lets go anyway. I want to talk to you. He caressed her neck with the tips of his fingers and looked into her eyes. Ah Harry, dont. Please dont. You know I cant do anything now.

He dropped his hands and stared at her for a moment then slammed back into his seat. O for christs sake! Whats wrong Harry? Nothings wrong, goddamn it. Nothing. Why dont you just leave me alone. . . .

Douglas Woolf

The Flyman

When the moving men had shoved and strapped the last piece, the last slippery convenience, inside the moving van, George Nader looked about him with very little sense of loss, for everything that remained, the flypaper, the swatters, and he believed the turtle bowl, was his. Had Zoe been divorcing him and taking along her legal property as dowry to another man, the division of goods would have been exactly this, except of course that she would then have been leaving George himself behind to enjoy the pure, seeming inconvenience of the house. He would never know what time it was: only sit at the backdoor and watch the cactus shadows on the sand outside, perhaps noting whether the sun or the moon was moving them. With the hours thus confused there would be no prompt, rude guests to demand his silent presence in the livingroom; their polished mahogany cage would be gone, not to mention their electricity. He would look without commitment at the mirrorless walls, for the loathsome electric razor would be buzzing the fuzz on some other cheek or the stubble underneath Zoe's arms. He would sleep, night or day, in the built-in bathtub, and survive on grapefruit and oranges and the neighbors' eggs. Delighted with such pictures, smiling upon Zoe's swollen rear, he took up a handy swatter and brandished it enchantingly until the men returned.

What he liked about the moving men was their pride in being watched. They spoke in low rough voices, cursing only humorously when his flypaper caught them up, pausing occasionally in their work to compliment Zoe upon this piece or that but once outside tossing her furniture quite insultingly among them as though it were simply so much stuff which they alone knew the real value of. At the very first, when they had stood in the livingroom wondering where to begin, he had said, 'Take everything with faces, or legs,' and had settled in a chair to watch how nicely it worked out that way, with the exception of a few planters of ivy and the pasteboard boxes of odds and ends. until they had taken the chair itself from under him. 'Easy now,' he had standing said, and when they smiled expectantly as though hoping he had found some failure in their work: 'Everything but me, that is.' And now he stood grinning as they shoved respectfully past Zoe at the door, where she hoped her presence would urge them to use a little more care, less skill, in their wild slippery sprint to the van, but as the van door cracked shut he sobered his face for her turn to him.

'Looks different, doesn't it?' he quickly said, not in sympathy or even sincerity but only wanting to take the words from her pursing mouth. 'Bleak?'

'It does, it does,' she agreed, forced to it, but hastily regained herself: 'We filled two-thirds of a van, you know.'

'Big baby too,' he shot.

'It was,' said Zoe.

He looked fiercely away from her fuzzy head, to the grey, permanent shadow of the departed television-radio. What had she expected of him once, that he had not given her? He supposed that at first it had been children, although as a struggling, wild-eyed veteran his reasons had been entirely economic, plausible, and she had agreed with him. Only in time, as he progressed, had the question become less economic than eugenic, and she had agreed again. How could she not. For it had grown increasingly clear that no child of his could have the common view, or chance. Today the question was no longer asked, yet he felt that secretly, in whatever depths she had, Zoe would have welcomed the pleasures of an abortion, the living proof that in fact she could create. Few men would help her prove it now, he and time had taken care of that. So they had settled on an easier enmity, as less harrowing, more mentionable, her loss of the housewife's sweet dependence which he had so easily usurped for himself. Deprived of her empty days, Zoe had filled her nights with appliances. Looked at in this way the unwieldy procession which he had just witnessed could not be said to betoken Zoe's unfathered children so much as a bitter, accurate accounting of Zoe's paychecks, and this cynical view of it made him able to turn to her again. 'Wait until we get up north,' Zoe said.

'Oh, wait.' He followed her zigzag course toward the kitchen, even he finding it oddly difficult to avoid the flypaper strips with the furniture no longer there to inhibit him, and he fancied he heard soft curses among Zoe's fat breaths. Watching her unwind from a gummy strip, he felt himself struck by a change in her appearance, the first he could recall in years. It was as though the moving men had carted off not only her movables but her very makeup itself, that pink, almost livid glaze with which she regularly hid from him and all the world the face he had loved twelve, maybe fifteen years before. And seeing in this abrupt way how dry and sucked of life she was, finally justifying her endeavor to look like anyone else but Zoe, he felt a sudden terror of time and reached his hand to her. 'Zoe.'

Zoe took his hand.

'I'm sorry, Zoe.'

She patted it, and now he watched her puffy fingers drape gummed paper along the soft, freckled flesh of his outstretched arm until it clung to the hairs there securely enough for her to draw free of it. Looking up from dead and drying flies, he saw her bright black eyes twinkle with something between defiance and disgust. 'Why this?'

'Because,' she said. 'It's yours, isn't it?'

'Ah.' His hand shot sidewise for a buzzing fly, caught it effortlessly in mid-flight and tossed it stunned to the floor for his ready foot to quash. There had been a time when Zoe would have watched this exhibition with genuine admiration, but today she turned sharply off as though he had belched or gassed the place. Well, as the doctor said, some men hate Mexicans and Republicans, some beat their wives.

'George, promise you'll have it all cleared out when I get back?'

'Back?'

'From the market, George.'

He suddenly smiled, at the picture of them following that two-thirds van of conveniences through eighteen hundred miles of ice and snow and stopping from time to time to eat cold canned goods beside the road. Certainly he would not build a fire, and he could not imagine heat from a fire of Zoe's. This was not a new thought, but he added to it now the one that Zoe would surely have packed the can opener away in the kitchen appliance box, and he spoke hurriedly lest she too might think of it. 'You hurry right along,' he said. 'I'll take care of everything.'

'Well . . .' He followed once more as she zagged through the kitchen, the front room, the hall, somehow this time escaping entanglement but turning finally at the front door to seek her purse. With all the furniture gone, there was nowhere for Zoe to hunt. Even at best things had been, as he thought, fuzzy around their home. For Zoe's talents were almost purely operative, or rather her affinities: she was a superlative driver of automobiles, unhampered by any comprehension of what made them run; she could twirl painful clarity from television sets, just so long as their extension cords and socket plugs were good; and of course over both their lives loomed that cryptically initialed machine, monstrously dialed, with which she made airplane parts whose names and places she did not know. Otherwise there was that fuzziness, that flapping, searching, beseeching, wasted fuss which made him grind his teeth and wince. But we do not hate people, he recalled, not even for enduring us, and grinned a wistful grin at Zoe before turning his attention to his papered arm. 'Look on the mantelpiece,' he said, and imagining Zoe's bleak glare of thanks waved his swatter graciously.

He felt her departure in much the same way that he felt the flypaper tear free of his hair and flesh, as a paradox of pain, relief. He tensed to the clattering porch, to the car's whamming doors, to the pitiable whine of a young motor overtaxed, and finally to the smothering cloud of dust that seeped through the fine-meshed screens, yet he was glad. When he turned it was almost as though Zoe had really left, scattering her own ashes behind her over the neighborhood; in twenty minutes, he knew, she would be back to stir them up again.

Meanwhile he did not mind too much what he had to do. It was the thought alone that had almost paralyzed him, when the furniture and Zoe had still been there, the thought of tearing down all his ingenious, tactically flawless stations without the possibility or necessity of ever replacing them. But now in the empty house his defenses hung like so much random paper, forlornly grouped, disorganized. What he did, quickly, was start at the front door and work his way in as nearly a straight line as possible along the south wall, yanking flypapers as he came to them and draping them in careless yet attractive disarray over the handle of the swatter which he still held. Then quickly back along the other wall and crisscross here and there about the room. When he had filled his swatter he reached for another, presently a third, but half a fourth finished the livingroom. The bedroom and kitchen yielded two swattersful apiece, one each for the bathroom, pantry, hall. Back in the livingroom he stuck his entire collection upended in the empty turtle bowl. Gathering the remaining, unused swatters, he added them one by one with flourishes to his bouquet, stood back to pass on it.

He was glad to have found some use for the turtle bowl. It had not worked at all. Despite weeks of enthusiastic experimentation, under the most favorable conditions he could devise, George had never known a turtle to catch a fly. Place twelve flies with two hungry turtles over night in a covered bowl, and in the morning twelve ummolested flies emerge. Put syrup on a turtle's nose, a fly may eat his sweets in peace. It did not work! Only if you dropped a fly into a turtle's water would it partake, and George refused to offer such sacrifices, dead or alive, simply that a turtle might stuff himself. He donated his turtles to the neighborhood and turned his attention to new pursuits. Chronologically the gyrotraps had come next after the turtle failure, and it was these he would attend to as soon as he had disposed of the mess in the turtle bowl.

Most weekends he did not go outside, except very briefly at lizard rotation times, for these were George Ingersoll's days at home. Not that he disliked the other George, he simply did not like the sense of driving him indoors. There had been a time when their weekends had been quite otherwise, they had become almost more than neighbors, finding several dependable interests in common such as their handicaps (mostly physical for the other George), their memories of beautiful, terrible northern winters which in past years they had somehow both survived, and more particularly their memory of North Africa and its big, blood-sucking flies which a man could look down upon, whether feeding on his own sores or on a corpse of whatever nationality, and say this is Evil, it isn't the Jerries after all. They had of course also had their common dismay at finding themselves banished by doctors to another Africa, a New World Africa, their sense of loneliness and exile in this wasted land and their exasperated fascination with its flora, fauna and insect life. Weekends they had fought the desert together side by side in their backyards, tearing up its cactus and tumbleweed, coupling their two hoses to lay its dust, attacking its blackwidows , scorpions, flies with lethal insecticides, all the while offering bitter, gasping encouragement to one another across the fence. But soon it had become clear that their intensities were not the same, that one could be satisfied with a mere surface tidiness that the other fiercely disdained. George Ingersoll spent more and more time resting on his canvas chairs, now looking contentedly at his swept backyard, now at George, his occasional shouted encouragement grown amused, polite. A certain restrain had grown between them as nowadays it so easily did (people no longer visited the Naders, they came in small explorative groups instead) and it ended with their reverting to a neighborly distrustfulness. George understood. The other still had the so-called job, was employable, while George himself had long ago lost the benign effects of the six-day purge. He understood, yet it surely hurt him that his neighbor no longer showed sympathy for what he was trying to do, neither took time to enquire about his experiments nor looked at them. Thus he was surprised, or a little angry, to find George on this last day lingering outside, hanging on the fence above the rubbish cans which they had found it easiest to continue sharing stealthily. 'Morning George ... Ah morning George.' They performed this ceremony solemnly, each glancing sidewise to see if the other still smiled at it. Neither did, though with George Ingersoll it was hard to say, for pain and the desert sun had long ago combined to draw back the brittle skin around his mouth into a permanent grimace. Whenever George looked up at him he was unpleasantly aware of his own soft juiciness. 'Hello, George,' he said again, and falsely coughed. 'How have you been?'

'Oh, fine, fine,' George Ingersoll said, and now he did appear to smile at a ghastly joke. 'And you?'

George also smiled. 'Haven't seen you around much, George,' he said, at the last minute muffling the 'for a year or two.'

'Yes, been busy inside,' was said. There was a pause, while George tugged at the stubborn garbage lid. 'Well, Zoe's transfer came through at last?'

'Yes, it came through,' George said, banging the lid with his free fist.

'Give it one on the side,' George Ingersoll advised, and George gave it a brutal one. 'No, one on the side of the *top*,' and George belabored it everywhere. He put down the turtle bowl, grasped the lid handle with both big hands and lifted the entire barrel off the ground, shaking it furiously from side to side. But we do not take out our anger on inanimate objects, and cursing he let the whole thing drop. The lid bounced off. 'Ah,' he said, swatters clattering in.

'I wouldn't mind having that bowl, if you're done with it.'

George passed the bowl over his shoulder, over the fence. 'It's no good,' he said, wiping his hands of it.

'Looks like just the thing for Miriam's fish.'

'Oh fish – I never did try fish.'

George Ingersoll patted the turtle bowl. 'I don't suppose you'll need any of this, up north?'

'No, none of it.'

Still patting George Ingersoll glanced at his neighbor's yard, then shamefully away again. 'What about your lizards, George?'

George, who had stooped for the garbage lid, straightened quickly to the sidewise face. 'You'd like them, George?'

'No no no, just curious.'

'Ah.' George came down hard, jamming the lid back on for George.

'I don't suppose they'd live through the winter there, even if you needed them?'

George shook his head, and it was almost as though he were shivering.

George Ingersoll too looked cold. 'George, what does the doctor say?'

'The doctor? Not much – it might be good for me.' Probably what the doctor had said to Zoe was that anything, even painful death, could be considered a benefice. But the doctor was no medical man, George had long ago passed them. 'They say there's work up there, you know.'

'I certainly hope so, George.' When they looked briefly at one another now, it was almost in their old way, with common memories. George Ingersoll put out his hand. 'I certainly hope the change of climate is good for you.'

'Well, thanks, George,' he said, taking the knotty hand reluctantly in his own soft freckled one. What he would like to have known before he took it was whether his eyes blurred at the sympathy of a friend or at the certain euphemisms of a hypocrite.

'We'll certainly miss you, George.'

'Oh, well now,' George said, and it almost blinded him, his dubious sentiment. He yanked free his hand to wheel away. '*Well* now, George.'

'I certainly ...' Fortunately some of the Ingersoll children were fighting now, and hugging the turtle bowl George moved to disentangle them. 'I'll see you, George.'

Oh oh oh, will you now, George thought, stalking quickly along the fence to the garage, the shop. He emptied the wheel-barrow of rusty tools and dragged it wickedly to the shop's locked door. He had the key, had it at all times on a string looped around his belt. Quickly inside, he swung the door on howling Ingersolls. Two years ago he had papered the ceiling and walls with flypaper (no paste, no waste, the flies make their own design) but now in the broken light of the one narrow window he noted how the ceiling curled and peeled, the walls writhed disgustingly, their glue had dried. The place smelled greyly of dust and wings, nor did the 200-watt ceiling lamp do much to clear the atmosphere. As it turned out, he would not have to redecorate.

His inventions lay everywhere, on the benches and shelves, and on the floor. These were mostly the gyrotraps, tiny razor-blade fans which he had connected in series to a motor sal-vaged from a Lionel train. Each fan was designed to fit snuggly into a No. 2 can liberally coated with marmalade. (These had worked, although their blades required daily honing and from time to time their shafts would gum.) Then too there was the syrup door: a delicate device which the weight of three in-verted flies could trip, slamming them against a red brick wall. (There were only three of these, for he had been unable to make them react to the weight of a single fly, and it had tor-mented him to think how many strays escaped.) There were several examples of the Infallible Fly Bath, simply a solution of molasses and hydrochloric acid (which he made himself by combining sulphuric acid with common table salt) in small glass tubs. These had worked very satisfactorily indeed, until neighbors began to understand what was happening to the noses of their cats. So it did not bother him very much to dump everything in a box and wheel it out for the garbage man. He did at the last minute leave one example of each behind, on the slim chance that some future scientist might find them a start-ing point, a useful groundwork for further exploration in the field. Not that this possibility greatly moved him either, for in his heart he knew that with the lizards he had come as close to a final answer to the problem as any man could, or would.

Here at last was what did hurt, having to gather his beer bottles now at the very time when he had finally perfected a formula for their rotation, a formula based on the observed frequency of flies at a given location at a given hour of a given day, as modified by such known variables as temperature, cloud covering, wind, humidity, and taking into account too such intangibles as the probable traumatic effects upon flies of his increasingly devastating war against their kind. Yet if the rotation formula was a marvel of deviousness, the trap itself was almost casual in its simplicity. Squeeze a small, vaselined lizard into an empty beer bottle, feed him just enough flies to prevent his escape ; now coat the bottle mouth with almost anything at all, and wait. (No electricity, no mechanical parts, after a few days at large a lizard may be used again.) He gathered the bottles quickly but gently, arranging them in neat tiers in the wheelbarrow, and he wheeled them smoothly out over the desert to a rock he knew. There he cracked each of the forty-eight bottles with deft little taps, being careful that the lizards were not cut by the broken glass. Even at that, and despite his practice of selecting his lizards for healthiness, one lizard had succumbed. Impossible to say how many flies he had taken first, although in death he did look well satisfied. George buried him. Now he stood for awhile watching the others staggering over the desert, their bloated bodies unwieldy on their stiff short legs. Facing his wheelbarrow toward the house, he steered with care among his glutted friends. Ahead Zoe's dust was in the air, and Zoe herself waited at the kitchen door for him. 'You did a nice job,' she said.

'Thanks, Zoe.'

'All ready now?'

Silently he looked about his experimental yard, a desert once again. He raised his eyes to an evilly buzzing fly, too high for him, and he did not move or speak until it came back again. He did not snare it at once but watched it cautiously circle his head, allowing it this last time the appearance of teasing him. When at last it settled on a freckled arm, he picked it off and held it out to view. 'When you are, Zoe.'

'Oh, why don't you get in the car,' she said, and she followed him.

'You've remembered everything?'

'Yes.'

It almost seemed she had. The canned goods lay boxed in the front seat, a shiny new opener visible. He knew their bags had been in the trunk for several days, and climbing into the car, into the back, he could smell the sweet insecticide. Despite the noonday temperature, all windows were tightly shut. He smiled at how narrowly Zoe opened the driver's door, how nearly flat she squeezed, how quickly she slammed once she was in.

'Mind if I open a window, Zoe?'

'Please, let's not.'

'It's hot in here.'

'It's hot everywhere.'

'It smells.'

'Let's wait until we're underway, at least,' as the motor howled.

'Ah.' Outside, George Ingersoll was leading his wife forward to see them off, and Zoe stopped the car to point the friendly neighbors out to George. All arms were raised; with the windows up the pantomimic mouths could have said anything, oh-oh-oh perhaps. Now the saving children must have yelled for the Ingersolls turned their wagging heads and ran. Releasing brakes, Zoe gaily blotted out the farewell scene.

'Now?'

'Wait until we're on the highways, George.'

So he sat waiting, his eyes closed to the dusty light, his breath almost closed off too, until he felt the car spring free of sand and heard the tires take up their gleeful howl on a highway paved with kitten fur. 'Now, Zoe?'

'Oh, *wait*.'

But he leaned forward anyway, not toward the window but

toward the driver's seat, his hand going up. He might have slapped down on her then and there, had Zoe not caught the movement in her overhead looking glass. He hung there rigidly.

'Did you see one, George?'

'No.'

'Well, please remember our frontseat rule.'

'Sorry, Zoe.' Leaning back again, tilting his head to rest, he continued to look at Zoe. But from the lower edges of his sight he could see his great short-sleeved spotty arms, folded across his chest, and from the fuzzy edges of his consciousness could hear his big hands slapping quietly.

'What now?' Zoe wanted to know.

'Don't worry, Zoe.' He watched her shaking head. 'You're happy, Zoe.'

'Well?'

'No, I'm glad for you,' he said. His hands were working harder now, moving rhythmically and conscientiously from freckle to freckle over his juicy arms, as Zoe turned round to him. Slap slap slap, he answered her, 'I'm really glad for you.'

'The temperature in St Paul last night was two below.'

'Oh, it was? Below?'

'Snow is probably falling now.'

'It *is*?'

In her looking glass she smiled at him. 'They say the winters are nine months long.'

'That's all right,' he said, and also smiled, for he would have lots to do.

The Cat

Claude walked on until he came to the largest neon sign in the city, red and purple, in the form of a cat, with his name on it. He turned in past the boys never too busy to deal him a smile, past the rows of ten dollar bills under the wipers, stopping by the little English roadster that said 'Guess my price and you can have me' just long enough to scribble the answer (£798 /6) and sign it not for himself but for Franklin Storrs, in care of the office. At the little white sales shack the folding chairs were tipped back against the front wall but unoccupied, the door generously open to nothing.

In the shack he paused before the door marked private long enough to place his facial muscles under rigid control, but even as he entered he knew he could not maintain it. For they, in their smiles and their shiny suits and their suntans and their generous stances, borrowing the illusion of unusual size from the sheer bulk of them together in this low-ceilinged room, swung as one to overwhelm him, like a team of all-American fatties welcoming a fan come to help them celebrate the start of the season. The centermost of them lumbered forward to press Claude's hand firmly (all their muscle was in their right hands) but the rest of the line, not qu-ite making it, leaned and/ or sat where they smiled, waving or lifting their highball glasses in greeting. To one side, on the bench, lay their cheer-leader Carlotta, flanked by some of the biggest backs and ends in the game. And over at the bar their coach, affectionately known as the Cat, squatted on a stool discussing the new plays with his co-captains. Crossing the red carpet Claude could almost believe he passed among buddies, not a few of whom had never seen him before, which was what finally made him lose all control. 'Hi,' he said, grinning, and the Cat himself sprang from his stool waving him forward.

'Come on in, pal.'

He was still the prettiest one of them all, even surrounded by the younger generation he looked big, if no longer tremendous, his shiny coat seemed to fit him more honestly than theirs for having been worn longer, and his long pants were full but not bursting with babyfat. He had the further advantage that his smile wrinkles were burnt indelibly into his face, so that at those odd moments when he was not using them they served as deep furrows of character. Topping all this was a sterling crown of tight curls, hand-wrought, highly polished, worn casu-ally. As a boy Claude had feared that given all these graces, plus his talent for meeting only the big men in the whirl and knowing them by name without knowing them, the Cat would someday be President, but he need not have worried. The Cat was too fond of his milk to be truly carnivorous, and the Cat knew it. That was why he spent his nights in the clubhouse with the boys, plotting his cunning plays, and flexing his smile muscles. That was why he leaned a little too far over the bar to offer his son what he could, a strong right hand and a jocular 'Pal, let me pour you a saucer.'

Seated beside the co-captains, his belly softly O-O-O-ing, Claude watched the Cat lace a large bowl of cognac with white creme de menthe, tenderly stir it. It was the Cat's favorite drink and he served it to Claude as a matter of course, as one of the family. He had made more than enough for them both, and now he brushed around the bar to claim his share. 'Stay where you are, boys,' he said, and the co-captains vanished. Making a gymnasium for himself of their stools, the Cat hunched forward to drink. When he had had all he wanted he reached intricately through rungs for a handkerchief and, still bent over, wiped his damp lips. Now sitting up straight he tucked the handkerchief into his breast pocket, stretched one arm out full-length on the bar, the other to the back of Claude's stool. 'O.K., pal,' he said, 'tell me the latest.'

'Well...' Claude felt for his cigarettes. For an instant the Cat crouched as though expecting a slap on the nose, but he quickly thrust the cigarette between his lips with the hand from the bar, whipped out his lighter and offered flame too with that hand. 'Where did we leave off last time?' Claude asked.

The Cat was stretched out again, his head tilted slightly back and aside to look past smoke at Claude. 'How have you been, pal? Still working for that paper?'

'No.'

'What was the matter, not enough money?'

'No, that part was all right.'

'They work you too hard?'

'Not that either. We didn't get along well, to put it some way.'

'Anything serious? I could speak to someone.'

'Don't do it,' Claude said, the Cat drawing back from his voice.

'Hell, I'll cancel my ad if the bastards are that bad.'

Claude smiled. 'Let me put it another way – I don't like what they print in their paper.'

'Ah, the news,' said the Cat, the lines in his face showing very white as he looked down at the bar. 'Nobody likes it.'

'They don't print it.'

'Oh?' The Cat watched Claude uneasily now, seemed to wait for him to continue, but nothing happening he moved over to drink, suddenly bored with their game. His thirst turned out to be real. When he straightened up it was as though he had forgotten what they had been playing, or hoped Claude had forgotten. 'What are you doing now, pal?'

'Nothing right now.'

'Well then . . .'

'Well no.' It was Claude's turn to drink, not very long. He looked up to see the Cat drop the end of his cigarette carefully into the ash tray, smother it with what seemed an excessive fastidiousness, especially in view of the sudden indifference with which he turned his back to it.

'Speaking of intra-office problems, I've had a few unfortunate experiences in the matter of personnel myself recently. I don't know, these always seem to come periodically, cyclically.' Speaking, he sat forward and tense on his stools, rather wide-eyed, rolling his big words out before him too deliberately and pausing to look after them too often, as though waiting to be asked for a translation. There seemed also a new quality in his voice, a new roundness, or perhaps Claude had simply been too young or near to notice all this when they lived together. Here at the bar they smiled almost bashfully at one another for a moment. But the Cat could speak in several voices, and the one he chose now suited him better: 'I had to ditch one of the boys just tonight, a few minutes before you came in. God knows I didn't want to do it, I kept him on longer than I should have, gave him every chance in the world to make good, but what he did was sit around in here boozing all day and then go out at night and cream one of my cars. It got so he was cream- ing more cars than he sold.' Did you give him his commission on the insurance? 'Hell, there was a day when if I had an opening all I had to do was snap my fingers and twenty good boys would come running – I mean real class, real beauties – but now . . .' Now fatties? 'I don't know what's the matter with the boys nowadays, whether they're getting soft or what. I give them a nice clean job with plenty of you-know, but they don't seem to show their appreciation. They don't want to work for their honey any more, they want alimony.' Have you sent Mother her check lately? 'I don't know,' he said, frowning. 'Maybe it's me, Claude . . . Claude, did you ever look at a tree in the forest?' No, never. 'I mean a big old tree long past its prime, so old that you said to yourself, "If I had an ax with me I'd chop that tree down"?' Hardly ever. '"All that old tree is good for is casting shade and getting in the way of others"?' Let's leave it. Let's face it, Claude – I'm not getting any younger I guess you know I'll be fifty next month?' He looked expect- antly at Claude, and Claude gave him a big smile for his birthday. 'O.K., enough of this sad talk. I don't like to be pessimistic, especially with you, pal,' he said, cuffing Claude's shoulder. 'I know I've been lucky. By that I don't mean to say I haven't earned every damned thing I've got – you could say that every car out there on the lot represents a good year of my life.' Come now, how old *are* you? 'Well, six months of my life, call it. Put that way, it makes you pause and think, doesn't it?' The Cat paused, but Claude could think of nothing. 'I don't kid my- self, a man doesn't put on this much fat all by himself,' he needs plenty of mice. 'He needs Guidance. "The Lord giveth the power to get wealthy." Maybe this trouble I've been having is just the Lord's way of reminding me that nothing in this world comes easy. Maybe I've had so many good boys all the way that He sent along a few bums, or poets, to show me how bad it can be.'

'You seem to have a full, well-rounded team here tonight,' Claude said, while the Cat bent to pour from the bowl.

'Oh sure, these are good boys,' the Cat said, looking them over. He had a gadget above the bar that buzzed whenever a car door was opened in the ordinary way by the ignorant public (salesmen opened them quickly, without touching any other part of the car); each time the buzzer sounded one of the team would peel off, rest his drink on the table or bar, and slip quietly out the door combing his hair. A few minutes later he would come back smiling to himself, combing his hair, shaking his head in bemusement at what he had seen out there. He was a good boy. 'These are all good boys,' the Cat said. There were no individual stars on this team: each played his part with the minutest possible deviations from all the others, visible only to experts. Thus most spectators were bored, although it did not seem to keep them away. 'That one that just came in – Harry?' Sure, I know Harry Halfenback. 'He works down at the C of C –' chamber of conners. 'This one in the tan suit, Eddie,' Eddie Fullerback, 'is employed at First Trust –' oh, anyone can tell. 'Elwood there is studying for his real estate exam . . .' Well! 'That big one, Clay There, is a deputy sheriff,' – mind if I pass? 'A good half of these boys have other jobs during the day, come over here five-six nights a week. I guess they represent just about every field you can name.' Insurance. 'Insurance, investment, real estate, radio-television . . .' I guess that about covers it. 'Food supplements. I even had a high-school teacher this winter – a real sharp boy he was too – but he had to go back home . . .' Hell. 'Arkansas, I think. I'd say nine out of ten of these fellows,' ten out of eleven, 'have been to college or business school. But there're still a few tricks they can learn from the Cat, that's why they're here. It's a pleasure to teach boys like these. They look up to me as a father image, and I don't mind telling you I get a bang out of it. I'd be proud to have any one of these boys as my son.' Could we arrange a quick deal – say you take Harry Halfenback there, I'll take that little English job you're giving away? 'Claude,' the Cat said, 'when these boys go home tonight they'll be able to look Him right in the eye and say, "Well Lord, I'm a little bit bigger man than I was yesterday," and believe me that's one of the best feelings there is in the world.'

Claude who had been playing with his drink, found himself suicidally lapping it now, slobbering, 'Where do most of them put up, at the Y?'

'Clown, these boys are family men. I like to hire family men, and I make it a point to visit each of them with their families, in their homes. They've got the nicest little wives in the world, a real bunch of dolls, and I'd say they average already three-four kids apiece, more on the way...' Who in hell do they get to do it for them? I mean even if they found the time, wouldn't it be a strain on their muscles? These are the kind of boys that carry their kids in the back of their pants, where they can exhibit them better. These are nice boys, well-mannered, with a well-rounded recreational program that leaves them no time or energy to play around with the girls. These boys aren't layers. They aren't cocks either, they're pullets. Harry there is a capon. I suppose there must be a few breeders still around, and if so you can bet these boys know where to find them. They have their little blue books in their pockets that give them the whole picture, list price according to style, make, and year, standard equipment or fancy. You know they get their proper commission. Do they watch? Or is that what they're all grinning about, giving themselves a little twiddle with imagining the doll at home on her back, some other wild posture, getting a good pecking at this very minute? '.. family men, Claude.'

'Then why aren't they home with their families?'

'You haven't been listening to me, Claude. It takes lots of honey to raise a family these days...' No, it isn't even that, these teddy bears don't like honey as much as they think they do. They think they're supposed to like it, the way they're supposed to like women and children. They think they're supposed to act like real grizzlies, but they don't feel it. You can't blame them, they just don't have it inside them. What they have, what they love most, is their memories: how the Coach used to shout niceworkpal whenever they caught the big ball or somehow hit the little one, how Dad used to wink when they caught one of his jokes, how when they repeated them he almost died laughing, so they told them and told them – if they told one really well he might do it. They memorized all the conversations verbatim, that about the pussies and the coons, the homers and the balls, the cams and the bearings. They're still memorizing. You can see them almost anytime you're out driving, there in the slow car just ahead, the young man at the wheel, the old man talking, the young man leaning a little to the right in order to hear better, the old man pointing out the properties, the young man looking and listening earnestly, straining to catch the old man's last word, the last joke verbatim, the last bit of know-how about the deals and the properties and the honey. When he thinks he's learned all he can from the old man, he'll shove him out of the car. You watch, next time you're out driving. '. . . these are the cream, Claude.' These are the all-American fairies.

'I had supper at Claudine's tonight, Dad.'

His father was behind the bar mixing a bowl, and Claude watched how tenderly he stirred it, how exactly he placed it between them before he came back to his stools. This time he waited until he was comfortably seated and stated before he stretched his arm behind Claude. 'How is Claudine, pal?'

'She's about the same as ever.'

'I've been meaning to go over some evening,' his father said, hitching one pantleg at the knee with his free hand. 'I'd like to see more of her. I don't know what it is, maturity, senility, or what, but I find that I've been bitten by the religious bug myself lately.'

'I thought I had noticed something.'

'Don't laugh,' and Claude felt the palsie cuff on his neck. 'This isn't the mushy kind, you know me better than that. This is the straight cuff, Claude. What we do is send Bibles overseas, place Bibles in the homes that don't have them ... Are you laughing?'

Claude, over his saucer, shook his head wretchedly, to show

the Cat that he wasn't. 'Go see her,' he begged. 'She'll be pleased.'

Now the Cat took his hand from Claude's back, flicked it out of its long sleeve to look at his watch. 'Oh-oh,' he said, and bent down to drink. Quickly finishing what there was, he shook his head while wiping his lips. 'Pal,' he said, chucking him, tucking his handkerchief, 'I'm due on the air in a minute to show off a few of our specials. Why don't you take a turn on the lot while I'm gone, give yourself a chance to put on a little fat. I'll speak to Harry.' He gave Claude a last big one as he hopped off his stool.

'I won't do it,' Claude called, but the Cat was already across the room speaking to Harry, and Harry Halfenback was already nodding his head, looking sharply at Claude, and smiling generously. That settled, the Cat chucked Harry Halfenback's arm. 'Come on, Princess,' he called to the bench, and Carlotta bounced up. She was wide like the rest of them, but no man could fairly say she was too wide. The most that could be said was that she did not have much further to go before she would have to start squeezing it in and strapping it up, which she clearly did not do now. She let it hang where it was, and it did very nicely by itself. As she passed among the boys they looked her over with unconcealed envy, as though they knew she had something they didn't have but were not quite sure what it was. One thing certain, she got more exercise than they did.

The next to be noticed were her braids, they hung forward over her terrain, ignoring as much as possible her contours, like two shiny black meridianal lines demarking her longitudes as far down as the equator. It was not hard to imagine oneself spending a long lifetime on that bare island alone, with no plan or ambition, too overcome with the heat to continue on south to the pole, far less return to the continents. Nothing productive could ever be accomplished there, but there would be comfort such as few men have known, there would be torpor. The body swelled with such thoughts, the mind shrank from them, and the longing eyes traveled finally up north, to where those meridians came together at a point above a bland white area vaguely charted, with few landmarks, no doubt sparsely inhabited. Here the imagination halted.

Her mouth was positively a mouth and no more, neither ruby nor rosebud nor dormant volcano. Her eyes might have been anyone else's somewhat over-exposed. She had the ears and the nose. People said she looked like an Indian princess, and it was not hard to see her that way, Pocahontas of the jigsaw puzzle, a nighttime scene, her full skirt blending unfairly with the black of the lake and the green-black of the forest, her pebbly toes easy to find, her hands also obvious, her head, like the moon, a round piece, in this case somewhat pointed on top. Once Claude had looked forward to seeing one of her pictures on television, but by the time he thought of it again the Cat himself dared no longer to present them. It did not matter, he believed he knew pretty well how she did it. There are actresses who learn their first entrance so thoroughly that it does no good to write them new ones, which is not to say that the first was not worth writing.

'Princess, you remember your line?'

The Cat and the Princess stood at the mirror, where she now wrung her hands low down before her with such ecstasy that her braids were caught together in the plump pinch of her elbows, her eye shadows sprang up, and her mouth became suddenly a round mouth. The attitude was not subtle, but very very genial. 'Ooooh, what a big one,' she cried, and, 'Will you give it to me, Daddy?'

Grinning at the mirror, the Cat chucked her behind. 'You've been practicing.'

She curtsied, the Cat bowed to the mirror. Encircling her with an arm, boldly landing on her island, he led her onstage waving and smiling aside all offers of luck. They would not need it, they had a dumb audience. Claude, afloat on his stool through all this, had drunk more milk than he realized. He was laughing. Even so he would have poured himself another but for the sudden call of the buzzer and Harry Halfenback's quick o-k-pal grin. Landing on his feet on the carpet, he made a kind of way through the boys. They all smiled, but nobody wished him good luck as he slipped out the door without combing his hair.

He spotted his mice at once, at a green one not far from the shack, for these were country mice who went directly to whatever they liked without snuffing everything else on the way. He was seated inside with one leg outside, she standing close by clutching her pocketbook. He showed her the gearshift, which seemed to impress her. Now he showed her the radio and the bounce of the cushions, but she only muttered, for she had observed Claude's approach. The man heaved himself out, and she bent stiffly forward to brush at a spot on his shirtsleeve. Looking down at his arm he shrugged her off, looked up grinning slyly at Claude. Claude nodded. They stood facing the green car for a moment, she brushing hard at that spot again. Now she tucked her pocketbook under her arm, held the material taut with one hand while she brushed with the other. She scratched with her fingernail next. That was grease.

'How much is this one?' she asked, looking at Claude, the man looking with sly embarrassment at Claude's ear.

'Doesn't it say on the ticket?'

The man said, 'I couldn't find it there nowhere.'

They both looked inside, neither finding it there. Then they got out and walked slowly around the car together, the woman following them.

'Does that ten dollar bill come with the car?'

Nodding, Claude lifted the wiper and picked at the bill stuck to the glass with cement.

'Hey, I'd like to be here some night when it's raining,' the man said, his wife cackling at that.

Claude took them around back to show them the trunk. It was locked, so he went up front for the key. He held the trunk door for them while they peered inside.

'I don't see no spare in there,' the man said.

Claude bent to look too. He held the door up and felt on both sides, but there was no spare to be found. He stood back so the woman could look for herself.

'Maybe we better try another one,' the man suggested.

They chose another green one, and the man got inside to feel the gearshift and the bounce of the cushions. Finally he thought to glance at the ticket, his wife too looking as well as she could over his shoulder; but this time they did not ask Claude for clarification. He got the trunk key and led the way around to the back, held the door high.

'Let's try another one,' the man said.

They found a green-and-white one this time, and then another a little farther down the line, but after that they began looking at just any car they came to, Claude letting them open the doors, and opening them once more himself with both hands when he went after the trunk keys. At the end of the lot, the man turned to look back down the long row they had tilled.

'I guess we want to shop around before we decide, Mom?'

'Yes.'

The man gave Claude a friendly little smile and wave. 'We'll probably be back.'

'Pleasure to have you,' Claude said, waving farewell.

By now the entire team was out on the field hunting for mice; Claude, finding himself no longer needed, slunk around the sales shack to catch the end of the act. He arrived just in time to see the Princess muff her line, stare sullenly at each camera by turn, lift her hands in a knot to her mouth and then drop them as quickly back to her lap, fold suddenly forward so far that each braid became a shaky exclamation point to each hysterical breast. The Cat was delighted. He stood with one hand low, palm up beside a braid, gave each camera a full minute's shrug, a smile both candid and askance. They were standing so, the Cat trying to decide what attitude to assume next, the Princess no doubt getting a cramp in her back and surely a chafe up in front, when the Cat spotted Claude. 'Folks,' he said loudly, raising his hands over his head, 'boys and girls, I know you're anxious to get back to the show, see what happens in that next reel, but I beg your indulgence just long enough to introduce to you another member of the Cat family. He's talented too. Would you like to meet him? Thanks, folks. Come on, pal. Come right up here, son. Come say hello to the folks . . .'

The Princess had remained folded, but now she straightened herself to look with the Cat past the cameras for Claude, smile enthusiastically at him. 'No!' he said. He would not do it, of course, no matter what, and he shook his head fiercely at the Cat's palsie wave, his 'Come on up, pal. Come say hello.' He would not, would not do it, and he was still shaking his head as he stumbled among wires to the beckoning hand, the pleading, 'Come on up, son,' the almost humble supplication of his father's smile . . .

'That a boy. Stand right here, pal.' The Cat put his arm around Claude, which was well, for he found himself leaning dangerously toward the cameras and he dared not lean back. 'Folks, this is my youngest,' the Cat said, tipping his head to look up at Claude. He did not have to look far. 'Claude Junior is a veteran of three years in the service, eighteen months overseas, and now he's through with his college and about ready to make his way in the world. He's been out on the lot tonight getting acquainted with a few of you nice folks who've dropped by to see us. . . . Well, son,' he said, tilting to attract Claude's attention, firm his back, 'have you been doing any good tonight?'

'No.'

'No? You mean you didn't send that last party away with a new used car?'

'No.'

'Well, son, suppose you tell the Cat all about it, and maybe he can give you a few pointers. What kind of a car were they interested in?'

'A green one.'

'A green one,' the Cat said, patting Claude proudly, but showing the audience his utter stupefaction, chagrin 'Did they find a green one they liked?'

'They said they wanted to shop around first.'

'Shop around where!'

'They didn't mention.'

'Did they say they'd be back?'

'They said so.'

'Good boy,' the Cat said. 'Here's a hundred for your trouble,' he said, handing Claude a bill with his right hand and reaching around him to take it back with his left. 'You can have that when they come back.' He winked at the cameras. 'The mice always come back to Claude the Cat. Folks, you watch, the next time you see this boy he'll be wearing a suit. He already has a nice pair of shoes. Boys, give the folks a peek at those shoes,' he said to the cameramen, and the cameras dove to Claude's feet. 'You can see that this boy is starting at the bottom and working his way up – pretty soon he's going to buy him a belt to hold up those pants,' the Cat said, the cameras creeping up to stare at Claude's crotch. 'Then one day he'll get him a tie,' and the cameras prodded Claude's throat. 'No, folks, the next time you see this boy you won't hardly recognize him. Will they, son?'

The cameras glared Claude straight in the eyes. 'I hope not,' he said, closing them.

'Princess,' the Cat called to the Princess. 'Come here, Princess. How about giving this boy a little you-know for his trouble.'

The Princess went at once into handwrung ecstasy. This time she wrung so thoroughly that it was easy to picture beneath her full skirt the plump knees pinched together in exact imitation of her elbows, though of course clasping no braids. 'Oooh, what a big one!' she cried flawlessly. 'Will you give him to me, Daddy?' She rose to her toes before Claude, the Cat steadying him, and settled her round mouth over his. 'Mmmm,' she said, resting one hand on each of Claude's cheeks and drawing him down to her level, by suction. The Cat watched them a moment, and then he looked at the cameras. 'That's fine, Princess.' He tapped her on the shoulder, but shrugged reassuringly at the cameras when she did not respond. 'It's all right, folks, she's his stepmother.' He was perspiring; they were all perspiring. 'There, that'll do fine, Princess. . . . Folks, why don't you come down and get in on the party. Oow, we've got some big ones ... Princess ... Boys, turn out those lights!'

The lights did seem to blink out. When they were glaring again the Cat had his supporting players firmly in hand, one at each side, and he was bowing. Now he released them; the cameras had swung for a shot of his big red-purple sign.

'Hey, son, come here. ... Where are you going?'

'I'll see you.' Wiping his face with a sleeve he stumbled among cars like a blind mouse in a playroom.

'Hey ... Come back here, pal. I've got something for you!' The Cat was blind too, he could hear him painfully thrashing and thumping behind him. 'Son ... Stop a minute!'

He drew up against a fender and waited for the Cat to catch up with him. At first his father too leaned against the fender, panting, then he pushed himself straight, brushing his trousers, shaking his head as he peered at Claude in the gaudy dimness. 'Where the hell were you going in such a hurry?'

'Home. I'm tired.'

'No hard feelings?'

'Don't worry.'

'You could have waited a minute,' his father said, still breathing heavily. 'I wanted to give you this hundred.'

'No, I don't want it ...' It was in his shirt pocket.

'You earned it, keep it. That was the best show we've put on since we started.'

'No, I ...'

'Shut up,' his father said, tucking the bill back in Claude's shirt. 'Will I see you tomorrow?'

'That's what I came over to tell you. I'm going to Arizona.'

'Arizona!' The Cat had heard of the place. 'You got a job out there or something?'

'No.'

'What's out there then, a girl?'

He did not think his father could see his face in this shadow.

'Who is she?'

'You don't know her.'

'Hell, if that's all it is ...'

'Let's skip it.'

'Hell we can fix you up here. Your stepmother knows plenty of girls, nice ones...'

'Let's drop it.'

'Well, Arizona,' his father said, wiping his face with a handkerchief. 'How were you thinking of getting out there?'

'I was thinking of driving.'

'You're in the market for a car?' asked the Cat, tucking his handkerchief.

'I was hoping I could make one of your deliveries.'

'Ah. Well,' the Cat said, 'I hardly ever have one going to Arizona...'

They were walking toward the sales shack now. 'Anything out in that direction?'

'I don't have more than two-three going out to Arizona a year.'

'Any in that general direction?'

'Well, I might have one to Okla City...'

'What you can.'

Claude followed the Cat toward the sales shack, stopping just long enough to slip the hundred under the wiper of a green one. The Cat met him at the door with a little card in his hand. 'Ya, I've got a '59 Thunderhead going to Okla City for a lady.'

'I don't suppose she'd mind if I stopped off along the way for a few days.'

The Cat thought about this, studied the card. 'Why should she care? You'll be buying the gas,' he said finally.

'O.K. What kind of A-1 shape is this beast in?'

'You don't care, you aren't buying her.'

'Well, let's take a look.'

'She's around back,' the Cat said, handing him the key and the card. 'The red one in the corner.'

Even in the dark he had no trouble finding her. Her antennas stood very high up in front, aslant in the back, her crazy spotlights looked everywhere up at the sky and down at the ground, white and jet black was her top, and the red paint of her lowslung body was more than bright, luminous. Claude held the little card to the glow, reading it over. Then he stood off eyeing her a moment before he opened her trunk.

'O.K., pal?' the Cat called from the shack.

'I'll take her.'

The battery might have started her had there been enough gas, but the Cat had five or six of the boys roll her over to the pump for a couple of gallons, a little shove with the pickup. Now she started off like thunder and lightning, and Claude stood up on the brakes to the end of the lot while the Cat walked beside holding the doors. The boys stood along the side-lines, cheering, and Claude reached under the dashboard to give them a blast with the wolf whistle.

He braked her to a stop at the entrance, let her idle. 'What sort of lady is this Mrs Merritt?' he called, and the Cat cupped his ear.

'What?'

'What's with this Mrs Merritt?'

Shoulders up, 'I never saw her.'

'Say, did anybody ever guess the price of that one?' he called, jabbing his finger at the roadster.

'What? Oh no, not yet,' the Cat answered. 'Guy by the name of Harry Halfenback came close, but we never did find him.

'You say he only came close?'

'What?'

'How close?'

'Oh, within a few shillings,' mumbled the Cat. 'I don't remember the details.

'Would he have won it?'

'What?'

'Would you have given it to him?'

'I don't get you.'

'Would you let a man have it?'

'Hell, yes,' the Cat said. 'If we could find him.'

Waving, Claude released brakes and eased the beast out on the street to a paternal thump on the fender and a gay 'Take it easy!' He could see all the waving boys, their smiles somewhat magnified in his looking glasses, but he did not have time to give them the whistle. Ahead an old man hopped back up on the curb and stood lightly there on one foot waiting, smiling and nodding at Claude; his plump plaid bowling ball bag affording him balance. Claude did not stop for him. He gave the beast her head and she went for a caution light, loudly making it. All the leftover leaners were noticing him now, he could see them already turning to look in the block up ahead, looking in the block he was passing, and, in his magnifying glasses, several blocks back. At the next corner he came to with no stopsign or signal he headed her north. Oh, she could take corners. Climbing the steep hill past the office he had to contain her, she muttering angrily. Going down under rein she almost exploded. Two blocks from the room he pulled her off the road at a standard corner, bringing the pink-faced monkeys out of their glass house in a hurry. They pranced before her, coaxing her onto the rack. Claude remained inside for a while, until he was sure she was resting, then hopped out beside them. 'Go over her carefully,' he told them. 'She's had a hard life.'

WILLIAM S. BURROUGHS

Was born in 1914 in St Louis. After graduating from Harvard, he traveled in Europe, returned to America where he worked at various times as a private detective, an exterminator, a bartender, and at many other jobs. In recent years, he has lived mainly in Tangiers, London, and Paris, and from time to time, in homes for narcotic addicts.

Of himself, he says: 'I have learned a great deal from using junk: I have seen life measured out in eyedroppers of morphine solution. I have experienced the agonizing deprivations of junk sickness, and the pleasure of relief when junk-thirsty cells drank from the needle. Perhaps all pleasure is relief. . . . I have learned the junk equation. Junk is not, like alcohol or weed, a means to increased enjoyment of life. Junk is not a kick. It is a way of life.'[1]

BOOKS: *Junkie: Confessions of an Unredeemed Drug Addict* (1953), *Naked Lunch* (1959), *The Exterminator*, with Brion Gysin (1960), *The Soft Machine* (1961, 1966), *The Ticket That Exploded* (1962), *The Yage Letters*, with Allen Ginsberg (1963), *Nova Express* (1964).

CENSORSHIP

What i am saying has already been better said by Mr Henry Miller in his essay 'Obscenity and the Law of Reflection' – Censorship is the presumed right of governmental agencies to decide what words and images the citizen is permitted to see: that is thought control since thought consists largely of word and image – What is considered harmful and therefore censored will of course depend on the government exercising censorship – In The Middle Ages, when the church controlled censoring agencies, the emphasis was on heretical doctrines – In Communist countries censorship is close in the area of politics – In English-speaking countries the weight of censorship falls on sexual word and image as dangerous to an economic system depending on mass production and a large public of more or less uncritical consumers – In any form censorship presupposes the right of the government to decide what people will think, what thought material of word and image will be presented to their minds – I am precisely suggesting that the right to exercise such control is called in question.

The excuse usually given for censorship is the necessity to protect children, impressionable, unstable and stupid individuals – However, this impressionable being is already subjected to a daily barrage of word and image much of it deliberately calculated to arouse sexual desires without satisfying them – That's what advertising is all about as anyone on Madison Avenue will tell you, and much popular fiction falls into the same category – And he is continually subjected to word and image deliberately calculated to arouse aggressive impulses on TV and radio, in movies and comic strips – I can not see how he would be harmed by reading the work of Rabelais, Petronius, De Sade, Henry Miller, Jean Genet or my own work (unlikely that he would read these works if they were available to him being in many cases virtually illiterate).

What would happen if all censorship were removed? – Not much – Perhaps books would then be judged more on literary merit and a dull, poorly written book on sexual subjects would find few readers – As to whether people will be sexually stimulated by reading a book? – We know from Pavlov's conditioned reflex that people can be sexually stimulated by almost anything through association – I think that if censorship were removed fewer people would be so stimulated by the mere sight of four-letter words on a printed page –.

The anxiety of which censorship is the overt expression has so far prevented any scientific investigation of sexual phenomena – Few investigators have asked the question: What is sex? – and taken the necessary steps to find the answers – So far as i know the only scientific work on this subject was done by Doctor Wilhelm Reich – As a result he was expelled from a number of countries before he took refuge in America where he died in a federal prison – His experiments indicate that sex is in all likelihood an electromagnetic phenomenon, that physicists and mathematicians could discover precise formulae of sexual energy and contact leading to a physics of sexual behaviour – It would then be possible, on the basis of precise knowledge, to determine what sexual practices were healthy and what practices were not healthy with reference to function of the human organism.

The Future of the Novel

In my writing i am acting as a map maker, an explorer of psychic areas, to use the phrase of Mr Alexander Trocchi, as a cosmonaut of inner space, and i see no point in exploring areas that have already been thoroughly surveyed – A Russian scientist has said: 'We will travel not only in space but in time as well –' That is to travel in space is to travel in time – If writers are to travel in space time and explore areas opened by the space age, i think they must develop techniques quite as new and definite as the techniques of physical space travel – Certainly if writing is to have a future it must at least catch up with the past and learn to use techniques that have been used for some time past in painting, music and film – Mr Lawrence Durrell has led the way in developing a new form of writing with time and space shifts as we see events from different viewpoints and realize that so seen they are literally not the same event, and that the old concepts of time and reality are no longer valid – Brion Gysin, an American painter living in Paris, has used what he calls 'the cut up method' to place at the disposal of writers the collage used in painting for fifty years – Pages of text are cut and rearranged to form new combinations of word and image – In writing my last two novels, *Nova Express* and *The Ticket That Exploded*, i have used an extension of the cut up method i call 'the fold in method' – A page of text – my own or some one elses – is folded down the middle and placed on another page – The composite text is then read across half one text and half the other – The fold in method extends to writing the flash back used in films, enabling the writer to move backwards and forwards on his time track – For example i take page one and fold it into page one hundred – I insert the resulting composite as page ten – When the reader reads page ten he is flashing forwards in time to page one hundred and back in time to page one – The deja vu phenomena can so be produced to order – (This method is of course used in music where we are continually moved backwards and forward on the time track by repetition and rearrangements of musical themes –

In using the fold in method i edit delete and rearrange as in any other method of composition – I have frequently had the experience of writing some pages of straight narrative text which were then folded in with other pages and found that the fold ins were clearer and more comprehensible than the original texts – Perfectly clear narrative prose can be produced using the fold in method – Best results are usually obtained by placing pages dealing with similar subjects in juxtaposition –

What does any writer do but choose, edit and rearrange material at his disposal? – The fold in method gives the writer literally infinite extension of choice – Take for example a page of Rimbaud folded into a page of St John Perse – (two poets who have much in common) – From two pages an infinite number of combinations and images are possible – The method could also lead to a collaboration between writers on an unprecedented scale to produce works that were the composite effort of any number of writers living and dead – This happens in fact as soon as any writer starts using the fold in method – I have made and used fold ins from Shakespeare, Rimbaud, from newspapers, magazines, conversations and letters so that the novels i have written using this method are in fact composites of many writers –

I would like to emphasize that this is a technique and like any technique will, of course, be useful to some writers and not to others - In any case a matter for experimentation not argument – The conferring writers have been accused by the press of not paying sufficient attention to the question of human survival – In *Nova Express* – (reference is to an exploding planet) and in my latest novel *The Ticket That Exploded* i am primarily concerned with the question of survival –, with nova conspiracies, nova criminals, and nova police – A new mythology is possible in the space age where we will again have heroes and villains with respect to intentions towards this planet –

Notes on these pages

To show 'the fold in method' in operation i have taken the two texts i read at The [1962] Writers' Conference [at Edinburgh] and folded them into newspaper articles on The Conference, The Conference Folder, typed out selections from various writers, some of whom were present and some of whom were not, to form a composite of many writers living and dead; Shakespeare, Samuel Beckett, T. S. Eliot, F. Scott Fitzgerald, William Golding, Alexander Trocchi, Norman Mailer, Colin MacInnes, Hugh MacDiarmid.

Mr Bradly – Mr Martin, in my mythology, is a God that failed, a God of conflict in two parts so created to keep a tired old show on the road, The God of Arbitrary Power and Restraint, Of Prison and Pressure, who needs subordinates, who needs what he calls 'his human dogs' while treating them with the contempt a con man feels for his victims – But remember the con man needs the mark – The Mark does not need the con man – Mr Bradly–Mr Martin needs his 'dogs' his 'errand boys' his 'human animals.' He needs them because he is literally blind. They do not need him. In my mythological system he is overthrown in a revolution of his 'dogs' – 'Dogs that were his eyes shut off Mr Bradly–Mr Martin.'

My conception of Mr Bradly–Mr Martin is similar to the conception developed by William Golding in *Pincher Martin* and i have made a fold in from the last pages of his book where Martin is destroyed 'erased like an error,' with my own version of Bradly-Martin's end – the end of Mr Bradly–Mr Martin is the theme of these pages – As regards The Writers' Conference i shared with Mary McCarthy a feeling that something incredible was going on beyond the fact of people paying to listen – I could not but feel that it was indeed The Last Writers' Conference.

Nova Police besieged McEwen Hall

The last Writers' Conference – Heroin and homosexuality war melted into air – the conferents are free to come and go visiting the obscurity behind word and image – Mr Martin was movie of which intellectual and literary elite asked the question: What is sex? –

'Hear Mr Burroughs or his answer?': Flesh identity still resisted the question and that book in his memory erased the answer.

On reflection we can discover cross references scrawled by some boy with scars – The last invisible shadow caught and the future fumbles for transitory progress in the arts – Flutes of Ali in the door of panic leaves not a wrack of that God of whom i was a part – The future fumbles in dogs of unfamiliar dust – Hurry up – Page summons composite mutterings flashing forward in your moments i could describe – The deja vu boatman smiles with such memory orders – Shifted with the method of composition, i have frequently left no address – Some pages of straight narrative beside you – Moments i could describe left other pages more comprehensible than the original texts that were his eyes – Inherit these by placing page deals: 'Hurry up please – Heavy summons, Mr Bradly–Martin, with texts moved or conveyor belts retained and copied my blood whom i created.'

You are writer since the departed choose the juxtaposition beside you – The image of the hanged man shut off, Mr Bradly–Mr Martin, to fashion heavy summons – Too much comment and the great boatman smiles – Growing suspicion departed have left no address – Falling history beside you – Dogs that were his eyes inherit this – Let them stray please, its time – And they are free to come and go – Fading this green doll out of an old sack and some rope – The great streaks of paint melted into air – Out of the circle of light you are yourself bringing panic or chaos – Heavy hand broken, erased like an error, fading here the claws in The Towers – The great claws, Martin, caught melted into air – Their whole strength with such memories still resisted – Mr Bradly–Mr Martin was movie played the vaudeville voices – These our actors visible going away erased themselves into air – Adios in the final ape of Martin – just as silver film took it you are yourself The Visiting Center and The Claws – They were our Towers – A Street boy's courage resisted erogenous summons muttering flesh identity – For i last center falling through ruined September beside you erased like an error–

A Russian scientist has said: 'Martin disaster far now' – Shifted with travel in space – Writers were his eyes, inherit this travel in space and time – Areas opened by the heavy summons, Mr Bradly–Mr Martin – I think they must close your account – New and definite my blood whom i created leaves not the third who walks with the past and your dust now ended – These techniques that have been war melted into air – Hurry up in human survival – My last summons Nova Express – Reference is to the ticket that exploded your moments – Nova Police – Heavy summons, Mr Bradly–Mr Martin –

Cross references scrawled by some governmental agency decide what the citizen is permitted to see in Scotland since thought consists largely of the arts – Zero time to the sick areas of politics protecting unfamiliar dust – In English speaking countries, hurry up – Page summons sexual word and image – Consumer's orders shifted – Any form of censorship left no address – Thought material of method proffers precisely the texts that were his eyes – De Sade, Henry Miller are free to come and go – Censorship is the necessity of chaos for stupid individuals advertising to thin air the story of one absent – Like an error fading here the claws we know from Pavlov – Mr Bradly–Mr Martin was movie of which sex is the overt expression – Voices asked the question: What is sex? – and erased themselves into the answer – Flesh identity, of which censorship is the overt expression, still resisted the question What is sex? and some boy's memory erased the answers – he had come muttering things i used to say over and over as Mr Martin Weary my blood whom i pent – Then i raised my eyes and saw words scrawled by some boy – Hurry up – Page summons composites – Get it over with – I have never known you moments, but the rages were the worst such memory orders – Shifted with me frequently left no address – Hurry up please – Heavy summons – Voice all day long muttering moved on conveyor belts very low and harsh no wonder shut off – But let me get on with this day and they are free to come and go without sore throat of an old sack and some rope – These flashes out of things i used to say over and over as yourself bringing panic or chaos – Never loved anyone i think fading here in The Towers – Same old things i don't listen to – These our actors going away on the final ape of Martin – Mr Bradly–Mr Martin voice all day long muttering sick lies – Closed your account – Not even mine it was at the end –

This brings me respectable price of my university – The Kid just found what was left of the window – Pages deal what you might call a journey – Its fairly easy thrash in old New Orleans smudged looking answer – Sick and tired of Martin – Invisible shadow tottering to doom fast – Dream and dreamer that were his eyes inherit this stage – Its time – Heavy summons, Mr Bradly–Mr Martin timeless and without mercy – You are destroyed erased like my name – The text of that God melted into air – Mr Bradly–Mr Martin walks toward September weary good bye playing over and over – Out of the circle of light you are words scrawled by some boy with chaos, for a transitory ape of Martin understood Visiting Center and Claws – He had come muttering flesh identity – His dream must have seemed so close there, whole strength to grasp it – He did not know that it was still resisted, falling back in that vast obscurity behind memory as the boatman began to melt away – Enchanted texts that were his eyes inherit this continent – Mr Bradly–Mr Martin was movie played to thin air – Vaudeville voices leave the story of one absent – Silence to the stage – These our actors erased themselves into good night far from such as you, Mr

Bradly–Mr Martin – Good bye of history – Your whole strength left no address – On this green land the pipes are calling, timeless and without mercy – Page summons the deja vu boatman in setting forth – All are wracked and answer texts that were his eyes – No home in departed river of Gothenberg – Shadows are free to come and go – What have i my friend to give?: An old sack and some rope – The great globe is paint in air – (1962)

ROBERT CREELEY

I was born in 1926 in Arlington, Massachusetts, and grew up in New England. I was at Harvard during the war years, in some confusion, and left to go into the American Field Service. That took me to India and Burma, and returning then to college, I married shortly after and left, short of a degree. We traveled a great deal after that, living in New Hampshire, France, and Spain. Finally, in the middle fifties, I came back to the States and taught at Black Mountain College, and from there went west to New Mexico and then San Francisco, and then back to New Mexico. There I taught in a boys school for a time while getting an M.A. from the University of New Mexico, and subsequently took a job teaching on a *finca* for two years in Guatemala. Next I taught for a year at the University of New Mexico, then at the University of British Columbia in Vancouver, and since 1963 at the University of New Mexico.

It seems a scrambled mess, but I remember seeing Stefánsson on television speaking with another man of a small cape both knew, and loved the beauty of, some hundreds of miles straight north within the Arctic circle. I remember place in the same way, as particular senses shared with some few other men and women. These relations are much more the facts of my life than I can simply record here.

BOOKS: *The Gold Diggers* (1954), (Published by Calder, July 1965, 'The Musicians,* in *Short Story* 3 (1960), *For Love: Poems 1950–1960* (1962), *The Island* (1963)

PREFACE TO THE GOLD DIGGERS

Had I lived some years ago, I think I would have been a moralist, i.e., one who lays down, so to speak, rules of behavior with no small amount of self-satisfaction. But the writer isn't allowed that function anymore, or no man can take the job on very happily, being aware (as he must be) of what precisely that will make him.

So there is left this other area, still the short story or really the tale, and all that can be made of it. Whereas the novel is a continuum, of necessity, chapter to chapter, the story can escape some of that obligation, and function exactly in terms of whatever emotion best can serve it.

The story has no time finally. Or it hasn't here. Its shape, if form can be so thought of, is a sphere, an egg of obdurate kind. The only possible reason for its existence is that it has, in itself, the fact of reality and the pressure. There, in short, is its form – no matter how random and broken that will seem. The old assumptions of beginning and end – those very neat assertions – have fallen away completely in a place where the only actuality is life, the only end (never realized) death, and the only value, what love one can manage.

It is impossible to think otherwise, or at least I have found it so. I begin where I can, and end when I see the whole thing returning. Perhaps that is an obsession. These people, and what happens to them here, have never been completely my decision – because if you once say something, it will lead you to say more than you had meant to.

As the man responsible, I wanted to say what I thought was true, and make that the fact. It has led me to impossible things at times. I was not obliged, certainly, to say anything, but that argument never made sense to me. (1953)

A NOTE ON WRITING

I find myself increasingly less able to explain why it is that I write something. I have no sense of *subject* more than some elemental one concerned with the need for distinction and the fact we are all alive. The story, as it were, comes with its own occasion, and orders me as much as I may it. At times – most often with a feeling of complete trust – I say something in the writing that I know, in the sense that it is made of a series of words which each have a meaning I can locate, but don't at all *know* in the sense of some final understanding, if that should ever be possible. The story continues, making that use of me.

One grows tired of writing intended as a specious example, compact of some dulled acknowledgment, time-ridden, excused with endless sentimental emphasis. I am tired of all that would *explain* me in some 'sociological' or equally perverted sense. I want to use, to be used by, what exists as complementary to my own life, and to be rid of that painful sense of self-conscious singularity (as if understanding really were the final 'sin') which such perversions of life have led to.

Words are common, and language knows more than one man can speak of. I delight in this possibility – not in what I think *I, isolated, can say*. I have in fact, not the least sense of what I would 'say' – were that choice ever to be given me. (1963)

EDWARD DORN

Born Illinois, 1929. My father I have never known. Mother of French parents – Ponton. Lived on the farm mostly, and attended one room schoolhouse, but my grandfather was a railroader. I played billiards with the local undertaker for a dime a point when I was in high school, away from school for weeks on end. Went up to the University of Illinois for two years. Then to Black Mountain. After that I did nothing much – sometime during travels around the country I started to write.

BOOKS: *What I See in the Maximus Poems* (1960), *The Newly Fallen* (1961), *Hands Up!* (1964), *From Gloucester Out* (1964), *The Rites of Passage* (1965), *Geography* (1965)

STATEMENT ON PROSE

In my own writing now I desire a 'formality' of tone and presence. It seems to me that Kerouac took care of all of what the informal range of the personal ruminator can do with our material. He continues to do so. I value his writing very much. But it is only partly satisfying. His syntax is quite dull. It allows the use of the 'I' only one device. This limitation could perhaps be traced to Thomas Wolfe although Wolfe is not so modern in his perceptions. Indeed that, among other things, is what's wrong with Wolfe. Kerouac has the courage of his own movement. And he knows where the best, most yielding material is. But the limited presence is perhaps our greatest problem.

The first part of chapter 3 of Melville's *Confidence Man*, the paragraph beginning 'Thus far not very many pennies...' shows a strain that brings that prose and that man right into our world. Much more than the fairly recent writing of *Billy Budd*. This syntax is able to hold those variations Melville needs to keep his very complicated machine going simply and smoothly. The *tensions* deriving from very conscious delays. What he has to say at the end is 'buttons.' This extreme involution is of course the point only in so far as its use registers control. The *sound* of that syntax is too far off.

I have been instructed by the sound of W. H. Hudson's writing in *Idle Days in Patagonia*, *Purple Land*, *Green Mansions*. Hudson was able to 'say' relatively little and certainly didn't have any of the sense of 'mask' that Melville did. But what is important for me is that prose in this century has not been significant for its hold on form. The only formal men of our time have been the poets.

What life is now is more important for prose than poetry. In its shorter windedness verse is nonetheless able to range, perhaps because of this shortness, wherein there are great dispersals, the milkweed pod, to all that men are. Prose is singleminded. It needs an adaptive I.

When the point comes up as to what and where the materials, there is sometimes a confusion of 'class' or 'what people are' or what their goals, trials, and so forth. In the *New Yorker* magazine, August 27, 1960, Whitney Balliett says, 'The fortunates of the world are another matter; happy, faceless clams, they demand strenuous digging from a novelist before yielding their secrets, which paradoxically, are usually twice as rending.' (From a review of *Tristessa* and *Miguel Street*.) Sounds like a statement by the agent of the middle class. Those rending people still will have to wait for a writer who will stick with them. The great prose writer may be middle classed (Burroughs) but he's not going to spend much time there. As prose gets its new formalities more in hand, the writer is again going to dictate *all* the terms to the reader. (1963)

WILLIAM EASTLAKE

Was born in New York City in 1917 and spent his early years in Liberty Corners and Caldwell, New Jersey. He served in the Army from 1942 until 1946 and after the war spent three years studying and traveling in France, Italy and England. Upon his return to this country, he purchased a ranch in New Mexico where he now lives with his wife. His chief interests are good cattle, good horses, and the plight of the Navajo Indians.

BOOKS: *Go in Beauty* (1956), *The Bronc People* (1958), *Portrait of an Artist with 26 Horses* (1963), *Castle Keep* (1965)

You write for posterity even though you won't be alive to enjoy. The writer makes the supreme gesture of faith. Not only he will not be around, but all the evidence seems to point to the deduction that there will be no world. So, in writing, the writer is the supreme optimist, the denier of all evidence. The writer is a creator who has built things and cannot face the tragedy of their destruction.

What drives a person to become a writer – to write? I believe people are born artists and then are shaped by rejection. Because the writer is incapable of cooperation, of joining anything, he has been pushed a little outside the human race and he stands there, a permanent voyeur watching it all go round.

And writers never grow up. The artist is forever a child, a child in that he has that first wonder for the world. Writers exist so that people can try to recapture their youth, their fresh vision. When William Faulkner died he still had that aggressive, joyful, ecstatic cry of the extremely young. Mark Twain was called Youth on his deathbed and the outside world always frightened Gogol and Swift.

Someone has got to believe in a future. Someone has got to give us a religion we can go by, and the truth is defeatist. Only the artist can give us the emotional ecstacy, the defiance in face of facts, the joy of life that will make us conquer ourselves and go on into the future, a future as bright as a mirror and colored with all the imagination of the young. If there is no future then the artist will make one. It is the unique ability of man and the supreme triumph of the artist. The artist is the best in us all. He is the true creator and art is the only religion worthy of man.

LEROI JONES

Born October 7, 1934 in the dumb industrial complex of Newark, New Jersey, the son of Coyette L. Jones, a postal supervisor, and Anna L. R. Jones, a social worker. Went to school in Newark in guise of skinny prim middle class Negro, i. e., lower middleclass American, but drifted about the 3rd Ward slum to meet junkies, whores, drugs, general dissolution, and thus protect myself against the shabbiness of 'black bourgeois' projected social progress.

Went to Rutgers, Howard, New School, Columbia. Secured to phenomenology and religion. All of this interrupted by the air force, where I served as a weather-gunner and read a great deal. Began to publish after release. Then began the magazine, *Yugen*, and Totem Press. Married a middleclass Jewish lady as protection against Bohemia, produced, in quick succession, two beautiful mulatto girls. Writing nonfiction books and teaching at New School. Aspirant political agitator with a tapped phone.

BOOKS: *Preface to a Twenty Volume Suicide Note* (1961), *Blues People* (1963), *The Moderns* (editor, 1963), *The Dead Lecturer* (1964), *Dutchman and The Slave* (1964), *The System of Dante's Hell* (1965), *Home: Social Essays* (1966)

STATEMENT

Pieces from *The System of Dante's Hell* are all part of musical-literary scheme. And all the stories after *Dante* use much of the same technique. *Dante* 'stories' are from later part of the work, and have literally come together as narrative after the accretion of single images, silences, and what I called 'association complexes.' These are the individual sounded notes and phrases that build to form motifs that are jammed together to make straighter narrative. But all the writing is 'variations' on whatever abstract concrete themes (or pictures or memory epics) come readily to me. So the image and the catalyst form the phrase, and the 'sense' is what the variation is played against. This, I hope, provides different thicknesses of meaning, that finally solidify, to the kind of narrative that 'The Heretics' represents. Where earlier, single images and associations are strung together or are heard together, and give an extended sense of the whole.

My influences have been Joyce, Dante, Burroughs, Ginsberg, Olson, Heidegger, Mao Tze-tung, and Negro music. As, listen to the beginning of Sonny Rollins' *Oleo*, new version, to get a sense of the first part of *Dante*, or Cecil Taylor's *Of What* to discover the total rhythm form I collect my words around. Also *Risk* is something I need, a 'romantic' concept to my liberal/fascist friends. (1963)

JACK KEROUAC

Parochial schools gave me a good early education that made it possible for me to begin writing stories and even one novel at the age of eleven. These schools, in Lowell, Mass., were called St Louis de France and St Joseph. When I got to public schools and college I was already so far advanced I set new records cutting classes in order to go to the library and read all day, or to stay in my room (at college) and write plays. Evidently the progressive education system is wrong, because you only have to learn to read and write, and then you're on your own from the age of 12 or 13 on, from the point of view of 'higher' aims, which can't be taught, only elicited from you by circumstances and influences not necessarily confined to the classroom.

BOOKS: *The Town and the City* (1950), *On the Road* (1957), *The Subterraneans* (1958), *The Dharma Bums* (1958), *Doctor Sax* (1959), *Maggie Cassidy* (1959), *Mexico City Blues* (1959), *Visions of Cody* (1959), *Tristessa* (1960), *Lonesome Traveler* (1960), *Book of Dreams* (1961), *Big Sur* (1962), *Visions of Gerard* (1963), *Desolation Angels* (1965), *Satori in Paris* (1966)

BELIEF & TECHNIQUE FOR MODERN PROSE: LIST OF ESSENTIALS

1. Scribbled secret notebooks and wild typewritten pages, for yr own joy
2. Submissive to everything, open, listening
3. Try never get drunk outside yr own house
4. Be in love with yr life
5. Something that you feel will find its own form
6. Be crazy dumbsaint of the mind
7. Blow as deep as you want to blow
8. Write what you want bottomless from bottom of the mind
9. The unspeakable visions of the individual
10. No time for poetry but exactly what is
11. Visionary tics shivering in the chest
12. In tranced fixation dreaming upon object before you
13. Remove literary, grammatical and syntactical inhibition
14. Like Proust be an old teahead of time
15. Telling the true story of the world in interior monolog
16. The jewel center of interest is the eye within the eye
17. Write in recollection and amazement for yourself

18. Work from pithy middle eye out, swimming in language sea
19. Accept loss forever
20. Believe in the holy contour of life
21. Struggle to sketch the flow that already exists intact in mind
22. Dont think of words when you stop but to see picture better
23. Keep track of every day the date emblazoned in yr morning
24. No fear or shame in the dignity of yr experience, language & knowledge
25. Write for the world to read and see yr exact pictures of it
26. Bookmovie is the movie in words, the visual American form
27. In Praise of Character in the Bleak inhuman Loneliness
28. Composing wild, undisciplined, pure, coming in from under, crazier the better
29. You're a Genius all the time
30. Writer-Director of Earthly movies Sponsored & Angeled in Heaven

ESSENTIALS OF SPONTANEOUS PROSE

SET-UP. The object is set before the mind, either in reality, as in sketching (before a landscape or teacup or old face) or is set in the memory wherein it becomes the sketching from memory of a definite image-object.

PROCEDURE. Time being of the essence in the purity of speech, sketching language is undisturbed flow from the mind of personal secret idea-words, *blowing* (as per jazz musician) on subject of image.

METHOD. No periods separating sentence-structures already arbitrarily riddled by false colons and timid usually needless commas – but the vigorous space dash separating rhetorical breathing (as jazz musician drawing breath between outblown phrases) – 'measured pauses which are the essentials of our speech '– 'divisions of the *sounds* we hear' – 'time and how to note it down.' (William Carlos Williams)

SCOPING. Not 'selectivity' of expression but following free deviation (association) of mind into limitless blow-on-subject seas of thought, swimming in sea of English with no discipline other than rhythms of rhetorical exhalation and expostulated statement, like a fist coming down on a table with each complete utterance, bang! (the space dash) – Blow as deep as you want – write as deeply, fish as far down as you want, satisfy yourself first, then reader cannot fail to receive telepathic shock and meaning-excitement by same laws operating in his own human mind.

LAG IN PROCEDURE. No pause to think of proper word but the infantile pileup of scatological buildup words till satisfaction is gained, which will turn out to be a great appending rhythm to a thought and be in accordance with Great Law of timing.

TIMING. Nothing is muddy that runs in time and to laws of *time* – Shakespearian stress of dramatic need to speak now in own unalterable way or forever hold tongue – *no revisions* (except obvious rational mistakes, such as names or *calculated* insertions in act of not writing but *inserting*).

CENTER OF INTEREST. Begin not from preconceived idea of what to say about image but from jewel center of interest in subject of image at *moment of* writing, and write outwards swimming in sea of language to peripheral release and exhaustion – Do not afterthink except for poetic or P. S. reasons. Never afterthink to 'improve' or defray impressions, as, the best writing is always the most painful personal wrungout tossed from cradle warm protective mind – tap from yourself the song of yourself, *blow*! – *now*! – *your* way is your only way – 'good' – or 'bad' – always honest, ('ludicrous'), spontaneous, 'confessional,' interesting, because not 'crafted.' Craft *is* craft.

STRUCTURE OF WORK. Modern bizarre structures (science fiction, etc.) arise from language being dead, 'different' themes give illusion of 'new' life. Follow roughly outlines in outfanning movement over subject, as river rock, so mind-flow over jewel-center need (run your mind over it, once, arriving at pivot, where what was dim formed 'beginning' becomes sharp-necessitating 'ending' and language shortens in race to wire of time-race of work, following laws of Deep Form, to conclusion, last words, last trickle – Night is The End.

MENTAL STATE. If possible write 'without consciousness' in semi-trance (as Yeats' later 'trance writing') allowing subconscious to admit in own uninhibited interesting necessary and so 'modern' language what conscious art would censor, and write excitedly, swiftly, with writing-or-typing-cramps, in accordance (as from center to periphery) with laws of orgasm, Reich's 'beclouding of consciousness.' *Come* from within, out – to relaxed and said. (1957)

JOHN RECHY

I was born in El Paso, Texas. I was drafted into the army, and I served most of that time in Germany. Since my release, Ive lived mainly in New York and Los Angeles – with shorter interludes in San Francisco, New Orleans, Chicago. But I always return to El Paso: This is where I look back and write. . . . The prose writers I admire most are Dostoevsky and, among the Americans, Poe, Hawthorne, the earlier Faulkner. . . . Concerning my own writing: Although I believe Ive written better, I have a special affection for the 'The Fabulous Wedding of Miss Destiny' (which was published as a short story in *Big Table* No. 3 and which appears, in an expanded version, as a chapter in my novel *City of Night*, published in 1963 by Grove Press.) . . . I'm now working on a novel, tentatively entitled *The Vampires*, which uses as a framework – loosely, in a contemporary setting – the vampire myth: the myth of the victim and the victimizer – and which is which. Ive also begun work on a play based on *City of Night*.

Like all other writers, I write for many reasons. But one of the main ones, for me, is the result of an obsession for 'framing' life.

By way of background: Very early (when I first felt inundated meaninglessly by life), I became fascinated by Mirrors. (For one thing, the framed image separates me enough so that I can think: 'I always have Me.') Too, as a child, I would sit for very long inside our house and look outside through a window – another frame much like that of a Mirror. Later, as part of this obsession, I added movies, books; and I would spend hours drawing pictures – pictures recurrently entitled 'Long Ago.'

Ive analyzed this 'frame' obsession as an attempt to place life in an understandable perspective, so that I can see it (as I can see myself only in a Mirror, a photograph), so I can try to know *why*, try to discern reasons.

Because:

Reality moves too unreally, too swiftly, too fiercely, too illogically, too complicatedly to be trapped.

For me, art became the re-enactment of reality for observation.

To movies, books, paintings – even when these contain elements of mystery – one can always return, re-view, re-read, try to understand them, or what they represent, at an at-least-unchangeable point – within the frame itself. Now reasons may be looked for, the results studied slowly, now at least possible of resolution.

I want to see the pattern of destiny, and destiny manifests itself only in retrospect, within the frame of memory.

Art slows life down, injects meaning into it, orders the horrible, brutal chaos. (1963)

MICHAEL RUMAKER

I was born in South Philadelphia in a Preston Retreat charity ward on March 5, 1932. My mother helped pay for her keep and my getting born by peeling potatoes in the kitchen of the

Retreat. Reared in an Irish-Polish Catholic background, I have seven brothers and one sister. I was in between.

When I was six years old my family moved to a sleepy little backwater town of about 2,000, National Park in southern New Jersey on the Delaware River, and there I grew up.

After graduating from Woodbury High School, I won a half-scholarship to Rider College in Trenton in the School of Journalism. The rest of that summer of 1950 I worked as a linerman on an oil tanker at a shipyard in Camden, New Jersey, with my father, before going to Rider.

After hearing Ben Shahn speak enthusiastically of Black Mountain College during a lecture at the Philadelphia Museum, I made application to the college and was granted a work scholarship, i.e., in return for four or so hours of work a day a work-student was given tuition and board. I went to Black Mountain in the fall of 1952 and graduated in 1955. While there I had my first two stories published in *Black Mountain Review*.

Since then I have lived in Philadelphia, hitchhiked across country to San Francisco where I lived until 1958, moved back to New York City and now live in Grand View, on the Hudson River in Rockland County, New York. Scribner's published a novel, *The Butterfly*, in 1962, and, earlier, in 1959, 'Exit 3', a collection of stories in *Short Story* 2. [*Exit 3* was published in Penguin Books in 1966]

THE USE OF THE UNCONSCIOUS IN WRITING

Story can be, obliquely, a map of the unconscious, its terrain and peopling. The physical can be made to yield psychic responses.

The unconscious nests the actual.

The landscapes which draw one are the landscapes of the self. Actual or imagined, the unconscious one posits itself on the physical one, invisibly permeating it. Each moving, in the act of writing, concurrently, creates an open structure in which one is free to invent, bound neither strictly to unconscious nor to conscious, but drawing from each – an interchange of the powers of each in which the tactile lifts as the psychic contents respond. All is believable within the framework of the story since all is created between those two poles of force.

It's as though experience resides in the unconscious as layers of silt – each the essence of the actual event heaped in layers of memory and non-memory.

It's as though the unconscious stores up, gathers into itself, as a slow accumulation, all our experiences. The more poignant, the more deeply does it imprint itself there. There is that other, as a residue, which we can't account for personally – there, in the unconscious as a kind of carryover of non-memory which we inherit with our blood at birth. It seems this residue only manifests itself according to the degree of intensity we bring to bear upon our own lives as the cross-forces of life touch us – as we act and are acted upon. It will sleep, if we sleep.

The psyche, in quietness, absorbs the energy of its contents, a thickening process that gathers for charges. They will be manageable or unmanageable according to how equipped and prepared we are.

The process is a conscious working at the substance of the unconscious whenever it manifests itself, in dream or in wakefulness. As a ruined site, tripe rests, indiscriminately, amongst valuable content there. Quality will depend on the closeness of sifting, will depend on how close and precise one has made known to the self its contents. That no barrier, impasse, is ducked. That one is involved in his known and in the known world about him.

If the unconscious has appeared in writing, it has been mainly by accident. Here is a rich field of content. To be acted upon consciously. To be made known.

Seized by the sight of an object, an intensity of seeing, brings up other, psychic contents charged with meaning beyond what the eye, as instrument, registers to the brain.

Although the root is in language and what men say, what their bodies do – yet, this other thing, which is unseen, quiet and unquiet, needs also its own equivalent language to make it known – by image, images as precise as those found to present the actual.

To get the thing there, in the words, with that same swift heightening, that sharp penetration, which strikes meaning from an object. But that the object remain the object, stated as such, with the same spareness and preciseness which is the heart of intuition. That the object be allowed or made to yield its meaning but not be despoiled. That is, not used simply for self-expression.

Not so simple. Too often the temptation is to imbue the object with personal meanings and effusions which force the object to be mouthpiece for the expression of the writer's reminiscences, ideas, private bellyaches, etc. – the qualities and characteristics of the object set aside, the object itself disturbed, taken out of its context to serve the writer merely as an instrument to express himself. Whereas the writer must act upon the object in such a way that it gets said, and the other, under meaning, without its being tampered with. The object must remain in its own context, as you, the writer, must also. Objects in a story must be given no more than their weight – that their lift or drop in the prose be equal to their substance – that the writer develops a sensitivity to the degrees of intensity with which they strike the psyche – that a point is reached where he can say, and know, 'Yes, there, there I go in.'

This is the quality of flatness: to present the thing no more than it is. It is not to equal objects, people, out, in a dull stringing. There must be intensity. There must be sensitivity.

In such a story meanings get there which aren't put there consciously. And if not consciously, they must stem from the unconscious. Meanings don't get there by accident. There is also operant an under-logic – not the conscious one – that brings about an interlocked structure of things within the story, in the face of the consciously willed one. It's also as though this intense preoccupation with the physical, with the self and with story, sets up an involitional force which is the unconscious, its contents moving parallel with the known contents as the narrative progresses. A rhythm, as car gears meshing, grabbing and gibing, each causing the other to move, to prompt and to yield the substance and power of each – an absolute rhythm of movement, instantaneous, going. (1958)

HUBERT SELBY, JR

Born 1928. I went to sea at the end of W W II, sailed a few years then spent 3 years in the hospital with T B, the details of which are boring. Read a book when I was about 23 and enjoyed it. As to what Im trying to do – well, Im trying to write a good story. I dont think theres any sense in going into details about my esthetic, there are only a few who would be interested & understand & they already know, through their own existence, what its all about.

BOOKS: *Last Exit to Brooklyn* (1964)

DOUGLAS WOOLF

Began in lower Manhattan in 1922, and at a tender age was taken to the foot of Rockingstone Hill, in the suburbs. Moved back and forth until I went to Massachusetts for school and Harvard. Left childhood scenes for three years in A F S and A A F, as ambulance driver and airplane navigator, and have seldom returned except for short visits. Tried L.A., Denver, Miami, Chicago, joined by my wife on the way. Two daughters followed, and a degree from the University of New Mexico. Was born in 1951 in a lookout tower on Cibola National Forest, and returned next two summers, during the last and best of which I wrote *The Hypocritic Days* in three sleepless months sitting on a ruptured disc. Have since moved through most of the far and southwest states as itinerant worker in ballparks, coliseums, icecream trucks, beanfields, etc, etc, settling for as long as a year at a time. Was born in 1956 in an Arizona ghost town, where I wrote most of *Fade Out*. Was born in an Arizona copper town in 1958, and wrote *Wall to Wall*. Born in an Idaho lead and zinc town, 1960 and in San Isabel Forest, 1962, but it gets harder every time. Died Spokane in 1964, when *John-Juan* was born.

BOOKS: *The Hypocritic Days* (1955), *Fade Out* (1959), *Wall to Wall* (1962), *Signs of a Migrant Worrier* (1965)

PROSIT

Writing novels in Century Twentyone is a desperate anachronism. Novels are about people, for people. Where, amid all the politico-scientific machinery, are they to be found? I try to think they have joined the Peace Corps, will be back in 1965. Yet the greatest peace corps of modern times, José Clemente Orozco, never for a moment leaves a man feeling so alone, and he himself is dead. And you, Albert Camus. I fear that no one will think to pipe the music of Thelonious Monk into the factories in time to save us from all those parts the workers are making there. Samuel Beckett has probably salvaged more souls than any other writer still active, yet does all this good begin to balance the harm done by the reporters, underwriters, and copymen who put hard covers on their politics and call them novel? A dozen little magazines and advance presses have done more in recent years to sustain the human spirit than all the quarterlies, monthlies, weeklies and hourlies the machines can bomb us with, yet more subscribers are being born today than on any previous day and how many more will be lost before the next issue of Outland comes out than before the last? So like everything else, it becomes a matter of numbers finally, and balances. I have noticed that in my own writings a stop usually comes at whatever point some kind of balance is reached, a point at which the people involved can pause to examine the odds against them. Nothing is ended, my people are left to see for themselves – or the reader for them. Where is he? I don't know how much longer I'll keep after him, it always seems too sad a time to stop. (1963)

More about Penguins and Pelicans

Penguinews, which appears every month, contains details of all the new books issued by Penguins as they are published. From time to time it is supplemented by *Penguins in Print*, which is a complete list of all books published by Penguins which are in print. (There are well over three thousand of these.)

A specimen copy of *Penguinews* will be sent to you free on request, and you can become a subscriber for the price of the postage. For a year's issues (including the complete lists) please send 4s. if you live in the United Kingdom, or 8s. if you live elsewhere. Just write to Dept EP, Penguin Books Ltd, Harmondsworth, Middlesex, enclosing a cheque or postal order, and your name will be added to the mailing list.

Some other books published by Penguins are listed overleaf.

Note : *Penguinews* and *Penguins in Print* are not available in the U.S.A. or Canada

Canadian Writing Today

Edited by Mordecai Richler

Writing Today is a series devoted to current literature, in verse and prose, from countries and continents all over the world.
'Where it seeks to counter the insularities of our taste and the unwillingness, in all but a few places, to study literature comparatively, it is an admirable venture' – George Steiner in the *New Statesman*.

Canadian Writing Today includes poems, short stories, articles, and extracts from plays, books and novels (some translated from French) by over forty writers, predominantly of the younger generation. Among these are Marie-Claire Blais, Leonary Cohen, Northrop Frye, J. K. Galbraith, Mavis Gallant, Margaret Lawrence, Brian Moore, Pierre Trudeau, David Wevill and George Woodcock.

The Writing Today Series

The following volumes are also available

Australian Writing Today
Writers in the New Cuba
England Today : The Last Fifteen Years
New Writing in Czechoslovakia
Italian Writing Today
French Writing Today
South African Writing Today
Polish Writing Today
Latin American Writing Today
South African Writing Today
German Writing Today

To Simon   1983
    Best wishes
        Stephen

Penguin Books
New American Story